FROM VENICE WITH LOVE

BY
ALISON ROBERTS

CHRISTMAS WITH HER EX

BY
FIONA McARTHUR

All aboard for some seasonal magic on

The Christmas Express!

These gorgeous docs never expected to
ind love…especially in time for Christmas!
During a magical train journey on the opulent
Orient Express, from romantic Venice to
cosmopolitan London, their ride of a lifetime
brings lifesaving drama and the chance for
their hearts to be finally unlocked!

FROM VENICE WITH LOVE
by Alison Roberts

CHRISTMAS WITH HER EX
by Fiona McArthur

FROM VENICE
WITH LOVE

BY
ALISON ROBERTS

First published in Great Britain 2013
by Mills & Boon, an imprint of Harlequin (UK) Limited.
Harlequin (UK) Limited, Eton House, 18-24 Paradise Road,
Richmond, Surrey TW9 1SR

© Alison Roberts 2013

ISBN: 978 0 263 89926 9

Dear Reader

Do you have a bucket list?

I do :-), and a year or so ago I was lucky enough to tick off one of the bigger items—travelling from Venice to London on the Orient Express.

It was the culmination of a fabulous trip. Along with writing friends Fiona McArthur and Trish Morey I had attended the Women's Fiction Festival in Matera, Italy. Then Fiona and I headed off to tick off *her* bucket list item of a Mediterranean cruise, which just happened to finish in Venice and dovetailed perfectly with my dream train journey.

Being a writer has a unique advantage. I don't have to rely solely on photo albums or journals to remember a special time. I can weave my memories into a story.

Come and share my trip of a lifetime. Let's start in Venice and finish in London and see what happens on the way to the cast of characters I chose—Charlotte and Nico and Charlotte's loveable gran Jendi who, like me, has always wanted to travel on the Orient Express.

And, just to make it even more special, let's make it happen at Christmastime.

Enjoy—and Happy Christmas!

To Fi, with lots of love.
Here's to friendship. And memories xxx

Alison Roberts lives in Christchurch, New Zealand, and has written over 60 Mills & Boon® Medical Romances™.

As a qualified paramedic, she has personal experience of the drama and emotion to be found in the world of medical professionals, and loves to weave stories with this rich background—especially when they can have a happy ending.

When Alison is not writing, you'll find her indulging her passion for dancing or spending time with her friends (including Molly the dog) and her daughter Becky, who has grown up to become a brilliant artist. She also loves to travel, hates housework, and considers it a triumph when the flowers outnumber the weeds in her garden.

Recent titles by Alison Roberts:

**These books are also available in eBook format
from www.millsandboon.co.uk**

CHAPTER ONE

THE SOUND OF more than one person shouting got steadily louder as Nico Moretti turned into the narrow Venetian alleyway that would get him to his destination a little faster.

He tried to ignore the sound. He was in a hurry and it wasn't as if the sound of shouting was anything unusual for a large Italian city but he could feel his frown deepening. It was a disturbing echo of what was already occupying too much of his head.

The noise was loud enough to have people stopping in the street now. Turning their heads and asking each other what they thought it might be about. The slowing pace and knots of people forming made it harder to move forward and Nico heard a growl of frustration escape his own throat.

He could tell them what it was about if he had either the time or the inclination. It was about people who wanted different things. People who were passionate about what they believed in. People who weren't prepared to even try and understand each other and left broken lives in their wakes. But he didn't have the inclination. Not when he felt so out of place in this city of

his birth and with the sound of his childhood language surrounding him and reinforcing that exclusion. And he certainly didn't have the time. Not when the real reason for his return to Venice was due to start in less than thirty minutes.

At least he had the advantage of his height. And plenty of practice in cutting through obstructions to get to the heart of an emergency. All he needed to do was take on the mantle of an expert consultant en route to an urgent call in an emergency department or at an accident scene.

'*Scusi.*' The word was a command, not a request, and, as always, it had the desired effect. A path appeared through the gathering crowd. Those closest to him actually stopped talking to stare at him but that only made the sound of whatever was happening ahead clearer.

Whatever it was about, it wasn't simply a misunderstanding or disagreement. There was a language barrier as well. He could hear English being spoken by a forceful, female voice.

'Stand back. Don't move him yet. Call an ambulance. *Ambulanza.*'

More shouting. In Italian. Had someone called an ambulance? Where was it? Why wasn't it here yet? They were right beside the Grand Canal, for heaven's sake. Practically a highway in Venice. Where were the police? Where was a doctor when you needed one?'

'*Sì.*' The English woman had understood something in the furore. '*Dottoressa.* I'm a doctor. Let me get close. I have to find out if he's breathing.'

'He's not,' someone close to Nico muttered. 'He's

dead. He has to be, falling off the roof like that. He must have broken his sorry neck. Who does that English woman think she is? An angel who can work some kind of miracle?'

'It's almost Christmas,' a black-clad Italian grandmother said sagely. 'A good time for a miracle to happen.'

'*Scusi.*' Nico schooled himself not to show any personal frustration as he recognised the inevitability of what he had to do. He raised his voice and spoke in Italian. 'I'm a doctor. Let me through. What's going on?'

Charlotte Highton heard the commanding male voice that overrode the almost hysterical barrage of Italian around her. She could also hear the faint sound of a siren. Please, God, she breathed. Let that be an ambulance.

Getting caught up in an accident scene had been the last thing she'd needed after getting lost in the back alleys of Venice, trying to take a shortcut to her destination near St Mark's Square, but what could she have done? She'd seen the man fall from the scaffolding. More than that. She'd been caught by the way he had been doubled over and clutching at his chest seconds before he'd fallen. There was no chance of him surviving any injuries the fall might have caused if he'd already been in cardiac arrest before it had happened.

But they wouldn't let her near and precious seconds were being lost. One of the man's workmates was probably the first-aid officer for the building company and he'd decided that the fall had caused a spinal injury. He

was holding the victim's head still and shouting at anybody who so much as bumped the unconscious body.

Now he was shouting in response to a query from the newcomer, who Charlotte couldn't see because other people were also trying to tell him the story and some were gesticulating madly—pointing to the roof of the house and circling their arms in the air to represent the fall. For a crazy moment Charlotte almost smiled.

Here she was in this beautiful, ancient city with the water of a canal lapping almost at her feet. Surrounded by the sounds of a language she loved but had never had the time to learn. Caught by the passionate involvement of people who were, for the most part, probably complete strangers to the unfortunate man who had fallen. This would never happen in England. It was *so* Italian.

Then a single, curt word from the newcomer and everybody fell silent. And shifted enough to make an opening. The man who stepped in to fill the gap was as Italian as everything else. Tall and dark. Strong featured and exuding a masculinity that was supremely confident. Such a stereotype that, for another crazy moment, Charlotte was sure she'd met him before.

Or maybe she just recognised that kind of confidence. It didn't come from any awareness of his effect on women. This kind of quiet power came from being in a situation where he knew exactly what needed to be done.

'You're a doctor?'

'Yes.'

'And you speak English?'

'Yes. I'm a specialist in emergency neurology.' He

was bending over the unconscious man now. 'Did you see the fall? Has he been moved at all?'

'Yes, I saw the fall.' Charlotte was right behind the man and she was reaching for the victim's neck. The newcomer caught her wrist in a grip that was as powerful as everything else about this man. His confidence. His voice. The eyes that were locked on hers right now.

'What do you think you're doing?'

'I *saw* him fall.' Charlotte spoke the way she would to anyone who was preventing her doing her job. Or some unfortunate junior doctor who was getting the basics dangerously wrong. 'I saw him *before* he fell. He clearly had severe chest pain. He didn't trip. He *collapsed*. I need to see whether he's got a pulse.'

For a stunned heartbeat the dark eyes continued to hold hers. Charlotte could see how swift his comprehension was. She actually felt the moment when he stepped back from confronting her action and they became a team. He let go of her wrist.

Rapid instructions in Italian followed. The Italian specialist took over holding the man's head and guided a log roll that had the patient on his back with his airway opened in an admirably short space of time. The nearby siren was getting louder but it wasn't yet close enough. Charlotte was crouched with her cheek against the patient's mouth, one hand on his neck with her fingers searching for a pulse and the other resting gently on his diaphragm seeking the movement that would indicate breathing.

'Nothing,' she snapped. She wasn't exactly dressed for performing CPR. She had to hoist up her slim-fitting skirt so that she could kneel on the rough cobblestones

of the alleyway. Her equally neat-fitting blouse beneath the skirt's matching blazer hadn't been designed for vigorous movement either. Charlotte felt a seam ripping within the first seconds of pushing her body weight down hard enough to depress the chest of the large man.

Her unexpected medical colleague was still communicating in Italian to those around him. Explaining what was going on perhaps. And then he was showing the person who'd been guarding his patient so effectively from Charlotte how to support the man's cervical spine but do a jaw thrust at the same time.

As she stayed in position, with her body weight directly over her straight arms, Charlotte could look sideways. She saw the way he demonstrated the required position, with his large hands splayed, the palms pushing against the angle of the man's jaw and his thumbs resting on his cheeks. She knew the pressure required to keep that kind of hold and yet he made it look like he was being gentle with the critically ill patient.

And then he let the first-aider take over the hold and shifted so that he was kneeling right beside Charlotte. The shafts of pain from the movement of her knees on the cobblestones seemed to fade as his body lined up so close beside hers their arms were touching.

That eye contact was extraordinary. Reassuring and encouraging at the same time. The almost invisible movement of his head told Charlotte that he was in sync with what she was doing. That he was ready for her to pause so that he could deliver a breath. With an equally subtle nod, Charlotte began counting aloud. She had no idea how many compressions she'd done already but it was standard international protocol to deliver two

breaths for every thirty compressions and a lead-in was given so that minimum pumping time was lost.

'Twenty-eight, twenty-nine…thirty.' Charlotte raised her hands and sat back on her heels as her CPR partner bent down, pinching the man's nose and covering his mouth with his own. She watched the man's chest rise and fall. Twice. And then she was back in position and the compressions continued smoothly.

Wow. Not only could this guy get air into someone without disturbing the protected position of a C spine, he was prepared to do mouth-to-mouth resuscitation on a stranger. A risk very few medical people would be prepared to take these days. And compressions were deemed the more important component of CPR now. If an ambulance was on its way and the compressions were effective, you had a window of ten minutes or so before the lack of extra oxygen would cause irreversible brain damage.

Charlotte was impressed. She was also sweating despite the deep chill of Venice in December, and her knees felt as if someone had attacked them with a baseball bat. She'd never been more grateful to hear the sound of a siren so close. Looking up, as she paused to let another two breaths be delivered, she was astonished to see that it was a jet boat, arriving on the canal, complete with flashing beacons and a uniformed paramedic, with a defibrillator in his hand, waiting to jump ashore.

She knew better than to stop what she was doing and wait for these emergency medics to take over the scene. Automatically, she rocked forward, her hands back in position on the centre of the man's chest with one flat and the other locked around the wrist to give her extra

strength as she pushed down and began the count that would remain silent until the warning of breaths needed.

One...two...three...

Nico could hear the shouts of the paramedics arriving and securing the ambulance. Thank goodness! The discomfort of kneeling on cold, hard cobbles to perform CPR was truly unbearable.

Not that the English woman was showing any signs of discomfort. Nico had been watching her, waiting for the signal to deliver another couple of breaths but also because she was so...so *in control*. So very British.

She had that English peaches and cream type of complexion and the kind of reserve that always felt so foreign to Nico, but he had spent so many years away from Italy it was very familiar. So familiar, in fact, that he could imagine he'd met this woman before. He'd certainly met the type.

Virtually the exact opposite of the type of women he preferred.

It was perhaps unfortunate that he'd inherited his father's taste in women. He liked them small and dark, curvy and vivacious. With an appetite for life and fun that could negate any tendency to take life too seriously out of working hours. But as long as he didn't make his father's mistake of marrying a woman like this, he wouldn't end up abandoned and broken-hearted when someone on another continent offered something more exciting. Like when his father's beloved Irish wife had simply taken their only child and made off for greener pastures.

Nico shook off the thought. Normally, snippets of

family history would never distract him from a situation like this but his mind had been full of it until the moment he'd intervened in this rescue scene. Even now, he was aware of the small object in his pocket that the solicitor had insisted he take with him. It should be small enough to dismiss out of hand but unfortunately it carried a significance that could never be dismissed.

He had to push it firmly to one side right now, however. After a second glance to reassure himself that the paramedics were coming in the right direction, Nico took another look at the woman who hadn't missed a beat in performing the chest compressions.

Strands of her blonde hair had worked themselves loose thanks to her current physical exertion but the rest of it was still tightly bound into an intricate kind of knot that removed the feminine allure of long tresses. She had grey eyes that could have looked attractively smoky but she was so focused on the clinical aspects of this situation that they were devoid of an identifiable emotion.

Even now, as the paramedics set up the defibrillator and prepared to take over the management of this patient, he couldn't detect any sign of relief or distress, perhaps, that she'd been caught up in this traumatic event. She was watching what the paramedics were doing with hawk-like intensity. She might not speak Italian but Nico had the distinct impression that she wouldn't hesitate to correct these medics if she felt things were not being done to an expected standard.

He filled them in as they attached the patches to the man's chest. He provided the cervical spine support as preparations were made to secure the airway and

the first shock was delivered, but then a second crew arrived, along with the police, and Nico found himself stepping back and merely watching, along with the crowd of people the police couldn't manage to disperse.

The English doctor was in the same position. Nico saw her tucking the hem of her blouse back into the tight waistband of her skirt. He noticed the holes in her tights and the red, grazed skin of her knees. He could feel the ache in his own joints and it gave him an oddly powerful feeling of connection with this stranger. He tried to catch her eye and smile but she was looking at her watch and frowning, as though she was running late for something.

And then she looked over her shoulder and her frown deepened. Whatever she was looking for was obscured by the crowd of people who were watching in fascination as the resuscitation scene reached fever pitch.

The man's airway was secured and a paramedic was delivering oxygen via a bag mask unit. An IV line was in place and drugs had been administered. And then the shout was given to stand clear and another shock was delivered.

There was a collective gasp from the onlookers as the man's body jerked in response to the shock and then silence fell as everybody held their breath. Only those closest could see the blip on the screen of the life pack and then another and another as the rhythm picked up. One of the paramedics felt the neck of the patient and grinned at his colleague.

'We have a pulse.'

A cheer went up from the crowd and the atmosphere only became more excited as the emergency services

prepared to transport the man to hospital as quickly as possible. People were moving away in response to the shouted instructions of the police officer and Nico saw the English woman disappearing behind others.

He couldn't let her vanish. Somebody had to thank her for her contribution to saving the man's life.

'*Scusi.*' Again, Nico pushed his way through the human obstruction. He was going against the flow towards the canal and where they were trying to manoeuvre the stretcher that now carried the still-unconscious man into the ambulance, but that was also the direction in which the woman was going. She was still looking for something, her head bent as she peered around people, and suddenly Nico spotted what she was after. A black laptop case, propped against the wooden piling the ambulance launch had been tied up to.

He could get to it first. She'd have to stop and talk to him then and he could thank her. Get her address, maybe, and then follow up on the patient and let her know the outcome. With a determined effort Nico stepped in front of a man and reached for the case. He had it in his hand when someone bumped into him from behind with such force that his hand simply opened. The case fell, bounced on the cobbles and fell again, in a graceful arc, to land in the canal. For a second or two it floated on the surface. And then it sank.

Charlotte watched the laptop case disappear under the murky water of the canal, its disappearance hastened by the wash of the ambulance as it took off with its beacons flashing and siren sounding.

If she took her shoes and jacket off...

Good grief…was she actually considering diving in to try and retrieve it before it sank too far?

The downward glance towards her shoes had hammered home the reality of what was happening. Straightening and dusting off her skirt after she'd got to her feet hadn't cured the creases and streaks of grime. Her tights were shredded and one knee was grazed enough for a trickle of blood to be obvious.

Her armour had been dented.

But worse than that—far, far worse than that—her shield had been ripped away from her and destroyed.

'Oh…my…God…' Charlotte had about a heartbeat before she knew the fear would try and kick in.

The man was turning towards her, clearly appalled at what had just happened.

She couldn't let him see her fear. Couldn't let anybody see it because if they did it would become real. It would take over and she would be sucked back into that place where she was utterly powerless. Where she became nobody.

It wasn't going to happen. Charlotte fought back, gathering fury as if it could repair the amour. Replace the shield.

'You *idiot*,' she snapped. 'Have you *any* idea what you've just done?'

The dark eyes widened, startled by her ferocity.

'I'm so sorry,' he said. But the apology in his eyes was being replaced by something more like astonishment. Anger, even, at being attacked for something that had clearly been an accident.

Charlotte knew that. She'd seen the person behind being pushed and stumbling, only prevented from fall-

ing by the safety barrier this man's back had provided. It didn't help, though, knowing that the action had not been deliberate. How could it, when the effect was the same?

'That laptop has my presentation on it,' Charlotte snapped. 'The presentation I'm supposed to be delivering to an international symposium in…' She jerked her gaze to her wrist. 'In exactly *ten* minutes.'

His face was changing again, along with the expression in his eyes. He was putting pieces of a puzzle together with the same kind of swiftness that had been obvious when they had become a team, working in sync to try and save the life of the unfortunate man who'd fallen from the scaffolding in the wake of his cardiac arrest.

They weren't a team now. They were on different sides of a battle and Charlotte felt as if she was fighting for her life. He couldn't possibly understand how important this was to her but he obviously knew more than she would have expected.

'Not by any chance the symposium on critical interventions in the emergency department? Being held at the Bonvecchiata hotel?'

'Yes. I'm Dr Charlotte Highton. Due to open the symposium in…' Charlotte had to swallow hard '…*eight* minutes.'

'*You're* Charlotte Highton?'

'Yes.' Charlotte glared at the stranger, who was looking at her as if he'd seen a ghost. As if he couldn't believe she was who she'd said she was.

He gave his head a sharp shake. And then he held out his hand. 'Dr Nicholas Moretti,' he told her. 'Nico.

We've met before. Twice, in fact. At St Margaret's Hospital in London. And that night at The Cosmopolitan Club. It was a few years ago now…' His voice trailed off. He was frowning and still staring as if he could barely recognise her. As if he couldn't make sense of what he was seeing.

Well…no surprises there. He was talking about a lifetime ago. She'd been a different person then.

A person she couldn't afford to be reminded of because it would only make this situation even worse. How incredibly unfortunate was this? To not only lose the protection she depended on but to meet someone who had known her back then? Before…

Before her life had turned so sharply it had virtually doubled back on itself to take the path she was now on.

For just a moment Charlotte could remember what it had been like at that crossroad.

She could feel the fear.

She didn't remember meeting him. Oh…she'd felt the beat of familiarity when she'd seen him. She probably *would* remember him if she allowed her mind to go back to that time. To when she'd been the rising star of a prestigious London hospital and her academic brilliance had been enough to erase the shadows of a painfully shy youth. To when she'd had the world at her feet and she had been courted by albeit distant royalty and wined and dined at places like The Cosmopolitan Club.

A time that it hadn't even occurred to her that she might be reminded of today.

Not only reminded of but stripped of any protection she would normally have to ward it off. How long had it been since she'd felt this vulnerable?

To Charlotte's *absolute* horror, she could actually feel the prickle of tears at the back of her eyes. Tears that could unleash weakness that might undo her completely. She blinked. Hard. She dragged her gaze away from yet another expression she could read in this man's eyes. He had such an open face. He was probably a very nice person but she didn't need anyone to be *concerned* about her.

She could look after herself. And succeed. She'd learned that long ago.

A police officer had come to stand beside them. This man who had an Italian name that matched his looks but who, curiously, spoke perfect English with an Irish accent, translated his query.

'He wants to know if you need assistance of any kind.'

A snort of something akin to laughter escaped Charlotte. She alone was the only person who could provide the kind of assistance she needed right now. Unless by some miracle a police diving team could be available within seconds and an even more impressive miracle would reveal a laptop that could survive total submersion.

But a rapid conversation in Italian led to the police officer nodding and indicating, with a wave of his arm, that Charlotte should follow him.

Nick was also following. 'He's going to take us to the symposium venue,' he said briskly. 'In the police launch. It will only take a few minutes.'

Charlotte looked down at her ruined clothes. She couldn't appear anywhere looking like this.

'We will explain what's happened.' His hand was on

her arm, guiding her through the crowd that was only now dispersing properly. 'Please let me help if I can. I feel responsible for this unfortunate turn of events and I will do anything I can to put things right. Perhaps they can rearrange the order of the presentations. And do you have a back-up of your material?'

Having a man step in and try and solve this problem was the last thing Charlotte needed.

'Of course I do. It's on a flash drive.'

'Which is where?'

Charlotte focused as the police officer offered her a hand to step into the speed boat. She ignored the hand, climbed aboard unaided and then turned back.

She had to speak through gritted teeth. 'It's in the side pocket of the laptop case that you *threw* into the canal.'

It was a totally unjustified accusation in the wake of an obvious accident. It was also an undeserved slap in the face given that he was trying so hard to help.

But Charlotte didn't care. She couldn't afford to.

'Please don't concern yourself any further.' She turned away and nodded to the pilot of the boat, who revved the engine. Waved at him imperiously enough to indicate that speed was of the essence and it was time to leave. 'This is my problem and I will deal with it.'

Nico watched the police launch speed away down the canal.

He could walk to the venue in only a few minutes longer than the boat trip would take. He hadn't actually told her that he was booked to attend the sympo-

sium himself so he couldn't really take offence that he
hadn't been invited to share the ride.

Besides…he needed a few minutes to try and get his
head around this extraordinary development.

She might not remember him but he remembered
Charlotte Highton very well indeed. He'd been look-
ing forward to seeing what that dynamic young doctor
was like further down the track of her brilliant career.

Not that she'd been his type when he'd met her all
those years ago but he'd been able to appreciate her
attributes. The soft femininity that had been such a
delightful contrast to the skill and intelligence she'd
radiated as a young clinician. The sparkle of a woman
who'd had the world and most of its men at her feet.

Now she was a female clinician who exuded power
and control. There wasn't even the slightest hint of soft-
ness.

Or emotion, other than anger.

Except…just for a moment there, when he'd told her
that he'd met her before, Nico could swear he had seen
real fear in her eyes. A vulnerability that had been so
out of place with the external appearance of this woman
that he'd thought he'd been imagining things.

What he certainly wasn't imagining was the stark
contrast between the woman he remembered admiring
in the past and the one he'd just encountered.

What the hell had happened to Charlotte Highton?

And what was she trying to hide?

CHAPTER TWO

'CHARLOTTE...THERE YOU ARE! Thank goodness...I've been seriously worried about what might have happened to you.' The tall, grey-haired man was hurrying towards her. As he got closer, however, his step faltered and his eyes widened. 'Oh, my goodness. What *has* happened to you?'

The hotel Bonvecchiata had a water landing for gondolas and motorboats so Charlotte had entered the foyer moments after leaping out of the police launch. She knew she looked a fright but there'd been no chance to duck into a restroom and at least tidy her hair and sponge some of the mud from her clothing. Richard Campbell, the co-ordinator of this select symposium and the man who'd invited her to open it, must have been pacing the foyer as he'd waited anxiously for her to arrive.

'Long story, Richard. I'm very sorry, but I got caught up in an emergency. A man went into cardiac arrest and fell off some scaffolding right in front of me. I had to keep up the CPR until the ambulance got there.'

Charlotte was speaking quickly but her mind was working even faster. There were about fifty people

who'd been invited to attend this symposium. Where were they? Sitting in the conference room already, drumming their fingers on the tabletops and muttering about the substandard organisation of this gathering?

Richard was an old friend. Charlotte felt terrible about letting him down like this by being late and he didn't even know the worst of it yet. How was she going to tell him that she'd lost her presentation material?

He'd noticed her gaze sweep the foyer.

'They're serving coffee and cake in the restaurant for everybody. As soon as I knew you were running late I put back the start time for half an hour. There's a couple of attendees that aren't here yet as well.'

'Oh…' Charlotte nodded. She had been given a small breathing space. Now she had to decide if there was any way in the world she could rescue the situation. 'Richard…about my opening address…'

The older man smiled. 'Catchy title. "Miracles or Mutilation?" It's caught everybody's attention already, I have to say. But, Charlotte…' Richard was frowning now, looking down at her shredded tights and grazed knees. 'Are you going to be able to deliver it?'

Richard Campbell's reputation was on the line here. There were people from all over the world who'd chosen to come to this satellite symposium—a breakaway group from the much larger conference that had finished in Rome yesterday—plus others who had chosen to come to this forum without attending the main conference. They were all leaders in the field of emergency medicine. Exceptionally busy people who would not be happy to have their precious time wasted.

Charlotte's presentation had been researched meticu-

lously. The medical illustrations department of her university hospital had spent hours preparing the graphics that represented the facts and figures, the trends and the controversies about cost-effectiveness. It didn't matter how phenomenal her memory was, there was no way she could do justice to her presentation.

If she could get hold of someone at St Margaret's they could find the presentation on her desk computer and email it to her, but that would take too much time. They only had a matter of hours to fit in the other presentations and discussions before the symposium dinner this evening. And someone needed to open the day's programme.

How would it look it she backed out? Even with the best excuse in the world it would still dent her reputation as a young leader in this field, and Charlotte *needed* that reputation. It was who she was. The professional Charlotte Highton was strong enough to hide the *real* Charlotte. The inadequate, shameful one who wasn't a real woman at all.

She was caught between a rock and a hard place here. If she explained that there was no way she could do this, she would tarnish her reputation with the taint of failure and that chink in her armour might never be mended. It might grow, in fact, and eventually split open and the whole world would know what she was hiding.

They might look at her the way Nico Moretti had. As if they knew she was a fraud.

Charlotte could feel her heart thumping rapidly and there was a sinking sensation in her stomach that threatened to spiral into nausea.

'I've got a small problem,' she confessed to Rich-

ard. 'I've lost my presentation. My laptop ended up in the canal.'

'Oh…Lord…' Richard shaded his eyes with his hand. 'Can you manage without it?'

Charlotte opened her mouth to tell him how unlikely that was, but before she could force the words out she was distracted by the sound of her name being called from somewhere near the reception desk.

'*Charlotte Jane Highton…*'

The voice was as familiar to her as her own but Charlotte didn't want to believe that there was yet another problem she had to deal with. She kept her gaze on Richard, who gave her a rueful smile.

'Sorry. I hadn't got around to telling you. Your grandmother's here.'

Charlotte shook her head sharply. 'No. She's not supposed to arrive until tonight. After the symposium. We're travelling back to London together tomorrow.'

But the voice was much closer now. It couldn't be ignored.

'Charlotte Jane… What on *earth* have you done to yourself, child? You look like you've been run over by a gondola.'

Charlotte closed her eyes. She might be thirty-one years old but her grandmother could make her feel like a child again in a heartbeat. Flame-haired and larger than life, Lady Geraldine Highton was never one to stand on ceremony.

'Gran…what are you doing here?'

'I'm supposed to be here. I booked a room for us tonight.'

'Yes, but you were flying in this evening.'

'I changed my flight and arrived first thing this morning. I decided I wanted to hear you speak and this lovely man has told me I can sit in with all the translators and hear you on some headphones.'

Richard was nodding now and his smile was intended to reassure Charlotte that this problem, at least, had been dealt with. Clearly, he had been charmed by Lady Geraldine. Or intimidated. Either way, she had made arrangements that she now deemed satisfactory.

'But, Gran, you hate hearing anything about medical procedures. You've never wanted to hear me talk about my work.'

'Today's different.'

Something *was* different. With the kind of skill Charlotte found invaluable in her dealings with people in traumatic situations, she could sense that there was something important her grandmother was keeping to herself.

'I might not like hearing it,' Lady Geraldine continued, 'and I might not understand it, but it won't stop me wanting the chance to be proud of my granddaughter. Who knows? It might be the only chance I ever get.'

Yes. There was a shadow there in her grandmother's eyes. Eyes that usually sparkled with the determination to squeeze the best that life had to offer out of every opportunity. What was going on?

Charlotte knew she was staring. She also knew that her grandmother could read her like a book.

'We'll talk later,' Lady Geraldine said crisply. 'What we have to do now is get you tidied up. Thankfully, I have spare hosiery in my bag. And a hairbrush. Come on, Charlotte. Where's the nearest bathroom? There's

no time to waste. You don't want to keep all these important people waiting, do you?'

'But…'

There was a plea on Richard's face now. 'You don't have to give the presentation you prepared,' he said quietly. 'I have every confidence that you can think of something to say that would be an appropriate way to open this symposium. Could you do that, Charlotte? Please?'

The space between that rock and hard place suddenly got so small that it squeezed the breath out of Charlotte's lungs. She couldn't think. Maybe because she had no choice.

'I'll do my best.'

So it was that Charlotte found herself looking almost presentable again fifteen minutes later, standing in front of a room full of people who sat at a huge, U-shaped table. Some wore headphones to receive the translation service. Most had laptops or tablets on the table in front of them, along with pads of paper, pens, pitchers of iced water and even bowls of mints.

Charlotte had nothing other than a microphone clipped to the lapel of her jacket. From the way her heart was pounding and how exposed she felt, she could have been standing here stark naked.

She tried to smile at the group but failed. She did, however, manage to introduce herself and apologise for the delay in starting.

'I'm sure you've all heard by now of the reason why I was delayed and you, more than most, will understand that emergencies happen.'

Oh, help. Charlotte could hear the sound of her own voice, magnified by the loudspeaker system. Where was the calm, professional tone she always used in public?

What would her grandmother think of this? The niggling worry that there was something wrong that her grandmother wasn't telling her couldn't be allowed to surface until this was all over but it was impossible not to have a flash of shame that the pride her only living relative had taken in her achievements was going to be dented.

'Ah…' Charlotte stared at the group, totally at a loss for what she could say next. Please, God, let the ground open and swallow me up, she thought.

The ground didn't open but the door of the conference room did, to admit a latecomer. Everybody's head turned at the interruption but Charlotte's gaze had got there first and now it was stuck.

The worst moment of her life had just taken a dive to a new low.

How on earth could Nicholas Moretti have the nerve to show up here, knowing he'd ruined her preparation for this talk? He'd already revealed his disbelief that she was who she said she was. Did he now want to see if she was going to make a fool of herself and confirm that disbelief?

He was about to get what he came for, then, wasn't he?

Nico gave a very European hand gesture, apologising for his interruption as he took the empty space at the table. His body language conveyed complete confidence that he had the right to be here, though. That he was, in fact, eager to take part in the proceedings. And then his

gaze locked with Charlotte's and that weird spinning sensation in her gut seemed to catch fire.

Anger?

Quite possibly.

Charlotte Highton wasn't about to let the actions of a man even threaten to destroy her.

Not again.

She took a deep breath, jerking her gaze away from Nico and vowing not to let it return to that section of the table until she was finished. In a way, he'd done her a favour. His entrance had covered her stumble and now she was fired up. Whether it was from anger or desperation was immaterial.

'Some of you might be asking whether I should have let myself become involved in that emergency situation, especially when the result has deprived you of the audiovisual accompaniment you were supposed to have this morning.'

A ripple of sympathy went through the gathering.

'It's a fair question,' Charlotte continued. 'How far should any of us go in getting involved? How far should we go as emergency medicine specialists? Out in the field or in our own departments?'

Her words were clear and her tone as professional as ever now. Everybody was listening. Looking at her. She could feel one gaze in particular so strongly that she knew exactly who it was coming from. Good. Let him watch and listen. Let him see who Charlotte Highton was now.

'We can do so many things that can be done in an operating theatre in our emergency departments or out

in the field. Burr-holes, tracheotomies, amputations, thoracotamies, Caesareans.' Charlotte paused for effect. 'Extreme measures in desperate circumstances. How many are justified? Does the weight of evidence suggest we're performing miracles? Or guilty of performing mutilations?'

Another pause. This was the moment that would make or break this talk.

'I had a presentation that was full of statistics about these kinds of extreme procedures and graphics to show you the controversial relationship between patient outcomes and cost-effectiveness. Obviously it's not possible to do those facts and figures justice from memory, so instead…' The solution to this problem came to her in a flash of inspiration. 'I'm going to present a case history.'

Nico sat back in his chair.

He could feel the surprise of the people around him. What was this? They were all intelligent people who were hungry for new knowledge. They wanted to be presented with the results of cutting-edge research that they could use to improve what they did for a career. But they were going to be told a *story*?

'The man I'll call Bernie was forty-three years old,' Charlotte was saying. 'He went to the corner shop very late one night, because his pregnant wife had a craving for chocolate ripple ice cream. The timing was unfortunate. The shop was held up and Bernie got stabbed. A small knife with a short blade was buried to its hilt in his chest, deflected by the sixth rib, maybe five or six inches to the left from the midline.'

Nico could sense the interest picking up around him. The injury had been dangerously close to the man's heart.

'The ambulance crew knew not to remove an impaled object. Bernie's still conscious when they arrive but his blood pressure's dropping. Fortunately, this corner shop is only about two minutes' drive from St Margaret's hospital. They put a doughnut dressing around the knife to stabilise it, give Bernie some oxygen and load and go. They establish IV access en route.'

The way Charlotte had changed to the present tense drew them all into the urgency of this case. Clever. Or were they all drawn in, as he was, by the sound of her voice? Soft, but as clear as a bell. As under control as her hair was again, all scraped back into that complicated knot thing.

Nico had preferred it the way he'd seen it after that resuscitation scene, with enough loose wisps to suggest that the whole knot could be released if you buried your fingers in it, wiggled them and then dragged them gently through the length of the hair. How long was it when it was loose? he wondered. And then he sharply dismissed the errant speculation and concentrated again on what she was saying.

'By the time Bernie comes through our doors, he's lost consciousness. His BP's unrecordable. His cardiac rhythm goes from SVT to VF to asystole within thirty seconds of my team getting him hooked up to the monitors.'

Nico was really listening now. So this was a case that Charlotte herself had managed? He could imagine her there, in the emergency department of St Marga-

ret's. Wearing scrubs, probably, with a white coat over them. No…she'd been expecting a major trauma. She'd have a plastic apron on. And gloves. And a head covering that probably had a plastic face shield to protect her from blood spatter. She would have been in charge. In control. Her voice might have been louder than it was right now but just as clear.

'We know our protocols inside out but how do we start CPR? This man's got a knife in his chest that's probably punctured his left ventricle. He's bleeding out. We can pull the knife out and push fluids but there's a hole in his heart so that would be futile.'

Nico was holding his breath without realising it. Everybody here knew that the only option was to do one of the most invasive procedures that could ever be done out of an operating theatre. Cracking open this man's chest and getting to the heart of the problem, so to speak.

'He's dead already unless we do something major and do it fast.' Charlotte's tone told them she agreed with the conclusion they'd all reached. 'A thoracotomy is the only option but I know as well as everybody else in the team what the odds are for a successful result. Virtually nil. But, hey…we have to try, don't we? This man is about to become a father. Right now, his pregnant wife is probably wondering why it's taking him so long to get back with her ice cream.'

Charlotte seemed to straighten her back. 'I'm the one who has to make the call and, as far as I'm concerned, it's a no-brainer. We take out the knife and I do a clamshell thoracotomy. There's a gaping hole in the left ventricle and I suture it shut while we deal with more blood in a thorax than I've ever seen before.'

Nico closed his eyes for a heartbeat. He could picture it. A nightmare scene. The tissue of the myocardium would have been slippery. The visual field would have been impossible to keep clear with all that blood so you'd have to work almost blind.

'We start pushing fluids and begin CPR. I'm riding that stretcher to Theatre with my hand inside Bernie's chest, doing internal compressions and praying that my rough suturing is going to hold.'

Oh, Nico could imagine that scene too. Charlotte would have had to have been astride the man's legs, with one hand on the side rail to steady herself. Amongst the bank of monitoring and ventilation equipment that would have been in place. Speeding along with her team running to get them to Theatre as fast as possible.

It felt like he was standing in one of the wide corridors of St Margaret's right now, watching the dramatic spectacle rush past him. Opening his eyes again, he knew that he was looking at Charlotte with growing admiration. This was some woman.

'The cardiac surgical team is waiting for us. They do a much better job than me in repairing the damage. They replace the blood volume and get Bernie's heart started again. By this time his wife is at the hospital. Bernie's taken to the intensive care unit. He's still alive but what none of us know is whether we've done the right thing in saving him. Will he wake up? And, if he does, how much brain damage has been caused by the lack of oxygen? His wife is distraught and, just to add to the tension, she goes into labour three weeks before her due date.'

A soft groan came from her audience. This might be

nothing like what they'd expected as an opening talk but they were all invested in the story now. They had to know the outcome.

'I've told you this story because it does, unlike so many, many others, have a happy ending. Bernie did have a degree of neurological compromise. His cognition and speech were affected and he had a unilateral weakness on his right side.'

It was the first time Nico had seen Charlotte smile. He felt his own lips curve in an unconscious response.

'But his weak arm didn't stop him being able to cradle his newborn daughter a couple of days later. His difficulty in finding words didn't dim the way he could communicate his joy to his wife.'

Dammit. Was that a *lump* Nico could feel in his throat? He swallowed it away. His own career was full of success stories like this, wasn't it?

'The bottom line,' Charlotte continued quietly, 'is that our job is about the people who come under our care. Bernie was a miracle. But if he hadn't made it, that resus scene in my ED could have been denounced as unnecessary mutilation. We couldn't know how it would go before we started but is it just a coin toss?'

Charlotte was looking around the room. Nico was waiting for her gaze to cross his. He was oddly disappointed when it didn't.

'No.' She answered her own question. 'That's what our chosen specialty is all about. Working towards being the best we can be in our field of expertise. Knowing when there's a choice that pulling out the big guns is going to make the difference between life and death.'

Nico saw Charlotte take a deep breath. She was

wrapping up now and the unusual introduction had clearly been a huge success. Everybody was leaning forward, totally engrossed and eager to participate in the programme that was about to start.

He felt the same way so how on earth could he be distracted by the way that deep breath pushed Charlotte's breasts against the material of the plain blouse she wore under that tailored jacket? The way a hint of cleavage struggled to appear over the top button. Good grief. She was so buttoned up with that hairstyle and the fitted clothes she wore, it was almost as if she was trying not to look remotely feminine.

Maybe she was batting for the other team. Nico tucked the thought away with satisfaction. That would explain a lot. Maybe she had been trying to deny her true preference when he'd seen her out with that man in The Cosmopolitan Club all those years ago. And even if she was now comfortable with who she was, in her position Charlotte probably wouldn't want to come out of the closet and travel in the company of her girlfriend. Or wife, perhaps. It was none of his business and it didn't bother him.

So why did that curious feeling of disappointment in not making eye contact with her a second ago suddenly deepen several notches?

'The papers you are going to be privileged to hear today are from invited speakers who are leading their particular fields. I'm looking forward to hearing the discussions that will follow the presentations. Again, I must apologise for my unorthodox keynote speech but, on behalf of Dr Richard Campbell, our chairman for today, and the others involved in organising this satel-

lite session, let me welcome you to our symposium on critical interventions.'

Nico joined the round of applause. His neighbour leaned sideways to say something about how moving the story had been and how good it was to be reminded of the human aspects of their science. But Nico merely murmured agreement. He couldn't take his eyes off Charlotte. As if she felt his intense gaze, she looked up from her position at the front of the room.

So there, her gaze seemed to say. *I did it—even if you did do your best to stop me.*

After the awkward start to the day things were running smoothly. Richard was delighted. He smiled at Charlotte as they were preparing to follow the others out of the conference room for the lunch break.

'Do you know, I think your introduction has allowed for some very interesting questions to be raised that people might not have considered appropriate otherwise. You've given this whole forum an informality that has brought people closer together. It was a stroke of brilliance.'

'Thanks.' Charlotte rubbed the back of her neck, trying to ease the tension that still hadn't gone away completely. 'It could have taken things in the opposite direction. I was lucky.'

'I think everyone was impressed.'

Had Nicholas Moretti been impressed? And why did it matter so much that he had been?

'I'm sure they'll want to tell you that themselves, over lunch.'

Charlotte wasn't at all sure she wanted that to hap-

pen. She might be used to talking to colleagues while balancing a plate of food and eating but the idea of doing that in Nico's company seemed disturbingly…intimate?

Whatever. She had the perfect excuse.

'I'm going to skip lunch, if you don't mind, Richard. I'll grab a sandwich or something but I really need to check on my grandmother and make sure she's being taken care of. And that she has something to do for the afternoon. Goodness knows what kind of mischief she could get up to otherwise.'

Richard was grinning now. 'She's quite something, your grandmother. How old is she?'

'Eighty-two. Going on about sixteen, I think. I often feel as if I'm in the company of a wayward teenager.' Charlotte's smile was fond. 'And then, at other times, she comes out with the kind of wisdom and advice that only someone who's experienced life to the full could have. She's amazing.'

Richard patted her arm. 'Go and catch up. I'll give your excuses to anyone who asks.'

'Thanks.' Charlotte hurried out to the reception area, away from the dining room, and asked whether her grandmother had left a message for her.

'No. But she's had lunch delivered to your room. Would you like your key now?'

The room was massive and decorated in Venetian style with sumptuous drapes, bed coverings and deep armchairs all in tones of silver and soft bronze. There was a Persian rug on the floor beneath the chandelier hanging from an astonishingly high ceiling. A small table with spindly legs supported a silver tray that had

plates of delicate-looking sandwiches and cakes, a pot of tea and cups.

The first thing that struck Charlotte was that the tray hadn't been touched.

Almost at the same time she noted how tidy the room was. Where were the clothes strewn about that always happened when Geraldine was choosing her next outfit? The open guidebooks as she chose her next adventure?

And why on earth was her grandmother lying on a bed in the middle of the day? Lady Geraldine Highton might be eighty-two but she didn't *do* naps. 'Life's too short,' she always said. 'And it's getting shorter for me by the day. Why waste it by sleeping? I can sleep when I'm dead.'

'Gran…' Charlotte moved towards the bed. 'What's wrong?'

'Oh…' Geraldine clearly hadn't been expecting a visitor. She sat up swiftly, looking…embarrassed. No, make that *guilty*. 'Charlie…I didn't think I'd see you until this evening.' The odd expression vanished, to be replaced by a beaming smile. 'That was a wonderful talk you gave, darling. I can't tell you how proud I was. And I understood every word. Well, almost every word. The next speaker was terribly dull in comparison. I went for a walk and watched the gondolas for a while. I might go for a ride in one after lunch. It's been years…'

Charlotte sank down onto the edge of the second bed, facing her grandmother. Something here was off-key. Terribly off-key.

'Gran…' She reached out and took hold of a soft hand decorated with several diamond rings. 'What's going on?'

'Whatever do you mean? Nothing's going on, Char-
lotte. Come and have lunch with me.' Lady Geraldine
got to her feet but then her face changed. She couldn't
hide a grimace of pain and her hand went to her stom-
ach.

'You're not well,' Charlotte gasped. 'That's why you
haven't touched your lunch. Why didn't you *tell* me?'

'I'm fine. There's nothing wrong with me.'

'Lie down,' Charlotte ordered. 'I want to have a look
at you.'

For a long, long moment Geraldine looked unde-
cided. But then she quietly lay down and answered the
barrage of questions. Yes, she had abdominal pain. No,
it wasn't the first time. Yes, she'd been to see a doctor
about it. She'd had a scan. She was booked to have a
biopsy between Christmas and New Year.

A *biopsy?*

With absolute dread giving her a chill that almost
made her shiver visibly, Charlotte quietly asked if she
could feel her grandmother's tummy and when she did,
the hard edges of the mass she could feel confirmed
her worst fear.

'Did…did your doctor tell you what he thought it
was after the scan?'

'Oh, yes…' Lady Geraldine took hold of Charlotte's
hand with both of hers. 'He's sure it's some form of
bowel cancer.' Her voice wobbled. 'I didn't want you
to find out, darling. Not yet.'

Charlotte's voice was thick with tears. 'Why not?
You should have told me. I should have been there with
you when you had your appointments.'

'We've been planning this trip for so long. Going on

the Orient Express has been on my bucket list for far too long.' Unbelievably, Geraldine was smiling mischievously. 'And what better time to fulfil a bucket list item than when you've been told the end probably isn't that far off?'

'Gran… We can't spend thirty hours on a train. We have to fly back to London tonight. I'll talk to people. We'll find a way to bring that procedure forward so we can start treatment earlier.'

'No way, Jose.' The way Lady Geraldine's eyes narrowed was a warning that she was not about to be contradicted. 'I've taken some painkillers. I'll be as right as rain after a little rest. You're not going to spoil this for me, Charlotte. Are you?'

It wasn't really a question. And the look coming from those faded blue eyes wasn't disapproving. It was full of absolute love. The kind of love Charlotte had received from this remarkable woman ever since she'd been orphaned as a small, terrified child.

This was why her grandmother had wanted to hear her speak today. Why she'd wanted to tell her how proud she was of her. Well, that cut both ways, didn't it?

'Let's enjoy this time together,' Lady Geraldine added softly. 'Before we know anything for sure. Let's pretend you didn't find me like this. The way I wanted it to be. Go back to your conference, darling. I need a little rest and then I'm going to choose my outfit for the dinner tonight.'

Those words stayed with Charlotte during the afternoon's symposium proceedings and it was the hardest thing she'd ever done, to keep up her professional image.

The papers being presented were fascinating and the discussions lively, and Charlotte had learned long ago to firmly shut the door between her professional and personal lives, but today it was impossible.

Today had started badly. She thought she'd made the best of a bad situation and survived but now it felt as if the world had tilted far too sharply on its axis. What did her brilliant career matter if she was about to lose the person she loved most? The only person she truly loved, come to that.

The conference attendees were invited to a cocktail session before a break to get ready for the dinner but Charlotte quietly slipped away from the group. She had to pull herself together. Had to find the strength to deal with what was undoubtedly coming. Did she really want to deprive her grandmother of the long-awaited pleasure of the train trip tomorrow and whisk her back to London and into hospital? Did she have that right?

The balcony leading off the now deserted dining room offered a private space with the bonus of an idyllic canal view where more than one ornate gondola could be seen floating past.

One of the gondolas held a pair of young lovers who were locked in a passionate embrace, oblivious to their surroundings for the moment. Maybe they were practising. Wasn't there a bridge here in Venice and if you kissed while going beneath it, it meant that your love would last for ever?

If her grandmother was here on this balcony with her, she'd be poking Charlotte with a bony finger right about now. Clicking her tongue.

That should be you in that gondola, Charlotte Jane,

she'd be saying. *Kissing some gorgeous young man whose baby you can't wait to have. You don't know what you're missing, child, and it's the most important thing in life.*

But Charlotte knew all too well what she'd be missing far too soon and hearing her grandmother's voice so clearly in her mind was the final straw.

Tears rolled down her cheeks. Hot, burning tears that felt like acid. No surprise there. They were pretty concentrated given that she hadn't shed a tear for six years now. They were such a sign of weakness. Feminine weakness.

She knew there was no point in trying to stop them.

Thank God nobody could see her.

The room Nico had been given at the hotel Bonvecchiata was luxurious. He eyed the huge bed, pulled at his tie to loosen it, and looked forward to putting his feet up for a while before heading off to the symposium dinner.

What a day!

Shedding his jacket, Nico walked to the tall windows of his room and looked through the ornate iron grille to find he had the bonus of a canal view. A gondola floated past with a young couple locked in each other's arms.

Nico smiled. Nice. His gaze drifted lazily and then it caught.

His smile faded.

There was a balcony on the floor beneath his. Charlotte Highton was standing there, her shoulders bowed as if she carried the weight of the entire world on them.

And she was *crying*?

Dio, but this woman was so full of contradictions.

For a moment Nico stared in fascination. He would never have believed that she was capable of showing such a depth of emotion. But why was she so upset?

Did it have anything to do with being unable to present what she'd intended to present this morning?

Because of the trouble he'd unwittingly caused for her?

For another, long moment Nico kept staring, unsure of how to unravel the conflicting emotions being stirred in his own gut. Why did he feel such a strong urge to try and help this prickly, complicated woman? It was more than having contributed to a bad start to her day. More, even, than being curious about how someone's personality could have changed so much in just a few short years.

Being aware that there was some indefinable extra motivation should be enough of a warning to stop him getting involved any further, but did he want to listen to that warning?

He turned away. Stared at the huge, inviting bed for a moment. And then, with a soft growl, he turned on his heel and headed for the door.

CHAPTER THREE

OH...NO.

As if she could cope with her day getting even worse!

Of all the people to discover her at her lowest point in so many years, it had to be Nico Moretti.

Charlotte did her utmost to stem the tide of her tears. She turned her back on Nico and leant on the balustrade of the balcony, gripping the roughened concrete so hard she could feel tendrils of pain in her fingers that flickered into her arms. She fixed her gaze on the canal beneath and blinked again and again, trying to clear the wetness that didn't want to stop. Why couldn't it go back where it had come from, instead of continuing to roll down her face in these humiliating tears?

He didn't say anything. He just came to stand beside her. He, too, seemed to be gazing at the view and he spread his hands on the balustrade as if the only reason he was there was to admire their surroundings.

Charlotte's panic ebbed a little as he just stood there, a silent presence.

She'd never had company during the most unhappy periods in her life. Her first instinct, even as a young child so bereft at the loss of her parents, had been to

hide. To cry alone. And feel alone. To accept that life was a terribly lonely business and you just had to deal with that.

There *was* comfort to be found in simply being close to another person. To feel the presence of another living, breathing human.

The fact that Nico wasn't saying anything made it easy to accept his presence. She didn't have to try and find excuses or explain anything, and to have someone there who was clearly prepared to accept the state she was in made it feel as if it was okay not to be coping. As if she had support.

Strong support. Bit by bit, Charlotte found her thoughts creeping out from the dark knot in her head. She was aware of how big Nico was. Well over six feet in height and broad with it. His hands against the ancient concrete looked huge and powerful but his fingers were long and artistic looking. Clever hands, no doubt capable of performing the careful, intricate movements that were needed when you were dealing with something as precious as brain tissue.

Charlotte blinked again and, amazingly, her vision wasn't blurred any more. Without raising her head from its bowed position, she could study his neatly trimmed nails and olive-brown skin and the smattering of dark hair on the backs of his hands that disappeared under the turned-back cuffs of his white shirt.

Her head turned, as if her gaze was being pulled up by an external force. Up his arms, across his chest, where a loosened tie hung like a necklace and the top buttons of his shirt were undone. It was impossible not to flick her gaze up to his face now, but it was safe. He

was still staring down at the canal so Charlotte let her gaze linger for a moment on the strong profile. Unfairly luxurious eyelashes that brushed his cheeks when he blinked. A nose that made no apology for the space it took and deep creases on each side that ran down to meet a mouth that looked as if it smiled often and easily.

A jaw that looked like it hadn't seen a razor in a fair few hours. And a firmness to it that suggested tension. Was he gritting his teeth? Was he standing there not knowing what to say? Wishing he was somewhere else?

'I'm sorry.' The words came out as a whisper. 'I've had… It's been…' she had to take a tiny gulp of air '…a weird kind of day.'

'I understand.' Nico moved finally, but only his head. He angled it a little towards Charlotte. And then he smiled at her.

And…dear Lord…*what* a smile. Slow and so full of warmth. The most genuine smile she had ever seen. And it was for *her*. She had to catch her breath again.

'And I have a horrible feeling I might have contributed to your day not being the one you hoped for,' Nico continued. 'I really must apologise again.'

His voice was as warm as that smile. The Irish lilt was unmistakeable but, if he had been in Ireland, they would hear something else. An Italian inflection that made it unique. An astonishing accent colouring a depth that was as masculine as his size and aura of power.

How many women had fallen in love with that voice already?

Not that she was about to join the ranks. Charlotte cleared her throat.

'No…really. Losing my laptop was nothing com-

pared to…' Oh, help. Had she really been about to break one of her most ironclad rules and share personal information with a professional colleague?

'Compared to what, *cara*?'

It was the endearment that did her in. An endearment in a foreign language that somehow made it inoffensive and genuinely caring.

'My…grandmother is here. She's not well and…and it's possible she might not have…' Charlotte's intake of breath was a small sob. 'Might not have much time left.'

'Ohhh…' The sound was a drawn-out note of understanding. Empathy.

This man was a stranger even if they *had* met before. She would probably never see him again after today. So it didn't really count as sharing personal information, did it? Nobody would be giving her meaningful glances at work or gossiping about her in the cafeteria at St Margaret's. As if it would help with the anonymity, Charlotte fixed her gaze on the canal again. She could be simply talking aloud to herself.

'She's the most important person in the world to me,' she said softly. 'My parents both got killed in a horrible accident when I was eight years old. I was in the accident too and came out as a terrified shell of a child who wouldn't even speak to anyone for months. Gran never cared how tough it got, she was always so patient and so loving. So proud of any achievements I managed.'

'She would have had a lot to be proud of.'

Charlotte's breath came out in a huff of incredulity as she twisted sharply to glare at Nico. He was so used to giving women compliments, wasn't he? Meaningless

compliments that demeaned what she was trying to tell him about her wonderful grandmother.

'What makes you think you know anything about me?' The words came out tight and accusing. And then Charlotte shook her head and swallowed fresh tears. 'You know *nothing*.'

There was a flash in his eyes but, while he might be startled by the verbal attack, he didn't look away.

'I know that a few years ago I met a woman who would have made anybody who loved her immensely proud,' he said calmly. 'But you're correct...I know nothing about you on a personal level.'

His gaze still held hers and there was something else in his eyes now. Respect? Curiosity?

'So tell me,' he invited. And then he smiled again. 'I'm listening.'

She was about to walk away.

Nico could sense the internal struggle but, dammit, he *wanted* to hear more. He knew perfectly well he was taking advantage of finding Charlotte in a state that made her vulnerable but he wasn't about to use the situation to his own advantage. Quite the opposite! His only motivation for coming out to this balcony and interrupting an obviously private moment had been to offer assistance.

He owed her that, surely?

Even though she had dismissed any contribution he'd made to her having such a bad day, he knew he hadn't helped it get off to a good start. And it was frustrating not to be able to think of a way to make up for that. Nico Moretti was an expert in making other people's

lives better, even in the most dire of circumstances. He firmly believed that you could find at least a little patch of joy anywhere if you didn't take life too seriously.

Maybe that was why he knew he had the reputation of being a playboy. But play was the key, wasn't it? Like when he took the time to actually play with one of his smaller patients or do something silly enough to make them smile. And…good grief…he'd never encountered a woman who couldn't accept a compliment, even if it had been an automatic and possibly less than genuine response.

Nico had a strong sense that anything Charlotte told him would be completely honest, no matter how badly it reflected on herself. In his experience, this was an unusual trait, particularly for a woman on first acquaintance.

What really surprised him, however, was how much he wanted to hear more about her. His curiosity about Charlotte Highton was increasing rapidly. He remembered the brilliant young doctor. He'd seen the icy-cool clinician in action. He'd seen a speaker not only cope with facing an international audience having been deprived of her resources but engage them to the point where she'd had them in the palm of her hand.

And now he'd seen a glimpse of a loving granddaughter. Beneath all the layers he could detect there was an orphan who'd been a desperately unhappy child. A woman who currently looked alone. And lonely.

Just who was the real Charlotte?

He tried to send a silent message with his smile. And his eyes.

Talk to me. Please. You never know, I might be able to help. I'm good at helping.

It wasn't working, though. It was as though he was trying to hold a wild creature in his hands and it was struggling to be free. An injured wild creature that wanted to crawl away and lick its wounds somewhere it felt safe.

He needed something more to keep her here. He needed to tap into something that would give them a bond, however tenuous.

'I've met many people at many conferences over the years,' he told her. 'They are often accompanied by their husbands or wives. Or their lovers. Sometimes by their children. You are the very first I've met who is accompanied by a grandparent. That's…intriguing. Special.'

He watched Charlotte take a ragged breath. He heard her sniff and had to hide a smile because it sounded so… unprofessional. Childlike, even. It wasn't as if he'd never witnessed a grown woman crying, of course. They usually did, when he told them things were over, but this was different. The tears had nothing to do with him and they touched a spot in his heart usually reserved for those younger patients or their families. Something poignant.

'Gran *is* special,' Charlotte said, her words a whisper. Then she cleared her throat. 'But she doesn't usually accompany me. In fact, I'm not allowed to talk about anything remotely gruesome or medical when I'm around her. She says that you can always find something uplifting to talk about if you try hard enough.'

'A woman after my own heart,' Nico smiled. 'A

finder of joy who can make people around her feel better.'

He let out a quiet breath as he sensed Charlotte relaxing. He knew she was almost smiling herself because he was watching so carefully and he could see the softening of her lips. The imperceptible curling at their corners.

'She always has something to look forward to. A new adventure planned. That's why she's here. As soon as she knew I was going to be speaking in Venice she looked up the timetable for the Orient Express going from Venice back to London and when the dates were perfect she said it was meant to be and I couldn't say no because it was well up the bucket list.'

'The bucket list?'

'You know…' Charlotte really smiled this time, as she looked up and caught his gaze. 'The list of things you really, really want to do before you kick the bucket?'

'Kick the…? Oh…' Just occasionally, the fact that English was a second language tripped him up. '*Sì*…' The Italian word slipped out unconsciously as he contemplated the euphemism for dying. 'I understand.'

Her eyes were grey. A dark, stormy sort of grey at the moment. He always expected blonde women to have blue eyes so the colour struck him as different. As unusual as this woman was herself, perhaps?

'But it's a crazy idea. How can we take a slow train trip across Europe when she's so sick? We should fly back to London tonight. I could have her in a hospital by tomorrow, getting the kind of investigations she needs to plan treatment.'

'Is that what she wants? Your grandmother?' It was

a relief to be given a problem to solve at last and Nico was more than ready to focus on it, but he needed more information. 'What is her name?'

'Geraldine. Her friends call her Jendi.'

'And what are the symptoms of her illness?'

'I don't really know. She's kept this from me. I wouldn't have known about it at all yet except I found her resting and could see she had abdominal pain. And…I could feel a mass…'

'She has medication for the pain?'

'Yes. She seems fine now. She totally refused to consider cancelling the train trip and getting a flight to London. She told me to go away so she could have a bath in peace and get ready for the dinner tonight. She wants to dress up.'

'If there are no obvious signs that it would be detrimental to her condition, then maybe that's exactly what she *should* do.'

Charlotte's jaw dropped. 'And the train trip? You think that's a good idea, too?'

'Another day or two will not make any difference to the course of her illness,' Nico said. 'And look at it from her point of view. What would be better? To be lying in a hospital bed waiting for possibly a painful procedure or being able to forget about what lies ahead for a brief time and enjoying a wonderful experience in the company of someone you love?'

'But…' Charlotte caught her bottom lip between her teeth and tugged on it. It was another childish gesture that caught Nico in that soft spot in his heart. But then she let go with her teeth and soothed her lip with her

tongue and suddenly it was quite another, very unex-
pected spot that Nico could feel waking up. 'How could
I forget enough to help her enjoy it?'

'Because you have that kind of strength.' This time
the compliment was completely sincere. Nico already
knew enough about Charlotte to be convinced of it. 'You
can choose the part of you that you want other people
to see and the rest you can keep hidden.'

Something very odd flickered across Charlotte's
face. The kind of expression that suggested…guilt? As
though she'd been caught out trying to hide something
huge and important?

No. The expression was gone as fast as it had ap-
peared. And now Charlotte was turning away. Nico
wasn't ready to let her go. Not just yet.

'I think you should make the most of any time you
can have together. Be proud that you can help her
achieve this bucket-list thing. Maybe you can find out
what the other things on her list are too and tick an-
other one off soon.'

A rueful laugh escaped Charlotte. 'Oh, I know what's
on the top of that list and it's not something that's ever
going to be ticked off.'

'Oh?' Nico tilted his head encouragingly. 'They say
that nothing is impossible.'

'*This* is.' Charlotte was looking up at the sky now.
Assessing the clouds to see if the forecasted snow might
arrive or was she seeking divine inspiration? She flicked
Nico the briefest glance. 'Gran's greatest wish is to see
me get married. Settled down and ready to present her
with her first great-grandchild.'

'Ohhh…' Nico nodded slowly. 'That could be tricky.'

'Impossible.' The word was final.

'Hmm.' He had solved the problem of the train trip. Surely there was a way of at least getting around this one? 'Would there be any harm in letting her *think* it might be possible?'

'Gran's not stupid. She knows perfectly well that I'm not in a relationship. I haven't been for years. I'm hardly likely to get away with pretending I've met "Mr Right" within the next few months, am I?' She took a step away from him, raising her hand to smooth her already perfect hairstyle. 'And I really can't believe I'm having such an astonishingly ridiculous conversation.'

Nico had been distracted for a split second, wondering again what Charlotte's hair would look like if it wasn't so tightly coiled and clipped into place. He wanted to pull out some of those pins. To force her to loosen up a little.

'Because it's not so ridiculous,' he said. 'What if you attended this dinner tonight with…with your new boyfriend? How happy would that make your grandmother?'

This time it was real laughter that escaped. A delicious, totally unexpected chuckle of real mirth. 'Is there a "hire a boyfriend" agency in Venice that you know about?'

'There's no need to hire anybody.' Nico's grin stretched his mouth. 'It's the least I could do to make up for this morning's unfortunate happenstance.'

It was perfect. Here it was on a plate. The opportunity to not only make up for contributing to any dis-

tress caused by this morning's incident but to do it in a manner that would be *fun*.

Except that Charlotte was looking at him as if he was totally crazy.

This was surreal.

Just having a personal conversation with a professional acquaintance would have been weird enough but this incredibly good-looking stranger seemed to be offering to pretend to be her *boyfriend* for an evening.

Imagine that!

Unfortunately, Charlotte *could* imagine it. She could imagine herself introducing him to her grandmother as a…as a *friend*…and Nico turning on his most charming smile and Gran putting two and two together and letting wishful thinking make the impossible a reality.

Oh…God…how happy would she be?

The distraction of a train trip to take her mind off what was coming was nothing compared to the joy she would have if she thought Charlotte had finally found 'the one'.

It was crazy. Wasn't it?

'That's crazy,' she said aloud, hoping the spoken words would confirm it.

'It's only for an evening.' Nico shrugged as if it was no big deal. 'We could tell her we've met before, which is perfectly true. We could say that there's something about Venice being such a romantic city and we've realised we can't fight the attraction any longer. It was meant to be.'

Oh…my… If the look he was giving her right now

was any indication of the performance he could put on for her grandmother, she would be totally convinced.

For a skipped heartbeat kind of moment, Charlotte almost believed it herself. She could feel it right down to her bones. How could anyone be so good at looking as if they had just fallen madly in love with someone? It was doing very strange things to something deep inside her. A process that had to be stopped immediately.

He's acting, she reminded herself. And he's only this good at it because he's clearly had a lot of practice.

'You may be an expert in pretending,' she snapped, 'but it's not something I could carry off. I wouldn't even want to try.'

He was still giving her *that* look.

'I watched you this morning,' he said softly. 'I think you can carry off anything that's important enough to you.'

There was a glint of mischief in those dark eyes. Good heavens, he was actually *enjoying* this, wasn't he? He *wanted* to do it?

'You might be surprised at how easy it is,' he continued. 'You might enjoy it.'

Charlotte snorted. 'I don't think so.'

'And wouldn't you even want to try? For your grandmother's sake?'

'No. It would be completely dishonest.'

'Completely?' Nico injected a hurt tone into the word. 'Could you not summon even a tiny bit of attraction to me to work with?'

He tilted his head, moving it closer to her own, his gaze dropping from her eyes to her lips.

And, heaven help her, but Charlotte could actually

feel a curl of desire unfolding deep in her belly. It escaped from that place that was locked away. A place she could never enter because, if she did, she would have to remember… Have to face up to what was so wrong with her…

'*No.*' The word came out like the slamming of a door. It was time to get away from there.

Away from this man who was making her think about ridiculous things.

Feel things she had no desire to feel.

'At least think about it.' His words followed her as she almost ran to get off the balcony. 'I'll see you at dinner.'

CHAPTER FOUR

'OH, MY...'

'What's wrong, Gran? Are you all right?' The lighting wasn't so great in this dinner venue. A restaurant within easy walking distance of the conference venue, this ancient stone vault of a room had been transformed into a winter wonderland in honour of the season.

White church candles with multiple wicks, in a nest of holly leaves and poinsettia flowers, made a centrepiece for each of the small tables set for four. Sheets of fairy lights in icicle form hung from the high ceiling and, on one roughened stone wall, a slide show of Christmassy scenes was softly fading in and out as the scenes changed.

It was a beautiful setting for a dinner but the flickering light levels made it impossible to see things as clearly as Charlotte would have liked. She was convinced her grandmother had suddenly gone pale.

'Stop fussing, Charlotte, for goodness' sake.' Lady Geraldine gave her a surprisingly sharp poke with her finger. 'If you weren't half-blind, you would have noticed what I just noticed.' Her smile was almost gleeful as she lowered her voice. 'Eye candy...'

'*Gran*. Wherever did you learn an expression like that?'

'I blame television,' Lady Geraldine sighed. But she was still smiling. Still watching a point well beyond Charlotte's shoulder. The entranceway, most likely, because Charlotte had deliberately chosen a table as far away from the door as possible. A nice, dark corner. With a bit of luck, Nico Moretti would be late and either he wouldn't be able to spot her or the two unoccupied settings at their table would have been taken by another conference attendee and his or her partner.

But no. With a sinking heart Charlotte realised that to have grabbed her grandmother's keen interest, this 'eye candy' would have to be spectacularly good looking. And judging by the way her elderly relative was practically fanning herself with her hand now, he was coming in their direction. Slowly, she turned her head.

Oh, my…was an understatement. Dr Moretti was wearing a beautifully fitting dinner suit, which always made men look good, but so were most of the other male guests here. Maybe the soft lighting had something to do with the way he stood out. Or more likely, it was the man's sheer presence as he wound his way through the tables, pausing to smile at people he knew or share a few words in greeting.

He seemed to have a spotlight on him, in any case, and Charlotte knew her gaze was as transfixed as her grandmother's. As focused as every other woman in this room.

If Nico was scanning the room, looking for her as he kept moving, he certainly gave no indication of it. Anyone watching would assume he knew exactly what

table he was expected at. Charlotte could feel her grand-mother's interest sharpen into astonishment as he finally made a beeline for their corner, his face lighting up in a smile of sheer joy.

'Carlotta. *Cara*…' With his gaze locked on hers, Nico reached out and cupped one side of her face with his hand. It was an exquisitely tender touch. Overwhelmingly so. Charlotte had no hope of collecting her thoughts, let alone expressing them. His gaze suggested that if she didn't want him to play this game she only had to say the word, but how could she when she couldn't even draw a breath?

And she saw the moment the question in his gaze turned to delight.

Game on.

With a smoothness that suggested Nico was far too good at acting, he turned his charm onto the unsuspecting Lady Geraldine. He gently picked up the hand with its diamond rings flashing in the candlelight. He pressed his lips to it.

'And you have to be Carlotta's *nonna*. I've heard so much about you. This is…*such* a pleasure.'

And then Nico took hold of one of the two spare chairs and moved it so that it was as close to Charlotte's as possible. He sat down and adjusted the silverware and then nodded at a nearby waiter, who instantly came to fill his champagne glass.

Lady Geraldine was watching this little show with rapt attention and she seemed as lost for words as Charlotte. Until Nico raised his glass, tilted his head in a silent toast to the women, took a long sip and then… smiled.

'Um…Charlotte?'

'Yes, Gran?'

'Is there something you haven't told me?'

This was her chance to pull the plug on this crazy plan that Nico seemed perfectly happy to put into action. To pretend—in public—that they were a couple in love.

Trouble was, even for the short time it had been happening, it was casting a spell that was unbelievably powerful.

They said that falling in love was magical. Maybe even pretending to be tapped into some of that incomprehensible power.

Whatever. Charlotte could feel the waves of envy coming from the other women in this space. She could see the gleam of joyous disbelief in her grandmother's eyes. Worst of all, she could almost feel what it *would* be like having someone like Nico head over heels in love with her.

And, God help her, she wanted more.

Just for an hour or two.

Just enough to give her a bubble of whatever this magic was so that she could remember it when times were bleak.

And there *were* going to be bleak times ahead.

Could there possibly be a greater gift she could give her beloved grandmother than to let her die with the peace of believing that the child she had raised was happy at last? That she would be loved and cared for in her absence?

It was a very strange feeling, this…giving in. Living in the moment without trying to weigh up any consequences or complications. It was incredibly liberating.

Fun—like Nico had suggested it could be? Something was certainly lifting the corners of Charlotte's mouth.

'Gran…this is…Nico.' Her words sounded hesitant. Breathless. The way they would if someone was about to reveal something secret. Something personal and precious.

'Nico Moretti,' he expanded. He laid his hand over Charlotte's on the crisp, white linen tablecloth as he smiled at Lady Geraldine. 'I am Charlotte's…' He hesitated, clearly at a loss for the right word to describe his relationship to her, and she held her breath. Could he really pull this off?

Nico turned his head and she could swear his sigh was one of pure happiness. 'I am whatever Carlotta will give me the honour of being,' he murmured.

'Charlotte?' The gentle word belied the 'please explain' undertone.

'It's been s-sudden,' Charlotte stammered. 'I was going to tell you today, Gran, but…'

'But then you started worrying about me.' Lady Geraldine clicked her tongue. 'For heaven's sake, child. This is *far* more important. I want to know everything.'

Oh, help… Charlotte tried to buy some thinking time by picking up her champagne glass. The Italian prosecco being served was astonishingly light. Delicious. She took another long sip.

'We actually met years ago,' Nico said into the expectant silence. 'At St Margaret's in London. It was my bad luck that Carlotta was unavailable at that time.'

Uh-oh… It took Lady Geraldine less than a split second to work out exactly what time Nico was refer-

ring to and that earned Charlotte a glance she would rather have avoided.

Gran knew there had been far more to the break-up of that relationship—the only one she'd ever known Charlotte to have—than she'd ever been privy to. It was the only aspect of Charlotte's life she'd ever been shut out of and it was a cloud that had hung over them ever since. Something that was never mentioned but always there.

Charlotte drank the last of her wine and barely noticed the waiter refilling her glass as she listened to Nico continuing to talk.

Why hadn't she thought that this pretence could open that particular can of worms?

And it was too late to stop it now. She was already in too deep.

About to drown?

He knew he'd said the wrong thing.

Nobody could have missed that electric glance that Lady Geraldine had speared her granddaughter with when he'd said that she had been otherwise attached when he'd first met her.

What the hell was that about?

Never mind. He knew he could redeem himself. He'd been quite confident of pulling this off from the moment he'd walked into this exclusive restaurant and spotted the table he needed to aim for.

The table where the two most beautiful women in the room were sitting.

Maybe Charlotte often wore an elegant silver dress to such a formal occasion but Nico had a strong sense

that it was not usual practice for her to leave her hair loose like that—a tumble of soft waves that gleamed an ash blonde in the candlelight. Had she be thinking of him when she'd brushed it out and chosen not to wind it back into its prison of pins?

And the grandmother! Nico had expected an English dowager of some kind. Tall and forbiddingly aloof. He had smiled the moment he'd set eyes on the old lady sitting beside Charlotte. Even from a distance he had caught the flash of her bejewelled hands and even a small tiara nestled in fiery red hair. He could sense her interest in the people around her and an ability to see beneath the surface of social niceties. This was going to be a much more entertaining evening than he could have hoped for.

'I can't tell you how often I've thought about her since then,' he told Lady Geraldine with palpable honesty. 'And then fate brings us together in the most romantic city in the world.' He shrugged, his smile suggesting he hadn't made much of an effort to stand firm against the winds of fate.

Was he overdoing things? Judging by the mistiness in Lady Geraldine's eyes, she was swallowing this very happily, but from the corner of his eye he could see that Charlotte was simply sitting there, staring at him, her lips slightly parted and her expression dazed.

He still had his hand covering hers, so he picked it up. Such a soft hand. Such elegant, long fingers and neat nails that were not disguised by any unnatural colours. He touched his lips to her hand and then leaned forward as though drawn irresistibly to kiss her lips next. They looked soft, too, and when Charlotte uncon-

sciously dampened them with the tip of her tongue, Nico realised that he actually *did* want to kiss her.

Dio… That wasn't meant to happen. He closed his eyes for a heartbeat to take control of the unexpected shaft of desire but then he let his breath out in a soft sigh. Did it matter? Charlotte wouldn't need to know it was anything other than good acting and it would certainly make his performance more believable. He opened his eyes and focused on the owner of the hand he still had imprisoned in his.

'It was meant to be,' he said softly. 'I'm lucky enough to have been given a second chance and even luckier that this beautiful woman seems to feel the same way.' He added a few words in Italian, knowing how limited Charlotte's grasp on the language was, and hoping that it would add to the impression of sincerity.

It had more of an effect than he had anticipated. Lady Geraldine sniffed delicately and picked up her linen serviette to dab at the corner of her eye.

'*Bella*,' she said, her Italian accent flawless. '*Carlotta è una ragazza fortunate.*'

Beneath his fingers, Charlotte's hand stiffened with tension. 'What?'

'She said you are a lucky girl,' Nico murmured. 'That the story of how we met is beautiful.'

'At last…' Lady Geraldine smiled mistily at her granddaughter. 'Oh, darling. I can't begin to tell you how happy this makes me. This…this is the best night of my *life*.'

Charlotte's lips trembled but she managed to smile. In the instant before she turned to look at her grand-

mother Nico caught the flash of emotion in her eyes that
told him how huge this gift of happiness was.

And she couldn't have given her grandmother this if
it hadn't been for him. It made him proud.

It made him want to give *more*.

The interruption of the first course of their dinner arriv-
ing was a welcome distraction that gave Charlotte time
to try and collect herself. Not that she had the slightest
appetite and she couldn't help her gaze straying side-
ways to look at Nico at noticeably frequent intervals as
she wondered how he could be so incredibly good at
this pretence, but that was just the sort of behaviour a
woman who'd just fallen head over heels in love would
display, wasn't it?

No wonder Gran believed it all. Charlotte had been
sucked in herself. She'd totally forgotten the fear of the
conversation touching on that no-go period in her life.
And the way she'd felt when he'd picked up her hand
and kissed it… No. What had been utterly shocking
had been the way she'd felt when he'd leaned closer and
looked as though he was about to kiss her on the lips.

The hum of conversation around them and the el-
egant strains of the Christmas carols being played by
a quartet in the restaurant foyer had faded into noth-
ing more than background static. The flickering light
of the candles seemed to mirror the tiny flames lick-
ing her skin. Heating her blood and pooling somewhere
deep in her belly.

A moment's madness, fuelled by what she could
swear was an equal level of attraction in Nico's eyes.
But they were dark eyes and the light was low. She

couldn't possibly have seen his pupils expand and she must have imagined the electric charge that came through her fingers where his skin was still in contact.

The shock of hearing her grandmother respond to Nico in Italian had been enough to break the extraordinary spell being cast, which was just as well. Nico was enjoying himself quite enough. How appalling would it be if he knew he was having a genuine effect on her?

Lady Geraldine wasn't eating much either, and that was enough to send Charlotte's thoughts in a darker direction. Her grandmother might be in her eighties but she had always been a woman of amazing energy who lived life to the full. Nobody would deny her the maximum extent of whatever modern medicine could do to prolong that colourful life, but you had to balance additional time earned by what the quality of that life would be. Major surgery and chemotherapy would be a miserable time and it was possible that the end would not justify the means.

Something like despair gathered in a cloud over Charlotte as she toyed with her entrée. Thank goodness Nico and her grandmother were so engaged in conversation. Nobody would thank her for destroying the joyous atmosphere that had been created at this particular table.

'So your mother is still living in Ireland?'

'Yes. With husband number four.'

'Good gracious! What was wrong with the first three?'

'My mother has trouble resisting offers that seem to give her a better opportunity to experience the best that life can give. She is a free spirit, Lady Geraldine, who

is not bothered by what others think. A bit like your-self, I'm guessing?'

Gran actually laughed with delight. If she'd had a fan in her hand, Charlotte thought, she might have smacked Nico's hand with it. Instead, the old lady gave him an almost shy smile.

'You can call me Jendi, dear,' she told him. 'As my friends do.'

'I'm honoured…Jendi.'

'And your father? Is he still living, too?'

'No.' Charlotte saw the way Nico laid down his fork as though he had caught the lack of appetite around him. 'He died some years ago now.'

'Oh…' The sound was one of sympathy. 'Too young. Was it an accident?'

'A broken heart.' Nico's voice was expressionless. He was stating a fact.

Charlotte couldn't help her eyebrows rising at such a non-medical notion from a man with his training. She didn't say anything but maybe her breath had escaped with a disparaging sound because Nico flicked a glance in her direction. His words, however, were directed at Lady Geraldine. His new *friend*.

'They called it a heart attack, of course,' he said. 'But his heart broke when my mother left him and on every visit I made back here, I could see his slow decline.'

'That's terrible,' Lady Geraldine declared. She was frowning now. 'But at least it hasn't put you off mar-riage, Nico.'

'M-marriage?'

The word was so shocked that Charlotte knew the game might be up. Had it not occurred to him that it

was a natural direction for someone's thoughts to go in when faced by two people who were 'meant to be together' and had made the connection at last?

'Early days, Gran,' she said in a stage whisper across the table. 'Don't frighten the poor man.'

'Frightened? Me?' To give him credit, Nico recovered fast. He actually winked at Lady Geraldine. 'We men like to pick our own time, that's all. The element of surprise, you understand?'

'Oh, of course.' Lady Geraldine beamed at him. 'I promise I'll be surprised.'

She wouldn't be the only one. Nico was only supposed to be posing as her new boyfriend, that's all. Something that would make Gran happy because it offered hope for her not having a lonely future. This was getting out of hand. He was sharing family secrets as though he was already a prospective grandson-in-law.

How on earth was she going to explain what had happened here tonight if, by some miracle, her grandmother's treatment was effective and she lived for years after this?

The interruption of formal speeches in praise of the symposium and its organisers filled in the time between courses and prevented any further bonding between her gran and Nico, but it didn't lessen the increasing tension Charlotte was experiencing. It only got worse as people began to mingle between the tables and Richard Campbell came to say hello.

'Did you enjoy listening to Charlotte this morning, Lady Geraldine?'

'Oh, I did. So much. Thank you for arranging things,

Dr Campbell. I am the happiest woman in the world tonight.'

'So I see.' It was impossible not to respond to the glow her grandmother was exuding. No one would believe that she could be facing confirmation of a terminal disease within days. And the misty look she was giving the young couple at her table was just as easy to read. Richard's jaw sagged visibly as he followed her gaze.

'Charlotte? You and…?'

'Nico Moretti,' Nico said, extending his hand.

A new challenge, then. Could he pull off this pretence with the people who worked with Charlotte?

'Delighted to meet you, Richard. Although I think we met some years ago. At St Margaret's?'

'That was where he first met Charlotte,' Lady Geraldine put in.

'Mmm.' Richard was giving Charlotte a strange look and Nico's heart sank. He remembered that impression he'd had when he'd been listening to her speak this morning. That her playing down her femininity might reveal a sexual preference that didn't include men. Maybe her closest colleagues were aware of something that was kept strictly private. Something she didn't want her grandmother to know, either.

Was that what had been hidden beneath that absolute conviction that she would never be fulfilling her grandmother's dearest wish of settling down and having babies? Suspicion on Jendi's part might also explain that charged glance directed at her granddaughter, which he'd inadvertently provoked.

Charlotte certainly seemed bothered by something.

As soon as possible after Richard moved on to another table, she excused herself, muttering about needing a bathroom. He saw her ask a waiter for directions and then head out a door that led to a long balcony. Presumably the bathrooms opened off the balcony to one side of the restaurant.

Which meant that Nico could also excuse himself and head in that direction. He could catch Charlotte before she came back into the dining room and just check that he wasn't causing even more trouble for her, although exactly how to broach the subject of her sexuality in a sensitive manner was entirely beyond him at the moment.

The balcony ran right along the canal side of the restaurant. It was quiet out here with the added darkness that came from the still water of the canal. Nico didn't need to use the facilities so he paced back and forth, waiting what seemed an interminably long time for Charlotte to reappear. What was she doing in there? Twisting her hair back into some impossibly tight 'hairdo'? He hoped not.

A gondola drifted past below with just a single light making the ornate brass ornament on the prow of the boat gleam. A couple sat, wrapped in blankets against the cold and silent as they gazed in wonder at the magic of touring this city at night with only the ripple of the boat to disturb the serenity.

The tap of high heels on stone disturbed the moment for Nico. He turned and Charlotte's step faltered.

'What are you doing out here?'

'Waiting for you.'

The only light now that the gondola had passed

came from the fairy lights of the restaurant and a small Christmas tree that was being used to reveal where the door to the bathrooms was. Silver light that made Charlotte's dress shine and cast a spotlight on the way the fabric clung to her body and revealed noticeable curves. It also caught matching strands in her hair. It would look golden in the sunshine, Nico thought. Chameleon hair. He could imagine her eyes could create that illusion too. Maybe they would take on a blue hue under a summer sky. Or when she was happy?

Right now they were a stormy, slate grey.

'Why?'

She sounded nervous and added to that impression by pushing her fingers through her hair. The gesture ruffled the loose waves. It was a supremely feminine movement. Confusing, given what Nico was there intending to find out. The reminder made him shake off his focus on how unexpectedly attractive Charlotte was looking. He cleared his throat.

'I...um... It seems to be going well. Your *nonna* is happy.'

'Mmm.' He could see Charlotte swallow. A ripple that ran the length of her elegant neck. 'Too happy, maybe.'

'Is there such a thing? Especially at a time like this?'

Charlotte sighed. 'She *is* happy. I don't think I've ever seen her look so...so contented.'

'There you go, then. It's been a good thing to do. A reprieve from thinking about less happy things. One that you may be able to use for some time.'

Charlotte looked away, watching the tail end of the gondola as it turned a corner. 'But I didn't think things

through. I thought other people would just think you were sharing our table for dinner.' Her voice rose and the words sped up a little, revealing how unsettled she was. 'I didn't expect to start a rumour that will follow me back to St Margaret's. I have no idea what I'm going to do about that.'

'You don't have to do anything.' Nico paused, trying to select his words carefully. 'Unless it's going to cause personal distress?'

She frowned at him. 'What kind of personal distress?'

'Well…you might have someone in your life that wouldn't be happy to know about this…this illusion you're creating.'

'I don't…' She was trying to process his meaning. Then she made an impatient sound. 'I told you I wasn't in a relationship.'

'Not with *Mr* Right,' he murmured.

There was a moment's dead silence and then Charlotte's eyes widened. 'Oh, my God…you think I'm a—' An incredulous huff broke her words. 'Are you *serious*?' And then she turned away but not before Nico had seen a fierce sparkle in her eyes.

Oh…*Dio*… He'd really put his foot in it now, hadn't he? Was she about to start crying again?

No matter. He had come prepared. He reached for the neatly pressed handkerchief he'd pushed into his jacket pocket just before he'd left his room. He pulled it out and, as he did so, something glinted in the light and bounced on the stones with an audible *ping*.

Charlotte turned her head. 'What was that?'

'Nothing important.' Nico knew what it was. It had

been weighing his pocket down earlier today. But then he'd forgotten all about it after he'd arrived at the symposium. After he'd been swept along by listening to the story Charlotte had told them. Weirdly, it hadn't occurred to him to think about it again all day. Or remember to take it out of his pocket.

His grandmother's ring. The one his father had given his mother. The one she'd left behind when she'd broken the marriage and Nico's true family. Maybe it was better if it got left behind at the bottom of a Venetian canal. Drowned and lost. Like his belief in true love and marriage and happy families for ever had been lost so many years ago.

But no. This ring was the only thing his father had left him as his inheritance. The only link he could touch that went back to his early childhood. It was important. Nico ignored Charlotte and his gaze raked the rough stones as he searched for what he'd dropped. It must have come out of his pocket at speed, propelled by being caught in the folds of the handkerchief. Had it already bounced irretrievably into the waters of the canal?

Like Charlotte's laptop?

No. There it was, precariously balanced right beside a stone balustrade on the very edge of the balcony. He would have to be careful not to nudge it over the edge, he realised as he stooped. Trying to slow his movement, Nico dropped to one knee and reached for the ring.

'What on *earth* are you doing?' Nico could see the ripple of the long, silver dress as Charlotte stepped closer. He sighed and held the object up to show her.

'It's my grandmother's ring,' he said heavily. 'It's a long story…'

He wasn't going to get a chance to tell her any of it, however. A startling shriek cut through the night air.

'Charlotte! Nico! Oh, my goodness…' Lady Geraldine had come out through the restaurant doors and was standing there, her hands clasped in front of her as though in prayer. 'Is this…? Are you…? Oh…how *romantic*. A proposal. In Venice, of all places…'

It took a long moment for the full horror to sink in but, yes…here he was, on one knee. Kneeling in front of a beautiful woman with a backdrop of a Venetian canal, holding up what was obviously an engagement ring in his hand.

He bought a fraction of time by getting to his feet somewhat awkwardly. He caught the panicked look in Charlotte's eyes. They were going to have to confess now, weren't they? Ruin the happiest night of this sick old lady's life.

No. He could fix this.

With the ghost of a wink to let Charlotte know he had things in hand, Nico grabbed her hand and shoved the ring onto her finger. It was a tight fit but he gave it an extra push to get it over her knuckle. Was it pain that made Charlotte gasp? Maybe it was the shock of how fast he'd moved or this unexpected twist in the show they were putting on. That didn't matter either. Maybe people would think she was simply shocked at how quickly he had managed to sweep her off her feet.

He kept hold of Charlotte's hand and gave it a squeeze. She dragged her gaze up from the ring and met his eyes and he tried very hard to give her a silent message.

Trust me. We can get through this without hurting anybody.

And then he turned and pasted a smile onto his face.

'Jendi… What wonderful timing. We wanted *you* to be the first to know.'

CHAPTER FIVE

'I KNEW ALREADY.' Lady Geraldine was coming towards them with surprising sprightliness given her age and state of health. 'Nobody can hide the glow of true love…' Tears were running down her wrinkled cheeks as she got close enough to embrace Charlotte. 'Oh, my dear…I'm *so* happy for you.'

She must feel like she was hugging a tree, Charlotte realised, but she couldn't make her body soften. Or even raise the arms now hanging by her sides like dead branches. One of them was even weighed down with an enormous rock. No… She had to be dreaming. He couldn't *really* have shoved that ring on her finger, could he?

Still dazed, Charlotte lifted her left arm. It looked like she was returning her grandmother's effusive hug but, in reality, she was getting her hand to a position where she could see it,

Yep. There it was. On her third finger. A quite respectably sized solitaire diamond in an antique gold setting. Definitely an engagement ring. What on earth did Nico Moretti think he was playing at, walking around with an engagement ring in his pocket?

Words floated into through the sludge in her head. His grandmother's ring. *A long story*.

No story could be long enough to rescue her from this escalating nightmare. What was that saying Gran used to deliver with a wagging finger? Something about the complicated web you weave when first you practise to deceive. Charlotte shook her head to clear the mist. This had to end. Now.

'This isn't what is seems, Gran. I'm not engaged. This is…ridiculous.'

'Oh, I know, darling.' The grip Lady Geraldine still had on her increased a notch. 'You weren't expecting this, were you?'

'Of course I wasn't.' A snort of something like laughter escaped her throat. 'Nico and I have only just met. We're not even…' Charlotte raised her gaze as she searched for the right word to explain the total lack of a genuine relationship between them. It brought her line of vision directly over her grandmother's shoulder. And it locked with Nico's gaze.

He had one eyebrow raised and a curiously disappointed stillness to the rest of his face . What dismissive word was she going to come up with here?

That they weren't even *friends*?

That they weren't connected in any way, shape or form?

Except they were, weren't they?

They'd become connected totally by chance when they'd formed a united medical team to help the man who'd had the cardiac arrest and fallen from the scaffolding. Having him present when she had been floundering in front of so many distinguished symposium

attendees this morning had been what had given her the strength to give any kind of presentation at all. The thought that he might have been impressed had made her feel like she hadn't failed.

Having him right there when she had been already starting to grieve for Gran had been what had given her the strength to try and make whatever time her beloved grandmother had left as happy as possible.

And the way she'd felt when he'd looked at her like that at the table. As if he was in love with her. As if he'd wanted to kiss her.

Oh, yes…she couldn't deny a physical *and* emotional connection to him even if she didn't want it to be there. Somehow Nico had broken through her safety barriers. Despite the short time they had known each other—less than a day, for heaven's sake—he was already enmeshed in her personal life in a way that no man had ever been.

'I know, darling.' Lady Geraldine's soothing words took her back. Way back to when it had seemed that nobody could ever understand. Or put things right. And yet the words had always been sincere. And Gran had always put things right, no matter how long it had taken. 'People will think it's too soon. *You* think it's too soon.'

'Of course I do. It's…it's…' *Ridiculous.* But Charlotte's gaze was still holding Nico's as she tried to read the silent message he was sending. It was a reassuring message, whatever it was. How was she supposed to interpret that? Or believe that this was somehow okay.

'It's love at first sight, that's what it is,' Lady Geraldine said happily. 'The best sort. Wearing Nico's ring doesn't mean you have to get married next week, dar-

ling. It's just a promise of commitment. You can take all the time you need to make sure that it's perfect.'

All the time they needed to keep Gran happy for as long as she lived?

Time.

That's what Charlotte needed.

'It will take time.' Nico's voice was strong. Amazingly calm, considering. 'And you're right, Jendi. I have…what's that expression? Jumped the gun.'

Something about the way he recited the phrase made Charlotte think his choice of words was deliberate. He was reminding her of the euphemism she'd used about kicking the bucket. Reminding her of what was important here. And maybe it was a warning, too.

If she destroyed this illusion she would be ruining not one but two of the items on Gran's bucket list. There was no way the train trip could provide the slightest pleasure if the number-one item on the list was revealed as a deception.

Geraldine let Charlotte go with a final pat. She turned and looked up at Nico, who smiled at her.

'We will have to be apart a lot in the coming weeks,' he said sadly. 'I have commitments in the United States and Europe. In Australia, even. But I had to do something to make my intentions as clear as possible. To achieve what I know will make us *both* happy.' Make us *all* happy, his glance reminded Charlotte.

'Of course you did.' Lady Geraldine beamed.

Charlotte's mind was clearing rapidly. Nico was presenting an easy way out here. He could be her fiancé but he would be absent. She could keep her grandmother happily believing that a wedding was on the cards with-

out any further awkwardness of them having to keep up the pretence for real. Or, if she couldn't bear to be less than honest, she could say that things had fizzled out in a few weeks and use the excuse that it would never have worked. They would never have enough time together to keep the relationship alive.

'Mmm.' The sound came out in a strangled fashion. 'I'm still not sure—'

'Of course you're not.' Lady Geraldine slipped her arm through Charlotte's and began to lead her back to the restaurant. 'You like to be in control, child, and you've been swept off your feet.' She slipped her other arm through Nico's. 'Come on. We'll all go and have another glass of that lovely champagne and give Charlotte time to get used to this delightfully unexpected state of being an *engaged* woman.'

Dio mio…

What, exactly, had happened there?

It wasn't the unexpected twist of events that had led to Charlotte now wearing his grandmother's ring that was disturbing Nico most as he followed the women back to the restaurant.

No. It went far deeper than a pretence that was now a little more complicated than intended. Something had happened when Charlotte had been caught in that loving embrace and had looked at him over her grandmother's shoulder. When she'd been searching for a way of trying to explain that this was all a lie. That there was nothing of any significance between them.

She hadn't been able to, had she? Because she'd felt the same thing he had when their gazes had touched

and locked. Somehow, over the course of this crazy day, they *had* connected. And on a level that was totally alien to Nico. Inexplicable and deeply disturbing but, at that moment, he would have overturned heaven and earth to protect Charlotte. To extricate her in a dignified fashion from this mess he had created.

He had no idea what had triggered such a strong urge. Guilt from knowing he'd pushed her into this? Or maybe he'd caught another glimpse of that lost and frightened child in her eyes. He'd certainly seen desperation that had been coming from not wanting to hurt somebody she loved so much. Maybe that explained why he was feeling as though the ground was shifting beneath his feet and that the rules he lived by were no longer relevant.

Knowing that Charlotte was capable of that kind of love when, to outward appearances, she was incapable of that much emotion. Knowing that she was such a different woman from the one he'd met years ago. Curiosity was a powerful motivating force and Nico wanted to put as many pieces of this puzzle together as he could before he moved on.

Maybe when he had the full picture he would be able to understand why he was feeling as if he was caught in some invisible web. And then he would be able to avoid it happening again. He liked his life exactly the way it was, thanks very much. He did not like this feeling of long-held beliefs wobbling and his footing being less than secure in his world.

Back at the table, Lady Geraldine waved a bejewelled hand and waiters willingly rushed to refill glasses and serve exquisite-looking desserts. Charlotte was sit-

ting very still, staring at the chocolate creation on the small plate in front of her as though unsure whether it was, in fact, edible.

Or maybe she was unsure whether anything was real. Perhaps she was hoping to wake up and find that this whole evening had simply been a bad dream. Her grandmother was also watching her and then she turned to Nico and smiled. It was an expression of understanding. And reassurance. Charlotte just needed a little more time, the glance suggested. And then she would be able to embrace the joy of this new event in her life.

She certainly needed something. A gentle reminder of why they'd started this charade in the first place?

Nico smiled back at Lady Geraldine. 'Tell me about tomorrow,' he invited. 'I hear you have an adventure planned. On the Orient Express?'

Lady Geraldine beamed at him. 'It's been a long-held dream of mine. One of them, anyway.' She slid another glance at Charlotte and there was a moment's pause as she sighed happily. Then she collected herself and focused on Nico. 'Have you ever travelled on the Orient Express yourself?'

'No. I've heard of it, of course. It has a wonderful history, doesn't it?'

'Right back to 1883.' Lady Geraldine nodded. 'It's the world's most famous train and it's been totally restored to its original glory. You step back in time and travel in the kind of elegant luxury that only the very privileged could afford a hundred years ago. It's an experience everybody should have at least once in their lifetime, don't you think?'

'Absolutely.' Nico was happy to agree. This was what

this evening was about after all. To make Charlotte's grandmother happy. To encourage her to make the most of whatever time she had left in her own lifetime. To tick off those 'bucket-list' items. 'I hear that the food is amazing and isn't there someone that plays a grand piano in the bar?'

'Oh, yes.' Lady Geraldine's smile was misty now. 'Everybody dresses in their best and is on their best behaviour. We'll all be thoroughly spoiled as we glide through Italy, Austria, Switzerland and France and back to London just in time for Christmas.'

She eyed Nico over a spoon containing a tiny portion of chocolate mousse. 'I expect you'll be visiting your mother for Christmas Day, Nico?'

'Ah…no.' Nico shook his head. 'I believe her new husband has whisked her off to New Zealand to have Christmas in the sun.'

'But you have other family?'

Uh-oh… Any moment now he was going to be invited to have Christmas dinner with Charlotte and her grandmother. He needed to head this one off at the pass.

'Sadly, I have work commitments in London I can't break. That's partly why I'm taking a day or two at my leisure in Venice now.' This was true enough, wasn't it? He was always happy to work over family-oriented holidays to give his colleagues time off. He didn't have a family to spend time with. And he didn't want one. Nico shifted in his seat, which brought his knee into contact with Charlotte's. He heard her sudden intake of breath and she finally seemed to become aware of her surroundings again.

Good. He needed some help here to avoid being pres-

sured into joining the Highton clan for Christmas dinner. Who knew how many other distant but formidable relatives Charlotte might have waiting in the wings?

Lady Geraldine had a very benign smile on her face right now as she apparently enjoyed her taste of the dessert but Nico had the distinct feeling that the impression of a sweet old lady was probably deceptive. There was an ironclad will beneath that perfectly groomed exterior and that improbable red hair. What Lady Geraldine wanted, she would no doubt get. Except, maybe, the chance to live to an even riper old age.

He reached for his glass of wine. He increased the pressure on Charlotte's knee a little to encourage her to say something but she was watching her grandmother, who was shaking her head as she put down her spoon.

'Absolutely delicious,' she said sadly. 'But I can't eat it.'

Nico could feel the tension in Charlotte's focus. 'You've hardly eaten anything, Gran.'

'I'm too excited,' Lady Geraldine said.

'About the Orient Express?' This was a good direction to steer the conversation back to. A safe one. 'I'm not surprised. It's probably a good idea to save your appetite for all that wonderful food.'

'Mmm…' Lady Geraldine nodded thoughtfully. 'I *am* excited about the train trip but not nearly as excited as I am about this engagement.' She reached over and took hold of Charlotte's hand, bending the fingers so that the diamond ring took centre stage. 'I don't think I've ever been so happy.' She was locked in eye contact with her granddaughter. 'You will be, too, Charlotte Jane. I just know you will.'

Charlotte's indrawn breath was ragged. 'But...'

'I know, darling.' Nico could see the way Charlotte's fingers were being squeezed. Lady Geraldine's voice was soft. 'And it doesn't matter if I don't live to see the wedding. This is enough. To know that you've met such a wonderful man and the attraction is strong enough to be totally irresistible. It's a promise of a happy future for you...and I intend to enjoy every single moment of it.'

She straightened in her chair and turned her gaze to Nico. 'I have two cabin suites booked on the Orient Express,' she said unexpectedly. 'I wanted both Charlotte and myself to enjoy this trip as much as possible, without being cramped.'

'Good thinking.' Nico nodded. Thank goodness the topic of conversation was getting back onto safe territory. 'I'm sure you'll enjoy every moment.'

'Oh, I will. Especially now.'

There was something in the gaze from those faded blue eyes that made Nico feel like a small child again. A small child confronted by someone in ultimate authority.

'Because of the engagement?' Nico's smile was a little forced. He should be pleased because this represented exactly what he'd set out to achieve but he had a sinking feeling that he wasn't going to get off quite this easily.

'Exactly,' Lady Geraldine purred.

Maybe he was. Nico's smile widened.

'I can't think of a better way to celebrate,' Lady Geraldine continued, 'Can you?'

'No. What could possibly be a better way to celebrate

than the very best of food and wine while you travel in ultimate luxury?'

'I'm so pleased you agree. I'll let the train manager know that you'll be joining us.'

'What?' Both Nico and Charlotte uttered the horrified exclamation simultaneously.

'It's perfect,' Lady Geraldine said calmly. 'You don't have commitments until Christmas Day, Nico, and we'll be back in London by Christmas Eve. As you said yourself, what better way could there be to celebrate? It sounds as though you and Charlotte are going to have a lot of time apart in the near future and I'm sure we all agree that we should all make the most of every moment we can have together. Who knows how many of them there will be?'

Her voice wobbled just a little as she finished speaking. Charlotte's jaw had been dropping but now it snapped shut.

'You can't do this, Gran,' she said slowly. 'You can't use something like your illness to make people do what you want them to do. It's…it's emotional blackmail.'

'Nonsense.' Any hint of frailty vanished from Lady Geraldine's demeanour. 'It's common sense, that's what it is. You're both important, busy people. You'd never make the time for something like this unless someone pushed you into it. And this is a once-in-a-lifetime opportunity. Do you have any idea how hard it was for me to get a booking on this train? And *two* cabins. If it had only been one, I would have given up my place so that you and Nico could have done the trip together.'

'But this is *your* dream, Gran.' Charlotte was shak-

ing her head now, looking bewildered. 'Why would Nico and I want to do it?'

'Because it's the most romantic journey on earth,' Lady Geraldine said. 'You've found each other in the most romantic city and by astonishing good fortune you now have the chance to build on that by travelling together to the destination you were both heading for anyway. I'm not going to take you away from Nico the day after you've just become engaged, Charlotte. This is my engagement gift to you both—some more time together. If he won't come with us on the train, then you can stay here and I'll go by myself.'

'No...you can't do that. I won't let you. You're not well enough.'

It was a stand-off. Nico didn't need the combined effect of both women looking at him to know he was expected to say something to defuse the tension but, for the life of him, he couldn't think of anything to say. For heaven's sake, all he needed was an excuse that would keep him at least somewhere in Europe for the next twenty four hours but his mind was blank. Stunned at the way this...diversion had taken on a life of its own. Moving at a pace that appeared as unstoppable as the train he was now expected to board tomorrow.

Tables were being cleared around them and any moment now the waiters would come and interrupt this awkward silence, but clearly it wouldn't be soon enough for Charlotte. She made an exasperated sound as she pushed back her chair and got to her feet.

'I need some air,' she announced. 'I'll leave *you* to talk to Gran, Nico.'

Her tone suggested that he was unlikely to get any-

where but that it was his problem. He'd got himself into this mess and now he could get himself out of it. Her body language as she headed towards the balcony suggested that she was washing her hands of the whole situation because it was clearly uncontrollable. The slump of her shoulders said that she didn't believe he could do it without causing harm.

And maybe she was right. Maybe now he was going have to confess his part in this deception. Was there a way he could do that and convince Lady Geraldine at the same time that it had been done with the very best of intentions and that Charlotte had only gone along with his stupid idea because she loved her grandmother so much?

Nico took a deep breath and opened his mouth but Lady Geraldine got there first to fill the silence.

'Oh, dear…' she murmured. 'And there I was, hoping that she'd finally got over it all…'

Nico couldn't help himself. 'Over what, Jendi?'

Lady Geraldine looked uncomfortable. 'That's the problem, Nico. I've never been able to find out.' She raised her eyebrows. 'I was hoping you might be able to tell *me.*'

'*Scusi?*' The Italian word popped out, as they often did in moments of great stress or surprise.

'There's only been one other occasion when I've thought that Charlotte might have found the right man for her. The person she was going to spend the rest of her life with. To raise her own family with. And it was *years* ago. Back when she was just a baby doctor and everybody could see how brilliant she was. *Is,*' Lady Geraldine corrected herself but she was frowning. 'I

don't know what went wrong,' she continued softly, almost as if she was talking aloud to herself, 'but Charlotte…changed.'

Yes. He was getting to the heart of the mystery now.

'That was the time I first met her,' he confided to Jendi. 'When she was the star of the emergency department and nobody could sing her praises highly enough. And she was so happy. There was a sparkle about her that lit up a room. A smile that advertised such confidence…' His voice trailed off as he realised the extent of how radically Charlotte had changed.

The confidence was still there but it was only professional. Cold. That's what had hit him this morning—that lack of sparkle for want of a better word. It was only when he had pushed himself beyond any acceptably professional boundaries that he'd seen a hint of a woman capable of *real* emotion. That buttoned-up outward appearance was like a suit of armour around the old Charlotte.

Whatever had happened had killed her personal confidence. Her hopes for a future outside her work ambitions. Had she been brutally dismissed by a man she'd been deeply in love with?

How could the man have been such an idiot to pass up a woman like Charlotte?

And why did the thought of her being passionately in love with another man stir up a nasty sensation in his gut that he couldn't identify? Was it jealousy? No. That was absurd. He had never felt jealous in his life.

'I saw her out with that man,' he told Jendi. 'At a very exclusive London club. I think we were even introduced. Was he a *prince*?'

Lady Geraldine made a dismissive sound. 'That's what he called himself. He was a long way down the tree of some obscure European royal family. He was certainly a very charming young man. And very sure of himself.'

'So what happened?'

'Charlotte will never talk about it. I didn't see her for a few weeks. She said she had flu and didn't want to pass it on. And then she always had an excuse of being too busy at work to come to see me and when she finally did I was…shocked.'

'Why?' Nico leaned forward, unconsciously holding his breath.

'She looked…ill. So thin. And…' Lady Geraldine shook her head very slowly and when she raised her gaze to Nico's he could see tears in her eyes. 'You hit the nail right on the head, my dear. Her sparkle had gone. It was like it had been when she first arrived in my care as an orphaned child. When she was so lost and unhappy that she wouldn't even speak. For *months*.'

'She wouldn't speak to you?'

'Oh, no. She wasn't a tiny child any more. She would talk but only if we didn't talk about *him*. Siegfried. All she would say was that the relationship was over and it wasn't important. The only thing that mattered was her work.'

Lady Geraldine looked away. 'I thought if I gave her enough space that she would eventually talk to me about it, but it's been nearly six years and after the first attempt or two I had to give up. It's the one thing that's never discussed but is always there. The elephant in the room, you know?'

'The elephant?' How many odd English phrases were going to test him today?

'The huge thing. You can't ignore it because you always have to walk around it to get anywhere. But you're not allowed to mention it because, if you do, the door gets slammed shut and you can't get anywhere at all.'

'Hmm…' Nico was digesting the information. He was silent for a long time and when he spoke, his voice was uncharacteristically grim. 'He hurt her,' he said softly. 'He hurt Charlotte badly, this *Siegfried*.'

'Yes.' Lady Geraldine dabbed at the corner of her eyes with her napkin.

'Physically?'

The gasp was shocked. 'Oh, *no*… If he'd done that, she would have gone to the police, surely?'

'But you said she looked unwell.'

'She'd had flu. There was a very bad flu going around that year. One of those bird varieties, I think.'

Nico wasn't listening. How could anyone have wanted to hurt Charlotte? She had been so beautiful. A girl testing the wings of womanhood. In love and totally trusting. What kind of bastard had he been and what had he *done* to her? Nico didn't believe the 'flu' excuse for a moment. And something was telling him that the pain of the broken relationship had not been simply emotional.

'I need to talk to Charlotte,' he said, his chair scraping on the stone-flagged floor as he pushed it back.

Lady Geraldine caught his arm as he turned to leave. Her age and state of health disappeared from Nico's awareness as he read her expression. It was the look of a mother as well as a grandmother. Ageless. She needed

to protect her child and she wasn't sure if she should have spoken about her concerns. There was a plea in her eyes that Nico could read only too well.

'I'm not going to hurt her.' The words came out like a vow and Nico meant every one of them. 'I never would. That I can promise you.'

Charlotte was freezing.

An evening dress was entirely inadequate for a winter's night in Venice but she couldn't go back inside. She could see that the evening was winding up now and people were leaving.

Good. If she waited a little longer, there would be no audience for when she had to go back in and face her grandmother after Nico had explained why he couldn't accompany them on the Orient Express.

She could see them through the tall, arched window. Their body language was intense as they leaned towards each other, oblivious to anyone else in the room. The fairy lights made the room seem like another world and Charlotte could see the Christmas images still scrolling against the far wall. Snowmen and sleighs. Christmas trees and prettily wrapped parcels. Happy people. Families. Parents with excited children.

Parents who had once been lovers. Engaged couples.

Charlotte was twisting the ring on her finger without realising it. She gave it a tug. Good grief…it was a tight fit. She was going to need soap to get it off. Maybe she should go into the bathroom and find some.

But then she saw Nico get to his feet abruptly and she saw the way her grandmother caught his arm. For a moment that seemed suspended in time she saw the

way they looked at each other and the light was enough for her to see the expression on Nico's face. Such a *kind* expression. Loving. Intense. The kind of look someone might have if they were making a promise they intended to keep.

Or maybe he'd been apologising. Was he coming out to tell her it was safe to go back in now?

Charlotte's heart picked up as Nico came out onto the balcony. He moved with such grace, this man. A calm assurance that he could command his environment and protect anyone within it. Powerful but not intimidating because there was a softness about him. That slow, easy smile. The glint in those dark eyes that advertised the ability to find joy in life. To play.

That's what they'd been doing tonight and Charlotte couldn't deny that, for a while, it had been…fun. No. Fun wasn't the word. What had drawn her in had been the illusion. The need to taste something that was so seductive it was irresistible. The illusion of being in love.

With Nico.

She had to turn her head and stop staring at him as if the charade was still continuing.

'Did you talk to Gran?'

'I did.' Nico was close to her now.

'Did you tell her the truth? Does she understand why you can't come on the train with us?' Charlotte couldn't repress a shiver. Was it the cold or the disappointment of failure?

'Not exactly.' Nico was shrugging off his jacket. He stepped closer and draped it over Charlotte's shoulders.

Her first instinct was to shrug the garment off with a dismissive shake. She wasn't a child who needed some-

one to take care of her. She could look after herself,
thanks very much.

But the gesture had been unexpectedly thoughtful.
Caring.

And the warmth was astonishingly comforting.
Charlotte could feel her fingers creeping to the edges
of the jacket to pull it closer around her. The warmth
was the warmth of Nico's body. The slide of the silk
lining against the bare skin of her arms and shoulders
made it feel as though *he* was touching her.

It was disturbingly intimate now. Charlotte could
even catch a whiff of a scent that was pure male. Pure
Nico? She had to close her eyes for a heartbeat as she
tried to stop herself inhaling deeply.

'Your grandmother loves you very much,' Nico said
quietly. 'She does not want you to be hurt…again.'

Again? Her eyes snapped open. Oh, my God…what
had they been talking about in there? But Gran didn't
know the truth so she couldn't have told Nico. She was
safe.

So why didn't she *feel* safe?

'W-what did *you* say?'

Nico looked more serious than she'd seen him look
all day. Even when he'd been arriving at a potentially
fatal incident. The subdued look didn't sit well on a
face that was made for laughter. Her heart skipped an-
other beat.

'I told her that I would never hurt you.'

'So she still thinks that we're…we're *engaged*?'

Nico's mouth twitched. 'I'm afraid so. I couldn't
bring myself to cause her pain.'

It shouldn't be such a relief. Not when Charlotte couldn't see any way out of this.

'And the train?'

Nico shrugged. 'I have a free day. I have to get back to London. Why not?'

'Because…it's impossible. How could we keep this up for thirty hours?' Charlotte had another try at tugging the ring off her finger, looking away from him as she did so.

She could see past Nico to where the final guests for the evening were leaving. Only her grandmother remained and the maître d' was looking concerned, helping the elderly woman to her feet. Lady Geraldine was pointing towards the balcony. And now she was walking towards the door.

'Nothing is impossible,' Nico was saying.

'She's coming. She'll guess. She's not stupid.'

'She won't guess if you stop trying to remove that ring.' Nico caught her hands. 'If we…'

His hands moved, pulling hers up to his neck before he let them go. His hands kept moving, though, burying themselves in her hair. Cupping the back of her head and tilting it as he leaned in to cover her mouth with his own.

He was *kissing* her.

Just for show. To cover an awkward moment when Gran might have picked up on the tension between them.

Except…it didn't feel like a pretend kiss.

Or maybe it did, for that first, startled moment as their lips made contact, but then Nico's lips moved with a kind of question that Charlotte couldn't help respond-

ing to on some deep, instinctive level that totally over-ruled any conscious thought. Her lips parted beneath his and when she felt the touch of his tongue against hers all ability to control her thoughts vanished.

A fleeting hope that her grandmother would see them and stay well away to give them a private mo-ment evaporated, along with any awareness of what was around them. Charlotte was completely lost in this kiss. Transported to a place she'd never been. A place where passion and tenderness combined to create an all-con-suming fuel that could burn away anything and every-thing and leave only peace and fulfilment in its wake.

A kiss that promised everything. So much more than this touch of lips and tongues.

More…

And that was when Charlotte stopped being lost. She couldn't do more. If she tried, Nico would find out and he would know what was so wrong with her.

That she could go so far and no further. Because she was not a real woman. Real women liked going further. They weren't…*frigid*.

That did it. Just the tiniest echo of that hateful word was enough. Charlotte wrenched herself back from Nico's touch. His jacket slid from her shoulders and puddled on the stone terrace. She could turn to see what had happened, scoop up the jacket and try to collect herself before acknowledging her grandmother stand-ing in the restaurant doorway.

'Oh…Gran… I'm so sorry. I…lost track of time.'

'So I see.' Lady Geraldine's smile warmed the win-ter's night.

Nico was rubbing his lips slowly with his forefin-

ger, staring at Charlotte, but now he also turned towards the door.

'You must be tired, Jendi. Let me see you both back to your hotel.'

'That would be lovely, Nico. Thank you. We have an early start tomorrow. I think we have to be at the Santa Lucia station by nine a.m. to catch the train.'

It was Charlotte's turn to stare at Nico but he didn't meet her gaze. Instead, he put an arm around her waist as they began moving.

'No problem,' he told her grandmother. 'I'm an early riser.'

CHAPTER SIX

'WHERE IS HE?'

'I don't know, Gran.' Charlotte allowed a small seed of hope to blossom that Nico might fail to show up in time. Or maybe that odd squeeze in her chest was disappointment?

Yep. There was definitely an internal struggle going on here. The safest thing was to never see Nico Moretti again and that's what she should want. And, yes, she could try and convince herself that she only wanted him around, continuing this pretence of a relationship, because it was such a joy to see her grandmother so happy, but there was no way of hiding the real truth. Part of her—a big, rebellious part of her—simply wanted to be close to him again.

'Maybe something came up.' Like a bout of common sense? 'He doesn't have our phone numbers so he might not have been able to let us know.'

The train was already here at the station, the sleek, dark blue carriages with the gold trim, the coat of arms featuring two rampant lions and the lettering announcing that this was, indeed, the Venice Simplon Orient Express. As if anyone could mistake it! Among the or-

dinary modern European trains in the station, this one
stood out like a beacon. So did the attendants. The gold-
trimmed blue uniforms looked positively military and
the pillbox hats the stewards were wearing made them
look ready for a fancy-dress party.

The check-in desk stood out on the grey concrete of
the platform in equally startling contrast. A red carpet,
of all things, with brass posts holding tasselled ropes to
create an oasis of luxury amidst the mundane. Even the
people milling around looked different. Like that young
woman in a long coat that belonged to another era, its
fur collar turned up around her neck. The people were
generally better dressed, certainly, but that wasn't the
only difference. There was an air of excitement that en-
cased this part of the station and separated it from the
rest. From the real world.

'I knew we should have offered to let him share our
water taxi.'

'It would have been a bit of a squeeze with all your
luggage, Gran.'

It had, in fact, taken an impressive tip to get the
water taxi driver to leave his boat tied up and carry
Gran's bags up the daunting flight of stairs leading into
the train station from the road beside the canal. 'You
did know you're only supposed to have one cabin bag
and one piece of luggage to be checked in, didn't you?'

Her grandmother sniffed. 'If you're going to do the
Orient Express, it must be done in style. Everybody
knows that. Goodness knows how you get away with
nothing more than an oversized handbag.'

Cabin luggage hadn't been all Charlotte had been
carrying on her way to Venice, of course. She'd had

her laptop bag to contend with as well. An accessory that was now lying on the bottom of a Venetian canal. She could remember the expression on Nico's face as he'd realised what had happened. So apologetic, even though it hadn't exactly been his fault. The willingness to do whatever he could to put things right.

He was a kind man. And a generous one. The tailored suit jacket Charlotte was wearing again today suddenly felt tight. Scratchy, almost, as her senses replayed the sensation of the silk lining of Nico's jacket against her bare skin. A sensation that morphed almost seamlessly into remembering that kiss.

How kind was he? Kind enough not to reveal astonishment…*disgust*…when he found out what Charlotte was lacking?

And then there was that very tiny seed of what was definitely hope because that kiss had made her feel things that no other kiss ever had—even Siegfried's. And if just a kiss felt that different, maybe other things would feel different too and maybe…just *maybe*…she'd be able to—

Oh, *help*… Wasn't it enough that her memory of that little scene had kept her awake virtually all night? She couldn't allow it to keep distracting her like this. Charlotte balanced her cabin bag on top of Gran's biggest suitcase and grabbed the handle of the other with her free hand. With a determined shove she began moving the luggage towards a check-in desk that looked suspiciously like an antique mahogany piece. Lady Geraldine pulled the handle of her smaller bag as she followed.

'You're going to have to wear the same dress for dinner tonight that you had on last night, aren't you?'

'What was wrong with my dress?' It had been the first time Charlotte had worn the slinky, silver number but she'd been delighted with how it had looked when she'd put it on. How good it had made her feel.

'It's a lovely dress, dear. You just need more than one of them.'

It was a lovely dress. And if Charlotte was honest, she'd felt way more than simply 'good' in it. The way Nico had run his eyes over it more than once, as though the experience was a pleasure all in itself. Yes…that dress had made her feel *beautiful*. An odd experience for a woman who did virtually nothing to enhance her appearance in order to attract the attention of the opposite sex.

'Nobody's going to know I'm wearing it two nights in a row.' Charlotte smiled at the woman behind the desk and handed over the tickets.

'Apart from your fiancé.'

The woman behind the desk was smiling. 'You must be Lady Geraldine. We got your message. We're delighted to be able to welcome Dr Moretti on board to accompany you and your granddaughter.'

'Um…there could be a small problem…' Charlotte began. But the woman wasn't listening. She wasn't even looking at her and the expression on her face suggested that she was looking at something far more interesting.

A tall and extremely attractive man, perhaps?

'Cara…' The endearment was a caress. 'I'm so sorry I'm late.' Nico pulled Charlotte into his arms and then bent to brush her lips in a perfectly acceptable kiss for a public place. Except it lingered for just a heartbeat too long. And his eyes lingered on hers even longer. Char-

lotte dragged in a breath. The part of her that wanted to be close to Nico was winning. Doing a happy dance inside her chest that made her heart thump and send extra blood up to warm her cheeks. The wash of relief was unmistakeable and hot on its heels was something she hadn't felt in years.

Excitement. The kind a small child would have creeping downstairs too early on Christmas morning and seeing the magic of the gifts under the tree. Gifts for *her*.

Did she dare to pick one up and rattle it? Tear off a tiny piece of wrapping paper to see if she could guess what was inside?

But what if it wasn't what she wanted? Maybe the anticipation was better than reality.

'I went to the hospital,' Nico explained. 'I knew you'd want to know how our man from yesterday was getting on.'

To her shame, no doubt due to the emotional roller-coaster the day had presented, Charlotte had barely given the man another thought. So much for her heart-felt presentation yesterday about the medicine they practised being about the people. But Nico was right. She could feel her face light up in her eagerness to know the outcome. This was the kind of excitement she was used to. *This* was what she needed to focus on.

'He's doing well.' Nico's smile was one of pure delight. 'He had an angioplasty and half a dozen stents put in. His broken leg's been sorted and he's sitting up in the coronary care unit and you'd never know he'd been dead for a while. No evidence of any brain damage even.'

'Really? That's…astonishing. Our CPR must have been up to standard, then.'

'A little more than that, I think.' Nico put his arm around Charlotte's shoulders as he turned towards Lady Geraldine. 'We are an amazing team. And here we are, about to have an adventure. I am the happiest man on earth.'

Lady Geraldine was beaming at them. The check-in clerk was smiling mistily but then she collected herself. 'Here are your boarding passes. We'll take care of the suitcases and you can take your cabin baggage with you. I wish you the happiest of journeys.'

Lady Geraldine merely nodded. 'It will be,' she said softly. She winked at Charlotte. 'All that remains to be seen is which of us is the happiest *woman* on earth today.'

Lady Geraldine needed some assistance to climb up the steps and negotiate the narrow corridor of the train carriage. The first impression was the glow of polished wood and brass. And lights. Lamps casting a soft glow. Fairy lights in honour of the season, looped at ceiling height on the internal wall and twinkling merrily. The doors had small wreaths festooned with artificial cherries and tiny golden bells.

Even more overwhelming than the warm glow of the wood and lights was a sense of confinement. The cabins were tiny with no more than a richly upholstered double seat and a tiny table beneath the window. A washstand was cleverly incorporated into a corner.

For most passengers this would have been their total space but with a suite, a door beside the washstand cabinet was open, leading to the adjoining cabin where the

seats had already been turned into comfortable-looking bunk beds with crisp white linen and soft-looking towels folded on the ends.

For one person, it would have been the ultimate in spaciousness aboard the train. For a couple, it still would have been more than enough. To share this amount of space with Nico Moretti was something entirely different. There didn't seem to be enough oxygen in the small spaces.

Their personal steward served champagne as the train pulled out of Santa Lucia station while Charlotte was checking that Lady Geraldine was settling comfortably into her suite. Nico joined them as the steward pointed out features of the cabins, including the bell that would summon him for assistance at any time of the day or night.

'The maître d' will visit your cabin soon to take your lunch and dinner reservations. Our restaurant cars have tables for two or four people.'

'We are a party of three,' Charlotte informed him. And how lucky was that? No chance of an intimate table for two with soft lighting and too much champagne. If she could put up good enough barriers around that part of her that was so drawn to this man she would be safe from making a complete fool of herself.

Was that a significant look that her grandmother was sharing with Nico?

'This is your gift,' Charlotte added, for good measure. 'And we intend to share every possible moment of it with you. Don't we, Nico?'

Nico seemed to be relishing the champagne and he merely lifted his glass in a toast of agreement.

There wasn't room for three people to sit in one cabin. Charlotte sat beside her grandmother as they opened and perused the map of the journey. Nico stood near the door, apparently enjoying the scenery through the corridor windows and chatting to other passengers as they went past.

They chose the first sitting for lunch and it was Nico who insisted on helping Lady Geraldine negotiate the route and cope with the sometimes jerky motion of the train. It took a long time to get through several carriages and through the bar car before they got to one of the restaurant cars, especially when everything had to be explored and admired.

'The bathroom is amazing,' Lady Geraldine declared after their first stop to wait for her, which was right beside her suite at the end of their carriage. 'The toilet seat is made of mahogany and everything else is brass. Even the cover for the paper. And it's all so clean and shiny.'

The resident pianist was not yet playing the baby grand piano in the bar but they had to stop there as well.

'Play something, Charlotte,' Lady Geraldine commanded.

'I can't do that.' Charlotte was horrified. 'I haven't played a piano for years and I'm quite sure it's not allowed, anyway.'

But the handsome young man polishing glasses behind the wooden bar grinned. 'Go ahead,' he invited. 'It's too early to bother anyone.'

'Please, Charlotte.' Lady Geraldine was heading for a nearby seat. 'For me? It's so long since I heard you play.'

And she might never hear her again?

'Yes… Please, Charlotte.' Nico's smile was mischievous. 'I'm curious about your splinter skills.'

Oh, for heaven's sake. Charlotte realised she wasn't going to win and the best way of avoiding stress in getting through this voyage was clearly going to be taking the path of least resistance. She slid herself onto the piano stool and raised the lid on the gleaming keys. She had taken lessons for years as a child and playing for pleasure had been a feature of every visit to her grandmother's house. Until…until her life had changed overnight.

Her hands shook for a moment as she held them over the keys. Maybe the least stressful response would have been to refuse to do this but now it was too late and if she didn't, she might be expected to provide an explanation.

Flicking a glance upwards Charlotte knew that Nico had seen the tell-tale tremor of her hands. She willed them to be still. Willed herself to continue, much as she'd forced herself to start that presentation in Nico's presence yesterday. The only piece she could think of to play by heart was Beethoven's 'Moonlight Sonata'.

The first notes were tentative but the piano was beautiful and within a few bars Charlotte was drawn in to the haunting sound of the music. Her stiff fingers relaxed as she remembered the release that this had once brought her. The pleasure of doing something for herself that had nothing to do with work. Mindless and satisfying and restorative. Just…pleasure…

'Bravo…' Nico's eyes were full of admiration as the last notes died away.

'I knew those piano lessons were worth every penny.'

Lady Geraldine held her hand out for Nico to help her to her feet. 'Now, let's go and have some lunch.'

The lunch was three courses of beautifully prepared and presented food but Lady Geraldine only picked at hers and didn't touch the tarte tatin served for dessert.

'I'm a little tired,' she confessed. 'I think I'll go back to my cabin and rest for a while.'

'I'll come and keep you company,' Charlotte offered immediately.

'No. I might need some help to get back without being knocked off my feet but I need some quiet time. I might have a nap.'

Charlotte felt her level of concern ramp up. Gran hadn't eaten much and now she looked pale. Was she in pain?

It was Nico's arm that Lady Geraldine chose to lean on to keep her balance and they had to stop at frequent intervals to allow other people to pass on their way to the restaurants.

One of those people was another elderly woman whose head turned in surprise as she took another look.

'Lady Geraldine? Jendi?'

'Oh, my goodness. Winsome Black. What on earth are you doing here?'

'I could ask you the same thing. What an astonishing coincidence.'

Lady Geraldine's head shake was incredulous. 'It's a small world, isn't it?' She turned to Charlotte. 'Winsome's an old friend that I haven't seen for years. We worked together once on a huge fundraiser for that children's charity.'

'One Last Wish.' Winsome nodded at Charlotte.

'Such a worthy cause. They made wishes come true for terminally ill children.'

'This is my granddaughter, Charlotte,' Lady Geraldine said.

'And this is my grandson, Connor.' The good-looking young man, who was clearly aware of how much space they were all taking up in the narrow corridor, smiled at Charlotte and offered her his hand.

She shook it with an equally conspiratorial smile. They had something in common, didn't they? Here they both were in the company of grandmothers with…personality.

'Charlotte and her fiancé are keeping me company,' Lady Geraldine was confiding in Winsome. Her smile was poignant. 'This trip is my last wish…'

'Oh, surely not.' Winsome smiled. 'I seem to remember you telling me that age is only an attitude.'

Lady Geraldine opened her mouth but then noticed the human traffic jam they were creating in the corridor. 'We'd better get a move on,' she said. 'But we must get together, Winsome, and have a proper chat.'

'That would be lovely.'

'How about afternoon tea? We could meet in the bar at, say, four o'clock?'

'See you then.' With a smile, Winsome continued on her way.

Charlotte wondered if the arrangement might be too much given that her grandmother had already said she needed a rest, but the sparkle in the elderly woman's eyes chased away the worry that her condition was deteriorating and that this trip would prove too much for her.

'Oh, look…the queue at the gift shop has gone. Let's see what they have.'

Charlotte was quite happy to linger and look at the souvenirs available. The more time they spent doing things like this, the less time she would have to spend with Nico, alone in their cabin while Gran had a rest.

You could buy hand-blown crystal glasses and crockery with the Orient Express insignia. There were salt and pepper shakers, travel accessories in blue velvet, photo frames and even jewellery.

Lady Geraldine chose a specially bound copy of Agatha Christie's *Murder on the Orient Express*. And then she ordered Charlotte and Nico to choose a gift for themselves.

'A selection of wine glasses would be a lovely engagement present,' she suggested.

'You are celebrating an engagement?' The tall man with a heavy accent who ran the gift boutique sighed happily. 'I tell everybody that this is the train of love…'

'This trip is the gift, Gran. Remember? We don't need anything else.'

But the tall man was putting things on the counter in front of Nico. 'For your beautiful lady?' he murmured. 'A special memory, perhaps?'

Blue velvet cases were being opened to display pearl necklaces on silver chains that had clasps engraved with the train's insignia. Silver and gold bangles were similarly engraved. A chain bracelet had tiny silver charms like a train carriage, a conductor's whistle and a pillbox hat but Nico was picking up another bracelet. He held it up to show Charlotte.

'Do you like this, *cara*?'

Tiny silver hearts linked together. A delicate piece of jewellery.

Romantic.

Charlotte opened her mouth to tell him that she didn't wear jewellery but out of the corner of her eye she saw the way her grandmother was pressing a hand to her throat. Holding her breath as she witnessed evidence of the love her granddaughter had finally found?

'It…lovely.' Let him buy it, she told herself. She could reimburse him later.

Nico not only purchased the bracelet, he insisted on putting it on Charlotte's wrist. His fingers brushed her skin as he fed the rod of the clasp through the silver circle engraved with the name of the train.

He smiled at her then. Just the way he had when he'd sat at their table last night. As though she was the only woman in the world for him. As if he was so deeply in love that nothing else mattered.

She knew he was going to kiss her. The tall man wanted it to happen. Her grandmother wanted it to happen.

And, God help her, *she* wanted it to happen.

It was just a kiss and her lips were ready for it this time, already soft and slightly parted. If she sat down at a piano any time soon again, she would probably find that her fingers were instantly ready for the release of music too. The pleasure to be found. The connections between her fingers and her brain and her heart had unexpectedly been woken up after a very long sleep.

Like her lips had been?

Not that it was a passionate kiss, of course. Just a gentle pressure. But the promise was there. And no mat-

ter how fiercely Charlotte told herself that she didn't want this and couldn't go there, her body was defying her. The shaft of desire was so much more intense after last night. How on earth was she going to cope with the rest of this journey? Where were some new barriers when she needed them?

At least Nico left her alone to do some more exploring after Lady Geraldine was settled back into her cabin behind a closed door. It gave Charlotte time to try and rebuild her defences. To plan how she could get through the next hours. Maybe one of them could sleep in here, on the seat? At the very least she could choose the top bunk so that she wouldn't have Nico climbing past inches away from her face. What did he wear in bed? Oh, God…imagine him climbing up wearing nothing but a pair of silk boxers or skin-hugging cotton knit underwear. And even with the highly unlikely possibility that he had a pair of flannelette pyjamas in his bag, she'd still be aware of him sleeping beneath her, wouldn't she? She would hear his breathing. Feel the warmth of his presence. *All* night.

Heavens, it was warm in here. Charlotte adjusted the central heating radiator beneath the window and even opened the top window a little for some fresh air. She was just beginning to feel calmer when Nico returned to the cabin.

He was carrying a bottle of champagne in a silver ice bucket. Two crystal glasses dangled from his other hand. He leaned against the door with a smile of invitation curling the corners of his mouth.

What woman would be able to resist?

Charlotte, that's who, with her grandmother safely

shut away and all the good work of calming herself down undone in an instant.

It wasn't hard to glare at Nico as though he was committing an unpardonable sin. 'What on earth are you thinking?' she snapped. 'I hope you're not planning to get me drunk so you can take advantage of me again.'

Again?

Nico shoved the cabin door shut with his foot. The champagne had seemed like a good idea. They were supposed to be celebrating their engagement, weren't they? They didn't have to drink the damned stuff. And what was wrong with trying to make this journey as pleasant as possible, anyway?

What *was* Charlotte's problem?

'Take *advantage* of you?' He kept his voice quiet but allowed it to cool noticeably. 'Is that how you see this?'

Her voice was small. 'No.'

At least she had the grace to look embarrassed but it wasn't good enough.

'On balance, I suspect most people would consider you to be taking advantage of *me* right about now.'

'You agreed.' Charlotte had two bright spots of colour on her cheeks and her tone was accusing. 'This was all *your* idea—'

'I have gone out of my way to help you,' Nico interrupted, dumping the ice bucket and glasses on the table by the window, oblivious to the glorious scenery of the Italian Dolomites rushing past in the distance. 'And it is *not* because I have any intention of "taking advantage" of you. You are the complete opposite of the type of woman I find attractive.'

A curious expression changed Charlotte's features. She looked…hurt? Disappointed? Surely not. The expression was gone as quickly as it had appeared but it took the wind out of Nico's sails. His anger evaporating, he sank down onto the seat beside her. 'Do you want to know the real reason?' he asked.

'Mmm?' The sound was somewhat strangled but Charlotte was looking at her hands, which were clasped tightly together in her lap.

'You fascinate me,' Nico said simply. An honest statement, dragged from a deep place, possibly against his better judgement.

There was a long moment of silence but Nico let it ride as he tried to shut down the implications. Why did this interest feel so very different from the attraction a woman usually had for him? Was it a threat?

Very slowly, Charlotte finally raised her head. Her eyes were a dark, stormy grey and they were wide and puzzled. Fearful, almost.

'Why?' The word was a whisper.

Why indeed?

'You're a beautiful woman, Carlotta.' The Italian version of her name came to his lips unbidden. 'You are also very intelligent and successful. I have a great admiration for your professional abilities.' He could feel a corner of his mouth quirk. 'You are also surprisingly talented at playing the piano.'

A snort of mirth escaped Charlotte as she shook her head, encouraging a lock of hair to escape the tight ponytail she was wearing today.

Nico couldn't resist catching that lock and smoothing it back behind her ear. 'I believe that people come into

your life for a reason,' he added quietly. 'I find myself in an extraordinary place, if only for a limited time, and I have to wonder if fate has brought us together because we have something we can learn from each other.'

She was looking at him now as if he'd grown two heads. 'Like what?'

'I don't know.' Nico shrugged. 'Maybe it's your astonishing grandmother I was destined to meet. To learn how one can make the most of life until the very end. Or how to face the prospect of that end with such dignity and courage.'

'Oh…' Charlotte caught her top lip between her teeth but it wasn't enough to stop tears rushing to her eyes.

Dio…he hadn't intended to make her cry. Nico extracted one of her still-clasped hands and held it between his own.

'Or maybe I need to learn about family,' he said. 'The love you have for your *nonna* touches me very much. Right here.' He brought her hand up to press it against his heart. 'I don't have a bond like that. Perhaps I pushed my mother away because of the childhood sadness of losing my father. Maybe that's why I never want to marry or have a family of my own because I can't imagine inflicting that kind of pain on children.

'But half of me is Italian and it doesn't feel right. I've ignored that sense for many years but seeing you with your *nonna* opened my eyes.' His smile was wry. 'I don't know if it will change how I live my life but it feels right to be helping you.'

'But you wouldn't inflict that pain on your own children.' He could feel the pressure as Charlotte started holding *his* hand instead of just letting hers be held.

'Because you'd know what it was like. And even if the marriage didn't work, you'd still keep your bond with your children. You'd fight for it. And win.'

She believed that. She believed in *him*. It gave Nico an odd frisson of…what, pride? Invincibility? Oh, yes… he could conquer the world if a woman like Charlotte truly believed in him. Except…

'It's not going to happen…' The admission was being torn from somewhere that had been so well locked away maybe he hadn't even been aware of it himself. 'The kind of love that leads to marriage…and children…can only happen if you can fall in love. I think…I think that I'm not capable of doing that.'

There it was. His deepest, darkest secret. Something that he'd never said to anyone. From the shocked expression on Charlotte's face she must realise the significance of his confession. But she didn't believe it.

'Why not?'

Nico had to swallow hard. Why was he putting himself through this? Because it seemed like a pathway to get Charlotte to open up about herself? If he stopped now, he'd never reach his goal.

'I love my mother,' he said quietly. 'I can't blame her for wanting to find happiness in her life and the men she falls in love with don't seem to be able to provide that for very long. But I loved my father too and, even as a child, I could see that he was destroyed by losing the woman he loved so much. Falling in love can create so much pain. You either end up being destroyed yourself, like my father, or destroying others, like my mother has—more than once.'

'That doesn't have to happen. Not if you choose the right person who can give you what you need.'

'What if you don't know what it is that you need? How can you possibly make the right choice of a person to be with for the rest of your life?' Nico shook his head. 'No. It's safer to never fall in love. Perhaps I'm lucky that I have that inability.'

Charlotte was still staring at him, a crease of concern between her brows.

'But you don't want to end up like Gran,' she said, with a wobble in her voice. 'Old and sick but with nobody to care about you. No child. No grandchild.' Her voice trailed away as if Nico wasn't supposed to hear her next words. 'That's what terrifies *me*...'

'So why are you alone?' Nico turned so that he could look directly at Charlotte. 'A beautiful, talented woman who should be thinking of having children of her own so that she can have grandchildren one day.'

There was no response other than a withdrawal Nico could both see and feel. As if the white witch from Narnia had waved her wand and turned his companion to stone.

Nico had bared a part of his soul here. A part that had never been shared before and never would be again. Charlotte wasn't going to be allowed not to take her turn.

'Tell me about Siegfried,' he said.

'No.' The refusal was absolute. Charlotte pulled her hand away and turned to stare out of the window.

Nico leaned back against the seat, letting his head rest on the lace-covered cushion. 'I'm a patient man,' he said lightly. 'We have the rest of today. And *all* night.'

He couldn't miss the way Charlotte's chest heaved as she gasped silently. Struggling for control? Interesting. He was getting somewhere, at least.

Nico watched her profile closely. 'We are in this extraordinary place and time and we never have to see each other again after tomorrow. I believe I have something to learn from you, Carlotta. And I think that maybe you have something to learn from me.'

He touched her arm and she flinched. Nico sighed. He should give up. Accept that Charlotte wasn't prepared or ready to learn anything. Except he didn't believe that. She just had to unbutton herself a little more. And if she did that, maybe he would get the answers to the mystery of why she'd changed so much. And then his fascination with her would fade and his life could get back to normal.

'In order to learn something,' he offered carefully, 'maybe you have to be prepared to admit that there's something you don't know. To be open. And honest. Being honest makes you vulnerable, I know that. But I've been honest with you.'

Charlotte nodded. 'You have.'

'More than honest. I've told you something that I've never told anyone else. That I never *will* tell anyone else. Something that I see as...shameful. What kind of man am I if I cannot fall in love or be the kind of husband and father a woman would want?'

She was still struggling. Did she even realise that she was shaking her head very slowly? That her hands were gripping each other tightly enough to have cut off any useful supply of blood?

'You have the power to hurt me, Charlotte, if you

chose to share that information with anyone. I'm trusting you not to do that.'

The slow headshake turned into an equally measured nod. A promise.

Nico lowered his voice to something just above a whisper as he touched her again. And this time she didn't flinch. 'You can trust me.' He cleared his throat and spoke more strongly. 'So…will you do me the honour of being honest with me?'

Dio, that had disturbing echoes of some kind of marriage proposal. Except it wasn't, of course, so he didn't need to feel as if he was getting completely out of his depth.

Even when Charlotte raised her eyes to his and he could see that she wanted to tell him.

Wanted to trust him.

She was just having to gather so much courage that it broke his heart to watch.

'I loved him.' She finally choked the words out. 'I thought he loved me. But he wanted… I couldn't…' There was agony coating the words now. 'We weren't… *compatible*.'

There was another message in her eyes now. One that said Charlotte was unbearably alone in the world but that there was nothing she could do about it.

Nico sighed again, more heavily this time, as though utterly defeated. He held out his arms and gathered Charlotte to his chest.

And held her while she cried.

CHAPTER SEVEN

'THERE'S NOTHING LIKE a *proper* afternoon tea, is there?' Lady Geraldine sighed happily as she stirred sugar into her second cup and listened appreciatively to the sound of silverware tapping against real bone china. 'Did you know you can buy these lovely cups and saucers from the gift shop?'

'I'll have to have a look. I'm planning to go there after this.'

Lady Geraldine couldn't help noticing the glow of Winsome's smile. Her old friend certainly looked very happy these days. She could return the smile easily. She had a lot to be happy about herself at the moment.

Like meeting an old friend unexpectedly. Being on her once-in-a-lifetime dream journey. Actually sitting in this famous bar carriage with the pianist now in residence playing some soft, classical music interspersed with Christmas carols. Remembering Charlotte playing on the beautiful instrument earlier when it had been the first time she'd heard her in so many years. Could it be that it was Nico who was bringing back the part of her granddaughter she'd been missing for so long?

She picked up the elegant white cup with the blue

ribbon pattern around its rim and the VSOE logo under a small crown. 'Maybe a set of these would make a lovely engagement gift for my Charlotte and her Nico.'

'You said they'd only met yesterday? In Venice? When they both saved that man's life?'

'Yes…' Lady Geraldine pushed aside that tiny niggle of doubt. 'But they'd met before. Years ago, at Charlotte's hospital. Fate has just thrown them back together and…' She sighed again. 'It's obviously meant to be. Like your Connor and…what was her name again?'

The conversation paused for a moment as the steward removed the plates that had contained tiny sandwiches and replaced it with a platter of warm scones, adding small silver pots of jam and clotted cream.

'Mmm…' Lady Geraldine eyed the cream. 'Proper Cornish clotted cream, by the look of that.'

'Kelsie,' Winsome said as she followed her friend's example and picked up one of the scones. 'Kelsie Summers. But I don't think she and Connor are about to fall into each other's arms like your Charlotte and Nico. She jilted him, in fact, fifteen years ago and I have the feeling he hasn't forgiven her.'

'*Really?*' Lady Geraldine had spread the jam and clotted cream onto her scone and was just about to take her first bite but the conversation had just become more enticing than the calorie-laden treat. 'They must have been very young. Oh, *do* tell…'

They both dropped their voices to a more discreet level and Lady Geraldine listened to the story with avid interest. Young love could be such a fragile thing, couldn't it? She had to hope that there wouldn't be

any unforeseen twists in the road ahead for Charlotte and Nico.

She finally turned her attention back to her scone but her expression was thoughtful.

'We might be able to help things along,' she suggested.

'What do you mean?'

'The dinner seating is very strict, I hear.'

'It certainly is. I've tried to change tables at the last minute on some of my previous journeys and it almost never happens.'

'It's not the last minute yet,' Lady Geraldine said firmly. 'And if we both had a little chat to the maître d', I'm sure we could persuade him to juggle things a little.'

'In what way?'

'By making an extra table available. We've still got a lot of catching up to do, haven't we? We haven't even started talking about that terrible business with Deirdre Wilkins defrauding the charity so that she could run off to the Maldives with that "personal" trainer of hers.'

Lady Geraldine knew her smile would reveal how much she enjoyed an occasional bit of juicy gossip. 'If we asked to be seated together, that would mean leaving both your Connor and this Kelsie and my Charlotte and the lovely Nico alone at their tables.'

'Yes… If we could make sure they gave them a table for two or didn't put another couple to join them at one of the bigger tables.'

'It would be so romantic, wouldn't it? Everybody dressed up and the lighting all soft and lots of delicious champagne to add to the atmosphere?'

Winsome was smiling. 'Why don't we ask our nice

steward to go and see if the maître d' might be able to spare us a minute or two?'

Charlotte drifted towards consciousness with reluctance.

She had never felt so comfortable. So relaxed. So *safe*. She was floating, supported by a strength she knew she could trust. Cradled against it and it was warm and…moving?

Yes. A steady, gentle movement like breathing. And there was an equally steady but gentle thumping against her ear.

A sound she normally only heard through a stethoscope.

Awareness of where she was kicked in. Or should that be who she was with?

Asleep on, in fact?

'Ohhh…' Charlotte pushed herself upright with a groan. 'I fell *asleep*?'

'You did.' There was amusement in Nico's tone. And a tenderness that touched something that felt raw inside Charlotte.

The last thing she remembered was bursting into tears and Nico holding her. She'd expected him to want more information about what had gone so wrong with her relationship with Siegfried. For her to define what she'd meant by being incompatible. But he hadn't asked anything. He'd offered her comfort instead, as though he understood. As though everything could somehow be put right.

And it had been too much for Charlotte. Her defences had collapsed completely and she'd sobbed out the tears

that had been bottled up for years and years. And then she must have been overcome by sheer exhaustion and fallen asleep.

And he'd just continued to hold her?

'How long?' Charlotte put a hand to her hair, which felt like a rat's nest. She closed her eyes in disbelief and found that her eyelashes felt all clumpy when she blinked. She probably had mascara all over her face. She opened them again. The short winter's day was ending already and it was dark outside but their cabin was glowing in the soft light from a lamp on the table. 'How long have I been asleep?'

Nico was tilting his head to one side and then the other, stretching his neck. 'I wasn't watching the clock.' He smiled. 'I may have dozed off myself, in fact.'

Charlotte could feel a smile stirring. A joke about them sleeping together forming.

'Only until the steward woke me to tell me about Jendi.'

The smile and joke evaporated. 'What? Oh, my God…and you didn't wake me? What was wrong? Why—?'

Nico put a finger against her lips and the gentle pressure stopped her anxious flow of words.

'He merely came to ask if I could accompany her to the bar for the afternoon tea she had arranged to have with Mrs Black. As soon as he saw that I was…ah… otherwise occupied, he said it was no problem, he would accompany her himself and ensure that she didn't lose her balance.'

Charlotte couldn't believe she could have slept through the whole exchange. 'I'm sorry,' she muttered.

'I must have been more tired than I realised. I…um… didn't sleep much last night.'

'Of course not. You're worried about your *nonna*.'

'Mmm. That, too…'

She saw the flash of understanding in his eyes as he considered what else might have been keeping her awake. Like that kiss…

Distraction was needed. Charlotte looked around. The bottle of champagne was still sitting in the bucket. There were a few small cubes of ice floating on the water inside. Nico must have followed her glance.

'It may still be cold enough,' he said. 'Shall we have a toast?'

'To what?'

'To making this evening as enjoyable as possible? For everyone involved. It will be time to get ready for dinner before long, I expect.' Nico was dealing with the foil on the champagne bottle. 'We need to prepare ourselves to put on a good show.' The cork came out with a satisfying 'pop'. He smiled that slow, easy, irre-sistible grin as he filled the glasses and held one out to Charlotte. 'Dutch courage?'

'Will I need it?' And then Charlotte remembered what her hair and face must look like and she smiled ruefully. 'Don't answer that. I know I look a complete mess.' She took a sip of her drink. 'It's just as well I won't see you again after tomorrow. I would be morti-fied. I can't think of anyone who's ever seen me look this terrible.'

Apart from Siegfried, of course. Charlotte took a longer sip of the wine.

Nico touched his glass to hers. 'You are beautiful, Carlotta.'

He looked as though he believed the words. He was giving her *that* look again. Like the one he'd given her last night. And again, in the gift shop. But why? There was no one around to see. He didn't have to pretend here.

And hadn't he told her that she was safe because she was so completely not *his* type?

She wanted to be his type. Heaven help her but she wanted Nico to kiss her again.

Dammit. Where were her safety barriers when she needed them? At the very least she needed to break their eye contact but it seemed impossible.

Charlotte searched for a barrier she could put up to protect herself but couldn't find a trace of one. All she could find was a memory of how it had felt to know that Nico had shared his shameful secret with her and how cathartic it had been to finally share her own with another living person. How it had felt to wake up in Nico's arms.

How was it possible to feel so vulnerable and yet so safe at exactly the same time?

She still couldn't break the eye contact either. And Nico wasn't looking away. Charlotte could feel the distance between them closing. The kiss that she wanted so badly was only a heartbeat away.

Until a knock sounded on the cabin door.

'Dr Moretti? Dr Highton?' The steward sounded as if the matter was urgent. 'I'm sorry to disturb you, but you are both needed.'

* * *

It was just as well the moment had been broken by the interruption.

Perhaps it had been a mistake to let Charlotte sleep in his arms for so long but what else could he have done?

The depth of pain he'd heard in those words '*not compatible*'. They couldn't have had anything other than a sexual reference and for it to be so hard for Charlotte to have uttered them meant they were the key to the puzzle of what had changed her so much.

A horrible suspicion had formed in Nico's mind. Something unthinkable. So dark it couldn't be given a name. So horrific all he'd been able to do was hold onto this damaged woman as he'd tried to fit in the other pieces of the puzzle and control the rush of pure fury on her behalf.

He had to control it. Nico hadn't known if his assumption was correct. Maybe Charlotte would never tell him and even if she did, what on earth could *he* do about it?

Nothing, that's what. It was none of his business. Not his problem. But it would provide an explanation to the mystery and that was what he'd wanted, wasn't it?

So Nico had done nothing. Said nothing. As the minutes had ticked by he'd continued to do nothing and that was when he'd felt Charlotte's heartbroken sobbing subside. When the exhaustion in her body had taken over. When she'd slipped into a peaceful, bone-deep slumber.

He could have eased himself away at that point, found a pillow and blanket to make her comfortable on the seat. Or carried her to a bunk, maybe, and left her to sleep for an hour or two. What was it about this

bizarre situation he'd been caught up in since early yesterday morning that made it impossible to walk away?

He could have ignored Charlotte when he'd first seen her crying on the terrace below his window. He certainly hadn't needed to come up with the dangerous notion of posing as her lover, let alone shoving a ring on her finger. And he could have found an excuse not to accompany the women on this train journey.

But he hadn't. Every step of the way he had hesitated and then been drawn in deeper by something he couldn't explain. And if the steward hadn't rapped on the door at that particular moment, he would have kissed Charlotte again.

More than kissed her, actually. He could have asked gentle questions with his mouth and his hands that would have confirmed what he suspected was the answer to the puzzle that had intrigued him ever since he'd recognised Charlotte on that cobbled Venetian street.

He would have got answers to those questions, he was sure of that. Just as sure as he was of the fact that Charlotte had *wanted* him to kiss her. He had seen that desire darken her eyes and soften her lips and he'd felt that knowledge kindle his own flame because it was part of what intrigued him so much. The contradictions. The ice queen on the surface and the woman capable of such deep emotion within. Was the single, ultimately professional doctor desperately in need of physical release, possibly without being consciously aware of it?

Whatever. The desire had been wiped from her eyes the moment that sharp rap had sounded on the door and the tone of the steward's voice had told them that they were not only needed but needed urgently.

Charlotte's assumption was, of course, that Jendi had become ill. She moved swiftly to wrench open the cabin door.

'It's my grandmother, isn't it? She needs us?'

The steward nodded. 'Only you, Dr Highton. She's asking for assistance to get dressed for dinner.'

'But you said you needed both of us.'

'Yes. I'm hoping that Dr Moretti could come with me to see another passenger in the carriage who requires a doctor. He thinks he might be having a heart attack.'

Nico could actually feel his professional persona taking over. Smothering anything personal, like his desire to kiss Charlotte. There was still a flicker of something personal there, though. He stepped closer, needing to touch her, and put his hand on her shoulder.

'You go and help your *nonna*,' he told her. 'I'll deal with this.'

'But…' Was it his imagination or did Charlotte lean into his hand a little, as if she was trying to return the touch? Her gaze caught his and he could read the message so easily. She was reminding him of what he'd told her grandmother only hours ago. That, together, they made an amazing team.

'I'll send for you,' Nico said softly. 'If I need you.' He stepped past Charlotte into the corridor, where the steward was waiting anxiously for Nico to follow him. The last personal thoughts evaporated. 'What equipment do you have on board?' he queried. 'Oxygen? A defibrillator?'

'Yes. We have oxygen. And an AED.'

'Good.' Nico picked up his pace as they made their

way to the cabin at the far end of the carriage. 'Show me which cabin and then fetch them for me, please.'

The man in the end cabin was in his sixties. His colour wasn't good and he was clutching a small red and white canister of glyceryl trinitrate spray in his hands. His wife was beside him, looking even paler than her husband and virtually wringing her hands.

'How long is it since the pain came on?' Nico asked.

The anxious woman checked her watch. 'Nearly fifteen minutes.'

'And how many doses of the spray have been taken?'

'Two? Maybe three... I've lost count.' The woman was struggling to hold back tears. 'It's not working and...and they said that if it didn't work it could be a heart attack and we'd have to get Douglas to the hospital as quickly as possible.'

Nico had his fingers on the older man's wrist. His pulse was a bit rapid but quite strong and regular.

'Tell me about the pain.'

'It's like a bus parked on my chest. Right here...' Douglas pressed a fist to his sternum. 'It's hard to breathe.'

'Just in your chest?'

'Yes.'

'Have you ever had a heart attack?'

'Yes. Ten years ago. That's when this whole business started. But it's been stable. Always comes on the same way...and if I sit down and use the spray it... does the trick.'

He was starting to sound breathless. Thankfully the steward had returned now. He was carrying an oxygen cylinder in one hand and the small red case of an

AED in the other. Hopefully the automatic defibrillator wouldn't be needed but it was great to know that such a lifesaver was available if it came to that. Even with the best team in the world performing CPR, it could only buy time. The only way to restart a heart was through defibrillation.

The best team in the world. Unbidden, a memory of Charlotte working with him on the man at the building site flashed into the back of Nico's mind. He shook it off as he uncoiled tubing and fitted nasal prongs to give Douglas some oxygen.

'This may help the pain,' he said. 'Are you on any medications?'

'Yes. Too many.'

'Can you tell me what they are?'

Douglas shook his head, closing his eyes and screwing up his face as though the pain was becoming unbearable. A sheen of perspiration was beginning to show on his bald head. Nico's heart sank.

'I've got them.' The anxious older woman was rummaging in a small suitcase. She pulled out a plastic bag containing numerous packages of medication. They were all things that a cardiac patient could be expected to be on.

'Have you had your aspirin today?'

'Yes.' It was his wife who answered. 'He's taken everything.'

'Let's try another dose of the GTN.' Nico took the canister from the man's hands. It was a bad sign if the spray that normally worked on his angina was failing to be effective but was it possible that it hadn't been used correctly? Nico rolled the canister in his hands, mak-

ing sure the contents were mixed and then sprayed a dose into the air to check that the metered dose mechanism was working. The spray came out but, oddly, Nico couldn't smell anything.

He held the canister up and peered at the base. 'This spray expired two years ago,' he exclaimed.

'Oh, my goodness!' Douglas's wife clapped a hand to her mouth. 'Really?'

'Really.' Nico reached for the portable pharmacy in the plastic bag. Yes. There was a small box in there that contained a replacement canister. And the expiry date was a year away. He ripped open the box, took the lid off the canister and squeezed off a test shot. 'Open your mouth,' he directed Douglas, 'and lift your tongue.'

He gave Douglas two sprays under his tongue and then kept his fingers on his patient's pulse and watched his breathing while they waited. Within a matter of minutes Douglas started breathing more easily and deeply. The lines on his face relaxed and when he opened his eyes he actually smiled.

'It's almost gone,' he said.

'Oh…thank God…' His wife was crying. 'I'm so sorry, Doug. This is my fault. I should have thrown that old spray away as soon as we had the new one.'

'Waste not, want not.' Douglas patted his wife's hand. 'If you weren't so good at being thrifty we'd never have been able to afford this trip, would we?' He turned to Nico. 'Thank you, Doctor. I'm not having a heart attack after all, am I?'

'It certainly looks like nothing more than an episode of angina. Let's keep the oxygen going for a little

while and see how you go. Someone can always come and find me later, too, if you're worried.'

The only person looking worried now was Douglas's wife. 'I'm so sorry to have disturbed your trip,' she told Nico.

'It's not a problem.'

'Is it your first time on the Orient Express?'

'It is.'

'Isn't it wonderful? Are you enjoying it?'

'Of course.' But Nico had to consciously smile instead of allowing a puzzled frown to crease his forehead. Enjoyment wasn't a word that he would have chosen to describe his state of mind so far. He'd started out being intrigued and then he'd been impressed by Charlotte's piano playing. He'd had a spell of being angry when he'd been accused of planning to take advantage of her and then he'd had that cold chill of horror when he thought he'd guessed her secret.

But the overwhelming emotion that he would remember from this trip was going to be the way he'd felt sitting in that cabin and holding Charlotte while she slept. The feeling of protecting her. Of knowing that she trusted him enough to fall asleep in his arms like that. That he could trust *her* enough not to ever share the personal information he had given her.

A good feeling.

An incredibly powerful feeling.

Even more powerful than the desire that had kicked in when he'd realised that Charlotte had wanted him to kiss her as much as *he'd* wanted to kiss her?

Yes. Strangely, it was. He was used to desire and he

knew there were countless women in the world who could make him feel like that.

But that other feeling was completely unfamiliar. And deeply disturbing. Powerful enough to feel like it had a life of its own and could take control. Was this what falling in love was all about?

Nico couldn't answer that because he'd never been in this space before. He wasn't capable of falling in love. He knew that. But maybe he was getting a glimpse of what it might be about.

And it was disturbing enough that he never wanted to experience it again so maybe it was time to take charge and make sure he wasn't ambushed by any other strange emotions. The distraction of being a doctor for a little while was definitely helping. The fact that the train seemed to be coming to a halt was less helpful.

Had something happened? Maybe there was engine trouble or something on the tracks and he'd end up being on this train for a lot longer than expected. Just how long could he keep up the level of control he might need when he was sharing a compartment with Charlotte?

The steward, who'd been hovering outside the cabin while Nico treated Douglas, stooped to peer through the window. 'We're coming into Innsbruck,' he announced. 'I need to attend to other duties.'

Nico nodded. 'Thanks very much for your help.'

'I can put the AED away now?'

'Yes. Thankfully, I don't think we need it.' Nico raised his eyebrows as the train jerked and came to a complete halt. 'Why are we stopping?'

'We have to change engines whenever we come to an international border. This is a thirty-minute stop and

most people like to get off the train and stretch their legs a bit.' The steward hurried off, probably to open doors and then to stand, looking very smart in his blue uniform, to give people another photo opportunity.

Douglas certainly wasn't going to be jumping off the train to stretch his legs right now. Nico adjusted the setting on the oxygen cylinder and settled in to watch the progress of his new patient.

The contents of Lady Geraldine's larger suitcase were spread out over the seat and hanging from the edges of the bunks as she chose her outfit for dinner.

'The long black taffeta skirt,' she decided. 'With the black, silk camisole and the velvet bolero jacket.'

'Very Gothic,' Charlotte smiled. 'Shall I do your hair so that you've got a bit of fringe covering one eye?'

'Don't be naughty, Charlotte Jane. The black is merely a canvas to show off my diamond jewellery. I'm going to need my necklace and the brooch that goes on the jacket. And I've got my bracelet and best rings in my jewellery case. Oh…we mustn't forget that darling little tiara either. The one I wore last night, remember?'

'How could I forget?'

Lady Geraldine eyed her granddaughter suspiciously. 'I don't think you're taking this seriously, Charlotte. This is the dinner of my lifetime and I intend to look the part.'

'Sorry, Gran.' Charlotte kissed her fondly. 'I want you to enjoy tonight as much as possible. Are you sure you're feeling all right? Did you have a good rest?'

'I had a lovely rest. And then I had an even better

time having afternoon tea with my old friend, Winsome. We still have lots to talk about.'

'Maybe you'll see her again after dinner.'

Oddly, Lady Geraldine looked evasive now. 'Help me into my skirt, child. And then you'd better start doing something to get ready yourself. Fancy suggesting I wear my hair over my eye. Have you looked in a mirror recently? What have you and Nico been up to in your cabin?'

'Gran...' But Charlotte couldn't help thinking about the look in Nico's eyes just before the steward had interrupted them. About how much she had wanted that kiss to happen. Even now, the curl of desire the memory could evoke was enough to make her close her eyes for a heartbeat. To make her lips curl in pleasure at the memory.

If that kiss had happened, would it have stopped there? Would she have wanted it to? The bite of fear that kicked in was enough to make her shake her head as if she could banish the hateful sensation.

She needed to try and locate at least a shimmer of her old armour. To pretend to be in control. Normal. Maybe it would help to make a joke of it. 'Have you *seen* the size of those bunks?'

'You're young,' Lady Geraldine said with a smile. 'I'm sure you'll cope.' She reached out and stroked Charlotte's cheek. 'Oh, darling. You're so in love with him, aren't you?'

Charlotte had to turn away. To find something solid to focus on as she felt the ground shifting beneath her feet with a curious spinning sensation. She lifted the hanger holding her grandmother's astonishing skirt with

the ruffled hem down from the top bunk and pretended to notice some lint that needed brushing away.

In love?

Ridiculous. Nobody fell in love that quickly. She felt safe with Nico, that was all. He knew more about her than anyone. More than her grandmother, in fact, in a rather significant area.

She liked him. A lot. Who wouldn't? He was clever and kind. So kind that he'd sat, getting cramp, for hours, holding a woman in his arms because he hadn't wanted to wake her?

She trusted him, too. Who couldn't trust someone who put the kind of trust in you that led to sharing the kind of secret she could so well understand him wanting to keep to himself? Not that it was true, of course. Nico was more than capable of falling in love if he'd only let himself.

And that feeling when she'd woken up in those arms. As if she had been floating in the most blissful place on earth. She'd never felt so safe.

So *protected*.

Superimposed on that memory came that look of desire in Nico's eyes when their lips had been drifting closer together in the moments before that rap on the door.

That mix of safety and desire was a chemical combination that could only mean one thing.

That…yes. She *was* in love with Nico Moretti.

No. Maybe it meant two things.

She was not only in love. She was in trouble.

CHAPTER EIGHT

MAYBE IT WAS her new awareness of how she felt about Nico. Or perhaps it was the incongruity of him appearing in these surroundings looking impossibly gorgeous in his dinner suit. Whatever it was, it completely stole Charlotte's breath away when she opened the door of her grandmother's compartment to his polite knock.

Did her grandmother actually bat her eyelashes?

'It's been a long time since I was escorted to dinner by such a handsome young man,' she said with delight. 'Charlotte Jane? You can have him later but I really do need Nico's arm while we're walking. This train is remarkably jerky at times.'

'No worries, Gran.' Charlotte smiled. 'He's all yours.'

But then her gaze caught Nico's and the smile got stolen away like her breath had been. Oh…Lord…that look in his eyes.

'I love that dress,' was all he said. 'I'm so glad you've worn it again, *cara*.'

Lady Geraldine made a tutting sound. 'I'm trying to train Charlotte to expand her wardrobe, Nico. It won't

help if you tell her you're happy she's worn the same thing two nights running.'

'But it's true, Jendi.' Nico's smile for her grandmother was so warm and genuine that Charlotte's heart squeezed painfully. How could she not love a man who was clearly already so fond of her beloved gran? 'And I am an honest man.'

The comment did something strange inside Charlotte. Echoes of his voice telling her that he'd been honest with her and asking her to give him the honour of being the same with him. It was a bond she knew she could never have with another person. Did he feel the same? No. How could he when she hadn't shared the most shameful part of her secret? When she'd been less than completely honest?

But his gaze flicked past Charlotte's again. 'Most of the time,' he added.

All the time, Charlotte suspected. This pretence they were engaged in was an aberration. Sure, Nico had approached it as an amusing diversion but any control had been lost very quickly, hadn't it? At about the time he'd pushed that ring onto her finger, probably.

No wonder he was feeling uncomfortable but Lady Geraldine didn't seem to pick up on the loaded comment. 'I'm ready to go,' she announced. 'I want as much time to enjoy seeing everybody else dressed up as I can before I start feeling too old and tired.'

Or before she felt too sick and sore? Charlotte followed Nico as he carefully escorted Lady Geraldine through the rocking carriages towards the dining cars. She needed a break, she said, when they reached the bar car. She wanted to sit for a few minutes and enjoy listen-

ing to the piano. And…how nice…her friend Winsome was sitting at one of the side-facing seats and seemed to be saving space for her. Perhaps Charlotte could order a nice cocktail for her?

Charlotte perused the cocktail menu while Nico made sure her grandmother was seated comfortably. Heavens, but there were a lot to choose from. She'd never even heard of a Moscow Mule or a Planters Punch. Both her grandmother's favourites were there, though, so all she really needed to choose between was a Singapore Sling or a Gin Fizz.

Nico came back to the bar as she ordered a Gin Fizz. When he was only a step or two away the train gave a sudden and rather dramatic lurch. A cry rippled through the carriage as people spilt their drinks but the pianist didn't miss a beat of the Viennese waltz he was playing. And Nico's arm was right there to steady Charlotte as she lost her balance.

It was the first time he'd touched her since that almost kiss when they'd been interrupted earlier and it seemed to ignite a peculiar magic. How else could Charlotte explain the fact that a steadying touch morphed into an embrace that moved in time to the music?

They were dancing?

Yes. On a minuscule patch of blue carpet, in the space between the bar and the piano, Nico was very competently leading her through a confined version of a Viennese waltz. Charlotte could have laughed out loud. Except that this was giving her the same kind of feeling that she'd had when she'd woken from that deep sleep in Nico's arms, and she wanted to recapture that bliss for just a few seconds.

So, instead of holding her head in the correct position for a waltz as she'd been trained to do in those lessons Gran had insisted on when she'd been a teenager, Charlotte let herself droop enough to put her head on Nico's shoulder. And he tilted his head so that it rested against hers. It was no waltz now. Just a slow, close dance.

To anyone watching, and no doubt that included Lady Geraldine and her friend, they must look like a couple madly in love. Nobody, meaning Nico, needed to know that it was actually genuine on her part now.

And maybe that was a good thing. Maybe…just a very small maybe…this didn't have to end when they got off the train in London tomorrow.

No. That tiny, unbidden seed of hope died away as Charlotte remembered Nico saying he never wanted marriage or children. That she was safe because she was so completely not his type of woman.

Oh, well…at least if Gran lived long enough for her to have to confess that the relationship wasn't going to work long term, she wouldn't have to pretend to be heartbroken, would she?

Oh, God…she really was in trouble now.

Released from Nico's arms to a round of applause from the crowded carriage, Charlotte headed back to the bar. She was going to order one of those potent-sounding cocktails for herself because she needed something strong if she was going to cope with the rest of this journey. She needed some bottled courage. Or stamina.

Moving towards Lady Geraldine's seat to wait for the bartender to bring the drinks, Charlotte found that introductions were being made. Winsome's grandson Connor was with a young woman called Kelsie, who

was now sitting beside Lady Geraldine. They were discussing seating arrangements.

'Winsome and I have arranged a table for ourselves,' Lady Geraldine said. 'We don't want to bore you young things with our gossip.'

The implications were immediately obvious. Nico and Connor exchanged a glance as if they were measuring each other up and considering the prospect of a foursome for dinner. Kelsie was watching the older women as if she knew there was more coming. And there was.

'So, instead, we have three tables,' Lady Geraldine smiled. 'One for each couple.'

Charlotte almost groaned aloud. 'I don't think you're allowed to change arrangements like that, are you, Gran?'

Lady Geraldine merely tapped the side of her nose. 'Wait and see where the maître d' puts us all,' she murmured. And then she winked at Winsome. 'Being old doesn't entirely deprive us of our ability to charm men into doing what we want, does it, Winnie?'

'Not at all, dear. As you say, age is only an attitude.'

Charlotte caught Connor's gaze and his expression said it all. This was a done deal and there was absolutely no point trying to make changes now. She was now faced with the prospect of being alone with Nico for a dinner that might go on for hours. An intimate, romantic kind of dinner. Her heart sank. One strong cocktail was not going to be enough.

Nico had to admire the persuasive powers of older women. Tables had to be at a premium on the train, even if there was more than one sitting for dinner, but

here they were at a table that could seat four people and it was only set for two.

It was beautifully set with crisp, white linen, sparkling silverware and immaculate crystal that caught the soft light of the Tiffany lamp on the window side of the table. The carriage might be crowded with other diners but it felt like he and Charlotte were enclosed in a bubble of their own. He was glad that she hadn't had a different dress to wear because this silver sheath was gorgeous and so very appropriate for the season. It made her eyes look like a dark shade of silver instead of grey. Or was that because they were catching such a warm glow from the light?

Or perhaps it was the champagne he had ordered. She certainly seemed to be enjoying the Moët, even if she wasn't clearing her plate with each delicious course that arrived. He had polished off the entrée and then demolished the main course of traditional roast turkey with chestnut stuffing.

Conversation had proved easier than he'd expected, having been deprived of Jendi's company. They'd started out with the practical matter of sleeping arrangements for the night.

'I'll stay in the bar for a while,' Nico had told Charlotte. 'And then I'll come back to the cabin and sleep on the seat. You can close the connecting door when you go to bed.'

He'd asked if she knew what would happen tomorrow.

'We get to Paris around dawn,' she'd told him. 'When we get to the end of the French line for the Orient Express, we have to get off and there are special buses that

we stay on for the channel crossing. The English branch of the train takes us into Victoria Station. I think we get in at about five p.m.'

As the plates for the main course were taken away, Charlotte allowed her champagne glass to be refilled. Did her smile look a little forced as she held it up to Nico in a toast?

'What will you do?' she asked brightly. 'When we've arrived back in London? For Christmas Eve, I mean.'

Nico shrugged. 'I expect I'll go to work and catch up on any inpatients. I'm covering a big area for the next few days. I like to give my colleagues as much time as possible to be with their families over Christmas. And you? What will you be doing?'

Charlotte turned her head to look out the window, although there was nothing to see in the darkness.

'I'll go out to Gran's. Her estate is a good hour out of London. I'll stay with her for Christmas Day, of course, and then it'll be time to face up to what needs facing up to.'

Jendi's cancer. Dio…but it was going to be a difficult time ahead for Charlotte. Nico wanted to reach across the table and catch her hands. To offer to be there for her as a friend in the weeks or months ahead.

But this faux relationship wasn't supposed to continue, was it? Charlotte wouldn't want it to. Having her in a committed relationship with a potential family in the future might be at the top of her grandmother's bucket list but Nico could still hear the vehemence in Charlotte's voice when she'd declared that it was never going to happen.

So he said nothing. Instead, he followed Charlotte's

example and stared out of the window. There were sparkles of light swirling outside in a mesmerising kaleidoscope.

'Look at that,' he exclaimed. 'It's snowing. It'll be a white Christmas for some people.'

'I love a white Christmas,' Charlotte said softly. 'It makes you feel like you're living inside a Christmas card. I think the best Christmas I ever had was one where Gran and I got completely snowed in and the electricity went off. We ended up cooking the chipolatas that were supposed to go in with the turkey on sticks on the open fire. I was only about nine but I was so impressed that Gran knew how to do stuff like get the fire going and cook sausages.'

'Sounds special.'

'What's the best Christmas you remember, Nico? Was it white?'

'No. It never snowed in our part of Italy.' Funny that to remember his best Christmas he automatically wiped out any year after he'd been whisked off to Ireland. 'It would get cold, though. I think the best Christmas I can remember was outside. We had a terrace with a long wooden table that was under grapevines. In the summer it was leafy and cool and in the winter there was an open fireplace big enough to roast an ox. For some reason we had Christmas dinner outside that year. Possibly because so many family members had gathered. There were aunts and uncles and cousins I never knew I had.'

'How old were you?'

'About six.'

'Did you have turkey?'

Nico shook his head. 'That wasn't traditional. We

have the feast of the seven fishes on Christmas Eve and then on Christmas Day we have lots of pasta and then roast meat like chicken or beef. And potatoes.' He frowned. The food hadn't been what had made that Christmas memorable.

'There was music,' he continued softly. 'My father was at the head of the table and he was *so* happy. Between courses he would drag my mother away from the kitchen and dance with her in front of the fire. There were so many people. So much laughter. So much love…'

'Family.' The word was a whisper and Charlotte's eyes were as bright as he'd ever seen them when Nico turned from the view of the snow. 'It's what Christmas is all about, isn't it?'

'It was once…' Nico had to clear his throat. The memory of that particular Christmas was disturbing because it evoked a yearning he'd thought he'd put behind him many, many years ago. Part of the heartbreak he would never want to inflict on a child. Or a woman. Or have inflicted on himself ever again.

Dessert of a classic plum duff with crème anglaise and brandy butter came and went with a noticeably more sombre mood at their table. It was a relief when a steward came to tell him that Lady Geraldine was ready to be escorted back to her cabin whenever it was convenient for him.

'Or I can arrange another escort?' The steward tilted his head to include Charlotte. 'If you and your fiancé wish to stay longer?'

'No.' It was Charlotte who spoke up quickly. 'We

can finish now.' She didn't meet Nico's eyes. 'If that's all right with you, Nico?'

'*Sì*. Of course it is.

The last thing Charlotte expected when she returned to her suite after helping her grandmother get undressed and settled into her bunk for the night was to find Nico still there.

She had thought he would be long gone. Having a nightcap in the bar and ready to wait until he thought she was safely asleep before coming back to get what rest he could on the seat in this compartment. Not that she expected to get much sleep herself but it would have been a relief to shut the connecting door and have a space entirely to herself for a good few hours. No chance of losing control and making a fool of herself that way.

Now she was distinctly unsettled. Not only was Nico here but he'd taken off his dinner jacket and rolled up the sleeves of his dress shirt. His bow-tie was undone as well, hanging down beside the undone top buttons of his shirt. His hair was rumpled, as if he'd thrust his fingers through it more than once, and it was long enough since he'd shaved to give his jaw a dark shadow. He looked ever so slightly disreputable lounging on the padded upholstery of the seat.

And ultimately desirable.

Maybe that was why Charlotte's words came out more sharply than she'd intended. 'I thought you were going to the bar.'

Nico raised an eyebrow. 'It occurred to me it might be a good idea to wait until Jendi was asleep. What if

she wanted to go to the bathroom and saw me abandoning my beautiful fiancée?'

Oh, God…this was getting way beyond a joke. Charlotte had had enough.

'It's not funny, Nico.'

'No…it's not.' Nico got to his feet. 'Shall I tell you the real reason I haven't gone to the bar?'

He took a step closer and Charlotte was pinned by the heat in his gaze. She still had a hand on the door to help her keep her balance as the train rocked, and Nico was swaying on his feet but his gaze didn't waver in the slightest.

She couldn't respond to the question but it didn't seem to matter. Nico was going to tell her anyway.

'I didn't want to,' he growled.

Charlotte didn't have to ask why not. She could see the see the answer in his face. Could feel the flicker of heat spiral deep in her belly. The words forced themselves out anyway, though, as she tried to buy enough time to process what was happening. 'W-why not?'

'Because I wanted this instead.' Nico closed the gap between them. He steadied himself with one hand over Charlotte's against the door but he slid the fingers of his other hand behind her neck and then up into her hair as he cradled her head and dipped his own so that their lips could touch.

His mouth felt familiar now. Safe. Charlotte knew that the touch of his tongue against hers would provide a pleasure so intense it was almost pain but her lips parted eagerly and her tongue met his halfway to begin the dance. And this time the give and take of the kiss

changed into more than an exploration and taste of pleasure. This time it had an urgency that demanded more.

And that was enough to make Charlotte pull away. To snatch a gasp of breath and then shake her head.

'I…I don't understand…'

'Yes, you do, *cara*,' Nico said very softly. 'I want you.'

She shook her head again, more insistently. 'But… *why*?'

Nico leaned against the door. He still had a hand cradling her head and she felt his fingers move in a caress. 'Why wouldn't I?'

'Because I'm…not your type. You said so.'

Nico smiled *that* smile. The slow, lazy one. Except that this time it seemed to be gentle. Reassuring? 'I say stupid things sometimes.'

Charlotte had to drop her gaze. Dammit. The train seemed to have picked up speed and the way it was rocking made her more acutely aware of the proximity of Nico's body. Of how it would take nothing for her to fall just a little closer and mould her own body against his.

'This can't go any further,' she said.

'Why not?' The words were a whisper. A question, not an accusation. If she said the word Nico would stop but he genuinely didn't understand, and why would he? He must have seen her own desire for him. He had to be well used to reading those kinds of signals from women.

'Because…' Charlotte couldn't look up. She couldn't stop herself continuing either. Good grief…far from giving her the stamina to maintain control in a difficult situation, the amount of champagne she'd knocked back

this evening was having the opposite effect. Her control had slipped so far she'd lost the handle for the door behind which she kept her secret so well shut away. She hadn't been completely honest with Nico earlier, had she? *He* had been with *her*. Guilt bubbled up inside her and something snapped.

'I can't do it,' she whispered. 'I…can't have sex. I'm…' No. There was no way she could utter that horrible word. A shudder went right through her entire body.

Nico's hand slipped out from her hair and he let go of the door. This was it. He was going to excuse himself and go to the bar for a stiff drink, and who could blame him?

But, instead, he gathered Charlotte into his arms and held her close to him. His mouth was close to her ear and he spoke softly.

'You've been hurt, *cara*,' he said. 'I know that. You've been raped, haven't you?'

Charlotte's gasp was shocked. 'No…it…wasn't rape. How could it have been? He was my…my boyfriend. I had chosen to be with him. I'd chosen to go to his apartment. It might have been my first time but I knew what was going to happen.'

For a long moment Nico simply held her in silence. Then he spoke gently. 'But it didn't happen the way you wanted it to, did it?'

'N-no.' Unbelievably, the tears were gathering again. After not having cried for so many years, she was certainly making up for it now.

'And when you wanted him to stop, he wouldn't, would he?'

'H-he said it wasn't his fault if I was frigid. He wasn't

going to have his evening ruined by a—a tease.' There.
The word had come out all by itself. 'And—and he was
right. I hated it and…and when I tried again, more than
a year later, with someone else…I couldn't do it…so
he—'

'Was a stupid, arrogant bastard,' Nico whispered ve-
hemently. 'Who had no idea what he was talking about
and didn't deserve to be in the company of any woman,
let alone someone like you.'

Charlotte felt his lips press against the top of her
head. And then she felt Nico's hand under her chin and
a pressure that made her raise her face to meet his gaze.

'It's not true,' he told her. 'You are a beautiful, *pas-
sionate* woman and all you need to do is believe that.'

Maybe there'd always been a glimmer of hope deep
inside that that was true. Maybe when she'd tried again,
it had been too soon. Or with the wrong person. Char-
lotte had always thought that she might have conquered
her demons if she could have talked to someone profes-
sional about it but the shame of anyone knowing had
always stopped her.

And now Nico knew. And he was still here.

And he was gorgeous and kind and he'd said that
he wanted her.

They wouldn't be seeing each other again after to-
morrow so would it really matter if it didn't work. She
might never have an opportunity like this again. To
find out…

Charlotte licked suddenly dry lips. 'Did you really
mean it?' The words were incredibly hard to utter.

'That I want you?' Nico's eyes were so dark they
looked black. His hands on her back slid lower until

they cupped her bottom. He pulled her even closer so that she had no need of any verbal confirmation of his state of arousal.

'Oh…' Charlotte couldn't look away from his eyes.

'Do you trust me, *cara*?'

She didn't have enough breath to say anything. Instead, Charlotte stretched on tiptoe so that she could reach Nico's lips with her own. She slid her arms around his neck at the same time as she felt herself being lifted off her feet and carried into the adjoining cabin and a bunk that would simply have to be big enough.

Well…

He'd been right, hadn't he?

Not just about the reason why Charlotte Highton's personality had changed so much.

He'd been right about the fact that she was a beautiful and passionate woman.

It was well after midnight when Nico eased himself out of the bed that was far too small for two people to sleep together comfortably. He got dressed again and let himself quietly out of the cabin with the intention of going to the bar for that long-postponed nightcap.

Charlotte was deeply asleep again, which wasn't surprising. She'd been on an emotional roller-coaster for the last two days and she'd had rather a lot of champagne tonight.

Had he taken advantage of her lack of inhibitions?

Or would she thank him for proving what she should have been able to believe in all along? That there was nothing wrong with her. Nothing she needed to be afraid of or hide from.

That was a minefield in itself. Charlotte was a passionate woman. The way she'd responded to him had been a joy. No...it had been by far the most tender love-making he'd ever experienced. So overwhelming that he could only hope Charlotte hadn't noticed she hadn't been the only one with tears wetting her cheeks in the aftermath. The way he'd felt when she'd started to touch him back... To offer herself so completely...

Even now Nico had no idea what to do with the sensations that made it hard to breathe. It had made him feel like he was the most special person on earth. As though she was the only woman in the world he ever wanted to be with again because he would never experience anything like this with anyone else.

He knew how ridiculous that was. The world was full of beautiful women who were eager to share his bed. But Charlotte was naïve in such matters. She might believe he was the only man who could make her feel like that. She might mistakenly believe she had fallen in love with him when she was now capable of having a fulfilling relationship with any man she chose.

It didn't have to be him.

He didn't want it to be him.

So why was he feeling so...uneasy? So in need of a stiff drink?

Because there was a voice in his head that was trying to insist that being with Charlotte for just a little longer wouldn't hurt? That he could, at least, have one more night like last night? Just to check whether it had actually been so extraordinary?

He knew perfectly well how wrong that would be. *That* would, without any doubt, be taking advantage of

Charlotte, and Nico had far too much respect for her to even consider it.

The strange sound Nico heard as he made his way through the seemingly deserted carriages in the early hours of the morning only added to his disturbance.

He'd heard that sound before. The cry of a baby who'd only just entered the world.

A newborn on the Orient Express? Impossible.

The echo of that cry of new life stayed with him, though, imagined or not. And Nico didn't like it.

He didn't want a new life.

He wanted his old one back.

CHAPTER NINE

CHARLOTTE KNEW SHE was alone even before she'd surfaced from sleep enough to open her eyes.

Had it been a dream?

Her memories certainly had a dreamlike fuzziness to them. Sensations rather than clear thoughts, and the gentle rocking of the train beneath her seemed to encourage her to close her eyes and explore them. She could feel each one as clearly as if it was happening all over again.

The surprise of finding Nico in the cabin when she'd finally got Gran settled, so closely followed by a breath-robbing fascination generated by seeing him with his shirt buttons undone and his tie hanging loose. As if she'd interrupted him in the process of getting completely undressed...

The explosion of that sensation that had sent shafts of desire into every cell of her body when she'd seen the reflection of her own desire in Nico's eyes. When she'd felt his fingers steadying her head for the kiss that had sent her straight over the edge.

Into that abyss of fear and self-loathing. The feeling of falling without a parachute, knowing that death was

inevitable, as she'd uttered the words that had been her confession of her inadequacies as a woman.

The soft cloud that had gathered and cushioned that fall…first with Nico's words of reassurance and then the physical invitation to see how right they'd been.

And…oh…Charlotte had never known it could be like that. Maybe she'd had fragments of glimpsing it from haunting, erotic dreams but this had been reality.

Or had it?

Shifting a little in her bunk, Charlotte could feel the sweet, inner tenderness that could only be the result of having been passionately loved. With a small sound that was almost a groan, she let herself sink into the last sensation she remembered. Of falling asleep in Nico's arms again but this time feeling as though it was the only place in the world she could ever want to be. Falling asleep with the utter bliss of knowing those arms would still be around her when she woke.

Except they weren't.

How had Nico managed to extricate himself from this tiny space without waking her? He must have been very determined not to, which meant that he'd wanted to be alone.

Why? Did he regret what had happened between them?

Well…why wouldn't he? For heaven's sake, he'd been sucked into her private life because of her meltdowns in front of him. She'd cried all over him. Twice! He'd seen her with her panda eyes and he'd heard all the sordid details of her mortifying past. He must think she was needy and pathetic virtually all the time.

Did he think that she might remain clingy? That she

would try and keep him in her life longer than the period they'd agreed on? Ask him for more than he was prepared to give?

It was odd but the notion of being seen as pathetic and clingy was worse than revealing herself as physically frigid. Nico had shown her that what she'd believed about herself had been so not true.

What she needed to do was show him that any fears about how else she might behave were also untrue. She was in love with him, certainly, but that was *her* problem. It didn't need to be Nico's and he didn't deserve it to be. Not after giving her a gift so far beyond price by restoring her self-esteem.

Creating the magic that had been her night on the Orient Express.

She would have to thank him, of course, but she had to do it in a way that let him know he was not under any further obligation to her. And she needed to make him believe it. To present herself in a way that showed confidence and independence. The way she presented herself at a conference might be a good start.

With a determined shove Charlotte got rid of the bed covers and climbed out of the bunk. Finding herself naked was a reality check that made her blush. She'd never slept naked in her life and the comfort zone of well-fitting clothes had to be her first priority. Washing her face in the tiny corner basin a short time later, she eyed herself in the mirror. The smudged make-up and rat's-nest hair that advertised a night of totally wanton behaviour were the next things she had to take control of. Only then would she be able to face her day.

And Nico.

* * *

He was going to have to face Charlotte at some point. Having caught a few hours' sleep on the seat in the daytime area of the suite and making sure he was not there when Charlotte woke up, Nico had successfully whiled away a good portion of the morning with coffee and newspapers in the bar car.

Brunch was being served already in the dining cars and there was still no sign of Charlotte or Lady Geraldine. It wouldn't be that long before they reached Calais and would have to board the buses for travel to England via the channel tunnel. There would be no private cabins on the train leg to London, during which they would apparently be served afternoon tea, and they would be going in different directions as soon they reached Victoria.

Nico could well imagine how chaotic it was going to be in that huge station on Christmas Eve. It probably wasn't going to be much less private from the time they had to share a bus with dozens of other people. If he wanted a conversation alone with Charlotte, he would have to do something about it now. Clearly, she wasn't planning to come and find *him* this morning.

Their suite was empty and Lady Geraldine's door was closed but Nico tapped on it anyway. It was after ten a.m. Surely Jendi would be up and about by now?

Charlotte opened the door. For a long moment they simply stared at each other. Nico had to process the startling change from when he'd last seen Charlotte, asleep with her glorious hair spread across the crisp, white pillowcase, her lips devoid of any artificial colouring and swollen from so many kisses.

He was facing Dr Highton right now. Dressed in that power suit he'd first seen her in when she'd been on her way to the symposium. She had her hair scraped back into that complicated knot arrangement that gave her the look of an air hostess and her make-up was perfect. No smudged mascara from tears being shed and her perfect lipstick made it look as though her lips had never been licked, let alone kissed.

And, apart from a flash of something that was gone too quickly to analyse, even her gaze looked professional. Impersonal enough to make Nico take a mental step backwards, at any rate.

'Is everything all right? It's…getting quite late.'

Charlotte wasn't meeting his gaze now. 'I can't believe I slept so late,' she said, loudly enough for her grandmother to overhear. 'No wonder you went off to find some breakfast. There's something about the motion of a train, isn't there? It makes you sleep so well.'

Nico raised an eyebrow. Surely Charlotte would realise that *he'd* had virtually no sleep.

'Is that Nico?' Lady Geraldine called. 'Bring him in, Charlotte Jane, for goodness' sake.'

There wasn't room for three people to sit. Charlotte remained standing as well.

'How are you this morning, Jendi?' Nico enquired politely. 'Did you sleep well, too?'

'Not bad.'

Nico could feel the tension emanating from Charlotte. She didn't believe that and she could be right. Lady Geraldine did look rather pale and she was gripping the windowsill with one hand, as though the movement of the train was making her uncomfortable.

'Apparently there was a baby boy born on the train last night, have you heard?'

'No…*really*?' Lady Geraldine turned and was unable to disguise her wince of pain. She ignored it, however, and her expression suggested that everybody else had better follow her example. 'How do you know?'

'The steward in the bar told me when he gave me the newspapers. He said that we'd be reading about the unexpected event on the Orient Express very soon. I actually heard it crying late in the night when I was walking through the carriage. Apparently the young girl had disguised her condition very well, by wearing a large, old-fashioned coat.'

'Oh…I think I saw that girl at the station in Venice,' Charlotte said.

'What on earth were you doing, walking around the train in the middle of the night?' Lady Geraldine asked.

'I needed to stretch my legs,' Nico said, after a moment's awkward silence. 'The bunks are…rather small, aren't they?'

'Depends on what you're doing.' Lady Geraldine managed a smile. 'I'm delighted that Charlotte felt the need to sleep in, I must say. It's probably been years since she hasn't been up at the crack of dawn.'

There was a very noticeable flush of colour on Charlotte's cheeks now and when she flicked a glance towards Nico the shutters were down. She was most definitely thinking about what had kept her awake last night. The relief at seeing what he now knew to be the real Charlotte peeping out was enough to make him try and hold that gaze. And convey the message in his

smile that he agreed it was well worth remembering. Unforgettable might be closer to the mark.

'Oh, for heaven's sake…' Lady Geraldine flapped a hand at them. 'Go and make sheep's eyes at each other in your own cabin and leave an old lady in peace.' The tone was authoritative but she was still smiling as she delivered the order.

Charlotte looked as though she was about to refuse but then shook her head and signalled Nico to go ahead of her. He stepped into their suite and she barrelled in straight after him, closing the door behind her.

'I don't want to leave her too long,' she said. 'I'm pretty sure she's not feeling nearly as well as she's trying to make out.' Biting her lip, Charlotte stared down at her hands. 'I *think* she wants me out of the way so she can take another dose of her painkillers.'

'Is there anything I can do to help?'

'I don't think so.' Charlotte shook her head. 'But… thank you…'

Nico had the distinct impression that the hesitation meant that Charlotte had something else she wanted to say. So he waited. Sure enough, her chin rose as she took a very deep breath.

'I don't mean just for offering to help with Gran…' The movement of Charlotte's facial muscles suggested acute embarrassment. 'Thank you for…you know…'

Nico raised an eyebrow. Was this it? So much for fearing that Charlotte might think she'd fallen in love with him! Was last night going to be a polite 'Thank you' and 'You're most welcome' kind of exchange?

He felt distinctly piqued even though he knew he

should be relieved. But it deserved something more than that, surely?

He stepped closer. Close enough for them to be breathing the same air. He bent his head as if he was about to kiss her but stopped halfway there.

'I can assure you it was very much my pleasure.'

Her eyes widened and he heard her catch her breath but then she stepped back. Only a tiny step, admittedly, but it was enough to send a very clear message. Charlotte didn't want to be kissed again this morning. And there was enough tension in the air to make Nico wonder if she was trying to get back into her old comfort zone. That might explain the way she was dressed and the hairstyle that defied anyone to try and run their fingers through those long tresses.

'Don't….' The word escaped from him as a whisper. A soft groan almost.

'D-don't what?' she stuttered.

Nico had to close his eyes for a heartbeat. He hadn't intended saying this but maybe it needed to be said. 'Don't dismiss last night as a one-off.'

Oh… *Dio*…would she think he was asking to see her again?

Maybe he was…

With a mental shake Nico forced a smile to his lips. 'Don't ever stop believing that you're special. That what you have to offer would be more than enough for any man you chose to be with.' He straightened his spine and tried to keep his smile from faltering. 'There's a whole world of men out there, Charlotte. You'll find someone one day and you'll know he's the person you

want to share your life with. Don't let your past hold
you back.'

She was nodding. Blinking hard as though deter-
mined not to cry. And when she spoke, her voice was
remarkably strong.

'Back at you, Nico Moretti.' Okay, her smile was a
bit wobbly. 'Don't be afraid to fall in love in someone
or let your past hold *you* back. You need to trust your-
self and find someone who can appreciate all you have
to offer because…it's a lot.'

Find someone?

Someone else, she meant.

It was Nico's turn to nod. To smile. This extraordi-
nary connection they had was because they'd shared
things they'd never shared with others. It was a new
experience—much as this train journey was new. To-
tally unrelated to normal life and it couldn't be expected
to continue. They both knew that. At least, this way,
they could part with special memories of their brief
time together.

Charlotte was twisting the ring on her finger. 'I
should give this back,' she said.

'There's no rush.' Nico shrugged. 'Despite your wise
words, I'm not about to go hunting for a wife. And even
if I found someone, I don't really think she'd want to
wear such an old-fashioned ring.'

'It's a beautiful ring,' Charlotte said immediately.
'A family heirloom. A symbol of what's held you back
even. *I'd* wear it.'

'You *are* wearing it.' He had to smile. 'Not that I
gave you much choice about that.'

Charlotte's breath came out in a huff. 'I mean, you'd

have to make sure that whoever you really give it to understands its significance. The promise. You'd have to tell her everything you told me.'

As if he was ever going to find someone to share soul-deep secrets with again. Once was enough. Like this train journey.

They were both staring at the ring.

'I'll have to take it off as soon as I get back to work,' Charlotte said. 'I wouldn't be able to wear a ring like this even if I *was* engaged.'

'There's no rush,' Nico said again. 'Just see how things go with your *nonna*. You know where I work.'

Charlotte nodded again. 'At the Hammersmith, yes?'

'Yes. And it doesn't matter if I'm not there for some reason. You could just leave it with my secretary.'

'But…' There was a lot not being said here. About how long she might want to keep up the pretence. How long it would take for her grandmother to die. Her lips trembled. 'But it's precious…'

'I trust you.'

It wasn't hard to sound sincere. He'd trusted Charlotte with far more than a family heirloom, hadn't he?

The only sound for a long moment was the clack of the train wheels. Rhythmic and steady. Like a heartbeat. And then Charlotte raised her eyes.

'I trust you, too,' she whispered.

That was a lot bigger than the trust he'd placed in her, even by confessing what he knew could be seen as an inadequacy. Being a commitment-phobic male was far more socially acceptable than the stigma of having been labelled a frigid woman. Or having been raped.

He was holding a secret that could potentially wreck her carefully ordered world. It was huge.

A gift that no one else could have given him.

Like the one he'd given her by showing her that it wasn't true? Being the man who'd had the privilege of holding her as she'd come apart in someone's arms for the first time?

They were even. Equals.

And, as long as he didn't do something stupid and make a fool of himself, they could keep this respect for each other. Part as friends. They would get back to reality and their own lives soon enough.

It was time to lighten the atmosphere.

'I'm hungry,' Nico announced. 'Would you care for breakfast in the dining car?'

'Gran's ordered cabin service. I need to stay with her and see if she actually eats anything. You go.'

So the separation was to begin already. The countdown was on.

Fine. Nico knew that was sensible. What they both wanted. There would be plenty to distract them for the rest of the day because it was unlikely that they would be alone again together. They would probably never be alone together again. This was it. The last intimate moment he would have with Charlotte Highton.

He had to kiss her. Just a soft farewell.

'I won't forget.' It was a promise. A deliberately ambiguous one. Charlotte could assume he was talking about her wise words regarding his future. She didn't have to know that he meant *her*.

Her quiet words followed him like an echo that

seemed to be picked up by the train wheels as he made his way to the dining car.

'I won't either.'

The rest of the journey seemed interminable.

Lady Geraldine was keeping up a brave face but she ate virtually nothing of her brunch and didn't touch the champagne or afternoon tea on the English leg of the trip. The weather was cold enough to make her look pinched and it was clearly a struggle to join the excited conversations around them that were predicting a genuine white Christmas as fat snowflakes began to fall more and more heavily.

'I'm just tired, love,' she told Charlotte. 'But I wouldn't have changed anything about the last couple of days. Not a thing.'

And Charlotte had been able to smile back and tell her grandmother that she felt exactly the same.

Victoria was heaving with people desperate to get to where they wanted to be for Christmas Day. It was Nico who helped collect their luggage and carve a pathway through the crowd to where Lady Geraldine's chauffeur had arranged to meet them.

They offered Nico a lift but he declined with palpable regret.

'I've made an appointment with a colleague at the Hammersmith,' he told them. 'You need to go in the opposite direction and it'll be bad enough already. I hope you don't get caught in a traffic jam or the snow. If I can't find a cab, I'll take the tube.'

He took Charlotte in his arms to say goodbye. For her grandmother's sake? Was that why he said that he

was going to miss her and that seeing her again couldn't be too soon for him?

It wasn't why Charlotte returned his kiss and agreed that it couldn't be too soon for her either.

She meant every word.

The bleak feeling of watching the crowd swallow Nico only got stronger as they inched their way out of London.

Lady Geraldine took her hand and gave it a squeeze.

'I know it's hard, darling. It's such a shame that Nico's going to be so busy for a while.'

'Mmm...'

'You're lucky, though.'

'Oh?' Thank goodness her grandmother couldn't possibly have any idea of just *how* lucky her granddaughter had been.

'Yes. Much luckier than back in my day. You've got your mobile phones and...and Scope.'

Charlotte smiled despite herself as she sighed. 'Skype, Gran.'

'Whatever.' Her hand got another squeeze. 'It's not quite the same as the real thing, though, is it?'

'No. It's not.' There was an odd pain in Charlotte's chest as she tried to draw in a new breath.

Her heart starting to break perhaps?

CHAPTER TEN

CHARLOTTE'S FAVOURITE CHRISTMAS ever had been the one she'd told Nico about when they'd been snowed in and Gran had cooked sausages on sticks over the open fire in the drawing room.

Maybe, some time in the future, somebody would ask her about her *least* favourite Christmas and she knew that, coincidentally, it would also be one of the rare, truly white ones.

This one.

She stared out of the V-shaped gap in the snow piled on the sill of her latticed window and there was the eerie, early morning light that only a thick blanket of snow could create. There was nothing to disturb the perfection of the Christmas-card scene in the gardens of Highton Hall. The footprints on the lawn below had probably been made by a fox but if her grandmother had seen them in years gone by, she would have told a small Charlotte that they were the tracks left by Santa's reindeer.

The thought should have brought a poignant smile

to her face but instead Charlotte felt the lump in her throat get bigger.

She had never felt this…bleak.

This lonely.

This…*empty*.

As if she'd lost something huge that she would never have back again. Like her heart? Or maybe it was part of her soul. The part that she'd shared with Nico. Yes. That's what it felt like. He had brought light into the darkest part of her being and, by touching it, it had somehow become his, even if he didn't want it.

Was that what love was? Giving away the most important part of yourself?

No… Charlotte found her picture-perfect view becoming blurry. It was finding someone who recognised that part. Accepted it. Made it better than it had been before simply by being there.

And it wasn't one-sided, that had been the clincher. Nico had shared that part of himself with her. The lonely little boy who was still there deep inside. The one who'd been hurt and had seen people he loved get hurt, and was determined to never be the cause of such hurt himself.

Nico thought he didn't know what he needed. That he couldn't possibly make the right choice of a person to be with for the rest of his life. He thought he was incapable of falling in love.

And maybe he had the kind of strength to hold himself back from that kind of surrender but it was blindingly obvious what he needed.

A tiny robin, its bright red breast a decoration in it-

self, fluttered into view and landed on the windowsill, tilting its head and to give Charlotte a cheeky glance.

'He just needs what we all need,' she informed the robin. 'To be loved.'

The robin fluttered off like an echo of laughter.

As if it was that simple...

It was. Charlotte had found that person, hadn't she? She had given him that part of herself she could never give to anyone else.

But it was that impossibly difficult at the same time.

Because finding someone that you connected with at a soul-deep level wasn't enough. They had to feel the same way or it could never begin to work.

And Nico didn't feel the same way. How could he when they'd only known each other for a couple of days?

But he didn't even want to *see* her again. Good grief, he'd told her that she could leave the ring with his secretary, if he wasn't around.

It had meant nothing. A bit of harmless pretence to make an old lady happy before she died. Repayment for the imagined debt of losing her laptop. A bonus of a one-night stand as well?

Charlotte forced herself to move. She couldn't stand here dwelling on how miserable she felt. It was Christmas Day after all. And her toes were freezing. Dressing quickly, she chose clothes for warmth, donning black woollen leggings and an oversized crimson pullover on top of a black bodysuit. No doubt her grandmother would expect her to change for dinner but that was a

few hours away yet and it would be warmer downstairs when the open fires were stoked up.

Maybe Christmas dinner wasn't so far away after all. The rich aroma of roasting meat caught Charlotte's nostrils as she went downstairs. Betty, the cook, must be busy in the kitchen, probably under Gran's strict supervision. Charlotte would probably be given a laden plate of bacon and eggs and an admonishment about the perils of laziness and sleeping in.

The Christmas tree in the huge foyer of this grand old house had coloured lights twinkling merrily and there were gifts beneath, enticingly wrapped in pretty paper and tied with bows of satin ribbon.

It looked like one of the festive pictures that had played against the wall of that Venetian restaurant… good grief, only three days ago? On the evening when she'd given in to the temptation of pretending that Nico was her lover. When she'd accidentally become 'engaged' to him.

The ring was still on her finger. Touching it, Charlotte found she could twist it more easily now. Because she was away from the efficient central heating of the Orient Express and in a huge, chilly ancestral home?

Or was it because she felt so cold inside? So bleak…

Whatever. She couldn't take it off yet, could she? Not on Christmas Day, when it would be the first thing Gran would notice. She would have to find a solution to this situation but not today.

And she couldn't let Gran see how miserable she was either. Pasting what she hoped was a bright smile on

her face, Charlotte walked past the Christmas tree and went down the long hallway to the kitchen.

Betty was basting an enormous turkey. Her husband, John, was polishing silver serviette rings over newspaper spread on one end of the kitchen table. Her daughter was peeling Brussels sprouts and scoring an X into the stalks.

'I was just about to put some breakfast on trays and bring it up,' Betty said after Christmas greetings had been exchanged. 'I was getting worried.'

'Has Gran not been down yet?'

'Not a peep from her. And she's always the first up on Christmas Day.'

'I'll take her up a cup of tea,' Charlotte said. She was worried herself now. 'I expect she's just tired out after her big adventure.'

'You look a bit peaky yourself, pet.' Betty and her family had been a part of Highton Hall for as long as Charlotte could remember. They were more like relatives than staff. Family. Charlotte's smile was genuine this time.

'I'm fine, Betty. I just need a cup of tea, too.'

Betty had been patting her hand. Her jaw dropped.

'Oh…my…. Is that what I *think* it is?'

Charlotte held up her hand and the diamond flashed as it caught the light. Her heart sank. The game had to go on a little longer no matter how much worse it was going to make her feel.

'I guess I had a bit of an adventure myself, Betty. You'll hear all about it as soon as Gran's up, I'm sure.'

'I'd better.' Betty busied herself with a teapot and a

china cup and saucer. She added a couple of tiny gingerbread stars to the saucer. 'Go on…tell Lady G that we're waiting to hear all about it.'

Her grandmother's bedroom was still dark.

'You awake, Gran? I've got a cup of tea for you.' Charlotte balanced the cup in one hand as she drew back the heavy drapes to let the bright, mid-morning light into the room.

And then she turned, and didn't notice how much tea she was spilling on the Persian carpet as she raced to her grandmother's bedside and dropped the cup and saucer on the bedside table. Gingerbread stars floated in a saucer full of tea.

'Gran…'

Lady Geraldine was lying with her knees pulled up and the bedcover gripped between clenched fists. Her face was white with a sheen of perspiration on her forehead. Her pulse was racing. And weak. Her abdomen was swollen and hard to the touch. And it only took the lightest touch to make her cry out in agony.

'Oh…*God*…' Charlotte picked up the phone beside the half-empty cup of tea. She dialled only three numbers.

'I need an ambulance,' she said crisply as soon as her call was answered. 'It's urgent.'

Emergencies like heart attacks and strokes were no respecters of what day it happened to be.

Extreme weather was more of a problem on days when people simply had to be somewhere else for an important occasion and the number of accidents rose.

And there were plenty of people like him who had no family to be with and no desire to celebrate Christmas and carried on with stupid behaviour like getting into fights and getting beaten up or stabbed.

Worst of all, there were the people who found the season too much of a reminder of what they didn't have so the rate of attempted suicides always went up, too.

It was not a good day to be in charge of an emergency department but the staff always did their absolute best to make it as cheerful as possible, and Nico had always managed to join in and encourage them.

Why was it *so* hard this year?

Why did he feel so…bleak?

So…*empty*?

It was *ridicolo*. Ridiculous.

He had his life back the way he wanted it to be. *Needed* it to be.

So why did he feel so off-kilter? So *perduto*, almost?

And why was it always Italian words that came into his head when something stirred him deeply? The past was behind him and best forgotten. Even dredging up happy memories, such as the favourite Christmas he'd shared with Charlotte, was not a good thing to do. No wonder he couldn't settle into doing what he most loved to do and lose himself in the demands of his work.

He would go and do another thorough neurological check on the elderly gentleman in cubicle three who had fallen when he'd gone outside to sweep snow off the steps in preparation for his family arriving. He'd hit his head hard enough to need a period of observation before they could consider letting him go home

to his Christmas dinner. Maybe it hadn't just been the slippery steps and the fall responsible for him losing consciousness either. Perhaps a more thorough cardio-vascular work-up would be justified.

Imagine what would have happened in Venice if Charlotte hadn't been there to see beyond what others had seen?

'Incoming, Dr Moretti,' a nurse told him as she hurried past. 'Eighty-something-year-old female with an abdominal mass and acute bowel obstruction. She's tachycardic, short of breath and vomiting. GCS of thirteen.'

Dio… An elderly woman with a bowel obstruction that could potentially be due to a tumour? Was everything today going to remind him of either Charlotte or her *nonna*? They were probably sitting in front of an open fire right now. Drinking mulled wine or eggnog, perhaps and listening to Christmas carols. Maybe there was a piano and Charlotte would be playing carols. Or maybe they were opening their gifts to each other.

Or…maybe something terrible had happened. Nico could see the ambulance team coming through the doors of his department now. He couldn't see much of the figure on the stretcher because she was bundled up in warm blankets and her face was covered by an oxygen mask. The person holding the bag of IV fluids aloft wasn't part of the paramedic crew, however.

It was Charlotte.

No. Could this be the beginning of the end for Jendi? Surely not today, of all days…

'Resus One,' Nico ordered, before the triage nurse

had a chance to consider priority. 'And get a surgical consult down here stat.'

He ushered the entourage into the resus area reserved for major cases. There was no time for any more than brief eye contact with Charlotte as Nico listened to the handover from the paramedics and prepared to launch an investigative and stabilisation protocol that could deal with this emergency. There was no way he was going to let Lady Geraldine Highton die in his department on Christmas Day.

As awful as it was, this was just the kind of challenge he'd needed. That disturbing, *empty* feeling had completely vanished and Nico had never felt more in control. Or more determined to do his absolute best for his patient. And her family.

The waiting was the worst.

At least all the tension and drama and fear since the moment she'd found Gran in such a dreadful state had been balanced by the swiftness of action and the company of others. The paramedics had been brilliant, using a four-wheel-drive vehicle to get to the estate and then transferring Gran to a faster ambulance to get her into the city. The roads had been appalling with all the snow and traffic jams from a big accident on the M1. They'd had to stick to routes that had been cleared in the city and get to an emergency department that was not only open on Christmas Day but prepared to accept a major case.

It had taken too much time and all the while Lady Geraldine's condition had been deteriorating. It was

becoming hard for her to breathe and her level of con-
sciousness was slipping. By the time they'd arrived
at the totally unexpected destination of the Hammer-
smith—*Nico's* hospital—she was unconscious and the
situation was looking bad enough for Charlotte to be
unaware of anything except the relief of getting to a
place where they might be able to help her grandmother.

And then there'd been the drama of trying to get
Gran stable enough for the surgeon to consider that op-
erating might be an option on an eighty-two-year-old
woman. There'd been fluid resuscitation and ventila-
tion assistance, blood tests and scans and ECGs. Peo-
ple rushing in and out with the kind of controlled chaos
Charlotte was all too familiar with, but this was her
gran being treated and she'd never felt less like a doctor.

Waiting like this in an area set aside for the families
of patients undergoing surgery was a new experience
too. It was nerve-racking and felt interminable. There
were only one or two theatres being used for absolute
emergencies today and just a skeleton staff on duty so
it felt like she was completely alone and she'd been here
for what felt like hours. Surely the surgery was over by
now? Why hadn't someone come to tell her what was
going on?

Had they forgotten she was even here?

No… Charlotte could hear footsteps echoing in the
wide, empty hallway outside. Coming closer. Someone
was coming to see her and what they had to say could
possibly be devastating news.

She couldn't move. Could only stand there, with her

fingers pressed against her mouth to stifle a cry. Afraid to breathe. Unable to blink even.

And then a tall figure filled the doorway. A powerful presence entered the small space of the waiting room and…

And Charlotte wasn't alone any more.

'Carlotta…*cara*…' Nico gathered Charlotte into his arms and held her close. '*Grazie a Dio ho trovato voi.*'

He'd had to come even though he had no real news for her yet. Standing there, in the observation deck of the operating theatre, it had come back with a vengeance.

That empty feeling.

Had it really been the challenge of fighting for Jendi's life that had made it go away? The focus on medicine that was the most important thing in his life? Or had it had been because Charlotte was so close to him again?

He had to find out. His shift in the emergency department was finished and there would be no professional distraction for him now. If he found Charlotte and that empty feeling disappeared then he would know the truth.

And it had. *Dio mio*, but it had evaporated like mist in hot Italian sunshine as soon as he'd gathered her in his arms and held her close to his heart.

The truth was irrefutable. It wasn't work he needed like the oxygen in the air he breathed. It was this woman. *Charlotte*. Without her, he would have that horrible, empty feeling for the rest of his life.

'*Carlotta...*' The word was a breath that got lost in her hair.

'I don't understand,' she said.

Neither did Nico. But it was wonderful. So joyous.

'I can't speak Italian, Nico…' She was wriggling in his arms, pulling back so she could see his face. 'What's happening?' Her breath was a fearful gulp. 'Where's Gran?'

How could he be so selfish? Nico stroked her hair and focused enough to change languages.

'There's a break in surgery. They're doing a biopsy of the tumour. It will be a bigger operation if they decide to try and remove it all and it would be too much of a risk if it's…'

She knew what he was saying. If the tumour was aggressively malignant, they would only attempt a palliative procedure to deal with the bowel obstruction.

But Charlotte's eyes had widened. 'The surgeon thinks there's a chance it's not malignant? That it's… *benign*?'

Was it cruel to give her hope or a gift that he could share with her for at least a little while? The point was moot because she knew the answer. They wouldn't be interrupting surgery for the length of time it took to use a technician on Christmas Day if it wasn't a good possibility.

'Are you going back? Can you find out?'

Nico shook his head. 'They'll come and tell us. I want to wait here with you. I…I *have* to.'

'You *have* to?' Charlotte's tone was as odd as his had been. A note of wonder? '*Why?*'

'Because…' There was no point in being less than honest with her. There never had been and never would be. 'Because being with you…it makes the empty feeling go away.'

'Oh…' Charlotte's gaze was holding his and he could actually see it melting. Getting misty. 'It does… It *so* does, doesn't it?'

'*You* feel it too?' A surge of emotion was threatening to explode inside Nico's chest. Gratitude? Relief? *Hope*? No. It was bigger than any of those. 'I've never felt like this,' he confessed. 'I don't know what this is… but it's…it's…'

'I think it's love,' Charlotte whispered. 'I'm in love with you and that's why I have the empty feeling when you're not here.'

'I'm in love with you…' Nico tested the words out loud. Strange and new but…yes…they felt right. He tried them in Italian to make sure. '*Cara mia, innamorata di te.*'

And that made them real but still unbelievable. 'How?' he whispered. 'How did this happen? So fast?'

'I don't know…' But Charlotte was smiling. Almost laughing, but there were tears in her eyes at the same time. 'But it's Christmas…and it's the most wonderful gift I could ever have been given. I love you so much, Nico. I've never felt like this before. It feels like everything that's ever happened to me, even all the bad things, were worth it because it led me here. To *you*.'

He had to kiss her then. Slowly. Tenderly. The bursting feeling inside him intensified and turned to molten

joy. It was a long time before he could lift his head to look into Charlotte's eyes again.

'When I was in Venice,' Nico told her with a smile, 'a moment or two before I saw you at the accident scene I was having to push my way through the crowd and I heard this old woman and you know what she said?'

'No.' Charlotte was smiling up at him. A tear escaped and Nico let go of one of her hands so that he could brush it away for her. 'What did she say?'

'That it was almost Christmas. A good time for a miracle to happen. I think that's what this is, Carlotta. A miracle.'

Charlotte sniffed and the sound was so unromantic that Nico could feel himself fall even deeper in love with her. Had he really thought he was incapable of doing this? He was good at it. With a bit of practice he would be the best.

When Charlotte scrubbed at her nose, he caught her hand. The one with the ring on it. He seemed to remember it had been quite a struggle to get it onto her finger but it came off quite easily.

Charlotte went very, very still.

'You know what this is.' Nico had to clear the sudden gruffness of his voice away. 'Of all the people in the world, you are the only one who can know the symbolism of this ring. The...' His voice cracked again. 'The promise it carries.'

Her gaze clung to his. Her head dipped and rose again in a slow, solemn nod.

'I didn't give you a choice about wearing it before,' Nico continued. 'I'm giving you that choice now. Will

you wear this ring, *inamorata*? Will you accept my promise?'

'Oh…*yes*, Nico.' Her hand was shaking as she held it out for him to slip the ring back on her finger. 'But…'

He stilled her words with a gentle finger on her lips. 'It's like your *nonna* said,' he murmured. 'It doesn't mean we have to get married next week. It's a promise of commitment. We can take all the time we need to make sure it's perfect.'

The sound of footsteps outside the waiting room sent a sudden chill down Nico's spine. Someone was coming to give them news.

What if it was bad news?

The only way this could be truly perfect would be to have Jendi at their wedding, wouldn't it? To see her, at some point in the future, cradle her first great-grandchild in her arms.

To know that the biggest thing on that bucket list of hers had been well and truly ticked off.

It was the surgeon, who'd come straight from Theatre to find them. He'd stripped off his gown and gloves but he was still in his scrubs and white gumboots. He still had a hat covering his head and neck.

But he was smiling. 'Your gran's a real trouper,' he told Charlotte. 'Tough as old boots, in fact. She's come through this astonishingly well. You'll be able to go and see her in Recovery very soon.'

'Oh…thank God…' Charlotte was clinging to Nico's hand with a vice-like grip. 'And…and the tumour?'

'Benign. We got it all out. Can't see any reason why

she won't keep ticking along for a good few years yet.'
The surgeon's smile widened. 'Merry Christmas.'

Charlotte was sobbing in his arms now. Nico had tears on his own face.

Buon Natale, indeed.

The best ever, without a doubt.

EPILOGUE

CHRISTMAS WAS LONG GONE.

Lady Geraldine Highton didn't remember it at all. She remembered Venice, of course, and the magic of the Orient Express journey. How could she ever forget when it had made her most cherished dream come true? Her beloved Charlotte had found the love of her life.

And here they were, in the gardens of Highton Hall, in the springtime. Surrounded by daffodils and bluebells with the gentle perfume of apple blossom and tiny puffs of cloud in an otherwise blue sky making this day perfect.

Their wedding day.

They'd waited until she was fully recovered, bless them, and these last few months had been a gift in themselves. She hadn't been allowed to rely solely on the wonderful care Betty had co-ordinated. They'd both moved into Highton Hall themselves, despite the hassle of commuting to London for their busy working lives.

And somehow Nico had got out of all those overseas commitments that had threatened to keep him and Charlotte apart for the foreseeable future. They hadn't

had to rely on that new-fangled Scope thing at all. It had been, in fact, as if they couldn't bear to be apart from each other for a heartbeat longer than they had to.

And when they were together, they couldn't keep their hands off each other. Not that anyone minded today, of course. It was only expected that they would link hands when Charlotte had wound her way through the chairs set out in the bluebell woods under the ancient oak trees to join her husband-to-be in front of the celebrant. That Nico had immediately bent his head to place a lingering kiss on her lips might have been a tad premature but…he was Italian. What could one say?

And it wasn't as if Charlotte was wearing a veil to cover her face. She may have chosen a traditional, stunning white dress that made her look beautiful enough to bring a tear to anybody's eye, but she'd left her hair loose and flowing.

It had been a joke when Geraldine had offered her beloved tiara as the 'something borrowed' but there it was, sparkling in her blonde hair as a shaft of sunlight found a way through the unfurling leaves of the oak trees. A glint of silver on her wrist was the only other adornment Charlotte had chosen. That tiny ring of hearts that had the emblem of the Orient Express engraved on its catch.

Geraldine eyed the rings on her own fingers as she smoothed the skirt of her lovely new pink silk dress. Maybe she should tone down her own accessories? No. That would be tantamount to curbing all sorts of things. Acting her age even, and that would never do, would it?

She had to shift a little on her chair in the front seat

as the proceedings started. There were still moments
of discomfort as she recovered from the major abdom-
inal surgery that had removed that thankfully benign
growth but she would never complain.

This was more than a bonus of time that she hadn't
expected to have.

What had occurred during this last Christmas sea-
son had been the most amazing gift ever.

Although…

She'd interrupted something last night. A moment
between Charlotte and Nico that had looked like more
than an intimate goodnight on the eve of their wed-
ding. Nico had had the palm of his hand on Charlotte's
belly. She'd had her hand resting on top of his and the
look they'd been giving each other was one of those
that could speak volumes.

She hadn't let on that she'd seen them.

And she certainly wouldn't advertise the fact that her
bucket list now had a new item on the top.

She was already the luckiest woman in the world,
even though she knew her granddaughter would dis-
pute that title. It would be her secret that she would be
keeping her fingers crossed for another amazing gift
next Christmas.

A gift they could all share.

A *baby*…

* * * * *

CHRISTMAS WITH HER EX

BY
FIONA McARTHUR

MILLS & BOON

First published in Great Britain 2013
by Mills & Boon, an imprint of Harlequin (UK) Limited.
Harlequin (UK) Limited, Eton House, 18-24 Paradise Road,
Richmond, Surrey TW9 1SR

© Fiona McArthur 2013

ISBN: 978 0 263 89926 9

Harlequin (UK) policy is to use papers that are natural, renewable and recyclable products and made from wood grown in sustainable forests. The logging and manufacturing process conform to the legal environmental regulations of the country of origin.

Printed and bound in Spain
by Blackprint CPI, Barcelona

Dear Reader

Who can resist the romance and glitz of the world's most glamorous train journey? Certainly not Alison Roberts and I. So we travelled in *olde world* style from Venice to London on the famous Orient Express, always with the idea that we would write these books.

And what a magical journey it was. From the canals of Venice to the soaring Italian Dolomites, crossing snow-covered valleys and burrowing through the mountains of the Austrian Alps, with men in tuxedos and women in sequins… It's a journey we will never forget.

I'd love you to share the journey with my heroine, Kelsie Summers, an independent midwife who has always dreamed she'd ride this train one day, and Connor Black, the man she left outside the register office fifteen years ago.

Offering his seat to Kelsie in Venice two days before Christmas is bad, but leaving her alone with his meddling grandmother is a hundred times worse. Connor can't believe his bad luck, or the surge of emotion as he looks at the woman he crossed a world to get away from after she broke his heart.

Through the next thirty-six hours and into the night the train blazes a trail across the countryside, past the bells of railway crossings and the flashes of light, while its occupants sleep in their little beds until dawn outside Paris. Such fabulous fun as Kelsie and Connor rediscover and then lose each other again while the train shoots through the tunnel to England and the white cliffs of Dover, past keeps and stone walls and English backyards, until it reaches the bustle of London and the magic of Christmas.

I wish you a happy journey!

Fiona xxx

To my darling husband,
who watched our travels via internet banking,
with words of caution and judicious injections of funds,
and the fuzzy but fabulous use of Skype.

Mother to five sons, **Fiona McArthur** is an Australian midwife who loves to write. Medical Romance™ gives Fiona the scope to write about all the wonderful aspects of adventure, romance, medicine and midwifery that she feels so passionate about—as well as an excuse to travel! Now that her boys are older, Fiona and her husband, Ian, are off to meet new people, see new places, and have wonderful adventures. Fiona's website is at www.fionamcarthur.com

Also by Fiona McArthur:

These books are also available in eBook format from www.millsandboon.co.uk

PROLOGUE

THE SEAGULLS WERE screaming—or maybe it was him. Twelve-year-old Connor saw the wave lift his mother and tumble her over and over.

He was running but it was too late.

He should have told her not to go back. The words had been on his lips.

He should never have held them back.

'A quick look for Daddy's ring,' she'd said. 'I must have dropped it in the rock pool.'

But he'd known the tide was coming in. The last wave had made them run from the rocks. And now...

'Look after your mother,' Dad had said, and he hadn't. He should have said, *No! Dont go. The waves are too big. They'll sweep you out. You don't have time.*

The wave... And then another...

And then there were people—shouting, helping. Reaching his mother as he couldn't. They'd get her.

But, no. A man was carrying his mother towards the sand, and his mother was limp like the seaweed that washed this way and that in the waves.

Her long hair was touching the sand as they came

closer. He saw her face—and he knew nothing would ever be the same.

He knew he should have stopped her. He knew it. *He knew it.* Now…the way she was lying.…he knew something awful had happened.

He'd disobeyed his father. His mother was dying and he knew it was his fault.

CHAPTER ONE

As Kelsie Summers floated in her gondola past St Mark's Square she thought of last night's Christmas-themed mass at St Mark's Cathedral and she rubbed the goose-bumps on her arms at the memory it evoked. The strings of Christmas fairy lights over the Bridge of Sighs had winked last night and now, though extinguished, they still decorated the canals and bridges of Venice on her way to the station.

Her bag was full of nativity scenes in glass and gorgeous Christmas-tree globes for her friends.

Even the crumbling mansions on the Venice waterways had gorgeous glass mangers and angels in their lower windows and she watched the last of them fade into the distance as her gondolier ducked under the final bridge.

The end of two weeks of magic and her trip of a lifetime—and so what if she'd originally planned to share it with someone long gone, she'd still made it happen.

The bow of the long black boat kissed the wharf and the gondolier swung Kelsie's bag up onto the narrow boardwalk the same way as he held the craft steady,

with little effort. She'd chosen the strongest-looking gondolier for just that reason.

She stepped out, in not very sensible shoes but she was a little more dressed up than usual in honour of the coming journey, and then her tasselled-hatted hero abandoned her cheerfully as he pushed off.

Kelsie dragged her bag up the planking to solid ground, or as solid as she could get in Venice, and sniffed away the idea of tears.

Surely she wasn't weepy just because of the lack of gentlemen to help her move this huge bag! It was because she was leaving Venice. Because her lifelong travel dream was coming to an end.

Modern-day women didn't need male help, Kelsie told herself, but the Stazione di Venezia, and the Santa Lucia steps, mocked her as she glanced down with a grimace.

A passing Venetian 'gentleman' flicked his nicotine-stained finger at the tiny alley that ran up the side of the building for those who didn't want to hump their belongings up the steps and she smiled her thanks. Bless the inventor of suitcase spinner wheels, and her sense of independence was appeased.

She'd arrived in Venice in a blaze of anticipation via the front entrance to the railway station and it seemed fitting, she wasn't sure why, to be slipping home to the real world of work and her solitary flat more than ten thousand miles away in Sydney, out the back way.

Though once she'd dragged this bulging brick of a suitcase inside, the train she was about to board was

anything but the back way, and she felt her spirits soar again.

The last part of her journey—the one she'd dreamt of since a long-ago friend had mentioned his English grandmother embarked on it every year—had captured her imagination while she'd still been in school uniform. Venice to London via the Orient Express—the world's most glamorous train journey. And she'd finally made it happen.

Which was why she was wearing her second-highest heels and her new cream Italian suit. Maybe not so glamorous doing it by yourself, she conceded, but still very glam, and stiffened her spine as she entered the cavernous world of departure beside a tourist shop adorned with miniature gondoliers' hats.

Platform One. She'd entered at the correct platform, arrived at the specified time, so where was the blue and gold emblazoned wagon of the Orient Express?

Kelsie glanced around. Remembered the inside of Saint Lucia from arrival—like any other railway station—grey concrete, cold underfoot, traveller-filled bench seats, matching-luggage families huddled together. Finally she saw a small white sign, very ordinary, very unostentatious, that read 'Meeting Point for Venice Simplon Orient Express'.

Connor Black watched the shoulders of the smartly dressed woman sag as she peered under her dark cap of hair with the perplexed countenance of the unseasoned traveller as she turned her back to him. Her head dipped down at what must be a horrendously heavy suitcase.

It was almost bigger than she was, and he wondered if she'd dare try and perch on top of it.

He sighed and stood to offer his seat, brushing away the niggling feeling that he knew her. Of course he didn't. He was in Venice. And if he didn't offer her his seat Gran would poke him with her silver-topped cane as if he were a six-year-old until he did. Gran was his one big weakness and the only woman he loved. Unfortunately she knew it.

He caught his gran's eye as she nodded approvingly and bit back a grin. Despite her age she looked like a million pounds in her pink jacket and skirt with her snow-white hair fresh from her Venetian stylist. The pink Kimberley diamonds at her wrist and throat glittered under the electric lights. Lord, he would miss the old minx when she was gone. Had to be the reason he was standing here in the first place.

He had very special clients, the Wilsons, a couple he'd worked with for years, whose tenuous assisted pregnancy had been particularly challenging, and they were all on tenterhooks until Connie Wilson had this baby safely delivered. He'd promised her influential husband, and more importantly the nervous Connie, he'd be available twenty-four seven.

So he should be somewhere closer to them, instead of sitting on a train for the next thirty-six hours playing nursemaid to an eighty-year-old lady who should be at home, knitting. But then even he laughed at the idea of Gran doing anything of the sort.

The original *grande dame* inclined her eyes sideways

towards the woman several times and he settled her with his nod. And he'd better be quick about it.

Not used to taking orders from anyone, Connor decided this could prove to be a very long thirty-six hours as he stepped closer to the woman and spoke from behind her. 'Excuse me. Would you like my seat, madam?'

The woman turned, their eyes met, and recognition slammed him harder than being hit with a suitcase twice the size of hers. Sky-blue eyes. Snub nose. That mouth. The one it had taken him, admittedly in his callow youth, two years to banish from his mind. A face that seemed outlined with a dark crayon line instead of the blur every other face was.

Fifteen years ago. Kelsie Summers.

'Or perhaps you'd rather stand.' Luckily that was under his breath because his grandmother's eagle eye had spotted his reaction.

Stunned blue eyes stared frozenly back at his. He saw the movement in her alabaster throat as she swallowed, and then her tongue peeped out. Yes, you damn well should lick your lips in consternation, he thought savagely, when you left me at the registry office, cooling my heels.

He gestured to the seat beside his grandmother with all the reluctant invitation of a toddler giving away his last lollypop.

Damn if he didn't feel like sitting down again and turning his own back. But that would be childish and he hadn't indulged in such weakness for a long, long, time.

Stinking bad luck, though, to meet her here, and if he knew his grandmother it would be the perfect diver-

sion for the boredom that, despite her assurances, would ultimately descend on her before they reached London.

Kelsie felt like sinking into the grey concrete, maybe even through that and into the murky bottom of the Venice waterways that were probably somewhere under the railway station.

This was the first time she'd seen Connor since the day she'd run away.

She'd written, trying to explain why she thought she'd ultimately ruin his life if she married him, sent the tear-streaked missive, had watched from around a corner as he'd paced in agitation waiting for her to arrive, committed every line of his worried face to memory because she'd never see him again.

Though one glance at his face this morning when he'd recognised her and she could tell there still might be something he wanted to say to her about all that. As time had gone on she'd had a little more insight into how he might have felt. She swallowed nervously.

Fifteen years ago, as a teenager, she'd wanted to expect more from herself, too, had wanted her own career, and even then she'd had a core of sense and clarity that the more romantic Connor had lacked. She had wanted to be a wife who brought more to the table than hero-worship.

She'd seen, through eyes that had seen it before between her mother and father, that her deference and his growing tendency to take control might just bring more than order to her sometimes scattered life.

Connor would always be her hero, but as the wedding date had grown closer, slowly it had sunk in further that

she hadn't wanted to rely on Connor all her life. She'd wanted to be a woman her husband could be proud of and she wouldn't have been able to do that under his very protective wing.

Well, they were adults now. He'd morphed into a gorgeously handsome hunk with just a touch of silver at his temples—where had those years gone? she wondered in awe. He certainly wasn't nineteen any more, and they'd been far too young to elope anyway. Everyone had told her that. She was also a very different woman now, she thought as he gestured her, less than graciously, to his seat.

'Thank you,' Kelsie said. Not much else she could do. He didn't answer as she sat down, just looked at the older lady in the gorgeous pink designer suit next to her and raised a mocking eyebrow. 'I'm having coffee. Would you like me to get two, Gran?'

'Three.' The older lady turned a sweet smile her way. 'Do you take sugar?'

Kelsie blushed when she realised the woman's intent. No. No. He wouldn't want to buy her coffee, and when she glanced at Connor his smile had such a bitter sardonic tilt to it she lifted her chin. 'White, no sugar. Thank you.'

Connor couldn't believe his stupidity. He'd just wanted to walk away, get his head together—not that he wasn't over her, good grief it had been years ago, but it had been a shock—and coffee had seemed a good excuse. Of course, now the conversation was open there would be no stopping Gran from pumping Kelsie. Her name echoed in his brain and travelled through his body

and stirred every nook and cranny into alertness. He shook his head to be rid of it and sighed. Gran would burrow for all the information she could get.

If he'd stayed around and damped down the friendliness, instead of sloping off, he might have been able to hustle Gran onto the train and only bad luck would have made them meet again.

Too little, too late, too bad, and he'd just have to move on, he thought as he picked up the pace and clenched his fist in his pocket. Now he really needed the coffee to wash away the bitterness at the back of his throat.

Funny how feelings he'd thought he'd forgotten rolled in his belly like it was yesterday, and he searched for the anger that had finally obliterated the hurt of her no-show at their wedding. The one person he'd thought he could trust. Damn her.

The forgotten embers flared and the heat of it gave him pause. The rational person he was now frowned it down and locked it away. Douse it. It was water under the bridge, and there were plenty of bridges in Venice to let it wash away, quite symbolic really.

It was just the shock. Not a huge deal after all. He began to feel better.

Sitting uncomfortably on a seat she didn't want, Kelsie watched Connor Black stride away, the man who used to be her best friend, so tall, so rigidly straight, waves of disdain emanating from him like mist from the canals, and she remembered the last time she'd seen him.

She hadn't expected it would be fifteen years before she saw him again.

The elderly lady next to her leaned closer and the serene scent of Arpège perfume drifted across the seat. Kelsie inhaled it with a pang and the penny dropped that this must be the woman who rode the Orient Express whom Connor had talked about all those years ago. The reason Kelsie had sketched in this journey on her bucket list.

The elderly lady twinkled up at her, her faded blue eyes shone, brightly inquisitive, and despite the pit that had just opened Kelsie couldn't help a small smile back.

'I'm Winsome Black. And if I'm not mistaken, you know my grandson, Connor?'

'Kelsie Summers. I knew him a long time ago.' She sighed for the idealism of a young Connor and her part in fracturing it.

Winsome snorted. 'Must have been memorable because I rarely see any expression cross my grandson's face and that was a positive grimace.'

'Gee, thanks.' Kelsie couldn't help the rueful smile that escaped. True, it hadn't been a happy face on poor Connor, and she couldn't help another swift peek to where extraordinarily broad shoulders were just disappearing into the station coffee shop.

He'd changed. A lot. She blinked the last image away. He'd always been a favourite with the girls but she'd bet his wife hated having him out of her sight. Where would they be now if she hadn't run away?

'So you're that Kelsie!' It wasn't a question. 'How fascinating.' This was accompanied by a demure smile

and an even brighter twinkle in the eye of the older lady, and Kelsie almost wished she'd followed Connor. Her thoughts must have shown because Winsome touched her arm.

'Don't go. I'll be good. But it's Christmas in two days. You could humour an old lady's curiosity just a little.' Not waiting for permission, Winsome launched into her cross-examination. 'Are you married?'

Not a lot she could do about this, Kelsie thought as she accepted the inevitable, so she settled back for the interrogation with what composure she could muster. 'No.'

'Why not? A young, attractive woman like yourself must have had her chances.'

Kelsie shrugged. 'I didn't marry the man I did love. So I wasn't going to marry one I didn't.'

Winsome looked dubious. 'I think that makes sense.'

'And I love my independence and my work.' She hadn't meant to sound defensive. She wasn't feeling defensive!

'I know someone like that.' Winsome shook her head at a thought she didn't share. 'So you're not even engaged?' Inquisitive faded blue eyes twinkled at her again.

Kelsie lifted her chin. 'No.' Her life was good just as it was.

Winsome sat back. 'Connor's not married either.' She acknowledged Kelsie's narrowed gaze and obviously decided she'd pried enough. 'I'll stop.'

Kelsie raised her brows. 'You seemed to have ac-

quired the salient information.' And imparted a bit as well. Why wasn't Connor married?

'My *modus operandi*, dear.'

'I consider myself warned,' Kelsie muttered to herself, but there was food for thought in her new knowledge. How could that be?

As if she'd heard the thought, Winsome added, 'He's been very busy with his career.' Then she smiled and Kelsie wasn't so sure she trusted the unholy glee in the older woman's face. 'And here he comes.'

When Connor arrived he handed Kelsie her coffee without a glance and ignored her murmured thanks.

Winsome accepted hers with all-seeing eyes and directed her attention to her grandson and pretended to sigh. 'I'm disappointed with the waiting room for the world's most glamorous journey.' There was a special twinkle in her eyes as if she knew a secret no one else did.

Connor glanced at the tiny white sign alone on the concrete. 'Me, too. If only I could make it happen for you, Gran, I would.' He snapped his fingers.

As if conjured up, like Mary Poppins's sister, a young woman in a gold-edged royal-blue skirt and high-collared jacket high-heeled her way across the concourse towards them, pushing a tall wooden reception desk on wheels. Another equally well-dressed young woman pushed a covered luggage trolley.

Kelsie blinked. It wasn't luggage on the trolley. It was furniture.

The hostess directed her junior to unroll a plush,

deep red carpet stamped with a blue and gold insignia and then…magic.

Kelsie blinked again as within seconds a large circular waiting area sprang up in an empty space on the grey concrete. The beautiful oak reception desk, also sporting insignias, two potted palms in four-legged oak pots, also on wheels, a gold-edged name plate on the desk and a bowl of roses. Kelsie thought they looked suspiciously real.

The young hostess snapped open a box of labels and turned to the bemused crowd. 'Who is first?' She smiled and then disappeared from view for a moment behind the surge of patrons.

'I can see why you travel with him,' Kelsie whispered to Winsome as they stayed seated to allow the crowd to thin, and Winsome nodded complacently.

At that moment the unmistakable sound of a diesel engine and rattle of wheels on rails heralded the arrival of the world's most famous train and everyone paused to look.

Shiny blue carriages, with burnished gold edges and gold lettering, and gleaming panes of glass all came closer until the brakes screeched as the wheels locked on the rails and inched to a stop.

The anticipation in the air rose like the smell of diesel from the train.

Thank goodness for the distraction, Kelsie thought with relief. It was the perfect excuse to put some distance between her and Connor. She turned to Winsome. 'May I leave my bag here while I go and have a closer look?'

Winsome patted her leg. 'Of course.'

Kelsie stood hastily and without glancing at the man looming over her she carried her disposable coffee cup to the platform and began to wander up the length of the train.

Such shiny gold trim around the windows and gorgeous lettering proclaiming 'Express Eurpeen' above the glass, but it was that chance to peer in, that glimpse into a bygone era that attracted her. Each cabin held an ornate bench seat with tiny lace-covered tables and a dainty pink lamp next to a delicate orchid that danced in a slender crystal vase, and everywhere rich, dark panelling glowed in the dim light with exquisite parquetry. She couldn't wait to see which tiny cabin was hers.

Not to mention the relief of being able to hide her face from the steely glance of the man she'd jilted more than a decade ago.

Back on the bench Winsome Black raised her brows quizzically. 'She's very striking.'

'Hmm.' Connor didn't want to think about Kelsie Summers and he certainly didn't want to talk about her. He tried not to glance up the platform but his gaze strayed disobediently before he whipped it back. She still had the whippet thinness he remembered but had gained subtle womanly curves that beckoned anyone with a spoonful of testosterone without her even trying. Typical.

He snapped his teeth together. 'If you give me your ticket I'll check your baggage in. I imagine it will take

a while before all these people are checked in and the luggage loaded.'

His grandmother had declined to allow him to care for the tickets. He wasn't used to it. The whole 'not being in command' thing. And he knew she regularly lost things so he'd be glad when he'd secured the damn things and they were on the train.

His mind drifted unexpectedly. Kelsie used to lose things all the time too.

He snapped back to the present and the frown he sent his grandmother must have been more ferocious than he thought because she burst out laughing.

'And will you cut off my head if I don't?'

'What?'

'Give you the tickets. You have serious control issues.' She shot him a penetrating glance. 'Thinking of other things, were you?'

Lord, he'd forgotten how easily she read him. 'No.' He took the tickets she offered. 'And thank you,' he added, his voice dry. This journey could prove very tiresome if Winsome decided to tease him for most of it.

He moved into line behind a young woman buried in what looked like a 1940s ankle-length trench coat two sizes too large for her, and the fur of the collar was pulled up around her ears. When she darted a look at him all he could see was the bridge of her nose under her dark glasses and the thick black hair scraped back off her high forehead.

'*Buon giorno,*' he said.

'*Buon giorno,*' she whispered back, and turned away.

Maybe she was a very young secret agent? This trip

had the makings of a farce already, he thought sardonically, and glanced ahead to another older lady around his grandmother's age, though not as well looking come to think of it, accompanied by a younger woman.

He narrowed his eyes thoughtfully. That could be an answer. Distract Gran with a kindred spirit. Maybe arrange to have them sit together at dinner. He glanced at the girl. She had a nice smile so even if Gran tried to pair him off with someone else, it wouldn't be too bad. Anywhere away from Kelsie Summers.

Truth be told, he didn't understand why he was dwelling on such a chance encounter with a woman he'd once fancied in his youth. Well, maybe a little more than that but it wasn't like he'd carried her with him for all these years—or been celibate. Far from it.

Neither had he found anyone else he could think of joining his life with, a sardonic voice inside suggested, and he impatiently brushed that thought away. A full-time relationship was the last thing he required. He seriously didn't have time.

The line moved forward and he wondered idly where the luggage for the woman in front was.

Which made him shoot a glance back at where Kelsie's Suitcase-asaurus Rex was, and decided it was the biggest damn thing he'd ever seen and even she'd have trouble losing that. He wondered if she knew she couldn't have it in the cabin with her and then shrugged.

And why was that his problem? What was wrong with his brain today? Thankfully the line moved forward and he directed his thoughts to move on too.

His eyes drifted back when the line stopped again.

Her suitcase was still there. Might have been a stretch to think that someone would steal it anyway but…

She was back. Sitting next to his grandmother, and they looked like they were having a lovely conversation. He groaned and tried not to crush the tickets in his clenched hand. Kelsie had always been a great listener. He turned back to the line.

Insidiously, while he stared at the back of the head of the woman in front, his mind drifted to all those plans they'd had when he'd been young and stupid. Plans he'd built in his head during those impressionable teenage years that you never seemed to forget. No matter how hard you tried. The only one he had ever shared them with had been Kelsie because she'd been so much a part of his life then.

The first plan had always been—marry Kelsie. Keep her safe.

Then—become a doctor.

The third—take her to Venice on the Orient Express when they could afford it, because it was the one thing she really did have a fantasy about.

God, he'd been so stupid. He shook his head and returned to the present as the line moved forward again. But there had been other plans and he guessed he'd at least achieved them.

He was a research-based obstetrician. Dealing with infertility. Well respected. His gran would say world renowned but he would have said he was more recognised for being happy to share what he'd learnt. He'd been very busy during the last fifteen years so it was no wonder he hadn't married.

Gran had informed him she despaired he'd find a wife before she died. No doubt she was pretty keen to see it happen but as far as he was concerned there were a lot of research projects he'd be happy to leave the family fortune to.

In fact, he had a horrible feeling this whole trip had some romantic connotation he was missing and it wasn't really about diverting Gran's mind from her recent loss. Something along the lines of if he wouldn't marry for good sense then he'd better marry for love.

Couldn't see it happening on a damn train but she'd muttered about some bloke she'd fallen for in her distant past whom she'd met on this train, and he just hoped the old man hadn't turned in his grave when she'd dropped that little bombshell.

His grandfather had been the father he'd lost the same year he'd lost Kelsie and he'd always thought his grandparents perfectly matched at least. Funny how things in life weren't always as you expected.

Like meeting Kelsie again after all these years.

CHAPTER TWO

KELSIE GLANCED AT her watch. Ten thirty-five and the train left at ten fifty-seven. She should find her carriage but seriously she wasn't ready to sit down just yet.

Winsome and her grandson had boarded, and Kelsie carried her tiny overnight satchel—thank goodness for outrageously expensive wrinkle-free clothes—and she tried to slow her agitated feet to an inconspicuous amble.

She'd been almost the last to get her ticket, mainly because she'd wanted to stay well clear of Connor, and had walked up and down the platform ostensibly admiring the ornate carriages but really walking off her agitation at seeing him again.

Connor Black. She'd loved him like a brother since fifth grade when he'd moved from being annoying to mysteriously compelling. Not that all boys had been mysterious—just Connor.

For an only child, having Connor as her friend seemed an impossible dream, until he'd come across her being bullied by a mean-streaked older boy who'd found the purse she'd lost one afternoon, late in the spring.

She could almost smell the scent of falling orange blossoms, and blood, in the orchard where it had happened.

The ensuing bout of fisticuffs had left Connor with bruised knuckles and the other boy with a black eye and split lip, for which Connor had received a caning from the school principal the next day. The thought still made her cringe because it had been her fault.

But Connor had shrugged it off as no account and her hero-worship had been sealed.

She glanced into a window of the train and her reflection smiled ruefully back at her. He'd looked so heroic, his shirt torn, his eyes narrowed as he'd warned the other boy, his gentle grasp of her hand as he'd led her away.

For the rest of that year he'd taken to walking her home, the absolute best part of her day, and she'd never felt unprotected again, even when Connor had gone off to boarding school, because the letters between them had kept them close. Because home hadn't been such a grand place, with her mother gone and her dad not much use at conversation unless it had been to give an order.

Her dad had expected her to follow the rules, and had been worse since Mum had finally rebelled and left. Although thankfully the fighting had stopped, her dad was so distant Kelsie had felt rudderless in the world until Connor. She'd wash up, do the housework and her homework, and take herself off to bed at dark, and dream of escaping to the city with Connor.

Except for Connor's correspondence, hers had been a lonely existence, lightened when holidays had come

around and Connor would find her and the two would slip away to dream together.

Connor had always been full of dreams. His real mother had drowned in a tragic accident when he'd been twelve and he was always going to be a doctor, always going to save the world. And Kelsie had believed him.

When Connor went to university they would marry. Elope, Connor said, because everyone would say they were too young.

But she was content to wait until Connor said it was time and she began to have dreams of her own. To be a nurse. To be free of her father's dictatorship. Be with Connor and gladly follow him to the ends of the earth. He'd arrange everything because that's what he liked to do, and it was easier to say yes.

Finally the day arrived. Her dad forbade her to leave, Connor had forbidden her to be late, and the similarities suddenly dawned on her. Had she been using her romance to escape her father's control, only to fall into the same trap?

It was an uncomfortable thought that wouldn't go away now that it had surfaced. It was all so confusing when Connor had been so good to her.

He'd secured rooms for them near his new university, the registry office was booked, and he'd bought her a short white dress for her to wear on the train when she travelled to meet him. He'd admonished her not to daydream and miss the train. Not to lose the ticket. As if by mentioning it he could influence the vagrancies of fate.

She thought about that. And then the doubts crept in

just as the hands of the little watch Connor had bought her crept closer to the time they would meet.

She loved Connor. Could see the goodness in him. How much he cared about her. But was she ready to tie herself to another man who would run her life for her so completely? Was she always going to make Connor sigh when she needed rescuing?

Was that what she wanted?

If she was having these thoughts, was it fair to rush into this and maybe one day do what her mother had done and abandon ship?

Of course she didn't want that but she knew if she tried to explain some of these thoughts to Connor, he'd brush them away as nerves.

But the seeds of doubt grew into full-grown wisdom trees on the train as she twisted the hem of the white dress between her fingers and watched the stations flash by.

Until, finally arriving, Kelsie hung back.

She loved him. The man was a serious hero. Too much of one to spoil his chance of the career he was destined for by dragging him back by her doubts. Or expect him to marry her just because he'd proposed in an impulsive moment. So she sent a note saying she was safe but she wasn't coming.

They were both too young and she wasn't able to contemplate being a burden on him. Plus there was the matter of her threatened independence. He deserved so much more but she hadn't been brave enough to tell him.

She had already seen herself frustrate him when she

lost things, seen his doubts after he'd impulsively proposed, knew how much easier it would be for him to realise his dreams of becoming a doctor unencumbered by a young, unskilled bride.

The next day, after a lonely night in a sleazy motel she ran to her only other relative, her mother's much older unmarried sister, a midwife in Sydney, and that's when her life really began to change.

She'd come a long way since then. A long way.

All the way to Venice.

Kelsie blinked at the reflection in the window—the face staring back at her wasn't hers. A woman, eyebrows raised in disapproval at her invasion of privacy, stared back haughtily and Kelsie blinked. Wake up.

Her cheeks heated as she walked away. She'd been staring into the past—not the window. If she didn't watch out she'd spoil her once-in-a-lifetime trip worrying about a man who had every right to hate her.

Because maybe she should have waited to find out if Connor had agreed with her reasons. Talked about it with him. But by then it had been too late, and she'd lost touch and the confidence that he would forgive her.

And her career had taken off until the serene, confident maternity unit manager she'd become barely resembled the young girl who'd run away instead of getting married. Except for the occasional misplaced item when she was tired.

Kelsie strode purposefully up to the immaculately presented, blue-suited guard, his quaint round porter's hat stiff with its gold-trimmed peak, the whole confec-

tion jammed importantly on his head. She presented her ticket as he held out his white-gloved hand.

'Welcome to the Orient Express, madam.' He bowed, took her satchel, assisted her up the steps like precious cargo, and once she was safely aboard gestured for her to follow him up the narrow wood-panelled corridor.

Finally aboard the Orient Express, she could feel a smile plastered on her face.

'Come this way, please.'

The air inside swirled pleasantly cool around her still-hot cheeks and hinted of different perfumes and metal polish and cedar oil and old wood. Kelsie couldn't help glancing into the cabins as she followed him, in-terested in her fellow passengers, she assured herself, not nervously checking for Connor, and most of the passengers looked up and smiled back.

The cabin before hers held a young woman who seemed huddled in her coat, but the door was pulled shut as soon as she passed.

Kelsie winced. She was going to have a good time if it killed her or she had to kill somebody else—namely Connor Black for making her doubt herself.

The conductor stopped at her cabin and gestured grandly. 'Your seat, madam.'

Kelsie obediently sat. Not quite sure what she was supposed to do as the conductor gently hung her satchel on a big brass hook.

He stepped back, facing her, and smiled, his teeth even and white, his blond hair crew cut around his ears. 'Allow me to introduce myself.' He bowed again. 'I am Wolfgang. Your steward.'

Volfgang, she repeated to herself with an inner smile.

His English was precise and she guessed that, unlike herself, he was probably fluent in several languages. 'I vill be caring for your needs, and those others also in this car, on our way to Calais. There you vill change for the Tunnel crossing.' His precise English and accent matched his name and he suited the surroundings so appropriately, she had to smile, outwardly this time.

'Thank you, Wolfgang.' Kelsie perched on the long tapestry seat. The hanging neck pillows suspended by tapestry cords divided the seat into two. She realised she'd been lucky enough to face the direction they'd travel, thank goodness, and maybe she was even the single occupant for the next thirty-six hours. Hmm. She wasn't sure if that was a good thing or a bad one.

No. It was a good thing. She would imagine Agatha Christie with her and breathed in as she replaced the smile on her face.

Everything was perfect.

The little cabin was perfect, even prettier from the inside than it had looked when she had peered through the windows, and she noted there was only one crystal champagne flute on the pristine embossed Orient Express coaster on her tiny table so she probably did have the cabin to herself.

She sat in solitary splendour, surrounded by the different-coloured woods of the parquetry wall panelling as they glowed with light, and she noted more brass hooks holding the deep blue silk bathrobes and velour slippers, one of which she could don should she wish to slip into something more comfortable. How deca-

dent. Though perhaps not, especially at eleven in the morning.

'Observe there is a sink for washing your face and hands if desired.' Wolfgang pressed a lever and the tiny bench opposite transformed into a basin and taps. 'There is a water closet at both ends of the car.' He stared at a point at the top of the window to avoid meeting her eyes. 'It is preferred that passengers refrain from use while the train is at a station.'

Good grief. Now, that's a salubrious thought. She chewed her lip to hold in a laugh as she nodded. 'Of course,' she murmured.

He inclined his head. 'Then excuse me. When our journey begins I will return with champagne and also to record your preference for the first or second dinner sitting.'

Kelsie was tempted to ask which sitting the Blacks were on so she could choose the other but contented herself with, 'Thank you.'

She sat for a minute longer, trying to decide what to do when he left.

'Acqua Panna.' Kelsie sounded the words out on the complimentary water bottles on the bench of the washbasin hidey-hole. 'Acqua has to be water.' She picked one up, cracked the seal and took a sip as she surveyed the amenities.

Facecloths, a hand towel, a beautifully boxed cake of soap she might just keep to remind her of the journey, toothbrush and paste, an art deco folder holding postcards and embossed VSOE paper and envelopes.

Now she'd pretty well covered the contents of the cabin.

She put the bottle back and stared at the angled wooden divide opposite. They were really quite snug, these compartments, standing room only before the wall of the adjoining cabin. Someone coughed next door and she heard it quite plainly but couldn't distinguish the voices.

At least she didn't have an infectious companion locked in with her. She grinned to herself just as the train whistle shrieked a warning of departure.

Kelsie stood and reached hastily for the table to steady herself as the carriage jerked, and peered out the window. They were easing out of the station. Her grin was back and the excitement of finally fulfilling her dream made her want to laugh.

When she poked her head out of her cabin door other occupants had crammed into the corridor and were watching through the windows opposite as the world shifted, and she could imagine the wheels on the tracks below them begin to turn and pick up speed. They slipped past two bushy islands on their little spit of railway tracks on the way to the mainland of Italy.

With a sense of urgency to take just one last look at Venice, she squeezed past an older couple in the tiny corridor and walked to the far end of the carriage, where she was able to pull down the sash window on the door she'd entered the train by.

When she leaned out the cold wind blasted her face and she could see Santa Lucia station disappearing into the distance.

She looked the other way and a dark-haired man had his head out the window half a dozen carriages up. A very familiar face turned her way and Connor Black surveyed her coolly.

Only one thing to do. Kelsie waved.

CHAPTER THREE

CONNOR PULLED HIS head in and ran his hand through his hair. He'd stuck his head out to blow thoughts of Kelsie Summers away. Fine chance of that now!

At least she wasn't in their car—she was in the last one—and he hadn't wanted to know that. He just hoped they'd chosen the right lunch sitting to avoid her.

Funny how much importance avoiding Kelsie had assumed. He hadn't spent that much brain activity on a woman for years and far too much on her today.

When he returned to their connected double cabins the steward was there.

He waved away the offered champagne. 'No, thank you.'

His grandmother gasped and leant forward to take the glass.

'For goodness' sake, Connor. If you won't drink it, I will.' She waved at the man and the obliging fellow bowed and put the second glass next to the other one.

Great, Connor thought. Now Gran was going to get tipsy and she'd be uncontrollable. This trip was assuming nightmare proportions. 'I'll drink it.'

'Good.' His grandmother sat back smugly and he

realised he'd been conned and she'd never intended to have two glasses. He sighed and had to smile. She winked.

'Much better. You don't lighten up enough, my boy.'

He narrowed his eyes at her but he couldn't stay cross. She was a minx. 'It's my training. Normally, I'm responsible for people's lives.'

'You've thought you were responsible for people's lives since you were a child. Makes you bossy.' His grandmother shrugged that away. 'You've been too responsible for too long. You're becoming downright boring.'

Connor froze in the act of sipping and frowned at her. Did she mean that? Nobody else had complained—but, then, who else was there to complain?

There was a distance between him and most people that he'd acquired early, since the loss of his mother and advent of his stepmother, to be precise, and had never lost. His patients wanted him to optimise the course of their pregnancies. Fertility assistance required set boundaries of safety and precautions. Still, her comments seemed a bit harsh. 'You don't know the real me, Gran.'

'Hmph.' She snorted and he looked at her quizzically. So older ladies really did that?

She snorted again just to prove it. 'Hmph. Nobody knows you. Except maybe that girl at the end of the train.'

So this was what it was all about. And how the heck did she know where Kelsie was sitting? He'd bet Winsome had bribed the porters already, though goodness

knows when as he'd only been gone a few minutes. The she-menace had probably rung the bell as soon as he'd left.

She knew them all by name because she'd been on this train every year for the last twenty years with his grandfather. Her yearly birthday trip in February she'd missed this year because of his grandfather's death.

That had really knocked her badly and Connor, alarmed his grandmother might just fade away with grief, had hired a nurse to look after her for a few weeks to ensure she ate enough to survive. She'd begun looking much like her old self since he'd agreed to share a last journey on her favourite train.

But he was very aware this was her first Christmas without her husband and they'd decided this was as good a way as any to get over the lead up to festivities on her own.

So this was effectively a ten-month delay on her birthday train trip.

He didn't understand how she didn't get bored.

He was halfway there already, and it would be worse if it wasn't for the unexpected arrival of Kelsie Summers, and they were only a few minutes out of the station.

He sighed. So she was all over the fact that Kelsie was here! He should have known.

He enunciated carefully, as if to a child, 'You've blown it all out of proportion. She was a kid at my school and I was like the big brother she never had.'

His grandmother nodded and he could tell she wasn't listening.

She proved it. 'When you came to me you told me you'd been going to marry her.'

'Childhood nonsense. An impulse.' He shrugged. 'The girl is nothing to me now.'

She nodded, all sweetness and light, and his head went up. 'I'm pleased. I wouldn't like to see you upset.'

For some reason he didn't like the sound of that, or the way she'd said it. She glanced out the window and then back again and a horrible premonition hit him just before her next words.

'So it should be fine with you that while you were admiring the view I sent her an invitation to join us for lunch.'

Kelsie's golden envelope arrived, along with her glass of champagne, its embossed VSOE paper and the spidery writing giving a clue to its origin. She'd bet it came from Winsome.

Wolfgang hovered as she opened it and glanced at the bottom. Sure enough, the flamboyant W rolled into an exuberant salute. 'Please. Come!'

An invitation to join them for lunch at the first sitting. Fun. Not! How the heck did she answer this?

'Perhaps I should return for your answer in a few minutes?' Wolfgang wasn't slow on the uptake.

She guessed he'd been exposed to many such missives and their impact.

Kelsie smiled gratefully. 'Thanks, Wolfgang.' His head disappeared from the door and Kelsie looked down at the embossed paper again. So how did she decline politely?

She sipped her champagne, the golden fluid so surprisingly light and dry that the bubbles jumped and tickled her nose until she took it away from her mouth and looked at it. So this is what the other half drank?

Like drinking golden sunshine—no hardship at all—and she needed the courage to make a decision so she took a bigger gulp.

Or maybe she should go? Maybe that was what needed to be done. Surely inside Connor Black there was still a vestige of the hero she'd admired as a young girl and that man might understand her adolescent thinking all those years ago. He'd been her best friend and she had let him down.

The perennial questions of youth had been so important back then.

The indecision of it all. *Who does he think I am? Who do I want to be? And if I went with him would I have any choices left to me?* That had been the big one.

She still believed she'd done the right thing, but she shouldn't have been such a coward about it.

Maybe it wasn't too far-fetched that they could reconnect as friends. She hated the constraint she'd caused between them and the added bonus was she genuinely liked his grandmother.

If she sincerely apologised then surely a lot of the ill feeling would be over? It seemed he didn't mind if she came to lunch so that was a good sign.

And afterwards she could get on with enjoying her trip. Soak it all up in the way she hadn't yet started to do because of remembering her youth and Connor and her last-minute aborted wedding.

The whole trip would be over by tomorrow evening and she would have wasted it dwelling on the past.

She felt a strange sense of settlement as the decision was made. Funny how things worked out.

Wolfgang returned with the bottle of champagne and offered her a refill. She appreciated his generosity in the circumstances. 'You can tell her, yes, thank you.' She looked at her brimming glass. 'Just make sure I don't fall over on the way to lunch.'

He nodded with a smile. 'My pleasure, madam. I will return at five minutes to the hour to escort you to the correct dining car.'

'Lovely, thanks.'

Kelsie put down the glass and glanced at her watch. Eleven-thirty. And how long would lunch go on for? It couldn't be too long because the second sitting had been set for an hour and a half later and they'd have to reset the tables.

She glanced at her satchel, still unpacked. Clothes!

As the magnificent scenery of the white-capped Italian Dolomites passed, Kelsie refreshed her make-up, brushed her hair, and with a certain excitement hung up her clothes for the meal after this one.

Her aunt had always stressed it would be black tie for the evening meal on the train when she'd first mooted the idea of realising her dream, and Kelsie wanted everything to be ready when she came back after lunch.

They'd often laughed about Kelsie wearing off-the-shoulder velvet on the Orient Express, and while it wasn't velvet or off the shoulder, the black uncrush-

able gown was suspended by gold links of chain above her breasts and fell from beneath her bust to the floor.

Keslie studied the gown as it swayed gently on its hanger, almost Grecian in appearance, the accompanying chain belt dangling loosely at the side. The saleswoman had said it accentuated her height. She might need that if she was going to be passing Connor in the bar car.

Kelsie brushed the creases from her suit and changed the fine pale pink silk scarf for a Nile-blue one that made her smile and gave her confidence.

Her aunt had always promoted blue scarves or necklaces. 'Excellent for the throat chakra, you know. Allows conversation to flow.' Well, Kelsie thought, she certainly wanted to ensure her communication skills were premium. This could be a good day for blue.

She dived back into her jewellery bag and added blue earrings and a necklace, a little over the top, she conceded, but she wanted her mouth to function well and every bit helped.

Wolfgang arrived as she'd retouched her lipstick so she squared her shoulders and picked up her purse.

'Please follow me, madam.'

'Thank you.' I'd love to, she thought sarcastically as nerves fluttered in her stomach. No. This was going to be fine.

She wobbled a bit on her heels as they walked, though she did improve the further she went. Wolfgang didn't seem to have any problems with the slight swaying of the carriage but every now and then Kelsie raised her hands for balance, just in case, as they

rattled from side to side, and placed her feet carefully on the blue carpet.

At the end of each car the wood panelling reached new heights of intricacy, with the inlaid parquetry glowing with colour. Someone, maybe even Wolfgang, was handy with the cedar oil and polishing, but she had to admit the decorations were truly beautiful examples of a bygone era.

And then she saw the bar car. 'Oh, my.'

An absolute delight, the long curved bar was lit softly by lamps, and there was an ebony baby grand piano, the white ivory keys silent but, like the young passenger standing at the bar nursing his glass, waiting for the time it would be played.

Wolfgang inclined his head at the man, and Kelsie smiled as well. It wasn't hard. He was young, extremely good looking, with an admiring smile. Maybe she could spend some time in the bar before dinner.

Of necessity the carriages were all narrow, and the bar car was no exception. Tiny window seats for two slim people huddled together on one side of the narrow walkway, and on the other side a lengthwise set of couches that allowed people to sit side by side and look across the aisle and out to the magnificent scenery opposite. Tiny tables with ice buckets and wine or dishes of nuts were scattered along the length of the car.

They passed into and through the first dining car—plush velvet, crystal glasses, white-coated waiters—and into the next, which was just starting to fill with well-dressed patrons. And everywhere Christmas decorations had been discreetly tucked into unexpected

corners and there was a muted background of carols playing.

Connor and Winsome were already there and Connor stood as she entered, tall, broadly jacketed, and austere as Wolfgang stopped beside their table.

Then her new friend turned and deserted her, or it felt like desertion, and she fought the urge to follow Wolfgang as Connor indicated she should take the seat next to him. She hadn't expected that. She gulped.

Kelsie stiffened her spine and slid across to the window opposite Winsome, trying not to shrink away as her ex-fiancé sat back down beside her.

It was a good thing she didn't have to look at him, a very good thing, but the warmth from his leg radiated heat her way even though he wasn't actually touching her.

As the waiter flicked her serviette and floated it onto her lap in a stirring of air she could smell Connor's aftershave, tangy and very masculine.

'Thank you,' she murmured to the man, fingering the fine linen in her lap nervously, and then looked across at Winsome. 'Thank you for the invitation,' she said politely, like a little girl and then inclined her head towards the fourth setting. 'Is someone else joining us?'

The two exchanged a look but Winsome answered. 'We're not sure. Apparently the other single passenger is feeling unwell and may not join us for lunch.'

'Oh. That's a shame.' Truly a shame. A bit of diversion to leaven the stolid silence at the table wouldn't have gone astray.

'And who is your travelling companion in your

cabin?' Winsome asked. 'I always wondered what happened if you ended with someone terrible.'

She had to laugh at that. 'I'm on my own. It's lovely to stretch out.'

'Oh. How fortunate. But if you get lonely just come and find us.'

Kelsie smiled and murmured her thanks, but along with Connor she didn't comment on his grandmother's invitation.

'Would madam like a drink?'

How many hospitality staff were there? She hadn't seen the waiter arrive and she declined after a glance at the embossed wine list and thought of the glasses of bubbles she'd already downed. 'Water, please.'

'Sir?'

Connor raised his dark brows. 'Perhaps a glass of wine with lunch?' He glanced at his grandmother. 'We are celebrating your deferred birthday after all. Champagne?'

'Absolutely. Thank you.' Winsome obviously enjoyed the good life. 'Surely you'll share a glass with us, Kelsie.' Her eyes twinkled. 'It's a very belated birthday and I hate waste.'

Kelsie inclined her head to the waiter. 'One glass, then. Thank you.' What the heck. She might just need it because the vibes coming off the man beside her and even Winsome seemed strained.

It was beginning to look like Connor hadn't been too pleased after all with the invitation his grandmother had issued. She had the sudden horrible thought that

maybe he hadn't even known she was coming until she'd arrived.

A different waiter appeared and stood poised with pen over notepad as he took Winsome's order and then turned to her. 'Your preference for the meal, madam?'

Kelsie looked back at the menu in her hand. 'The broiled lobster and potato and chive whirls, thank you. And the Christmas pudding.' He nodded and lifted a brow at Connor. 'Sir?'

Kelsie glanced to her left out the window and counted to ten, told herself to relax, breathe, as Connor gave his order, and almost envied the freedom of the tumbling stream that ran along beside the railway line. It looked freezing outside and every now and then they passed another house with a decorated Christmas tree in their window. The cold outside would almost be preferable to the stifling atmosphere inside.

Connor had ordered, the silence lengthened, and his leg seemed to be sending off waves of heat from beside hers, until finally she turned to his grandmother with a forced smile. 'The countryside is lovely.'

Connor was at a loss. Damn his grandmother's meddling. He felt unexpectedly blown away by the pulsing awareness he could feel just sitting next to Kelsie and that awareness was consuming him.

But as he watched her struggle for conversation, despite his own turmoil he could feel himself soften as she tried to carry the conversation by herself. She'd always been more of an enthusiastic listener. He'd probably bored her silly over the years. He should lighten up and help her out, if only for Gran.

'So tell us about Venice.'

He said it at the same time as she turned to him and blurted out, 'I'm so sorry I hurt you, Connor.'

Good grief. He hadn't expected her to go straight for the jugular. He felt his face heat, something it hadn't done for years, and he didn't like it. Not one bit. He resisted the urge to turn his head and see if anyone else had heard.

All the frustration and anger he'd damped down at the station an hour ago rose again. The last place he needed it was right here in front of everyone, and now she'd apologised he'd have to be all amenable and say that it was fine.

Well, it wasn't! She'd gutted him. But he didn't want to say that either, so he wasn't going there, and hopefully, with a hint, she would just drop it.

'Perhaps we could leave that for a less public place.'

He heard the sting in the words as soon as they were out, and regretted it. The sudden blankness of her expression almost hid her shock—but he knew it was there. A part of him even mourned the Kelsie who would have shown every emotion, but this new woman was made of sterner stuff, it seemed, and for the first time he wondered if she would give as good as she got if he really let go.

But she said, 'Of course,' and he watched her long fingers play with her scarf, his senses ignoring his cold logic of disliking her, and marvelled that the material was the exact colour of her eyes.

Then she smiled with apparently unruffled composure at his grandmother. 'Venice was gorgeous with

the decorations and fairy lights, wasn't it? Where did you stay?'

They carried on the conversation without him.

CHAPTER FOUR

CONNOR WISHED NOW he had sat opposite Kelsie so he could see her face because while her profile, he had to admit, was achingly familiar, he wanted expressions and he wasn't getting any.

Not that he deserved what he wanted after such a harsh come-back to her apology. Not at all like him to speak before he thought and be unkind. He couldn't remember that last time he'd let his mouth get away from him. Consideration was in his life blood.

He was known for his unflustered take on the most emotive issues and that was why he did so well with infertility issues. Someone had to offer a clear mind. And keep it that way.

His grandmother was expounding on the virtues of the Hotel Cipriani, across the Grand Canal from the Doge's Palace, and he listened with half an ear as his libido poked him and suggested that even if he didn't want to talk about it maybe it would be a good idea to work out just why Ms Summers had left him high and dry all those years ago.

It wasn't like the thought hadn't crossed his mind once or twice since he'd last seen her.

The one time he'd tracked her down, after a mutual acquaintance had mentioned her on one of his visits back to Australia, he'd phoned and spoken to a fellow named Steve, her fiancé apparently, and that had been that.

He glanced at her bare fingers and wondered dryly who'd run away this time? Him…or her again?

Maybe she was one of those serial bride-to-bes who made a habit of leaving at the last moment.

He remembered a movie his grandmother had made him watch and steeled himself towards Kelsie again. He wasn't sure whether it was because of the past or in response to the definite attraction he could feel pounding between them, but he was finding it hard to concentrate on anything else except the woman sitting so close to him.

He didn't like that either.

'So you spent the whole time on your own?' The voice was his but the tone belonged to a different person. Not what he'd intended and he saw his grandmother lift her brows in reproof.

Kelsie coped admirably. 'I joined tour groups and made friends at the hotel.' She raised her own finely arched brows at him. 'I'm a good mixer.'

And let him think what he likes about that, Kelsie fumed, with some acerbity. Connor Black had obviously turned into a self-important boor.

She'd learnt it was always good to keep people guessing what went on in her head, especially men, but she couldn't help feeling disappointed that her unlikely dream of being friends with Connor had slipped out

the carriage window and was lost somewhere in the snow on top of the Dolomites.

Winsome looked crushed by her grandson's attitude. And it was her pseudo-birthday.

One of them had to make an effort to give the birthday girl a good time. 'Your grandmother says you deal with infertility?'

'Not personally.' He said it so dryly that she had to laugh.

Well, at least he had a sense of humour and despite the hard going at the table she was genuinely interested in his work. Winsome looked slightly relieved that Kelsie had started a conversational ball rolling that Connor might want to play with.

Funny, when what she really wanted to do was eat her lunch—or not—and get back to her cabin, but that wasn't going to happen for at least an hour. The time would pass more quickly if they chatted and she could do chat. A skill she'd learnt through her work.

She felt Connor ease his chair to the side, turning to face her a little more, and she kept her expression interested while she fiddled with her scarf below the level of the tabletop. The silk had better do its verbal soothing with her part of the conversation because she could feel words drying in her throat at the thought of carrying the whole conversation.

But it seemed Connor had finally decided to help out. 'I'm involved in research. Occasionally I work for short periods in participating hospitals and I have a few private patients.'

His voice had softened and she saw him glance at

his grandmother in apology. Maybe he wasn't as bad as she'd feared. 'Did you become a nurse? I seem to re-member you fancied that.'

A wee fancy for the little woman? Patronising pig. 'Hmm. Yes. And later a midwife—which is the area I work in now. So we do have a little in common.'

Thank goodness. She could talk about her work. Un-derwater, if needed, she loved it so much.

'I run a programme that caseloads pregnant women from their homes. Each midwife takes thirty women through the year, sees them through their pregnancies and into labour and then visits them at home for six weeks after their baby is born.'

She saw an odd expression pass across his face. 'Do they deliver in the hospitals?'

'Most *give birth* there.' She made the distinction with a little emphasis and Connor grimaced wryly at her ter-minology. 'A majority of the time they do, but if they want a home birth, I support them in that too.'

His eyes narrowed on hers and she could feel the current as if from another conversation simultaneously running on another level. 'Is that challenging?'

'I find it rewarding.'

'You find the challenge rewarding?'

Did he expect her to back down? 'That too.' She smiled coolly and this time he smiled back at her. Right into her eyes, and she felt herself falter.

Damn if he didn't still have it. Her stomach kicked and she looked away as the sensations swirled through her bloodstream like the stuff in her glass.

His grandmother was watching them with a spec-

ulative gleam in her eyes. No distress there. Well, at least one of them was happy with the way the meal was progressing.

She focused on the question, not on the grey eyes that were assessing her response. 'But mostly the privilege of seeing a woman in control, in her home environment, is the ultimate reward. Women need to make the choices and wield the power in their own labours.'

And then the train whooshed past Verona station without pausing, lunch arrived, and she was saved. Eventually her pulse rate settled.

By the time they'd eaten lobster, and Christmas pudding, and finished off the bottle of bubbles, it was all okay. Even though the conversation hadn't flowed quite as smoothly as the wine it had proved less of a chore than she'd feared.

Connor had even made her laugh once or twice more and Winsome looked quietly pleased with herself.

Well, don't be thinking I'm coming to dinner, Kelsie thought to herself, and she felt Connor shoot her a glance. Good grief. Had she said that out loud?

Judging by the spark of ironic humour in those grey eyes, she just may have. It was time to go before she said something even less discreet.

She stood up. 'If you'll excuse me, I think I'll head back to my cabin and just soak in the fabulous countryside. Thank you for the wine.'

She'd seen the price on the menu, practically the price of a small car, and was quite happy that she'd earned her keep. Connor could pay for it with her blessing.

Connor watched her go. Assured, elegant, no shy young woman, this, calling to something inside him that he flatly denied, worlds away from the Kelsie he'd known.

Lord, they'd been young. She'd been the first girl he'd ever kissed! It had taken him all day to work up the courage.

His grandmother tapped the table and he snapped out of the past, stood up quickly, and eased around behind her to pull out her plush velvet chair.

They had to pause at frequent intervals to allow other people to pass on their way from the restaurant car.

One of those people was the elderly lady he'd seen on the station. Her head turned in surprise as Winsome took another look. She wore a red jacket over a white silk shirt. The russet tones sat quite well with her flaming hair, he thought, but still it was startling.

'Lady Geraldine? Jendi?' Connor stopped and waited for the inevitable exclamations.

'Oh, my goodness. Winsome Black. What on earth are you doing here?'

'I could ask you the same thing! What an astonishing coincidence!'

Lady Geraldine's headshake was incredulous. Her red hair shone as she shook it. 'It's a small world, isn't it?'

She waved a ring-encrusted hand at the young woman accompanying her and Connor remembered seeing her at the station too.

'Winsome's an old friend that I haven't seen for

years. We worked together once on a huge fundraiser for that children's charity.'

'One Last Wish.' Winsome nodded at Charlotte. 'Such a worthy cause. They made wishes come true for terminally ill children.'

'This is my granddaughter, Charlotte,' Lady Geraldine said.

'And this is my grandson, Connor.' Connor shook hands with the young woman and they both smiled at each other in mutual indulgence of people they cared about.

'She and her...fiancé are keeping me company...' Lady Geraldine's smile was poignant. 'This trip is my last wish...'

'Oh, surely not...' Winsome smiled. 'I seem to remember you telling me that age is only an attitude.'

Lady Geraldine opened her mouth but then noticed that they were creating a human traffic jam in the narrow corridor. 'We'd better get a move on,' she said. 'But we must get together, Winsome, and have a proper chat.'

He heard his grandmother say, 'That would be lovely.' No doubt it would be excruciating but he was in for the lot.

'How about afternoon tea? We could meet in the bar at, say, four o'clock?' So he wasn't invited.

Connor bit back his smile as he heard his gran's, 'See you then.' And both elderly ladies continued on their way. No doubt he could find something to amuse himself with. Or just sit in peace.

Back in her own cabin, Kelsie curled her legs up on the seat and leaned on the window to stare out. She

was exhausted and yet felt strangely alive after such a fraught lunch.

Twitchy even, when wine usually made her feel sleepy.

She needed to walk but there was nowhere to go except towards a whole row of little compartments that just might contain the Blacks, and she wasn't ready to know which cabin was theirs.

Lulled by the passing countryside, the time passed in fuzzy daydreams of long walks holding hands, stolen kisses and the protectiveness of Connor's arm around her shoulders when she'd been a heck of a lot younger than she was now. She didn't want to remember and she finally stirred herself to distract her mind.

Thankfully, afternoon tea, tiny fruit custard tarts and Earl Grey tea, plus scones and cream, arrived via Wolfgang and a silver tray. She'd be ten kilos heavier by the time she finished this trip, she thought as she poured herself a long aromatic stream of tea from the silver jug he offered. She waved to a magazine on the table.

'There's a brochure with signature items for sale. So is there a shop on the train, Wolfgang?' Window shopping. Always a sure-fire way to divert her thoughts.

He smiled. 'Of course, madam. A boutique,' he corrected gently. 'In the foremost car. The boutique manager will be happy to help you.'

'Excellent. Then as soon as I finish this I might go for a wander.'

'Certainly. In a few moments the train will change direction and the bend in the track is very famous. If you watch as we navigate the curve, at one point you

will be able to capture the whole train in one photo-graph at the correct time.'

It seemed that was a compulsory achievement as a passenger so Kelsie nodded and patted her camera until Wolfgang nodded approvingly.

'Then in one hour we stop in Innsbruck for thirty minutes to change engines. You will be able to walk around the station for a short while as well, before you dress for dinner.'

Obviously her attire wasn't suitable for the evening meal, Kelsie thought with a spurt of amusement. She wondered if she should reassure him that she would pay the proper respect to the dress codes but no doubt he would already have seen the hanging dress.

Meanwhile, afternoon tea in the bar car was even more civilised than in the carriages, and the two older ladies settled down for a lovely gossip.

'There's nothing like a *proper* afternoon tea, is there?' Lady Geraldine sighed happily as she stirred sugar into her second cup and they both listened appreciatively to the sound of silverware tapping against real bone china. 'Did you know you can buy these lovely cups and saucers from the gift shop?'

Winsome didn't like to say she'd been on this trip so many times she knew every corner of the boutique. 'I'll have to have a look. I'm planning to go there after this.'

Winsome hoped Lady Geraldine couldn't notice her nervousness. Now that she'd shaken off Connor, after their tea she was finally going to the boutique to see Max.

But in the meantime this was lovely. Meeting an old friend in the bar carriage, with the pianist now in residence playing some soft, classical music and the occasional Christmas carol thrown in.

Geraldine said, 'Maybe a set of these would make a lovely engagement gift for my Charlotte and her Nico.'

Winsome shook her head. 'You said they'd only met yesterday? In Venice? When they both saved that man's life.'

'Yes…'

She wondered if that was a tiny niggle of doubt in Lady Geraldine's voice.

'But they'd met before,' Geraldine said. 'Years ago, at Charlotte's hospital. Fate has just thrown them back together and…' She sighed again. 'It's obviously meant to be. Like your Connor and…what was her name again?'

The conversation paused for a moment as the steward removed the plates that had contained tiny sandwiches and replaced it with a platter of warm scones, adding small silver pots of jam and clotted cream.

'Mmm…' Lady Geraldine eyed the cream. 'Proper Cornish clotted cream, by the look of that.'

'Kelsie,' Winsome said, as she followed her example and picked up one of the scones. 'Kelsie Summers. But I don't think she and Connor are about to fall into each other's arms, like your Charlotte and Nico. She jilted him, in fact, fifteen years ago and I have the feeling he hasn't forgiven her.'

'*Really?*' Lady Geraldine spread the jam and clotted cream onto her scone and was just about to take her first bite but the conversation became more entic-

ing than the calorie-laden treat. 'They must have been very young. Oh, *do* tell...'

Their voices dropped to a more discreet level until Lady Geraldine turned her attention back to her scone, but her expression was thoughtful.

Their voices became generally audible again. 'We might be able to help things along,' she suggested.

'What do you mean?'

'The dinner seating is very strict, I hear.'

Winsome knew that for a fact. 'It certainly is. I've tried to change tables at the last minute on some of my previous journeys and it almost never happens.'

'It's not the last minute yet,' Lady Geraldine said firmly. 'And if we both had a little chat to the maître d', I'm sure we could persuade him to juggle things a little.'

'In what way?'

'By making an extra table available. We've still got a lot of catching up to do, haven't we? We haven't even started talking about that terrible business with Deirdre Wilkins defrauding the charity so that she could run off to the Maldives with that "personal" trainer of hers.'

Lady Geraldine's smile revealed how much she enjoyed an occasional bit of juicy gossip. 'If we asked to be seated together, that would mean leaving both your Connor and this Kelsie and my Charlotte and the lovely Nico alone at their tables.'

Winsome had to admire her friend's ingenuity. 'Yes...if we made sure they gave them a table for two or didn't put another couple to join them at one of the bigger tables.'

'It would be so romantic, wouldn't it? Everybody

dressed up and the lighting all soft and lots of delicious champagne to add to the atmosphere?'

Winsome smiled. 'Why don't we ask our nice steward to go and see if the maître d' might be able to spare us a minute or two?'

'Afternoon tea was delightful,' Winsome assured Connor. Unfortunately he was already back in her compartment when she'd gone to freshen her make-up. 'Though Geraldine did look unwell.' Her own stomach felt a little queasy too but that was probably because it was nearly time.

Nerves. She was damnably nervous and she shouldn't be. It was ridiculous because she was eighty years old. But inside she didn't feel eighty.

She felt like a young girl on a first date. With a new boyfriend.

Thumping heart—Lord, she hoped it wasn't angina—and sweaty palms. At least menopause was long gone. She smiled grimly, but in fact she had nothing concrete to go on to assume the man she'd pushed to the back of her mind still felt the same as he had twenty years ago. Even then she'd been sixty, for goodness' sake. But their eyes had met and something had passed between them.

Her heart gave another flutter and she almost giggled like a little twit. She shouldn't have had so much wine at lunch but she'd needed the courage to face him.

It had been so many years of nods and handshakes, for goodness' sake, and they'd both been married at the time. It should never have happened but that lightning

bolt of ridiculous magnetism had never truly been dispelled in her mind. And every year she did still think there was a special glow just for her in his dark chocolate eyes.

Max.

Ten years her junior, so gallant, so gentlemanly, so loyal to his invalid wife, as she had been loyal and loving to Robert. It had been the only thing to do.

But his wife was gone now. And so was her darling Robert. And she didn't want to spend her last years alone.

Maybe she was mad to even consider being so forward, but she knew she'd be madder not to try. She just hoped Max felt the same.

After that first year when they'd been not all that much younger and very silly, they'd indulged in one solemn stolen embrace, one magic kiss that had accepted the vagaries of cupid shooting his arrow when neither had the freedom to fly. After a long angst-filled conversation that had acknowledged the truth in their reality, they'd never physically strayed again.

The whole thing could be her overactive, aging imagination but she didn't think so. For twenty years she'd wondered and today she'd finally find out.

She'd go now. Before she lost her nerve. He might take some persuading. 'I think I'll go and have a look at the boutique.'

To her dismay, Connor put his magazine down and stood up. 'I'll come with you, Gran. Perhaps I could buy you a gift for Christmas. It's your last trip.'

Impossible. 'No. No. You stay here. I don't need anything.'

He remained standing. 'Please allow me to do that.'

She looked at him. Swallowed the disappointment and accepted the reprieve from being brave. 'Of course. That's very sweet of you. Thank you.'

Winsome's eyes went to Max's as soon as she entered the boutique and she hoped it wasn't her imagination but suddenly it did seem as if they were alone.

Still gorgeously dark and straight-backed, Max was not as tall as Connor but a lovely height to look up to. He did look older. No doubt she did too. But he still looked wonderful. She could feel her smile, the warmth in her stomach. Such a lovely man. It shone from his eyes, and every year, when she came again, without even touching her, he made her smile. Soften. Warm.

'Mrs Black. Welcome back on the Orient Express. How lovely to see you again.' Max bowed low over her hand, like he'd done so many times over the last twenty years. 'And my sincere condolences on the loss of your husband. Mr Robert was truly a gentleman.'

'Thank you, Max.' Reluctantly she drew her hand away and glanced at Connor, who stood behind her, assessing the fine glassware, sparkling jewellery, even the bound copies of Agatha Christie's novel.

'Max, I'd like to present my grandson, Connor. He was kind enough to join me on my last trip. He's come to buy me a present.'

'For your belated birthday or for Christmas?' Max held out his hand and the men shook.

Connor looked surprised and Winsome thought iron-

ically there was a lot more he could have been surprised about. 'She did miss her birthday.'

Max smiled at Connor. 'For women as deserving as your grandmother, birthdays are sacrosanct.' Then he looked back at Winsome. 'Your last trip?'

She met his eyes and her voice lowered. 'I'm getting too old for jaunting around.' She saw his eyes soften and felt her knees tremble.

'Nonsense. Women half your age are too old. You will never reach that state.'

Winsome smiled, felt the heat in her cheeks, and turned to her grandson, hoping it didn't show. 'You see why I come here?'

'Absolutely.' His attention wandered and she relaxed. Saw him skim the contents of the jewellery case assessingly. 'Will you make a choice?'

About what? Then she remembered. 'Connor has promised me something from your boutique for Christmas.' Her voice sounded overbright to her own ears. She'd already said that, for pity's sake, and she tried to tone the squeak down as an idea formed and she touched her grandson's arm.

'Why don't you go away and have a drink in the bar car? I can have a proper look without you glowering at me to hurry up, then I'll meet you there and Max can wrap it for you to collect and pay for.' She laughed and smiled sweetly at him and he shook his head.

'You are incorrigible. But…' He grinned at Max. 'I don't need telling twice. Enjoy.'

Kelsie's walk up the long snake of the train was like something out of the movies. She clattered in and out of

doorways between carriages, passed people sideways in the corridors, bumping into walls when the track jolted a carriage unexpectedly, and always, outside, the countryside rushed past the windows.

The scenery was dotted with soaring cliffs and turreted castles and huge suspended motorways that curved like ribbons on stilts around the mountains.

She passed through three carriages of compartments, the bar car, two dining cars and another three carriages before she reached the end, and not once did she see a dark-haired Connor or his vivacious grandmother.

Congratulating herself on her good luck prematurely, she froze when she heard the deep timbre of his voice as she approached the boutique—and his grandmother's laugh.

Kelsie spun back the way she'd come, she really didn't need to gatecrash their party again, but before she could slip from the carriage Connor's voice halted her.

'Is that you, Kelsie? Don't change your mind on my account.'

The hairs on the back of her neck rose and prickled. Just the way he'd said her name made the last years flash past. She hadn't expected such a visceral response.

Kelsie turned but to her disappointment there was still a neutral mask on the face she'd once known like her own. She'd be dreaming to think anything would have changed. 'Are you sure? I thought you'd be sick of the sight of me.'

Was he that bad? Connor took note of the wariness in her eyes and the challenge of unravelling the mystery

of the real Kelsie Summers beckoned irresistibly—as long as he was careful.

He closed the gap between them and the expression on her face was hard to fathom. Not warm. Not cold. More assessing. But still she struck deep into his psyche in a way he remembered from all those years ago. Intriguing to imagine he did the same to her. He couldn't tell but he would like to know very much.

'It's my turn to apologise,' he said, seeking to find a way past the barriers he could feel between them. Barriers he probably deserved after their lunchtime conversation and the awkwardness he had been responsible for.

She raised those darkly arched brows and her eyes narrowed. 'For what?' It seemed she didn't trust him. Well, that was fine by him because he didn't trust her one inch. He doubted he ever would but he was damned if he could ignore her.

So she wasn't going to make this easy. Well, he was almost glad. He wasn't sure of his plan but he did know that for the first time since he'd stood up after lunch he wasn't tired. In fact, he could feel the air crackle with sudden tension between them and again wondered just how much chemistry was left from the long-distant past—on both sides.

She shrugged those slim shoulders and time seemed to stop. She'd always done that. He'd have recognised the movement as hers anywhere. His eyes were drawn to the gentle slope of her shoulders, centred on the swell of her breasts, followed the crease upwards to her throat, where a small pulse beat under the translucent skin,

and her neck rose enticingly swan-like from the cream of her silk shirt.

He wanted to slide that blue silk scarf slowly from her shoulders so he could watch it caress her neck.

'Hello? I said, for what?' Kelsie was looking at him strangely and he blinked. As well she might. He felt like slapping his forehead to wake himself up. Talk about ditherdream and dumbo. She could still scatter his thoughts.

Question? What had the question been? Ah, yes, what he needed to apologise for. 'Not making you as welcome as I should have.'

Connor considered his options. He should have added he was sorry for cutting her off in the dining car when she'd tried to apologise for the past, but he still had a bit of a knee-jerk reaction over that one. Wasn't happy with the idea she could dismiss destroying his youthful dreams with a quick apology in a public place.

But they couldn't stay here. No potential. Though why he was looking for potential in her case was a worry.

'Will you join me for a drink in the bar? My grand-mother is choosing her birthday present…' he inclined his head, indicating the boutique '…in there, and I have permission to leave her in peace so she doesn't feel rushed.'

He watched her absorb the words, and realised that watching Kelsie was actually an interesting pastime—he'd have to beware of that—and as she nodded he let out the breath he hadn't known he'd been holding.

'If you're sure you want to,' she said, and turned

around again and led the way. And Connor decided walking behind Kelsie was also a spectacularly pleasant experience.

He could smell some faint unfamiliar floral scent drifting back from her and he wasn't sure if it was perfume or something she washed her hair in. Either way, he decided it was his new favourite scent.

The Christmas fairy lights made her thick bob of auburn hair shine with flashes of brilliant red and a sudden memory of playing with long strands in the sunlight when she'd worn it past her waist as a younger woman rushed into his memory as if the train had rushed through an unexpected tunnel.

'You cut your hair.'

She paused and looked back over her shoulder. 'Ten years ago.' And once again the past shimmered between them as they both remembered.

She started off again her with neat little bottom swaying gently in front of him and unwillingly his lips curved. She'd been a funny little old-fashioned girl one minute and the next a gamine seductress, and he'd loved that about her. It had always turned him on and that was another place he'd learnt his restraint.

They'd never actually gone all the way, although plenty of times he'd been sure he'd die if he didn't. They had been saving the experience for their wedding night. Well, he'd blown that chance badly.

To be fair, maybe some of that had come from his father, who'd threatened him with castration if he got a woman pregnant out of wedlock.

And look where that restraint had got him. Someone

else wouldn't have been so slow to bed her—and it was incredible how bitter, even now when it shouldn't matter a jot, that thought was.

They reached the bar car without further words but it was as if they were having a conversation he couldn't quite hear. He saw her tension in the tell-tale stiffness in her neck and rigidity in her shoulders, and wondered if it was just him she was reacting to, or if she was normally a little uptight.

Or if, like him, she felt as though they were walking towards danger—becoming more delicious by the second, perhaps—but definitely danger.

Kelsie wasn't so sure this was entirely smart. It seemed to take for ever to get there and the whole time she could feel his eyes on her back. She was thinking about the dilemma of seating when they got to the bar and how to keep her distance until she'd figured out her body's responses.

The worst thing would be to knock knees on the opposing window seats where they faced each other—nowhere to hide there—and second worst would be the risk of brushing up against the full length of him if they sat together on the side lounges. She tried to remember if the fellow standing earlier had had a bar stool beside him at the bar. Yes, she thought he had. She'd head for that and see what happened.

CHAPTER FIVE

'HOW ABOUT HERE?' Connor's voice stopped her head-long dash for the bar stools. So close.

She closed her eyes then opened them before she turned with a bright smile pinned on her face. 'Sure.'

Window seat! Bummer. 'You sure your legs will fit under that table?'

'I'll manage.' He cocked an eyebrow at her. 'I'd like to see your face.'

Oh, goody. She'd been afraid of that. She slid in past the tiny table and rested her elbow on the window ledge while she jammed her knees together and pointed them at the wall.

He slid in and propped his arm on the window ledge as well. She wondered what they looked like to an observer. Probably a pair of wary dogs sniffing around each other, though a quick glance at his face showed him quite relaxed. Amused even, and she wasn't sure she liked the idea that he could be amused at her expense.

The waiter arrived promptly and Connor inclined his head towards her in mute query.

What did she want? Something that took time to

drink and that she could play with when she needed to look away. 'I'll have a long gin and tonic, please. With lime.'

'Certainly, madam.' The waiter wrote her order down and she wondered why when there were so few people in the car. 'And the gentleman?'

Connor ordered a Mexican beer and slid his credit card into the man's hand before he sat back. Darn. She would have paid for her own drink this time.

'It looks cold outside,' she said finally, and glanced up at him.

This was the first time she'd really examined Connor's face up close, dared herself to really look, and the tiny signs of maturity were there if she let herself see. His bones were clearly defined still, his jaw solid, with an even more determined tilt than she remembered, but there were a few tiny lines around his gorgeous grey eyes as if from long periods of intense concentration.

His sensual lips curved as he waited and for a moment she was that star-struck young sixteen-year-old gazing in admiration at this young god who had incredibly chosen her.

For those few brief seconds he seemed to pull at the core of her until she blinked and returned to the real world. The world where she needed to get it over with and apologise and get out of here with her dignity intact—but she had to wait for the drinks.

The waiter returned and Connor raised his glass to her with a glint in his eyes. 'What shall we toast?'

She drew a breath as the man walked away. 'To apol-

ogies. I'd like to apologise for what happened fifteen years ago.'

He shrugged. Took a sip and put his glass down. 'Feel free.'

Kelsie ignored that. 'I am sorry I was a coward, Connor. But I had second thoughts about getting married to you.'

He laughed with a tiny bitter twist of his lips. 'Obviously.'

He wasn't being helpful and she could feel her temper slip a little. This wasn't easy but it had been a long time ago and he didn't need to be sarcastic.

'It didn't help that you were so sure about it that I knew if I expressed any doubts you'd just sweep them away.'

He nodded judiciously. 'Ah. So it's my fault.'

She frowned. 'No. I said I'd come and I didn't. That was my fault and I apologise for hurting you. I was a coward for not telling you my reasons on the day but I was very young. I really should have told you why.'

He leaned back in his chair and studied her face and she refused to look away. Let him look his fill. She was no shrinking violet now.

'So why did you leave me standing on the steps of the registry office fifteen years ago?'

This was the hard part. But he deserved the truth. 'We were too young. And I didn't think I was the best thing for you at that time.'

He shrugged. 'Perhaps. I obviously had no say in the matter. I can certainly see now that maybe you were too young.'

The comment held a tinge of mockery that raised her temper another notch. 'But not too young to see I was going from one controlling relationship straight into another.'

Connor felt the words go right through him. Like someone had just knifed his hand to the table and he couldn't move. 'That's not true. I was all about making sure you were safe. I wanted to look after you. Be there for you.'

She shook her head and her hair slid like a cap from side to side. 'I wasn't strong enough for you then, Connor. You organised everything. You organised me. Dressed me. You railroaded me when I wasn't sure we were doing the right thing. I was in the train coming to you before I realised it was a little too close to home. Too like the way my father had treated my mother before she left. The way he treated me. As if I didn't have a brain of my own. Wasn't responsible for anything. I didn't want us to end up like that.'

It was her turn to shrug. 'So I got cold feet.' And the air between them was getting colder too. There was no curve to his lips now. No smile in his eyes. She'd hurt him again and she hadn't intended that.

Connor had a sudden memory of his grandmother telling him he was too carefully organised. Bossy, even. It wasn't true. If you didn't make sure things were done a certain way then bad things happened. He'd learnt that early on in life. In the worst possible way.

'I think you had it wrong. I only wanted what was best for you,' he said quietly.

She spread her hands. 'You're entitled to think that.

But I still think I was right. I should have confronted you on the day, I know that. Only I was too scared you'd sweep my fears away. But I am sorry I hurt you.'

You don't look sorry enough, Connor thought bitterly. 'Well, thanks for that.'

She stood up. At least it saved him doing it. Clearly, this conversation was only going to deteriorate from here.

'My pleasure,' she said, and internally he winced. Their little talk hadn't turned out quite how he'd hoped.

She looked down at her barely touched glass. 'Thanks for the drink. Enjoy the rest of the trip with your gran.'

She walked away, her dignity intact, and he wondered just how close she'd been to losing her temper. He had a sudden thought that she might have been very close to an explosion. He'd have liked to have seen that and maybe then they would have been on an even footing.

But Connor felt incredibly hard done by and actually quite wild on his own part. So it had been *his* fault for not listening when she'd had second thoughts about getting married? Well, if he'd realised just how cold her feet had been he would have listened. He wasn't a mind reader.

He'd been a romantic! He'd arranged flowers and chocolates for after the wedding back at their flat. A bottle of champagne he'd been unable to afford in the fridge because he'd thought she might need a glass before they made love for the first time. He'd wanted everything to be perfect for her.

And she'd said he was too organised! But someone had to be. Didn't they?

He downed his beer and picked up her gin and tonic. It tasted disgusting but he drank it anyway. Well, she was no immature girl now. She was fair game. So game on!

Half an hour later, as they entered Austria, Connor saw Kelsie sweep off the train in Innesbruck. Her long scarf trailed behind her as she strode up the platform and he decided a breath of fresh air would be just the thing.

He'd spent the last thirty minutes going over their conversation. Too bossy, eh? He was going to be so damn deferential he'd drive her crazy. He didn't know why it was so important to let Kelsie know she'd missed out on the catch of a lifetime but there was definite satisfaction in the thought, and the next twenty hours was a large amount of time to kill with nothing better to do. Then they would really be over.

A sardonic voice inside enquired if he was sure of that...

When he climbed down the steps she was sweeping up and down the platform like a ghost was after her and he had an idea his younger self may have been that illusion she was escaping from.

Well, he needed to banish that phantom too if he was going to win this little battle. He wasn't quite sure when it had become a war but he was in no doubt that he was planning one.

He'd walked the other way so that she was almost

ready to board again before he approached her, and he saw her eyes widen as he came near.

'Kelsie. Just one minute.' And he smiled. Very friendly. Slightly rueful. 'Can I apologise again?'

She raised those truly quite delightful eyebrows and he admired the view as he waited for her to speak. 'For what?'

They both watched Wolfgang polish the fingermarks off the handrail with his white gloves as he stood beside the steps.

He lowered his voice. 'My lack of manners. I'm sorry. I was less than gracious earlier and of course I accept your apology for not marrying me.' He smiled again.

It seemed she wasn't ready to board now, but maybe the impact would be greater if he chose to leave, so he inclined his head and climbed the steps, leaving her alone again. He could feel her eyes on him as he disappeared inside and he chewed his lip to stop laughing out loud.

He felt like that blasted nineteen-year-old again as he went in search of his gran.

The bar car was crowded when Kelsie moved through the doorway to join the pre-dinner throng and her long black gown clung lovingly to her breasts and thighs. At least it wasn't falling off.

She'd missed the first ten minutes of pre-dinner drinks when one of the gold-linked straps holding up the bodice had snapped and she'd needed an urgent repair.

One-handed, she'd called for Wolfgang, who'd

swooped to the rescue with a tiny pair of pliers on request.

She'd decided that taking the extra time to check and squeeze each link could be an investment in preventing her future embarrassment. Even with the repairs the bodice of the gown dived a little lower into her cleavage than she remembered but not as low as it would if the strap broke. The last thing she needed was Connor coming to her rescue from a wardrobe malfunction. He'd done that in the past too.

The bar wasn't full, but her aunt had been right about formal dress. Wow!

The pianist was in a velvet brocade jacket that would have done justice to a very swish couch cover and his music soaked the car with waves of pleasure like the scenery outside—sometimes soaring, sometimes gentle, always melodic and accompanying the sound of the rails below.

Scattered on small tables and along the curved bar were bowls of nuts, *petits fours* and canapés, and all the while through the windows she could see white-capped mountains and white houses with Christmas lights and church spires and tumbling mountain streams.

And inside, just as grand, the men were in dinner suits with bow ties. The maître d' wore black tails and the waiters wore formal white.

The same young man was still at the bar, a little less steady, and he leered when he saw her.

'You look beautiful, madam.'

Kelsie smiled back at him carefully, and decided he was too young for her, and a bit too effusive.

'Doesn't she?'

She had no idea where Connor had come from but he was by her side as he smiled at the man. His shoulders looked very impressive in his black dinner suit and the young man suddenly seemed insignificant. 'Would you like to introduce me to your friend, Kelsie?'

What on earth was Connor doing? 'If only I could,' she said, and held out her hand to the man. 'I'm Kelsie.'

The bar fly was happy to take her fingers. 'Winston Albert the Third.' He shook her hand and they both looked at Connor.

'Connor Black.' He glanced down the carriage as more people arrived. 'Ah. My grandmother beckons. Perhaps you'd like to join us, Kelsie? Or later?'

He didn't move off immediately, but there was no hint of pressure either way, and Kelsie couldn't help feeling a little abandoned, which might have been why she found herself taking Connor's arm as she nodded goodbye to the other man.

She had the feeling she'd been outmanoeuvred. She wasn't sure how when it had all been her choice, but the feeling persisted.

The train jolted suddenly, the whole carriage shifted and there was a small outcry, and she probably would have fallen if Connor hadn't caught her. He looked down at her and grinned as he steadied her against his chest for a moment as their bodies remembered one another. Instant, scorching heat flared between them as their eyes caught and held.

'Are you starting a new habit of saving me?' she asked with a shaky laugh, and he raised his brows.

'Do I need to?' he asked softly.

She blushed and looked away. On the tiny scrap of dance floor a young couple had turned a near accident into an impromptu waltz and their obvious absorption in each other cast a glow over the whole carriage, so people were smiling despite a few spilt drinks. There was a brief round of applause for the dancers when they separated.

Further down the carriage, Winsome, dressed in blue shot silk, had somehow managed to secure a full side-facing seat and sat with another elderly lady with flaming red hair who waved hands laden with diamonds.

Kelsie's fingers rested over Connor's arm and he drew her forward so she had no choice but to intrude on the older women. 'Lady Geraldine, this is Kelsie Summers. A friend from my school days.'

He gestured to the older lady. 'Kelsie, Lady Geraldine, who sat on a committee of a large charity with my grandmother several years ago.'

Lady Geraldine inclined her head, Kelsie smiled, and then sat when Winsome patted the sat beside her.

Why did she feel the jaws of a trap were closing around her?

'Winsome and I have arranged a table for ourselves,' Lady Geraldine said, as if continuing a conversation Kelsie had missed the start of. 'We don't want to bore you young things with our gossip.'

The implications were immediately obvious. Another man and Connor exchanged a glance, as if they were measuring each other up and considering the prospect of a foursome for dinner.

Kelsie was watching the older women as if she knew there was more coming. And there was.

'Instead, we have three tables.' Geraldine smiled. 'One for each couple.'

Charlotte, the granddaughter, looked as if she wanted to groan aloud. 'I don't think you're allowed to change arrangements like that, are you, Gran?'

Lady Geraldine merely tapped the side of her nose. 'Wait and see where the maître d' puts us all,' she murmured. And then she winked at Winsome. 'Being old doesn't entirely deprive us of our ability to charm men into doing what we want, does it, Winnie?'

'Not at all, dear. As you say, age is only an attitude.'

Winsome seemed surprised when Connor didn't demur at her seating arrangements. She wasn't the only one surprised. Kelsie hadn't thought Connor would enjoy being organised by someone other than himself.

'Absolutely. I'm sure you and Lady Geraldine have a lot of catching up to do. I'm quite fine sitting with Kelsie if that's what you've arranged. As long as Kelsie doesn't mind.'

Kelsie declined to comment but decided she needed a drink for fortitude.

Connor must have picked up on her thoughts because he disappeared and returned with a glass of champagne. He handed it to Kelsie as if it was his lot to meet her needs, and she decided something was going on here because the vibes were *so-o-o* different from those at lunch and certainly different from when they had parted that afternoon.

And now they'd have to sit together, alone, for a formal dinner.

She took another sip and wondered what the alcohol content in her blood was running at since boarding this darned train and whether it was interfering with her usual caution.

Conversation flowed remarkably easily until the gong went for dinner. The bar car had filled up, men and women flashed their jewels and fabulous clothes, stilted conversations merged into introductions as strangers tried to make conversation as they waited to be allocated their tables.

Kelsie felt the heat in her cheeks as Connor stood attentively beside her. People dodged the champagne buckets and others milled and chatted in the small space as they waited.

Finally the loudspeaker encouraged the patrons to go through to dinner, first in English and then in French, as the waiters checked off names. Kelsie stood with Connor and walked through to the next car and their table.

Connor beat the waiter to her chair and pulled it out for her, helping her to move it back in when she was seated, and she looked down at the table, suddenly feeling embarrassed. He'd always had such beautiful manners. It had been one of the lovely aspects of spending time with Connor away from home. He'd always treated her like a princess.

The table was crowded with crystal glasses—four sizes each and all engraved with the VSOE insignia—three sets of silver cutlery, fine china with the crest again and crested doilies under everything to stop any

hint of slippage from the motion of the train. She marvelled at the thought of the relaying of the tables for the next sitting.

Their waiter arrived, carrying Connor's champagne bucket, and he skilfully topped their glasses despite the sudden jolts. They both smiled at his dexterity.

Connor broke the silence between them. 'So my grandmother has been at work again.' Connor settled back into his chair and smiled. 'Can you stand another meal with me or would you like me to ask to be moved?'

'Of course not.' There wasn't a lot she could do about it now and it could have been a whole lot worse. She might have had to keep the bar fly under control. Instead, she had a handsome man who had once been her lifeline. 'I'll be able to handle it for one more meal. I think breakfast is in bed tomorrow morning so I'm safe.'

'I'll look forward to it.' His mouth curved, smiling and sexy, a deadly combination that encapsulated her in their private joke, and the room seemed suddenly a little too warm again.

'Even your grandmother couldn't arrange that,' she said dryly, and he smiled again. She almost wished he wouldn't do that. It was a devastating smile and if her shoes hadn't been so tight her toes might have curled.

He glanced down at the menu and then back at her. 'So, what are you having?'

She looked down, scanning the options you could purchase before she looked at the meal that was included, and gasped. 'I think I'd rather buy a coat at Harrods than a serving of Beluga caviar.'

He glanced at the price of the optional entrée and

winced. 'We could both buy a coat.' He grinned at the
à la carte menu for those too fussy to have what the
chef de cuisine suggested. 'Shall we have the Christ-
mas dinner menu, then?'

She nodded vigorously. 'Indeed. I'll have the tradi-
tional roast turkey with chestnut stuffing and dessert
of a classic plum duff with *crème Anglaise* and brandy
butter.'

'Good choice. I'm not a turbot fan myself.'

She laughed. He was funny. It was easy. They were
conversing as if all the tense conversations of the day
had been swept away and she could feel the stiffness
in her neck begin to subside. The feeling of relief was
heady. And he was charming. She might just have to
watch that.

'The fellow at the bar was right, you know.' His gaze
rested on her face.

'What?'

'You look very beautiful in that dress. In fact, you've
looked beautiful all day.' He wasn't looking at the dress.
He was watching her face and she felt the warmth steal
into her cheeks. 'You look even more beautiful than you
did fifteen years ago.'

Now her cheeks burned and she didn't know where
to look. The obvious place was at him. Dark dinner
suit, white shirt and bow-tie. Sardonically suave yet
with a twinkle in his eye. 'Thank you. You look pretty
hot yourself.'

'I was hoping you'd say that.' His face became more
serious. 'So why haven't you married, Kelsie?'

'Why haven't you?' she countered.

He shook his head. 'That's a cop-out and I asked you first. I had the impression you were a brave new you. Don't be shy. I'm sure it's not because you haven't found anyone who exceeded my charms.'

'Oh, you're charming, too, but way too old for me. I'm looking for a younger man now. Like our friend at the bar.'

She'd been trying to keep it light, not sure they were quite at ease enough to get down to real truth. That it would take someone pretty darned special to make her give up the independence that she'd fought so hard for.

She wasn't going to make the same mistakes her mother had made and if she never did get married and have a child at least she wouldn't walk away from them like her own mother had.

She was starting to feel more emotional than she wanted to. Here was this gorgeous man, flirting with her, and all she could remember was how she'd left him standing alone on a corner. How worried his face had been. It made her feel bad. And sad.

'So you think I wouldn't be able to keep up with you?' His hand reached across the table and he squeezed her fingers, stroked the inside of her wrist, and she shivered. There was that unmistakable frisson of awareness that assured her they still had far too much chemistry happening for her peace of mind.

His hand moved back away from her and instantly she missed the connection. 'I'm willing to bet I could.'

Her fingers tingled. It wasn't fair that he could do that with just a touch and she'd always thought the whole vibration in auras between a man and a woman

had been exaggerated. 'You seem determined to put a personal spin on all my words but you can never go back.'

Her mouth was saying things her body didn't agree with but it seemed appropriate when she wanted to create a distance he was trying to close. Her imagination wasn't helping with fantasies of finding out just what would happen if she crawled into Connor Black's lap and kissed him.

He was watching her face and unfortunately there was nowhere to hide. 'Today I was thinking about our first kiss.' His voice dropped and she leaned forward to hear. 'You were soft, like a kitten.'

She bounced back into an upright position, blushing like a schoolgirl, and it was her turn to hope nobody had heard or could see the pink in her cheeks. 'And you missed my mouth the first time.'

He smiled lazily. 'I'm better at it now.'

That made her smile and instantly the rapport was back. 'You weren't so bad even then, once I got over the shock.'

Thankfully the meal arrived and it should have been easier but her eyes strayed to his strong white teeth as he put the fork to his lips, that tilt to his wicked mouth and his strong throat.

She tried to work out what was pushing her buttons. He was unmistakably the full package when you put his undivided attention and the close proximity of their bodies together. Plus the memories of their slow awakening as they'd grown to adulthood together all those years ago.

Would things have been different if they'd made love before their wedding day? The room was getting hot again.

Connor watched the play of emotions cross her face. Every now and then he caught glimpses of the young girl from so many years ago. A vulnerability he thought she'd lost that made him want to protect her, but he stamped that down. No way. She didn't want him to, and had never wanted him to. That was why she'd left him, remember?

But that wasn't all he saw. He saw the pulse beat at her throat, the subtle lushness of a woman's body that stirred him like no other woman's had. He could still feel the silk of her skin when he'd squeezed her hand that had burnt right through his defences so that he'd had to let go. There was no doubt he was playing with fire but hopefully neither of them would get burnt.

He sat back and let the tension ease. They still had eighteen hours to go and he wasn't rushing into anything.

Selected cheeses, the plum duff with *crème Anglaise* and brandy butter, a sun-kissed dessert wine to be sipped and between them awareness swirled like the gold in the glasses as they smiled over firsts together.

First hand-holding—how nervous she'd been. First kiss—how nervous he'd been.

First fight and whose fault it was—not able to agree on that one.

Old memories. Good memories that had been overlaid by guilt and shame and a lack of communication that now they could only shake their heads at.

Both of them warmed to the shared moments that, despite the years, seemed like yesterday now they'd been allowed to escape.

He glanced away to where a tiny Christmas tree spun in a corner with fibreoptic branches lighting the heads of the people sitting nearby in subtle colours.

He tilted his head towards it. 'Do you remember?'

She glanced across and he saw the smile in her eyes as she nodded. 'It was the year before you went away to school. My father had thrown out the old tinsel tree we had and I was heartbroken we weren't having a tree. So you bought me a tiny little tree like that, with decorations and fibreoptic lights that came on when I plugged it in. I kept it in my room and it made me smile at night.'

'I was so excited when I saw it but your father hated it.' He smiled and shook his head. 'And he hated me.'

She shrugged. 'He hated everyone. It was a lovely thing to do. If it hadn't been for you Christmas would have been the same as any other day in the year.'

He thought about it. 'You made my Christmas special just by being there.'

Kelsie couldn't believe how light she felt. As if she'd found a dear friend she'd thought she'd lost. And that was what it was. Impulsively she reached across the table and took his hand. 'I'm so pleased we've had tonight.'

He brought his other hand over the top and held her hand on his. 'So am I.'

Then he lifted her hand to his lips and kissed it

gently, and suddenly she didn't want to be in this car any more.

He must have seen that. 'There's not a lot of places to go but would you like to walk?'

CHAPTER SIX

AWAY FROM PEOPLE? Should she?

Not that they'd do anything they couldn't in front of witnesses. Witnesses. She shied away from the word, like a wedding that hadn't happened, thank goodness she hadn't said that out loud—but, yes. She'd like to go somewhere quieter. More private.

Connor rose and pulled out her chair, waited for her to precede him in the direction of her cabin, not his, and then followed at her shoulder so she could feel him brush against her as she made her way past tables filled with crystal and silver and satiated patrons.

People she didn't see. Past his grandmother, and the red-haired lady, and the couple who had danced, and always Connor's hand hovered below her waist in case she lost balance with the rock of the train. So she was safe from injury but moving forward towards a different sort of delicious possibility.

Her senses seemed more alert. Her skin more sensitive when he brushed against her. Her peripheral vision seemed filled with him and it was a very strange sensation amongst a sea of sensations.

Connor leaned forward and opened the door for her,

and for a crazy moment she wanted to bury her nose in his shirt and have him wrap his arms around her.

She wasn't even sure he liked her but maybe there would be time for that later.

She couldn't help the smile that curved her lips as she looked up at him and his hand tightened on her shoulder.

'Best not to look at me like that when we're in public,' he murmured with a wicked hint of warning in his voice.

Her stomach kicked and her face flamed. What were the rules for a first date with someone you'd once loved? Someone you'd thought about on and off over the last fifteen years. Someone you'd once known as well as yourself and who'd always left you deliciously alert. She'd never known him that way—though they'd had a few close shaves—but Connor had always said he'd wait until they were married.

But that had been then and this was now. Now they were both consenting adults with no ties. She was no longer a virgin—and it would be highly unlikely that a gorgeous man like Connor would be one either.

They passed through the bar car and she didn't see anyone. Just a blur of obstacles to avoid. Was she being too forward?

Would he think she'd turned into a nymphomaniac if she asked him to bed? Because that was what she was thinking, though it could be problematic in a small train with very thin partitions between the cabins.

His hand stayed in the small of her back, hot and possessive and the tension eddied and churned between them and her belly swirled with a mounting ache that

had her squirming as she walked faster than she probably should have towards her cabin.

They came to a deserted corner between carriages and he leaned her against the wall and pinned her there. His face was all angles and intent and a hint of a smile in his eyes as he took his time studying her face.

'Now. About that first kiss…' This time he didn't miss and Kelsie felt her head bump back against the polished rosewood parquetry as she melted bonelessly against him. His mouth was strong and hot and demanding and she couldn't have denied him if all the passengers had trooped past them.

His hand was in her hair, absently rubbing where she'd bumped it, murmuring against her lips with a smile in his mouth, and she kissed him back with all the angst of fifteen years of regret and apology and finally pure desire, and became lost.

Then someone did come along, coughed and made a small joke, and they broke apart. Kelsie smiled down at the carpet, avoiding the face of the other passenger, and heard Connor's relaxed, 'Good evening.' How could he be so cool? She not accidentally, though unobtrusively, brushed his thigh with the back of her hand and heard his indrawn breath. Still able to smile and pretend nothing was going on, Connor?

She glanced up at him as the footsteps died away and his eyebrows hiked as he smiled down at her.

'My, my. Haven't you grown up?' He leaned in again and flattened himself into her so that she could feel the length of him pressed solidly against her. He grinned lazily. 'Has anyone seen Kelsie?'

'I'm here. And you've been practising your kissing.'

'Fortunately.' They both smiled as he stepped back, took her hand and led her into the next carriage, and then the next, until they stood outside Kelsie's door and she opened it.

Kelsie put her fingers to her lips. Inclined her head towards the cabin next door. 'Sh.'

He leant down until his lips just brushed her ear and she shivered as he whispered, 'I can do quiet.'

Kelsie decided there was something very intimate about whispering in a darkened compartment on the Orient Express.

Especially when golden chains of her dress had been lifted aside and Connor Black was spreading wonder over her bare skin as they stood pressed together in the darkness of her cabin. It was all a blur of whispers and touches but mostly it was feeling Connor's mouth against hers.

Every few minutes a bell would ring and lights from a railway crossing would flash lights across their faces, and once she opened her eyes to see him staring at her as he stroked her cheek.

Time passed. They kissed like they could never kiss enough. Whispered about their lives, their dreams, their regrets and their successes. Held each other, Kelsie even shedding a few tears, and they laughed very quietly. Reconnected.

Connor was trapped. He wanted to take Kelsie more than he wanted to breathe but he feared the exposure.

The ripping open of a protective shield he needed to survive.

He couldn't do it.

Already she'd burrowed under his defences more than he would have believed possible. Though he'd been young, he had truly loved this woman. Would have given her everything. The problem was he was whole now and he didn't trust her not to hurt him again.

He'd survived once when he'd lost her and he wasn't so sure he would survive again if she touched his soul in giving herself to him. Making love with Kelsie, the way they were sparking off each other tonight, promised to be no light undertaking.

He didn't know if he would ever really trust her again. Surely it would be a hundred times worse if they made love and she got off the train in London and walked away.

Yes. It would. He could feel his sanity return.

For a few moments there he'd been ready to burn in hell if he could bury himself in her. But he was damned if he was going to rue the day he met her again.

Connor pulled the gold straps back up her shoulders and kissed her once more.

Kelsie sat back and stared at him. 'Is something wrong?'

'Everything is perfect. Let's not spoil it.'

He saw her disappointment. Well, he had dibs on that one from a long time ago, and tonight he was right there with her. But he'd been burnt once by her. Severely, and he didn't do loss well.

And he wasn't going to do something he'd regret.

Funny how it had only been that way with Kelsie. Seemed he was better at denying himself than she was, which made him feel slightly better.

But this was the new Kelsie and again she surprised him.

Connor had drawn the line. Again. Heck, she'd thought he'd got over that, she grumbled to herself in the throes of frustration! She sat upright from where they'd ended up entangled on the seat, pushed back her hair and straightened her straps properly. For the first time in her life she'd actually been totally swept away. Scary, scary stuff.

She took a few good breaths and focused. 'Well, that's a turn-up for the books. It's usually me who stops the action. Different, but probably sensible.' She looked at him with a crooked smile. 'Thank you. I think.'

'And I think I'd better go.'

She arched her brows. 'Before I jump you again?'

He smiled. 'It is a worry.'

She wondered at the underlying truth beneath his jokey statement as she watched him leave.

CHAPTER SEVEN

FIFTEEN MINUTES LATER, ready for her solitary bed, Kelsie was feeling pleased with herself. She'd visited the end of the rocking carriage and marvelled at the flash of railway tracks below the white porcelain bowl with a sort of horrid fascination.

Wolfgang had been in and made her long seat into a snug little bed with starched white sheets and satin-bound woollen blankets. There was a delightful old-fashioned tin of sweets, of course in a blue-lined crested container, resting on her pillow, and the nightlight had been switched on.

Outside the window, snow flew in little flurries and the muted bells of the passing railway crossings added a soothing melody to the sound of the tracks clacking below.

But as she cleaned her teeth at the tiny basin, she stared at her pink cheeks in the gilt-edged mirror and wondered at the star-filled eyes of the woman who stared back.

She still reeled at the absolute mindlessness Connor could induce when he kissed her. Her cheeks glowed back at her as she thought about her lack of control.

Somewhere inside her the unsatisfied woman within grumbled and groaned at an ache that wouldn't go but still she marvelled that after all these years Connor was the one who could make her legs give way when he kissed her.

It seemed she wasn't uninterested in sex after all. Sex was pleasant, nice, occasionally great, but just kissing someone had never shaken her rafters like Connor had tonight. She grinned at the thought. Did trains have rafters?

A small smile teased at her lips as she dried her mouth. And to think that she'd wished she hadn't seen him in Venice. They wouldn't have much time when they got to London but maybe it wouldn't be a solitary Christmas after all. She had a few hours before she flew away. The possibility of spending a little more time with a very grown-up Connor Black before she left would be a bonus and she would be very interested in that.

Not that she minded being on her own for Christmas, as she usually worked and the thought of wandering around the deserted streets of London on Christmas morning had been part of the plan.

They hadn't actually spoken about what would happen when they arrived in London but they had hours of travel to go. It was perfect that she was leaving the next day because the tiny voice that wanted to start planning a life with Connor didn't have a chance. That was good. She enjoyed her independence too much to be answerable to any man. Even Connor Black. Especially Connor Black.

For the rest of the night she was actually quite look-

ing forward to some cheeky dreams in her rocking bed. She switched off the light above her bed and let the dimness soak into her. Despite her solitude, her cabin still seemed to hold the essence of Connor and she closed her eyes dreamily.

The crying started just as Kelsie's head sank deeper into the pillow. The darkness carried the soft weeping that came every few minutes and rose and fell like a tiny wave.

Her eyes opened again and Kelsie glanced at the luminous hands of her watch. The sound went away and she closed her eyes.

It came again. Three minutes since the last.

She knew about those tiny waves. Sat up and stared at the wall opposite.

The noise returned, intensified, and she tracked it to the wall behind her head—from the compartment that held the girl in the oversized coat.

She climbed out of bed and pulled on the blue silk robe and her soft Orient Express bedroom slippers and sighed. Though not sure of her reception when the girl had tried so hard to remain out of sight, Kelsie couldn't leave her to weep alone.

Especially when she had her suspicions as to why a woman might be crying like that.

Kelsie unlocked her compartment door and peered out into the corridor. Apart from the clatter of the wheels on the rails beneath them, the corridor was silent—until the girl began to weep again.

All of the hallway doors she could see were shut and she suspected that nobody else wanted to investigate.

It had to be well after midnight but the sound floated in tendrils down the corridor.

Kelsie tapped gently on the door next to her. The crying stopped and there was a shuffling noise and then the door opened a crack.

'Are you okay?' Kelsie whispered through the crack, and the door opened a fraction more.

A shaky whisper came back, 'No. I am afraid.'

Afraid wasn't good, Kelsie thought, and hardened her resolve to intrude. 'Can I come in? I'm alone.'

No answer for a long pause and then the door opened enough to allow entry and Kelsie slipped around the door and then pulled it shut quietly behind her.

The girl climbed back into bed and curled into the foetal position as if she could keep away the pains. Kelsie couldn't really do anything except stand over against the door or sit next to her on the rumpled bed.

She was young, dressed in a thin white nightgown, and when Kelsie looked down the obviousness of the pregnant belly confirmed her suspicions.

'I'm Kelsie. Can I sit for a minute?'

The slim shoulders shrugged and the woman sniffed, but she shifted her bottom further back into the bed so there was room for two. 'I am Anna.'

'Hello, Anna.' Kelsie peered into her face. 'Are you in labour, Anna?'

Anna shook her head in the negative, rapidly, and then sighed. 'I don't know.'

'How long have the pains been coming?'

Huge dark eyes stared solemnly back as the girl

pushed her thick long black ponytail off her neck. 'Since we left Venice.'

'Are they regular?' The girl blinked and didn't answer. Kelsie tried again. 'Do they come the same distance apart? Every few minutes.'

'I think so.' Her eyes screwed up and her hand flew to her belly. 'Another comes.'

The young woman began to whimper and Kelsie put her hand on her shoulder. 'It's okay. Just let it happen. Don't be scared. If you're scared then you feel more pain. Keeping calm means less pain.'

Kelsie listened to her automatic midwifery patter and mocked herself. *Or you could be scared because you're in a train in the middle of the Swiss Alps and there's snow outside. If something goes wrong, we're all in trouble.*

Instead she said, 'Just let it go. Let it wash over you like a big wave. Ride it up one side of the wave and down the other and let it go. Everything is fine. You're doing beautifully.'

She could feel the tension ebb away under her fingers as she squeezed the woman's shoulder gently and hoped to goodness this baby was a decent size because the tummy beside her didn't look that big.

'When is your baby due?'

'I don't know.'

It wasn't an answer she wanted to hear but there was nothing to do about that now. 'Have you seen a doctor at all while you've been pregnant?'

'The doctor would tell my parents.'

Who must be very well known? Or perhaps it was a small town?

Mentally Kelsie grimaced. There are doctors out there who don't know your parents, she thought, but tried again.

Obviously money wasn't a problem if she could hire a single compartment on the Orient Express. It had taken Kelsie three years to save up for this trip so the issue wasn't financial.

'Have you been well?'

'Until today when the pain started.'

'And do you remember when your last period was?'

'*Non.*' Anna's eyes widened again and she began to hyperventilate.

Kelsie put her hand back on the young woman's shoulder and talked her through that contraction as well. It seemed to last longer and be more powerful than the previous one, which was never a good sign on a train, Kelsie thought resignedly.

She was so young. As young as she had been when she'd left Connor. She could remember what that felt like. Terrifying. 'Does the father of your baby know you're pregnant?'

'*Non.* But I go to tell him.' Her eyes grew rounder. 'In Paris. He is meeting me.'

He might meet more than you if the contractions get much stronger, Kelsie thought, and decided it was time for reinforcements.

She shifted on the seat so the girl could see her face more clearly. 'Anna, I am a midwife. A nurse for babies. You understand?'

The girl nodded. 'I think perhaps you may have your baby in the next few hours. We have to get you to a hospital until after your baby is born.'

Vigorous shaking of the head ensued. 'No. I will be in Paris in five hours. I will wait.'

Kelsie smiled. I wish, she thought. 'Your baby may not wait.'

More head-shaking. 'Leave me. I will not get off the train!'

Kelsie could almost understand her reluctance. It was dark. Midnight or later. Goodness knew where they were and if anyone spoke a language this girl understood if she did get transferred to the nearest hospital. And how hard would it be to be transferred out again after the baby was born?

But the reality was it was a very tiny cabin. And this was a train! 'Look, I believe babies of healthy young women are generally born healthy. But if something did go wrong you have no back-up plan. No way to save your baby if he or she needed emergency help. No way to save yourself if you needed help.'

She pushed away the thought of Connor a few carriages away. Just because they had an obstetrician on board, it didn't mean they had anything else.

Anna shook her head violently and then began to breathe rapidly again as the next contraction built and Kelsie saw the wildness enter her eyes. It seemed Kelsie might just need back-up very soon.

'It's okay,' she whispered as she leaned forward and pressed the call button for Wolfgang. Perhaps he could talk some sense into their friend.

This contraction didn't seem to want to end and Kelsie suspected Anna could be almost ready for second stage. It seemed they'd need Connor after all. She doubted they'd make a hospital unless there was one beside the railway track and around the next bend. She could manage the actual birth but wanted someone else here in case the baby did something out of the ordinary.

There was a knock at the door and Kelsie stood up to open it. Wolfgang's hat was skew and his top button undone.

'I need you to find Dr Black. Is the train anywhere near a hospital? Anna is having a baby.'

Wolfgang looked more horrified than worried for Anna. '*Mon Dieu*. My seats. The carpet.'

'We'll try to be as clean as we can,' Kelsie said dryly. 'Or you could get the doctor and maybe Anna off the train.'

Wolfgang nodded frantically. 'Of course. At once.' He wrung his hands, spun back to her as if to ask another question, and then spun away again to hurry off in the direction of the front of the train.

Kelsie shook her head. She never could understand why people went strange when babies were coming. Surely he knew it was too late now to wish it away. Best to just deal with what came and worry about it later, she thought prosaically.

Anna was breathing heavily again and this time, at the end of the long contraction, Kelsie heard the little catch and hold of breath that signalled the change to second stage.

Uh-oh! Kelsie glanced around the compartment,

swept the towel from the hidden wash stand table and rested it on the ridged oil heater against the window to warm. At least she could have something to dry the baby, if nothing else.

The most important thing was to keep the baby warm, after the carpets, she thought wryly to herself.

Anna's nightgown had tiny buttons all the way down the front. It would do. 'You'll have to take off your knickers. Panties.' Anna looked helplessly at Kelsie. 'Underclothes.' Kelsie pretended to pull off her underpants.

She had a horrible thought that surely Anna knew where babies came from? It seemed she did when comprehension flitted across the girl's face. A small mercy.

Another contraction arrived just as she accompanied this feat with huge modesty and this time Anna's expulsive breath frightened both of them.

'What is happening?'

'Your baby is getting ready to come.'

'But it cannot. We are not yet in Paris.'

'Not sure that mindset did much for you not being pregnant either,' Kelsie muttered, and bumped her elbow painfully on a wall. 'These cabins are pathetically small.' She'd bet Connor and his grandmother had a double suite each.

She shifted the pillow from the door side of the bed to the window end. If Anna lay down again the table would be a problem to access and she might just need some room.

Anna moaned just as Wolfgang arrived back with a

plastic sheet and two raincoats. Kelsie refused to take them as she helped Anna to breathe calmly.

'Where is Dr Black?' she shot over her shoulder.

'Coming.' Wolfgang thrust the first raincoat at her. 'For the bed,' he implored.

'Okay.' Kelsie glanced at the distraught man. 'We need you somewhere more comfortable, Anna. Do you want to stand up? You might find the contractions easier to bear if you work with them.'

Anna shook her head doubtfully. 'I don't want to move.'

'Do you have pain in your back?' Kelsie asked patiently.

Instinctively Anna's hand went to the small curve in her spine. 'Oh, yes.'

'Then standing will help that and also help your baby to present the easiest way for your birth.'

'Oh. I see.' She struggled to her feet with Kelsie's help, and Kelsie slid the raincoat under the blankets to protect the seats while she was up. Anna stayed doubled over, leaning on the tiny table, as the next pain arrived, but she was listening to Kelsie's instructions.

The young woman seemed to have found an inner calm that Kelsie hadn't expected, though she shouldn't have been surprised—women continued to amaze her all the time in her work. 'You are doing so well. Wonderful.'

'I feel less frightened,' Anna whispered, and Kelsie patted her arm.

With the contraction easing, Kelsie urged Anna to straighten her back into the full upright position before

the contraction rolled on, and a sudden startled expression appeared on the girl's face as a thin trickle of pink water ran down her leg and onto the blue carpet in a growing puddle.

Kelsie shot an amused glance at Wolfgang, who gasped in horror then looked at her accusingly, before all the blood slowly drained from his face and he crumpled to his knees in a dead faint, blocking the corridor.

CHAPTER EIGHT

'WHAT IS GOING on here?' The voice of authority arrived before the face did, and Kelsie gave Connor a cool glance as he poked his head around the door as much as he could without stepping on the unconscious Wolfgang.

Kelsie frowned at him. The last thing they needed here were loud voices.

'Anna is having her baby,' she said matter-of-factly. 'You are here in case I need a hand.'

His eyebrows shot up but his voice was low. Teasing. 'Shouldn't you be the one giving me the hand?'

She raised her own brows. 'Catch thirty babies a year, do you?'

'More than you've had breakfasts.' He grinned. 'But I can be your support person.'

The past shimmered between them and the tension lessened in the tiny cabin as they both smiled. It seemed Connor didn't have control issues about this and the thought warmed as well as reassured her.

Connor was about to step over Wolfgang when he changed his mind. 'Give me a minute while Max helps me move our sleeping friend.'

Kelsie looked up from rubbing Anna's back and saw

a tall, distinguished-looking older gentleman nod before he turned away.

Wolfgang moaned and tried to sit up. His eyes rolled towards the much larger puddle on his immaculate blue carpet and then he slumped unconscious again.

Then, bizarrely, Wolfgang's head dragged along the carpet with little bumps as Connor and the boutique manager pulled him unceremoniously out of the doorway by the ankles and he disappeared from view.

Connor stepped back to the now unimpeded doorway. He raised one dark eyebrow. 'Status?'

'Anna's been having contractions since Venice, due date not known, no medical care, on the way to her unsuspecting baby's father in Paris. Her waters broke three minutes ago…' she gestured to the puddle '…much to Wolfgang's dismay, and I think we're almost ready to push.'

'Succinct.' Connor couldn't help admire the calm way Kelsie had managed the transfer of information. And the situation. He saw her glance with a measuring look at Anna. 'I haven't been able to assess the position of the baby.'

Their eyes met and he nodded and tried not to look at the wrong woman because Kelsie's blue gown was knotted at the waist and the soft swell of breast could be seen between the folds.

He looked away to her face and couldn't help thinking she looked so different from the soft and languorous woman he'd left an hour ago. She still looked amazing but there was decision and assurance in every line of her body.

Back on task, he reminded himself. 'We'll assume this baby knows the rules.' He turned to someone behind him. 'Can we get another light, please, Max? Or even a torch in case we need it.'

Connor glanced back along the corridor as the man hurried away. 'Max has seen a lot on this train in the last twenty years,' he said to Kelsie, but didn't mention that apparently that included flirting with his grandmother if the interrupted conversation they'd been having had been what he'd thought it was.

Anna breathed through another contraction and the subtle expulsive effort confirmed Kelsie's diagnosis. He would be right up there with agreeing with her assessment of the situation.

Kelsie looked up when the contraction had eased. 'Do you have a doctor's bag?'

He smiled wryly. 'I'm not the sort of doctor who carries a bag to catch babies away from hospitals.' He shrugged. 'So what have we got on the plus side?'

'Catching babies outside hospitals is right up my alley. And there's two of us.'

He felt his mouth curve. Working with Kelsie was different from what he was used to. 'Great pluses.'

She went on as if ticking off the points. 'Anna is focused and healthy, so baby should be healthy too. And at least it's warm in here.'

All good points. 'So what can I do to help?'

'I need you to take the baby if needed. Get your helper to find us some cord for tying off and scissors to cut the cord. And maybe a dish or a bag for the afterbirth.'

He nodded and spoke to the other porter, who was helping poor Wolfgang to sit up and then turned back to see if he could do anything else.

Kelsie had that far-away look in her eyes that he'd seen in midwives who could almost disappear in a room they became so unobtrusive, only to soothingly reappear when the woman needed them.

He waited until she refocused and passed her requested items across, and she put them on the small table by the window.

She looked back at him and smiled as if she was very glad he was there. He was conscious that his whole chest seemed to swell. What was it about this woman that touched him so much? Whatever it was, he'd better work out how to put up a force field or he'd be standing outside a registry office on his own again.

'Thank you. That's lovely.' Her voice was soft. 'I can concentrate on Anna. We don't have anything if she decides to bleed, though, but there's no reason she should.'

Connor wondered if she'd said that for Anna's benefit, his benefit or her own. So he agreed in case she needed reassurance. 'Of course she should be fine.'

It all happened very quickly after that. Anna was still standing when Kelsie peered under the hem of the nightgown, much to Anna's embarrassment.

Kelsie murmured, 'So, it is a breech. I wondered. We have our first tiny foot, and now the second has appeared.'

Trickier, Connor thought, but not a disaster, especially if Kelsie was right and both feet had come down together.

He kept his voice low and matter-of-fact, a mirror of Kelsie's, so they didn't alarm the mother. 'Of course it is. Nothing straightforward about a baby that wants to be born on a train.' He lowered his voice even further so that only Kelsie heard. 'Do you want to swap places?'

Kelsie thought about that and appreciated he'd given her the choice. She liked that. But now the birth was a little more complicated he was the more experienced here and they both knew it. She'd delivered a breech birth before but this was no time for glory and not the place to practise.

'Maybe.'

He slid in behind her and she edged away to allow him past so that he was in front of Anna. Kelsie took the towel to dry the baby after birth and spoke in Anna's ear. 'The doctor is taking over now. Everything is fine.'

Anna nodded, too intent on the overwhelming sensations to care, as her uterus contracted again and her baby shifted.

Connor looked up at Kelsie. His voice still low and slightly amused. 'I know what you midwives are like. Don't worry. I'm an advocate for breech babies knowing what they want to do without my interference, too.' He held up his fingers. 'So I'm keeping my hands off.'

Kelsie felt a glow of relief, and pride, and confidence. This was Connor, her Connor, and he'd matured into a caring and skilled man. Maybe he had even recovered from some of his control issues, she thought with a smile, and couldn't help wondering what the future held for them. For the first time she wondered if some time in the future they might even meet again. She hoped so.

He spoke gently to Anna. 'If you can stand the change, it would help if you were to sit on the edge of the seat, Anna. Right near the edge so baby's toes can dangle. We won't lift your skirt until we need to.'

Kelsie slid one of Wolfgang's raincoats onto the floor and Connor knelt beside Anna. The girl's eyes were closed and she was muttering prayers under her breath in an unending litany.

Kelsie decided that was as good as anything to do in the circumstances but everything seemed to be progressing normally—or normal for a breech baby wanting to be born on the Orient Express between countries.

With Anna's change in position her baby's little legs descended further until his hips were suddenly exposed and Connor folded back the nightgown so they could see the progress of the baby. Things would happen faster now.

Anna was having a son. Neither Kelsie nor Connor mentioned it, with the mother concentrating so deeply.

'If the hips fit, the head fits,' Connor said quietly, and Kelsie smiled at him.

'I hadn't heard that before. Very nice.'

Anna's eyes were closed and Max was standing outside the door, available but not observing.

Kelsie leaned out the door and spoke in an undertone. 'Can I get another couple of towels, please, Max?'

He nodded and disappeared up the corridor, returning in less than a minute with warmed towels.

'Impressive.' Kelsie smiled at him before laying one across Connor's knees for him to use if he wanted to wrap baby before it was born.

The descent of the baby continued smoothly, with the help of gravity and his mother bearing down, and Connor's knowledge to keep his hands off a breech baby in case he startled it or pulled, in which case a baby would throw up its head into an alert position, instead of being curled for birth.

Frightened babies ran into problems. It seemed Connor knew that. Kelsie knew that. Some less up-to-date accouchiers didn't know that.

Connor also knew that breech babies could be a little more dazed and reluctant to breathe than babies who came head first. His main concern in this scenario.

So he was much happier to be the catcher to hand the baby on to Kelsie for assessment because he was more used to having a paediatric registrar do all his baby resuscitation while he cared for the woman.

In Kelsie's working world, caseload midwives who caught babies in homes were often in pairs and the second person was always responsible for encouraging reluctant babies to breathe.

Anna's baby had turned a pale shade of blue by the time the head finally arrived and Connor handed the floppy little boy across to Kelsie while he waited for the next stage with the mother.

Kelsie took the limp little body, wiped him quite firmly with a towel, dried him all over so that his little arms wobbled, but after another few seconds a mewling cry was heard, much to Connor's relief.

He watched the mother seem to wake from her stupor at the sound, shake her head and focus on her infant. Then with a gasp she reached for her son, and with the

cord still attached he was gently eased into the open front of her gown against her skin.

Anna's son lay with his head on the gentle swell of his mother's breasts, facing Kelsie, so they could see the colour of his face and as he cried with gradually increasing indignation, suddenly pink-cheeked and vigorous.

These were the moments Connor savoured. And judging by the soft look on Kelsie's face, she did too.

He wondered if she regretted not having had babies and then pushed the thought away. Pushed away the concept of a fifteen-year-old child they could have shared because the thought tore at somewhere deep within him.

He returned to the job at hand as the final stage of birth was completed with no damage.

He could hear Anna murmur in Italian, saw out of the corner of his vision the mother stroke the dark fuzz on the baby's head, and then Kelsie tucked another warm towel over them both.

She caught his eye. She'd always caught his eye. This time she held it and for a moment they connected with the satisfaction of a wonderful outcome.

A special moment. Then she sent him a long relieved look and he was surprised because he hadn't realised the depth of her anxiety, but she allowed it to escape now the crisis had passed. Suddenly he wanted to hold her in his arms and reassure her that everything was fine. That she was amazing. But he didn't.

It was one a.m. on Christmas Eve and a baby was born.

Kelsie was the first to speak. 'Congratulations, Anna. He's beautiful.'

'A boy?' The new mother raised tearstained eyes and nodded as the knowledge sank in. 'I cannot believe he is here.'

Over the next sixty minutes tiny Josef had been nursed, dressed in a hand-towel nappy, and clothed in a signature bear outfit from the boutique, so amusingly he looked like Wolfgang in miniature, complete with little blue cap. A tiny naked brown teddy bear sat beside him.

Now sated and wrapped in an Orient Express cashmere scarf donated by Max and settled with his mother after another feed, he was a contented baby.

Wolfgang had recovered, apologised for his unprofessional fainting attack and hastened to offer refreshments, but Max had taken over his duties and sent him off to sleep.

Anna was clean and warm, pleasantly drowsy and tucked into the narrow little bed with her baby. Already she'd spoken to her at first shocked then ecstatic boyfriend on Connor's phone.

A doting waitress had been allocated to sit with the new mother as she rested, until they arrived in Paris in the morning, where she and her baby would alight. Kelsie had promised to drop in before they disembarked.

Connor had left instructions for them to wake him through the night if needed so all bases had been covered.

They'd both washed in the tiny basin in Kelsie's room and Connor took Kelsie gently by the arm and steered

her back to the bar car, where Max had procured them a pot of tea.

Max smiled and went on his way, ensuring all was back to normal on the Orient Express.

Suddenly they were alone on the long settee in the bar car and Kelsie watched Connor flop back in the seat.

She had to smile as he said with disgust, 'Moments of unusual interest. Babies!'

Kelsie put her head on his shoulder. 'Such are the dear wee things. You were awesome.'

'And you were incredible.' He leant her way and stroked her cheek and she felt like drowsily turning her mouth to his hand and kissing his palm, but she wasn't sure of her reception after the way they'd parted earlier. He might think she was jumping him again. Seemed she was still a coward.

Instead she said, 'So we have a mutual admiration society. Sounds good to me.'

She closed her eyes for a moment as she nestled beside him on the long couch. Not a night she would forget in a hurry. Then she forced her eyes open and sipped the tea. 'As good as this is, I think I'm too tired to drink it.'

She heard him pick up his cup and then a long swallow. Felt him move his head, as if realising the time. Funny how little things like that made him seem more real. As if them meeting like this had a purpose. Another long draught of his tea and he put his white and blue cup down. 'Then let's get you to bed.'

Ha. Kelsie pouted. 'It didn't work for me last time,' she murmured.

He smiled, put out his hand and pulled her into a standing position. 'You can't have everything you want.'

'What did you say?' she whispered as they crept along the darkened corridor.

She didn't think he would come in when she offered but he did. When her compartment door shut behind them she felt like giggling, but surely Anna and the waitress would hear her if she did.

'I should just kiss you and go,' Connor said very softly.

'I can do that without noise,' she whispered against his mouth, and she could feel his smile against his lips.

CHAPTER NINE

KISSING CONNOR WAS like diving into a hot whirlpool. Again.

Despite both their efforts to cool their ardour, their kiss deepened into something more after the tension and stress of Josef's arrival and the awareness already between them, until Kelsie surrendered to it…and to Connor.

In fact, it deepened into something that the joining of their mouths couldn't satisfy, and her hands began to seek, his followed and both their clothes became disarrayed, all silent flutters of their fingers but no less intense as the dramatic emotion of the night mixed with the unsatisfied emotion of the time before that.

Now it culminated in a flurry of silent desperation as both of them were touched by the past and then lost in the present, in a small swaying cabin in the dark as the snow fell outside.

Until Kelsie stood within the circle of his arms, her once tied dressing gown not designed for resistance, open to the waist as Connor feasted on the bounty within—and she had Connor's shirt pushed aside, baring his chest, her eyes shut, head thrown back. Still with

her eyes shut, grinding her teeth as his tongue circled her, while her hands slid across the inflexible muscles of his upper abdomen. Her fingers grazed the pebbled nubs of his nipples, travelled over his taut back and her body arched helplessly against the iron hardness of him and the onslaught of his mouth.

Belts undone, underwear discarded and suddenly everything slowed again and the remaining clothes were lost.

Time itself stopped as they gazed into each other's eyes, and in the background, intermittently, the lights from railway crossings painted them red and then green—and then silver in the snow light while they held each other tight.

Then he sank to sit on the bed, pulled her to kneel between his knees, spanned her waist with his long slender fingers, and inexorably pulled her closer.

This was a Connor she hadn't seen. Grey eyes dark and burning into hers, his hands and mouth sure and possessive, no hurry but no hesitation in steering them to the conclusion neither of them could now contemplate avoiding as she sank downwards.

They both gasped as she lowered, teased, hovered until Connor's hands tightened and she was brought inexorably onto him—all with the sway of the train—a slow and exultant joining, and together they scaled their own mountain as the train sped on through the night.

Afterwards, Connor lay stunned by the storm that had erupted between them, overwhelmed by the connection with the woman he'd always loved. But where was his clarity and responsibility and plain good sense?

That was the very core of his mantra to remain in control of his world. That litany had kept him sane from a time when everything had seemed lost at a very young age.

Kelsie made him lose that essential part of his being. Nobody else did. Reason and logic went out the window when he was around her. Look at the fiasco it had been when he'd tried to marry her as a teenager.

He should have been thankful one of them had had the good sense to back away if this tornado was what happened.

And now, when he was far too old to behave like an impulsive, libido-driven teen, he had used no protection. Let alone that he was too well known across Europe to go creeping around train carriages at night for assignations with beautiful midwives.

He couldn't bear the thought of a newspaper story on Kelsie, and already there was a risk of one of the passengers noticing with the obvious rumours of a baby having been born.

God, he was a fool. But first he needed to sort the contraception. All the while in the back of his head a voice was saying that none of those things mattered. He just wanted to lose himself again. And again. And what if he was lost in this and she wasn't!

Sandwiched together in Kelsie's tiny bed, her head on his chest, Kelsie lay in stunned disbelief. She squeezed the strong fingers curled in hers and for the first time she understood why she had never been able to fall

in love. Why there had never been any magic with other men.

Connor.

The deep, protected core of her heart had always belonged to the boy she remembered and now this gorgeous, sexy, fabulous man.

She snuggled in further, felt the glow that surrounded them both, and knew she would never be the same.

She was a different person from the woman who had stepped in such a carefree way onto this train from the canals of Venice.

The problem now was that she felt the fragility of finding something so special. That awareness of the rise and fall of the precious chest beneath her cheek and even the flutter of fear should the day come when it would disappear. How crazy was that?

It was as if a huge beacon of light had finally been switched on and she danced like a wraith in the glow. She'd given up long ago thinking that she would feel this way—had, in fact, felt quite proud she was immune to being dependent on a man for happiness.

Now she just wanted to lose herself in his eyes again, see the man she could finally admit could be the one to spend her life with, but it was too hard with her nose buried in his chest.

Her brain began to function again and with it came fear. Would she lose this, too?

They didn't have long but they had some time when they arrived in London. Not much chance of a future with them on opposite sides of the world but that was for later.

No hurry, the rational part of herself reminded her, they wouldn't arrive until late in the afternoon. She should just savour this moment for as long as she could. Maybe even till dawn. Or was she just imagining he felt the same?

Fear gnawed away at her. She needed to know Connor's thoughts and turned her head but couldn't see his face from this angle. He was strangely silent, though he held her in their tiny cocoon.

Finally she had to probe. Quietly. 'Are you okay?'

His hand tightened. She heard the smile in his voice when he answered. 'I'm supposed to ask you that.'

She stretched her toes and rubbed his ankle under the sheets. 'I'm feeling wonderful.'

'I'm glad. But we have to talk.'

She snuggled in. About…? And waited with anticipation. Christmas in London? They'd already discussed the past. Was it time to talk about the future?

'The train stops for almost an hour in Paris. I'll get off and find an all-night chemist. They'll have a morning-after pill. I can't believe I didn't use protection. I'm sorry. It's inexcusable.'

What? She blinked and her head lifted a few millimetres off his chest.

That's what he was thinking? What? Poor little Kelsie needed safeguarding from the big bad man without protection? Or maybe he was worried that she'd trap him! As in the opposite to dropping him fifteen years ago? Did he think she cruised through life unprepared?

Not what she'd expected to hear. Maybe because

she'd known she was covered pregnancy-wise but he hadn't even asked that.

Apparently she was still too silly not to have thought of contraception.

I'm on the Pill, she shrilled at him silently. And as for the other concerns she didn't think that, no matter how much he'd changed, Connor was the kind of man to give a sleeping partner a notifiable disease. Well, neither was she.

It was disquieting the way his mind worked, though. Did he trust her so little? Was he that worried about unwanted complications? Was that finally the price she would pay for her actions in the past?

Did he think she would escape in London and not follow through? Did he want to ensure all was settled before they parted?

Her bubble of euphoria deflated and disappeared like suds down a porcelain bowl onto railway tracks and she sat up. Slid from the bed and picked up her robe.

'You okay?' he asked.

Umm. No. But she didn't say anything. Slipped the robe on and belted it before she turned to face him. Saw the closed look on his face and tried to keep her own expression blank as she wondered how she could escape so she could figure this out by herself.

She poked her feet into her slippers and unlatched the door. 'Excuse me.' Smiled in his general direction and fled.

Connor jammed his fingers through his hair.

He'd truly lost it. Their lovemaking had been torrid. The last thing he wanted was Kelsie finding out

in a month she was pregnant and he'd ruined her life. Especially if this was only a one-night stand for her.

He pushed away the stupid idea that he could live with the incredible idea of Kelsie having his child.

A child? Imagine if she left him then!

He shuddered. He wasn't doing wives and children and family who could leave at any time. He needed to put his trust in his work. It was his job to make sure other people had families.

He slid from the bed and began to dress before she came back, though he doubted even his grandmother would rouse the train to look for him—though she hadn't worried about shocking him when she'd sent Max in to talk to him.

He hadn't even had time to digest that startling turn of events in the last crazy few hours. But he had his own dilemmas now.

Kelsie still wasn't back as he shrugged into his jacket, the better to hide his crumpled shirt he'd rescued from the floor—he couldn't believe he hadn't hung it up!—and he straightened his tie and checked his phone.

Looked again. 'Please call urgently.' Damn. The Wilsons. Another baby in danger. He highlighted the number and opened Kelsie's door but she wasn't in the corridor.

He couldn't phone here, with people sleeping in every cabin, and he moved swiftly in the opposite direction until finally he reached the dimly lit bar car and could phone without fear of disturbing others.

He listened to a tearful Connie beg him to call and reassured himself that of all people Kelsie would under-

stand when a mother needed him. Ignored the thought that flitted through his mind that he couldn't wait to get back to a situation in which he had some rules to follow. Because he was damned if knew what the rules were with Kelsie. He dialed the Wilsons' number.

When Kelsie came back from the bathroom he'd gone. She'd thought he might have.

Her shoulders drooped and she shut the door and locked it. Hadn't she been the biggest goose. All soft and squishy over the old boyfriend and he had just been there for the night. Thank goodness she hadn't said anything to reveal her feelings. But inside she was shrivelling.

Mourning the silly dream she'd indulged in when he'd never said anything about tomorrow. Thanked her stars it wasn't a ten-night train journey or it could have been really embarrassing.

But it was a one-night journey. Breakfast would be served in the cabin in four or five hours. She wouldn't even see him. Then would be the pause in Paris, when she'd say goodbye to Anna and Josef, and hopefully meet the new father and make sure all was fine.

Then no doubt she'd see Connor at that point, because he'd drop in her little parcel containing the morning-after pill.

She narrowed her eyes at that. Toyed with idea of saying, 'No need, I'm covered,' but decided against it. Let him tramp about Paris at six a.m. and find a pharmacy because she wasn't feeling charitable about that one.

She climbed back into bed and pulled the second pillow over her head so she could hide. Didn't hear the quiet knock as it came at her door. Or hear Connor walk away.

Oblivious, Kelsie was sternly analysing recent events. Did she regret that she'd seen and lost Connor again?

No, she couldn't. She'd had the chance to say her piece. Explain a little and apologise for the past. Something she'd wanted to do for a long time.

Did she regret meeting his grandmother—the actual woman who had inspired her dream of travelling on the Orient Express? No way!

Was she unhappy she'd opened herself to Connor more than she had to any man? It had been special! She wasn't believing anything else. So how could she regret that?

No regret in learning what amazing sex was, finally, despite the mortifying ending. No. And it wasn't so humiliating when only she had known how much it had affected her.

Stern talking to completed, she shifted the pillow from her head and hugged it. Tried not to notice the faint scent of his cologne, breathed slowly in and out until her body reminded her it was very tired, but she couldn't sleep. Eventually the clack of the rails lulled her and the next thing she knew it was dawn.

Or a slow increase of dawn. In the dim light as she peered through heavy eyes the window began to expose the houses, see the waking city on the outskirts of

Paris, the flash of a waterway between houses and a tiny curved bridge reminiscent of Venice twenty hours ago.

With the dawn they rattled closer and closer to Paris and Kelsie washed her face, dressed and unsnapped her privacy catch as the train slowed for the pause on the outskirts before they rolled into the station. What would she give for a hot cup of tea?

There was a knock at the door and, magically, Wolfgang was there, looking sheepish, holding her dream tray with steaming water and an array of teabags.

'I was told you wanted to see the young lady and her baby off the train.' His cheeks reddened. 'I wish also to apologise for my odd behaviour. I do appreciate all your help last night.'

'Wolfgang. You darling. You were fine. And thank you for this.' She took the tray and then hesitated, hadn't been going to ask but couldn't help herself. 'Is Dr Black going to see Anna off as well?'

'I believe Dr Black has already seen them, madam.'

How had she missed that commotion through the thin walls? 'Oh. Then I will too, as soon as I've had this.'

Stepping back onto the train after seeing Anna and tiny Josef tucked into a taxi outside the station, Kelsie felt at least one family was happy.

They'd headed off at Anna's boyfriend's insistence for the hospital to be thoroughly checked out before he took them home to his flat. Though she did wonder what the Venetian grandparents were going to say about their new grandchild's unexpected arrival.

Anna's compartment door was shut and no doubt Wolfgang was planning a huge spring clean. The thought made her smile, which was a good thing considering the fact that Connor had run far and fast as soon as he'd dropped her little package in her compartment while she'd been gone.

She picked it up, curled her lip and tossed it in the tiny waste receptacle. She hoped he'd had the devil's own time finding it.

Her own little bed had been packed up and the seat had been returned to the daytime configuration. She decided the least she could do was enjoy the rest of her trip. She needed to remember that was why she was here.

Breakfast arrived and Wolfgang placed the flower-decorated tray on her tiny table in front of the window.

The train still sat in the Paris station awaiting clearance. Above her head cars and pedestrians streamed past in the peak-hour traffic, and the world went on turning while she waited in solitary splendour in her compartment.

She glanced down at the food. Fruit salad, pastries and rolls, wonderful jams to choose from, deliciously evil curled balls of French butter, and freshly squeezed juice. Far too much for one person—especially one who didn't appreciate them. She resisted the urge to push it all away crossly as she thought about Connor and her inability to understand him.

She picked at the food as she watched the passers-by scurry along the streets of Paris from her stationary train carriage, watched the buses fly over the overpass,

and thought that soon she would be one of those hurrying off to work herself.

When she was back in the real world. The world she'd worked so hard to create for herself.

But that was for later.

After Christmas.

It was Christmas Eve, she reminded herself, and she would be in London later today, across the world from her home, and booked in at the Ritz for Christmas morning before she left for the airport. It had all seemed so exciting when she'd looked at her itinerary before she'd left.

At the moment it looked a little flat and she chided herself for being pathetic. She needed to work on that.

CHAPTER TEN

CONNOR SAT IN the large double cabin facing his grandmother, his head in a medical journal as he tried to catch up on the latest breakthroughs in fertility. There were two articles with his name to them in the current issue and he needed to check that they had been presented correctly.

But his mind was elsewhere. Not with the Wilsons, because that had been a false alarm, though he suspected labour could be drawing closer for them, but hopefully not until after he and his grandmother arrived in London. Hopefully, also, when his brain was less scattered.

His short opportunity for sleep and the lack of rest it had provided didn't help.

Partly because of the recurring dream, the one he hadn't had for several years now. It was always the same, the horror of light dying from eyes fixed on his, and he'd woken before dawn, heart pounding and in a lather of sweat, and had known fear like he hadn't for years.

Desperately disappointed at its return, because he'd hoped the nightmare had finally been banished, this

time instead of his mother's face the woman's face had been in shadow—and yet he'd known it was Kelsie, even though he hadn't been able to see her features.

God, he hated the power of dreams that could strike terror into his psyche when he was at his weakest. No control to be had there.

One of the reasons he'd never seriously contemplated even a sensible marriage, or stayed the night at any of his women friends' homes, was his horror of anyone finding out about this little weakness. He doubted anyone knew he suffered those dreams except his grandmother, who had caught him at a weak moment years ago when he'd been staying over and she'd heard him cry out. That moment still made him cringe.

This morning the nightmare had receded to an eerily distant threat, so much so that it still clouded his thoughts, which were already in disarray with his angst about Kelsie. Why hadn't she answered the door when he'd gone back? Had she been soundly asleep—or deliberately avoiding him?

He hadn't tried again when he'd been to see Anna and Josef early that morning in case she was still sleeping. At least that visit had been successful and both seemed unfazed by the baby's unusual arrival. Good to see someone was happy.

He'd written a referral to a medical colleague in one of the maternity hospitals in Paris for a follow-up visit.

But still the dilemma of Kelsie lingered. His eyes stared unfocused on the page.

Ah, Kelsie. The memories of that morning were still very vivid in his mind. Her glorious body, her ability to

tilt his world and spin it until he didn't know which way was up, the woman who could explore deeply sheltered parts of him that nobody else had access to. He hated that. Was terrified of it. Loved it.

So much so that he wondered if that was where the dream had come from.

He'd have to try and talk to her again. Try to understand what she was thinking. He'd always wished she'd let him into her thoughts more. He'd ruined the mood disastrously by talking about the morning-after pill. Maybe the idea of repercussions had been just as terrifying for her as it had been for him but second-guessing her was difficult.

He'd been unable to settle ever since he'd returned to meet his grandmother for breakfast.

'You're very quiet.' Winsome sounded bored and he put his journal down. Hadn't been reading the thing anyway.

Poor Gran. He was not good company this morning because all he could think about was the impact he was already feeling after the time with Kelsie. He suspected she was about to fly back to Australia and out of his life once again.

'Sorry. What would you like to talk about?'

'You won't like what I want to talk about.'

He smiled. She was probably right. 'Thankfully it's not your pseudo-birthday any more now it's Christmas Eve. So you have to spare me.'

She pouted and he grinned. 'Don't try your wiles on me. You're not talking to Max now, Gran.'

She smiled at that. 'He is a darling. Are you sure you don't mind?'

'Of course I don't. He seems a good fellow. But that's none of my business.' And she was safely diverted to another topic for the next fifteen minutes, and Connor hoped she'd take the staying-out-of-each-other's-business hint on board.

He'd got over the shock of his eighty-year-old grandmother finding companionable love and truly appreciated the benefits to her not living alone as she grew older. He had the feeling the two elderly lovebirds wouldn't waste much time sorting out their future arrangements.

Lucky them.

Shame he didn't believe the same could happen to him but with that thought came his resolution to find Kelsie and try to understand where they could possibly go with this—if, indeed, there was anywhere to go.

Kelsie was sick of her own company but trapped in the dilemma of not running into Connor somewhere on the train if she ventured out of her cabin. The last thing she wanted was to look like she was chasing him.

When Wolfgang came to remove her tray she pounced on him and, despite the risk of looking needy, she encouraged his continued presence.

'So what's on the agenda for today, Wolfgang?'

He bowed. 'A delicious brunch will be served in the dining car, madam, at eleven.'

Her stomach groaned. More food. 'In case I was

starving to death by now.' She nodded and Wolfgang looked slightly confused.

'I'm sorry. Not enough sleep for me.' He nodded and looked slightly guilty again so she hurried on. 'And what time do we arrive in Calais?'

'Around one o'clock in Calais. The Ville coaches will transfer you to the shuttle terminal at Coquelles. Then through the tunnel to Folkestone where, after a short wait, you will join the Pullman train for the journey to London.' He smiled at her. 'There will be a very elegant afternoon tea on that train.'

She grinned back. 'Of course there will. I will be as big as a house by the time I get off at Victoria. So we lose you at Calais?'

He bowed. 'Our hostesses will accompany each VIP coach and hand you on to the new Pullman Stewards.'

She'd miss him. Had enjoyed his blue-suited attentiveness and his staid good humour. 'Thank you for explaining that. I guess I thought we caught this train all through the tunnel to London.'

Horrified that 'his' train would go across the Channel, he exclaimed, 'No! No! It is the Pullman train you will transfer to for the final leg.'

There was something sad in that. She liked her blue wagon lit. 'I understand. So when we all leave you will go home for Christmas?'

He smiled. 'Yes. We all go home. It is the last trip of the year. Normally our timetable finishes much earlier but this trip had been rescheduled so it became a special journey.'

Lucky her. 'I feel very fortunate. So you're on holidays now?'

He nodded and she wondered vaguely how his hat stayed on with all his nodding and bowing.

Oblivious to her curiosity, he went on, 'All except those who have other employment. VSOE have many hotels and we can move between them if we wish.'

'I hope your Christmas is delightful, Wolfgang, though I'm sure I'll see you before I go. You do a fabulous job of looking after us.'

He bowed, hat still amazingly glued on. 'Thank you.' He gestured towards the front of the train. 'The bar car is open if you wish to change scenery.'

'Sounds good, but I think I'll try and get to the boutique again to buy something to remind me of my journey. I didn't make it yesterday.' And she doubted Connor would be hanging out in there again today just in case she turned up.

Wolfgang went on his way and Kelsie dug out her purse for a walk through the train. The bar car was filling up and she wondered if she'd manage to find a seat when she came back through again. It was still early and she wondered where Winsome was or if she was still asleep.

The boutique was the last carriage before the engine. Apart from Max, it was deserted.

'Miss Summers. Welcome.' So he remembered her when she wasn't dressed in her pyjamas. She smiled and could picture how unobtrusively helpful he'd been. He didn't look as though he'd been up all night. Still immaculate, distinguished, his Italian accent rolled vel-

vety and vibrantly and his chocolate-brown eyes were warm with welcome.

'Max, isn't it? Dr Black said you'd seen a lot in the last twenty years on the Orient Express. You were very good last night.'

He bowed. No hat to keep on. 'It is you who were excellent. But I enjoy people and the drama of the journey.'

She thought a breech birth on a train did justify the description. 'Well, we certainly had drama last night. That's for sure.'

Max nodded. 'I believe that is our first baby born on board.'

Kelsie laughed, picturing the scene. 'Josef looked so cute afterwards when he was dressed in the little conductor suit.' She looked at the teddy bears, all dressed as Josef had been, and then at the more exotic gifts like cuff links, VSOE diamond bracelets and gorgeous pearl drop sets. 'I bet you've seen some romance here as well.'

She actually thought he blushed. She wasn't sure because he went on in his beautiful accent, as if nothing was a problem, 'This is the train of love. People come time and again. Anniversaries. Weddings.' He gazed into pleasant past. 'I have seen men propose on bended knee in the crowded dining car and then buy expensive and beautiful jewellery from my boutique.' He shrugged with a smile. 'All of this makes me happy.'

Kelsie decided Max was a bit of a honey as well as a romantic as she tried to decide on the perfect memento of her trip.

Footsteps sounded at the door and whoever it was must have been a favourite face because Max's eyes

softened and his smile would have lit up the room. Kelsie turned to see Winsome smiling back at him and then the older lady seemed to tear her eyes away to beam at Kelsie.

'Hello, my dear. I thought you might be here. Max's little boutique is the best part of the journey.'

Kelsie wondered at the unmistakably flirtatious note in her voice, and wondered if Connor knew his gran had a thing for Max.

Another footfall and a deep voice. It seemed he did. 'Behave yourself, Gran. You're embarrassing Max.' When Connor entered, the relaxed and festive vibe for Kelsie seemed to be swallowed by the awareness of his powerful presence. And the way his eyes immediately searched for hers.

Max and Winsome didn't seem to notice anything, thank goodness, Kelsie thought as she mentally wrapped herself in a suit of armour to stave off the weakness she could feel creeping around her knees.

'Your beautiful grandmother only ever gives me pleasure,' Max said heroically to the man lounging at the door. Kelsie had to smile at Winsome, who fanned herself theatrically.

Maybe it was time to change the subject. And prove she was no wilting flower just because Connor had skulked away from her bed. 'Max is going to help me decide,' she said to the room in general. 'I'm stuck. So what should I have as a memento for my trip?'

Winsome winked at the manager again. 'Max is very good at that.'

Max bestowed a shake of his head on her but the af-

fection between the two was obvious. So Max had a thing for Winsome as well, Kelsie decided with an internal smile. Well, good on them. Nice if it all worked out for someone.

Max returned his attention to Kelsie. 'Perhaps you could point out those things that appeal to you?' The wave of his hand included the whole display. 'Include those that are outside your price range just for the fun of it.'

She looked around. Carefully avoided Connor at the door. 'I can't say one of everything because that would be too greedy.'

The crystalware caught her eye as it reflected the light in myriad colours. It would remind her of dinner with Connor, and she would dearly love a set of each of those. 'The engraved crystal glasses. I love them. And the decanter is gorgeous. At least one of the beautiful snuff boxes and of course any of the jewellery, it's all divine.'

She stepped closer to the glass cabinet that held the diamonds and gold. 'I'm particularly fond of the charm bracelet with the tiny train and conductor's hat, and the diamond earrings with matching pendant.' She moved along the cabinet. 'And I should buy one of these beautiful VSOE velvet jewellery rolls to keep it all in.'

She stopped and blushed. 'Lost it for a moment in the daydream.' Shook her head. 'But enough dreaming. I think I would like a silver guard's whistle and an Agatha Christie book. Thank you, Max.'

'Excellent choice,' he said, as he carefully removed the gold-edged book from the pile.

'Only one of a thousand printed in this edition.' He was too much a gentleman to look disappointed she hadn't spent a fortune. 'And the whistle is very popular.' He wrapped them swiftly and elaborately, his vast experience obvious. Then placed her purchases in a little gold VSOE carry-bag, along with a catalogue. 'In case you see something you would like to order online.'

'You are very good at this. Aren't you?'

He nodded complacently.

She could feel Connor observing it all from the door, though he didn't say anything. Couldn't stop herself babbling to fill the awkward pause, though she was probably the only one who felt the awkwardness of the moment. 'So you must be going home for Christmas, too, after we disembark?'

'Actually, I'm not.' He glanced at Winsome. 'I have been invited for Christmas in London. And yourself?'

Kelsie wondered if Connor knew that but he made no demur. What a delightful intrigue. Perhaps more than just a flirtation?

Then she realised Max was waiting for her answer. 'I'm having Christmas morning at the Ritz and then flying back to Australia later tomorrow. I discovered it's incredibly cheap to fly home on Christmas Day.'

Winsome looked horrified. 'Oh, no. You can't go on Christmas night.'

Kelsie smiled gently at the kindness she could see in Winsome's eyes. 'Of course I can. I've worked every Christmas the last few years. It's never really been a big thing for me. This year will be a treat and I get to sit back. Then I'm working every day for a week from

New Year's Eve.' She smiled at Max. 'Hoping to catch lots of babies who very kindly waited for me until after Christmas.'

She picked up her carry-bag and smiled vaguely in Connor's direction. 'I'll see you all later.'

She thought she'd got away with it but Connor leaned towards her as she passed.

'I'll accompany you.' Connor turned to follow.

Softly answered into his chest as she passed, 'I'd rather you didn't.'

'Tough,' he said quietly, so that only she could hear. So not like the young man she'd known.

She narrowed her eyes and muttered over her shoulder. 'I can't stop you.'

'No. You can't.' Whispered into her hair.

CHAPTER ELEVEN

WAS HE TRYING to be annoying or just obtuse? Kelsie had to wonder what had happened to the incredibly attentive man who had held her so tenderly after they had both rocked their little cabin, the man who she'd thought had become her lover and a best friend again.

'I'm going to the bar.'

She heard the laughter in his voice. 'Be careful. They'll feed you.'

She stopped, turned, and her mouth twitched. She had to smile. Suddenly it was easier. 'You're overly stuffed with food too?' Maybe he wasn't so over her. Or was hiding it so she would just fall for him all over again with the barest hint of encouragement.

He grimaced. 'I ache with food.'

Actually, Connor ached with something else. The urge to hold Kelsie and hug her to him. Grab her hand and race her off to her cabin—much more private—because this was the last opportunity they would have to be alone before they were transferred to the non-sleeper part of their journey—but that way lay madness. Or was it happiness that he was afraid of?

He wished he knew which it was, although the ghosts

from the past had such a stranglehold on him he had to assume the former.

Now he'd discovered she was flying out tomorrow night they had very little time. He'd been disappointed when that had come out but not shocked. They had less reason to be careful because she would fly away and now he knew. No doubt she would have mentioned it yesterday if he'd asked her.

In fairness to himself, his intention hadn't been to sleep with her and find himself teetering on the edge of where he'd been all those years ago—back under her spell.

Maybe it was a good thing she was going. Not enough time for the miracle of Christmas to take a hand. But they should at least part friends.

He owed her that. He actually thought he needed it, too.

'Perhaps we could talk privately?'

The blue of her eyes darkened doubtfully and he thought again how much he loved the way her face had matured into the woman in front of him.

'Why?'

He shrugged. He wished he knew. 'For lots of reasons—all of them nebulous.' But he couldn't rid himself of the notion that they were balancing on the edge of an important truth—no matter which way it went. 'Or just because I left without explanation this morning and it wasn't my intention to hurt you.'

She shrugged unwillingly. 'We can talk in the bar.'

'Of course.' Kelsie heard the resignation in his voice. She chewed her lip as she moved forward again

through the next carriage. Did she really want to talk in the bar? With Winsome about to descend on them at any moment and the possibility of others overhearing?

Or did she want to risk being in close, private proximity to Connor where physical things could happen? Had happened before. Ooh. Naughty but nice.

She considered her lonely flight home tomorrow, at thirty thousand feet, imagining scenarios in her head if she chose the wrong answer now.

Would she regret not giving him a chance to speak to her in private? Yes. Best not to wonder, then. 'Fine. Your cabin or mine?'

Connor smiled. 'Mine's closer. And larger.'

Her brows went up. She'd known it would be. 'Show-off.'

He looked down at her. 'Jealous bag.'

She laughed. 'You always were good at the comebacks.'

'You weren't too bad yourself when you plucked up the courage.'

'I've grown up,' she tossed over her shoulder.

'Oh, yes,' he said softly. 'You certainly have.'

He touched her shoulder, she stopped, and they were there already. More reasons to go to his cabin. He unlocked his cabin and gestured for her to enter.

'Madam?' He looked so tall as he smiled down at her. So big and achingly familiar, and she could almost taste the impending loss, because they would be a world away from each other very shortly. But that was her life and she loved her life.

She looked up into his face as she passed under his

arm and she remembered the last time they had been alone. Felt the twist in her belly and the warmth in her skin as she brushed against him. 'Come into my parlour, said the spider to the fly.'

He shook his head. 'To my mind it's more of a black-widow thing.'

With her being the black widow? Not very complimentary!

He must have seen he'd offended her. Good. 'Let's just say I'm pretty sure you can protect yourself if you want to.'

Ah. But right at this moment did she want to? Kelsie hoped those thoughts didn't show in her face as she looked around the spacious suite. Two large seats facing each other with a table between them. Twice the size of her cabin and at least that much more expensive. She'd never really thought about the financial disparity between them but that reared its head now as another reason a relationship wouldn't work.

'So is this all yours?'

'It connects through that door to my grandmother's suite, which is the same.'

'Nice.'

He crossed to the tiny refrigerator she'd missed in the corner. 'Would you like a cold drink?'

'Juice. Thanks.' Something to do with her hands was always good.

He sat down when they both had drinks. Opposite each other, the air heavy with unspoken thoughts, both with small smiles on their faces as they compared the

stilted awkwardness to how they had been just a few hours ago.

Connor started. 'I hope I didn't upset you this morning when I left without saying goodbye—'

Did he expect her to say yes? She interrupted. 'I admit I thought it was a little unusual but I'm not needy.'

Much. She so did not want to be needy. 'So what did you want to talk about?' She paused, thought and then said it out loud. 'Contraception, perhaps?' She wouldn't put it past him and would not get her hopes up it could be something a little more flattering.

'Did you get the package I left?'

Surprise. Surprise. 'Hmm.' Bite your tongue, Kelsie! Say nothing.

He leaned forward. 'So you've taken them.'

'No,' she said coolly, and stood up. She didn't want to do this. She wanted out. Now! 'It makes me angry you're so obsessed with something that isn't your business. I didn't need them because I'm already covered. It's what grown women do.'

He stood too. 'Wait.' Touched her arm, carefully, as if afraid she'd brush him off, his eyes perplexed. 'Why didn't you say so?'

She shrugged. 'Offended mostly. I thought you were very speedy at declaring the risk of not being protected because you were so sure I wasn't.'

Like she was still a silly little girl. Not a mature, professional woman. If she didn't get out of here soon she was going to cry and she did not want to do that! She'd spent the last fifteen years growing up. Growing a tough

outer layer. Fighting to be the independent woman she'd thrown away the young Connor to become.

'Okay.' So perhaps it had been a bad choice to leave her like that. 'I'm sorry. But there was other stuff going on.' Connor wanted to pull his hair out. At least she'd finally explained how she felt. Half the time he had no idea what she was thinking and it wasn't surprising he'd managed to upset her.

He thought of telling her about the phone call but knew he'd been glad of the excuse. So that was a cop-out. 'Though, to be fair to me, contraception or lack of it *is* my business. I don't know if you see me as a one-night stand or an old boyfriend but either way the honourable thing to do is ensure you don't become pregnant when I'm the one who's been irresponsible.'

'You've still got control issues.'

He stilled. Stared at her thoughtfully. 'No. You think I have but I don't. I have care issues. I'm beginning to think you're the one with the control problem.'

'That's not true. You're just sexist.' And she spun on her heel and walked out.

Connor looked at the empty doorway. 'Sexist?' He repeated it. 'Me? Sexist?' He adored women. He was a reproductive specialist, for pity's sake, and he respected and admired women immensely.

She had serious trust issues. He knew her parents had been very unhappy before they'd separated; her father had drunk a fair bit and maybe it wasn't about him at all. Maybe she was terrified of falling in love and committing to one person for ever? Well, she wasn't the only

one. His phone rang and he turned away from the door and stared unseeingly out the window as he answered it.

Kelsie swept out of his compartment with her cheeks hot but not as hot as her temper. Did he want her to say he wasn't a one-night stand? And why was it all about his honour? He made her so angry but she just couldn't pinpoint why. She'd said the one thing she'd known would alienate him and reminded herself why she hadn't thrown herself on his chest.

As she flounced through the bar car, she decided against any form of male company, ever, and she glared at Winston Whatsit the Third when he stood up and smiled at her until he shrank back in his chair.

His terrified reaction did something to restore her good humour. Yes. That's right. She was a woman to reckon with, wasn't she? A black widow. Thank goodness she didn't need a man to make her feel like she had a perfect life.

When she reached her compartment she resisted the urge to dig out her bottle of limoncello she'd bought as a last-minute impulse in Venice and pour a generous slosh into her glass. *Grrrrr*, she thought as she glared at the bottle made famous in the lemon groves of the Amalfi coast. She'd like to bury someone in the lemon groves on the Amalfi coast.

Connor sat with his grandmother and stuffed his frustration, anger and disappointment in Kelsie into a sealed box somewhere under his diaphragm, where it sat like a lump.

He saw his grandmother open the yellow envelope and then frown across at him. He was in trouble. Well, what was new!

Winsome pointed the paper at him. 'What did you do to that poor girl?'

What had she done to *him* was more like it! 'Which poor girl?'

His gran's eyes almost disappeared as she glared at him and for the first time in half an hour he felt like smiling. 'Don't play with me, Connor. You know I mean Kelsie.'

He couldn't believe he was the one being scolded when he had been the one ill used. The whole thing was the result of two incompatible people butting their heads against a brick wall. But he did hate to see his gran upset. 'Nothing. She's fine.'

The letter was waved his way. 'She's apologised for not joining us for brunch.'

He sat forward. Caught his grandmother's eye and held it. 'That poor girl has been forced into our company the whole trip. She's probably having lunch with Winston Whatsit the Third.'

His grandmother looked a little hurt that he'd suggested she'd forced their company on Kelsie. He saw the pang of guilt cross her face and truly regretted that. But before he could apologise she'd absorbed his next comment.

'Eh? With who? Who's he?' Diversion was always good with Gran. Lowered the blood pressure.

'Fellow at the bar. He fancied her, I think.'

Another death stare. 'And that doesn't bother you?'

Not at all. Kelsie wouldn't touch a man that drank to excess with a ten-foot pole. He knew that much. 'Why should it?'

His grandmother gave her most impressive snort yet. 'Hmmmph! Because you're damn well in love with the girl, that's why.'

The humour abruptly left the conversation.

He was seriously fed up with this whole situation. In fact, thanks to his grandmother and a certain person who would remain nameless, he'd probably acquired a phobia about trains for life!

'Kelsie Summers and I are not meant to be together. That's the end of it.' He stood up. 'I'm going to the bar.'

'Well, I'm going to lunch!'

'I hope you enjoy your brunch, Grandmother,' he said very calmly and quietly. 'I'm afraid I won't be joining you either.'

Kelsie picked at her brunch with a very nice lady who was recovering from cancer and had become a naturopath.

She talked to Heath, the waiter, who had also been born in Sydney, like she had, and a lovely couple who had saved for five years to enjoy the journey on their tenth wedding anniversary. Max must have loved them.

She struggled through fluffy eggs with Scottish salmon, lobster with truffle sauce and a small slice of white Christmas cake with VSOE chocolates on the side.

Oh, my goodness, she thought as she placed her hand

protectively over her stomach and put down her sil-
verware.

It wasn't gluttony, it was diversion from not look-
ing through into the next cabin where she could see the
back of Winsome's head. Or not searching for the dark
one that would be close by.

She was starting to dislike all food. Finally it was
time to return to her own compartment and pack the
last of her belongings into her shoulder bag before they
arrived in Calais.

As she glanced around her snug little cabin she never
would have believed she would be wishing this journey
to end, but that was how she felt. And it was all Con-
nor Black's fault.

Finally the train arrived and it was time to transfer
from the gorgeous Orient Express, bursting with tra-
dition, opulence and dignified pride, to a coach! How
unglamorous was that?

Half a dozen VIP coaches were lined up waiting for
them and at the bottom of each set of steps a busy, blue-
suited VSOE hostess carried a clipboard and checked
off names.

When Kelsie cast a lingering glance back at her pre-
vious transport Wolfgang was there lined up in front of
the last carriage with the other staff, posing for pictures.

There was Max, looking very distinguished, and the
head chef with his towering white chef's hat, and the
maître d', black-suited and standing very straight, and
Heath the waiter looking a little pink in the cheeks at
all the attention, as passengers took photos of the staff.

Kelsie had to smile when she saw Winsome thrust

her camera into 'that man's' hands and hurry forward for a photo of her with the official entourage as she squeezed in between Wilhelm and Max. Then she remembered the older lady had said it was her last trip.

Symbolically the end of an era for Winsome—though hopefully it was the beginning of a new spring with her time with Max.

For Kelsie it was just the end of a train journey. She turned away.

Connor took the snap of his gran, and had to smile at her waving him on to take another. It was a good thing he didn't have time to see which coach Kelsie was boarding. As he put the camera down his grandmother came up, beaming, beside him. At least they were coming to the end of this awful train journey where he'd just complicated the blazes out of his life, but despite everything he was truly glad to have seen his grandmother so happy.

His phone vibrated in his pocket and he frowned. Unexpected phone calls rarely heralded good news. 'Excuse me,' he said to Winsome, and answered. Listened. 'I'll ring you back,' he said, and ended the call.

'Gran?'

Winsome gazed around like a kid in a lolly shop, soaking in the moment, a brightness to her eyes that could have been excitement or maybe the shine of tears, and reluctantly she drew her attention back to him.

'I need to head straight to London as quickly as possible for the patients I told you about. The mother is bleeding and they'd like me to be there. Would you be all right if I left now and had you met at Victoria?'

He saw her blink and focus more fully on him. 'Now?'

'They're sending a helicopter for me.'

She frowned. 'Don't like helicopters. I'll take the train.' She glanced at him coyly. 'I can always find Kelsie and sit with her.'

Internal wince. 'Or Lady Geraldine. She'd love your company.' He resisted the impulse to warn her to stay away from Kelsie. But it would only encourage her. 'Would you like me to find Lady G. and Charlotte?'

'No. No. I'll be fine.'

'You're sure?' He looked at her. Her cheeks were overbright and yet the rest of her face was a little pale. It had been a huge twenty-four hours and she'd had a fair intake of food—and wine! Maybe he shouldn't go?

'Go,' she shooed him. 'Go to that poor woman. I'll be fine. I've been fine for eighty years without you hovering at my elbow. I'll be fine for the next six hours.'

He redialled the number but the whole time he waited for a connection he studied Winsome. She didn't seem to be flagging. Lord, the woman had more energy than he did.

Harry Wilson picked up.

'That's fine. If you send the helicopter I'll come now.'

Gran would be fine. He'd ask Max to find a hostess to watch out for her and arrange for someone to meet her at Victoria. And Nick, Charlotte's fiancé, was a doctor so at least there was medical help on the train if needed.

The Wilsons were his last patients with a baby due this year. His next wasn't due till February. So he could stay longer with Gran afterwards to make up for this.

He spoke to Wolfgang, who nodded, and his bag was identified and handed over and he was directed to a far corner of the car park where a large orange cross was painted on the bitumen.

Apparently it wasn't unusual for passengers to skip the Channel crossing and take a helicopter to London from here.

He didn't have to wait long before the beat of helicopter rotors could be heard, which only increased his respect for Harry Wilson's business arm.

As long as Winsome was okay, this had worked out well. He was glad to get away.

After he'd watched his grandmother helped aboard one of the big silver coaches he'd refused to look for any other people he might know. Specifically one who had labelled him a controlling sexist. No wonder she hadn't married him if she thought that. All he'd ever wanted to do was look after her. What was so heinous about that?

The helicopter drew closer and he cast a last glance across to the coaches. Which one was she on?

No! He was glad he could remove himself from the temptation to do something as monumentally stupid as he'd done all those years ago. It was a good thing.

Ten minutes later, as the helicopter took off he couldn't help but glance down. The train looked like a toy. As did the coaches as they began to pull out of the car park. He glanced ahead and the sky was grey and featureless. Not unlike his life stretching out before him.

CHAPTER TWELVE

KELSIE TURNED AWAY, brushed away the regret that she'd probably never see any of these people again, and made darned sure she was on a different coach from the Blacks. It was time to move on.

There was a brief hold-up, their hostess informed them all, while a helicopter took one of the passengers away.

Kelsie settled into her seat and glanced out the window as she waited to see what would transpire in the crossing. She watched a helicopter take off and wished she could get on her plane now and head back home.

She hadn't been sure what to expect of the next hour but it hadn't been coach travel and three border controls as well as immigration control, where they all needed to actually get out of the coaches, troop through the customs and immigration, and have their passports stamped.

It became less glamorous by the second as once everyone was back on board their driver navigated the maze of transit lanes and down into a train shell that encapsulated their coach for the trip under the Channel.

Kelsie felt a tiny twinge of claustrophobia as their

compartment was sealed and the coach engine switched off.

The hostess had handed out bottles of cold water and then picked up the microphone. 'All lights and air will be shut down now and just letting you know it can get hot if there are delays.'

There were groans from the occupants and she hastened on. 'Usually it only takes about thirty-five minutes once we've started.'

'But we haven't started yet,' the coach driver said cheerfully. Then proceeded to share. 'We'll be in the tunnel, which is about forty metres under the Channel. Coaches and vans travel in one type of railway carrier and cars have a double-decker carrier, while lorries have carriers with open sides.' He looked up into the rear-view mirror so he could watch the faces. 'And there is an emergency tunnel running parallel to our tunnel in case of fire.'

Kelsie shuddered and decided she'd fly across if she ever came to France again.

Half an hour later, without drama of any kind, they popped out the other end into the English countryside, and she even spotted the famous white horse of Dover on the hillside as their coach zipped them towards Folkestone.

When they pulled up in the station, despite the English sleet a brass band jazzed them onto their new train and the mood, flattened by the officialdom and dimness of the tunnel, lifted again as the hostesses pointed out a printed list on the station wall that allocated their carriage by name.

Kelsie was destined for 'Audrey', and she could see the white dining cars laden with crockery as she spotted the beautiful Pullman carriage that would carry her to London—on her own. Peacefully. Without Connor Black.

Except that Winsome found her. At least there was no Connor cruising along behind her, though she couldn't help a glance back to see if he was there.

'May I join you? I'm all alone. Connor was called away.' Winsome was puffing a little and Kelsie thought she looked a little pale. 'And I haven't got your address. Or given you mine.'

There'd been a reason for that. Then the end of the sentence clicked in. She blinked. 'Called away? From the station?'

'No. From Calais. In the helicopter. One of his patients may have gone into labour.'

'Oh?' Kelsie would have taken more notice if she'd known it had been Connor soaring off. She didn't envy him the crossing in this weather. Served him right. Black widow indeed.

'Apparently his patient rang him very early this morning and after brunch, so he thought he might need to go. It wasn't too much of a shock when he abandoned me.'

He'd abandoned me, too, Kelsie thought, or maybe I abandoned him? But she didn't say it. At least he'd told his grandmother he was going, but, then, his gran had probably been nicer to him than she'd been.

Later, when she had time to think clearly, she would have to consider whether that had been a factor in him

leaving her cabin so precipitously. Maybe even why he'd left? She needed to think hard about that. But Winsome was looking at her hopefully.

What was she thinking? Winsome was all alone. 'I'm sorry. You poor thing. I'd love you to join me. I was feeling quite sad that I might not see you again,' Kelsie said with a smile.

Winsome settled down opposite Kelsie in the big plush seat and they both gazed at the silver '1927' plate above the doorway.

'You haven't got rid of me yet.' It was said quietly and Kelsie wasn't even sure if she was supposed to have heard, and she chewed her lip as she tried not to laugh.

'I love these carriages,' Winsome said in a louder voice. 'The way they've created scenery in the wood. Look at that castle there. All made out of slivers of different-coloured wood.'

Kelsie pointed. 'You've got an island and palm trees above your head, there. Just under the luggage rack.' Winsome craned her neck and Kelsie hoped she didn't strain her back as the older lady bounced around in the seat to look at all the murals made of wood.

A tall, ridiculously handsome waiter in formal white tails trimmed with gold braid bowed, imparted his name as Samuel, and offered them a glass of champagne.

Surprisingly, even Winsome declined more bubbly, but nodded vigorously when he suggested tea.

Along came the silver teapots, sandwiches, caviar and quail eggs, pikelets and the inevitable scones and clotted cream. When the trolley with pastries and cakes

was offered, Kelsie could see that nearly everyone shook their heads and declined. She didn't blame them.

She was learning to taste the array of food only. Neither of them had spoken for the last five minutes and Kelsie felt obliged to open conversation. 'Connor missed another lovely meal.'

The quail-egg wafer stopped halfway to Winsome's mouth and landed back down on her plate as if she'd been waiting for just such an opportunity. 'I want to talk to you about Connor. Do you mind?'

Kelsie bit back a laugh. As if I could stop you, she thought, but it was a poor choice of topic, Kelsie admonished herself. 'Why should I mind?'

'How much do you know about Connor's childhood?'

Actually, he'd always been more interested in her childhood but she knew a little. 'That he lost his mother at a young age and he didn't get on well with his stepmother.'

Winsome was nodding. 'Both true. You know he was there when his mother died. Did he tell you that?'

Kelsie felt cold all over. 'No. Just that she'd drowned when he was twelve.'

Winsome looked sadly surprised. 'I thought he might have told you more. He changed from a happy-go-lucky boy to a serious young man that day.' She sighed. 'All of us changed.'

Winsome shook her head with regret. 'He told me once it was his fault. That he should have told her to come back. Shouted it out. It's funny how youngsters can blame themselves for something they have no control over.'

Winsome gazed into the distant past. 'I always blamed his father but really it was my daughter's fault. She was headstrong. Impulsive. She was always losing things. Took after me in the way she'd misplace things like her handbag, her purse, keys—it used to drive Connor's father mad but she'd just sail on serenely.

'The day she died she'd lost her engagement ring in a rock pool, and she left Connor on the beach, even though the tide was coming in.'

Winsome sighed. 'A freak wave came, she hit her head badly, and it didn't end well.'

Kelsie remembered the serious young man who'd been the Connor she'd known. How good she'd always felt when she'd made him laugh. How good he'd said he felt when he cared for her. 'He was always going to be a doctor.'

Winsome sighed again and looked at Kelsie. 'I think he felt at some deep level it was his life's work to care for the people he loved from that day on.' She smiled softly. 'Caring for people. He has been there every inch of the way since my husband died. I was ready to curl up and die then but Connor made me sit up and believe I still had a life to live. That's not a bad trait to have.'

'So the loss of his mother is what made him so controlling.'

'Controlling?' Winsome's head came up. 'He's not controlling, not in a negative way.' She laughed. 'He cares. Worries. Gives in all the time to me, but he worries all the same, and, yes, sometimes I humour that and allow him to boss me around a little. But that's not controlling. He doesn't do it for his own gratification.'

The old lady looked concerned. 'He might have seemed that way to you,' she continued. 'You probably did need time to spread your wings before marriage and luckily you were tough enough to take it. Sometimes you just have to trust your instincts.'

She shrugged. 'And it hasn't all been bad for Connor. He loves his work. Has made a difference to so many couples. And, yes, with the work he does now, he does have to weigh risks and make decisions so he can help a woman come to a viable pregnancy, and he's used to organising things.'

The faded blue eyes looked directly at Kelsie. 'But Connor's nowhere near controlling. What on earth made you think that?'

'My father was a very domineering man. Worse when he drank. My mother left him, one Christmas, when I was fourteen. She died not long after and I never saw her again.' She looked out the window where lonely countryside stretched away into the distance. 'I vowed I would never let someone run my life again. Or ruin it.'

Winsome shook her head. 'No wonder you weren't sure you were doing the right thing, getting married, if your home was unhappy.'

Then her eyes focused on Kelsie and her voice didn't waver. 'But Connor is a world away from how you say your father was. I think it would be quite normal to have trust issues after that.'

Was that true? Was that a big part of the reason she'd run that day? She'd thought about it a lot since then. Had she been scared to love because of her parents' bad marriage? 'It's probably why I've never really been into

Christmas since then, though Connor bought me a little tree once.' She thought about that and couldn't help but smile. 'It was very cute.'

Winsome studied her with sympathy. 'That's the sort of thing Connor does.' But she frowned as she thought it through. 'So you left Connor all those years ago because you thought he was like your father?'

Had she? 'I guess a few things were said when I left home that started me thinking. It seemed to fit into a few thoughts I'd already had about wishing I could just run my own life for a change. But blaming Connor doesn't seem quite as logical when I look at it now.'

Did it mean that Connor had never been the reason she'd run away? Was that how it had been? Was that why she'd still not found a man she was comfortable to share her life with? Or was it because she'd been waiting for the magic she'd experienced with Connor? She didn't want to consider that she'd blown it with him for a second time.

Winsome was gazing off into the distance. 'A good marriage is worth waiting for.'

Kelsie thought about the man Connor had become, how wonderful he'd been with Anna and her baby, his sense of humour, his sincere affection for his grandmother, the way he'd held her when she'd let him.

Then she thought about the way he'd organised her in the run-up to their wedding that had never happened. What if none of it had been his way of controlling her but all so it would be easier for her? And she'd balked and panicked unnecessarily when she'd let him down.

She thought about the last twenty-four hours, how

they had been able to talk and connect when they hadn't been fighting over silly things, how he'd made her laugh.

Winsome had reached the point of her story and Kelsie came back to the present. There was new determination in his grandmother's voice. 'He needs a life partner to give him balance.'

Didn't we all? But Kelsie wasn't going there. 'I hope he finds one.' She had such a lot to think about before they arrived.

Winsome didn't look at all put out by her noncommittal answer. In fact, she looked like the mischievous older lady from Venice all those hours ago. 'Oh, I think he will.'

Connor was having a day from hell.

His flight across the Channel had been horrendous, with turbulent wind gusts and heavy sleet, and he decided he hated helicopters almost as much as trains.

Plus he'd been unsure if he had done the right thing by his grandmother or by Kelsie, but at least they'd been on the ground. Safe in the damn train.

It hadn't actually snowed on the flight but it had been falling heavily on the wild drive to the hospital.

Connie Wilson's labour was being stubborn. Stuck in the on-off contraction phase that robbed the mother of sleep. Her uterus contracted irregularly and inconsistently in strength, and therefore she wasn't any closer to actual birth but a lot closer to exhaustion. It was a pattern of an hour of contractions, none for two hours, three hours of contractions, and then none.

Connie and Harry were physically and emotionally exhausted and stressed and he felt bad that he hadn't been there earlier to allay their fears.

'Latent phase of labour is unpredictable,' he explained for the third time in a quiet voice. 'It's much more difficult to look at this slow start as a natural progression, especially when you have gone through so many medical procedures to finally get to this stage.'

He crouched down beside Connie and looked into her frightened eyes. 'It is normal, though.' He didn't say it could go on like this for days.

Connie smiled damply. 'I know. They told us in prenatal classes. And again when we arrived here this morning. But I guess I needed to hear it from you. Thank you for coming. I do appreciate it.'

She shrugged. 'Maybe I don't have the faith in my body that I should have but it has let me down. We couldn't fall pregnant without help and I just worry I won't be able to give birth to our baby without help.'

He understood that. Wished he could do more. 'That's perfectly understandable but I believe in your body's ability to do this. And you can take comfort that it's a very common mindset from parents who have gone through assisted reproduction, like you have.'

She sighed. 'And you have kept telling me I'm not sick or a patient.'

Connor looked at the worried father. 'That's because everything is normal. The baby's monitoring has shown lots of reserves yet, but as her mum you need a good sleep.'

At least Connie was listening but he could feel the

tension vibrating from Harry and he'd bet Kelsie would say it wasn't helping Connie's body to relax when they all knew her husband was desperately impatient to see their baby and his wife safely at the end of this pregnancy from hell.

'Exactly!' Harry pounced on the opportunity to have input. 'She needs sleep. So let's do something about it. Can't we finish this business with a Caesarean?' Connor could see the anxiety he was feeling because of the cumulative stresses of many miscarriages—and here they were so close to having all their dreams come true.

And he was probably on the defensive for his wife whom he couldn't help, either physically by taking her pains or with his usual mental ability to solve problems. For a man used to running his multinational business and dealing with problems immediately, he looked like he was having a hard time being utterly powerless for once.

Connor could sympathise but he wasn't going to rush into a Caesarean just because Connie had prolonged early labour. This was his business and it was his job to make unemotional, yet correct decisions.

He didn't believe in unnecessary Caesareans because there were risks in every operation and these pregnancies were so hard to come by that statistically he dealt in choosing the lesser risk. Normal birth was much less risky for mother and baby.

Connor ran his hands through his hair, unsure how to help until unexpectedly the image of Kelsie, serene and confident, on the train came to him. He looked up

and caught both the worried parents' attention with his sudden smile.

Maybe it was time for a little midwifery magic. He just wished she was there to do it for him but he'd try his best.

'I believe Connie can and will do this by herself. When your baby is ready. You're doing amazingly well.' Connor recited Kelsie's words and the calm and positive way she'd said them. 'Both of you. Your baby is very determined, just like her dad and mum, but we have to wait for the labour to establish itself properly.' He pulled up a chair and sat down.

'Let me tell you a great story about what happened on the way over in the train.'

Connie's eyes grew wider as Connor explained about Anna's baby's decision to arrive between countries, in a train and feet first, and as he concluded his tale with how he'd seen them that morning before Paris and how well they'd both looked, Connie sighed back into the bed. He saw her search out her husband's eyes and nod.

'Maybe I could have one of those sleeping tablets we keep refusing and just have a rest. Wait for it to happen instead of being so determined it has to happen this minute. I do want a birth like that.'

Connor stood up. 'I want you to have a birth like that too.'

He smiled, could feel the tension dissipate in the room as they finally accepted a delay in their expectations. 'I can't promise you a train carriage but I can promise you a couple of hours' sleep.

'The good news is that a large percentage of women

do wake up in labour after a sedation at this point. So hopefully you'll be one of them.'

He looked at Harry. 'They have a desk you can use for work if you don't want to leave the building, but I do think you should leave Connie to rest when she gets the sedation. She could text you when she wakes up.'

Harry looked at his wife. 'Is that okay with you, Con?'

She nodded. 'I am very tired.'

'Let's get this sorted, then.' Connor glanced at his watch. The train wasn't due into Victoria for another two hours.

If Connie went into labour he'd have to arrange for someone else to meet Winsome. He'd set that up just in case. In the back of his mind he still had all his balls in the air. He knew where Kelsie was heading tonight and he still had time to talk to her before she left.

Back in the Pullman carriages, rattling towards London, Kelsie and Winsome had passed the towers and keeps of the English countryside during the meal, leaving behind the manors and ploughed paddocks of the country towns.

Passengers were dozing in their seats, replete or even having over-indulged, and the waiters had begun clearing the tables as they began to pass through more suburban areas.

Soon they would arrive at Victoria and Winsome had settled back in her seat with her eyes closed.

Kelsie was wondering if Connor had arrived in time to be there for his client's birth. She knew how scared

fertility-challenged parents could become. She'd had a recent client of her own who'd had IVF and had been an absolute mess prior to labour.

Shelby had had so many pre-conception visits, so much intense screening and medication to achieve conception, and then such a tense time dreading a miscarriage until the first three months had passed, that when her IVF clinic had sent her back to her old hospital as a now low-risk patient, she hadn't been used to being left to progress naturally.

Kelsie had coached Shelby and her husband in the prenatal classes, a weekend course, and the improvement in Shelby's self-confidence and positive birth outlook had been miraculous. She wondered if they had such classes in the UK and suddenly it was something she wanted to talk to Connor about.

Anyway, she didn't need to go there. She'd be flying back to Australia very soon. Shelby and her husband had had a gorgeous birth not long before Kelsie had come away. When she got home she looked forward to visiting that little family.

Home. Her comfy flat. Her friends. It was ridiculous to think she wouldn't settle back into it all easily just because she'd met up with an old boyfriend. One who might even be keen for her to stay around.

Who was she kidding? Not just met.

Slept with.

Actually, they hadn't slept. They'd made incredible, amazing, mind-blowing love. She'd glimpsed a world she hadn't really believed existed before.

Seen that Connor held a part of her that nobody else

would ever touch. And then they'd bickered their way back to being strangers. How had that happened?

You couldn't just forget that sort of encounter. But that was what she'd have to do or risk driving herself mad.

She looked across at Connor's grandmother, and noticed Winsome rub her chest and frown as her eyes flicked open. In fact, she did look a little pale and not at all happy.

'Are you all right?' Kelsie asked softly.

'I might just have a wee nap. Wake me when we get there.'

Kelsie narrowed her eyes and studied Winsome as she closed her eyes. The older lady's cheeks were white and the tiny frown on her forehead made the soft wrinkles there pucker more than usual.

'Are you in pain?' Kelsie didn't know whether to bother her or not.

Pale blue eyes fluttered open again, accompanied by a rueful smile as she rubbed her chest. 'I'm a bit sore in the chest. Probably from overeating but it's starting to bother me. I thought a wee nap might help.'

'Have you had it before?' Kelsie stood up and leaned over the older lady's chair. 'Let me check your pulse.' She took Winsome's wrist in her fingers and felt for the pulse under the soft skin. There it was. Bounding along a little faster than she would have expected.

'Sometimes I get reflux.' She glanced around at the quiet carriage and grimaced with embarrassment.

Kelsie regarded her shrewdly. 'And does this feel like that?'

Winsome began to look extremely miserable. 'It's getting worse.' Big eyes looked mournfully at Kelsie. 'My husband died of a sudden heart attack, you know. I can't help thinking of that, even though I'm sure it's not anything like that. I just wish Connor hadn't left.'

Kelsie squeezed Winsome's hand. 'We're almost at Victoria and we'll get you to a doctor.'

Winsome bit her lip to stop the quiver. 'I want Connor.'

Kelsie's heart squeezed. 'I know. You'll be fine. I'll stay with you until we find him again.'

One large tear rolled down Winsome's cheek and Kelsie clasped her hand. 'I'll find Connor for you.'

She pushed the service button and while she waited she thought about the food and alcohol offered over the last thirty-six hours and how Winsome had been magnificent in her capacity.

It could just be gastrooesophageal reflux. Her skin chilled. Or it could be cardiac chest pain. She didn't want to think that but she needed to get someone to see Winsome before Connor's grandmother did something Kelsie couldn't handle by herself.

Where was Connor when they needed him? She'd be very happy for him to take control now. He should not have left his grandmother alone. And she'd tell him so. For some strange reason she felt calmer after that decision, and not just because it meant she would see him at least one more time.

She looked back at her patient. 'If you were ever going to get indigestion, I imagine this would be a popular time.' She glanced around the cabin and saw most

of the patrons had their eyes shut. 'What do you usually take when you get that?'

'My antacid tablets. I forgot to take the prescription one this morning. But they're in the luggage compartment.' She glanced around as if searching. 'I wish Connor was here.'

Kelsie nodded. She did too, and moved back to her seat and reached up to the ornate silver luggage rack and pulled down her tote. In her bag she had some lozenges so she dug around until she found them.

'How about you take one of my little over-the-counter antacid tablets?' She glanced into her bag again. 'And two of my travel aspirins, which would be about half a normal dose of aspirin. That will cover both bases while we wait for help.' Aspirin was always a good first-aid suggestion with cardiac pain or clots. They had done a lot of sitting and maybe Winsome was in more danger than she thought.

Samuel, the steward, appeared at her elbow and Kelsie turned to him with relief. 'Mrs Black has chest pain. How long until we arrive in London?'

Samuel looked instantly concerned and frowned over Winsome's increasing pallor. He spoke quietly, for Kelsie's hearing only. 'About ten minutes. I can arrange for an ambulance to meet us, if you wish?'

Kelsie nodded just as Winsome whimpered and rubbed her chest again. 'Do you feel breathless?'

'Just with the pain.' She sounded more frail than Kelsie expected and her concern climbed. 'It's difficult to breathe deeply. I just want Connor.' Her voice faded away and she closed her eyes.

Kelsie's heart settled a little at that. Cardiac chest pain shouldn't get worse with inhalation, which made it more likely to be another cause. But it still needed checking. She looked at Samuel then back at Winsome. 'We'll have that ambulance, thanks.'

It seemed to take for ever for the train to pull into the station.

The loudspeaker boomed as they came to a stop. 'Would all passengers please remain seated for the first five minutes while we transfer an ill passenger off the train. Your luggage will be waiting for you once they have been transferred. Thank you.'

Kelsie followed the ambulance officers, who had fireman-lifted Winsome out of the carriage onto the bench seat of another small luggage train, and Kelsie followed onto the platform and the organised chaos of Victoria Station. A row of luggage trolleys laden with Christmas goodies from Europe had arrived and the porters were lining bags up in neat rows for identification and retrieval.

Kelsie saw her suitcase, which towered over the others, almost waving at her, and she grimaced at that problem for later. Winsome first.

They trundled through to a side entrance, where an ambulance waited.

She glanced back into the crowded station. Could she accompany Winsome?

She knew she wanted to but a glance inside the small emergency vehicle didn't seem to suggest a lot of room and she doubted they'd let her. That was when she realised the snow was melting on her hair and face. Land-

ing quite heavily on her and the snaking line of people at the cab rank.

It would be hell to catch a cab in this on Christmas Eve but she'd feel she'd let Winsome down if she abandoned her to strangers.

A young woman appeared at her elbow. 'I'm to meet Mrs Winsome Black. Was that who was just lifted into that ambulance?'

The young woman was dressed from head to foot in black suede, very chic, but Kelsie decided she looked almost like a seal. Even the scarf threaded around her neck was suede to match the cap she wore over her hair.

But seal or not, Kelsie pounced on her with relief. 'Yes. She has chest pain. Do you have contact with Dr Black?'

The girl's eyes widened in distress. 'I can get a message to him.' The girl scrolled through her contact list. 'I've already arranged with a porter to have her luggage collected.' The young woman looked up enquiringly. 'And you are?'

Kelsie blinked, calmed a little now that Winsome was in good hands, and replayed the girl's words in her head. Well, who was she?

She glanced once into the ambulance but Winsome was being assessed by paramedics and perhaps she wasn't needed now. She turned away. She almost said, 'No one important,' but before the words were out she was stopped by a familiar, if frail voice.

'She's with me.' Winsome's voice drifted from the rear of the ambulance and Kelsie had to turn and smile.

It seemed Winsome Black didn't miss anything—even when miserably unwell in the back of an ambulance.

Well, then. She'd better stay. 'I'm Mrs Black's companion until she's seen by Dr Black.' It was actually a huge relief because she would have worried all night that Connor hadn't managed to find his grandmother and that Winsome hadn't recovered with medical care.

'Please tell him that Kelsie has gone with her.' She saw the interest in the girl's eyes and ignored it. She'd suddenly seen a solution to another problem. 'There is a very large purple suitcase with a K. Summers nametag. Can you arrange for that to be collected, too, please? If possible, have it transferred to the Ritz. I'm booking in there later.'

The girl didn't seem fazed by the request and Kelsie supposed that Connor would hire efficient personnel. At least she wouldn't have to wrestle with her bag and if she lost it then it wasn't a life-or-death matter. Possibly unlike Winsome—until she could be sure.

She'd phone the hotel from the hospital when she knew Winsome was okay.

The paramedic tapped her on the shoulder. 'Excuse me, miss. Would you please reassure Mrs Black that you're coming with us? She won't let us shut the doors. You can travel with the driver.'

Kelsie's distraction evaporated. The most important person here was Winsome. 'Of course.' When she peered in past the folded doors her new friend's eyes were huge with fear and she leant in and clasped her hand. 'I'm here. I'll be in the front and I'll find Connor.'

'Tell them to take me to St Douglas's Private Hospital.'

Kelsie looked at the men. 'Can you do that?' It wouldn't work like that in Australia.

The paramedic nodded. 'The main hospitals are very busy and it would be quicker than through their emergency department anyway.'

CHAPTER THIRTEEN

At the same time, to Connor's relief, Connie Wilson woke up in strong labour and as far as her pregnancy went, the waiting was almost over. Thanks to all the stop-start contractions her labour progressed rapidly through first stage, and if he didn't get to meet the train he couldn't complain because he would meet the new baby Wilson and be there for her parents.

The room was quiet, peaceful, and Connor stood, apparently relaxed, at the end of the bed, waiting. It was always the same and the tension never left him until the baby was safe in its mother's arms but neither his patients nor staff ever guessed that.

'I love you,' Connor heard Harry Wilson whisper to his wife, raw emotion thick in his voice, and for one fractured second Connor felt a sudden surge of loss so great he actually flinched. Why didn't he have the chance to share this moment with the woman he had always loved?

But he pulled his thoughts back to the moment. He'd tried and failed and unless he did something soon, she'd be gone from his life once again.

When he glanced back at Harry the man's eyes were

suspiciously bright as they darted nervously to Connor and then back at his wife. But Connie was elsewhere, concentrating in her own world, as she strained to ease her baby down the birth canal.

There was a little while to go but the end was drawing closer and then everyone could relax.

A senior midwife appeared around the curtain and crossed to whisper in Connor's ear. 'You have a phone call at the desk.'

If it had been anyone less unflappable he would have glared a refusal but the midwife in charge was no fool. So what could be this important? 'Can you tell them I'll ring back?'

'It's about your grandmother. Apparently she's been admitted downstairs with chest pain.'

He closed his eyes. Looked back at Harry and Connie. Estimated the amount of time he had before the birth. There was no sign of the baby yet, Connie had just started pushing, but would it upset them if he left, even for a few minutes? The last thing he wanted was to stress Connie. But what if his gran was critically ill?

His grandmother had always been there for him and it was his responsibility to ensure she had the best care. It was his responsibility that everyone had the best care.

Unexpectedly Connie leaned up on her elbow and panted at him. Waved him away with her hand. 'For goodness' sake. Go and see if your gran is okay. We'll be here when you come back.' Connie waved him away again. 'Go. Hurry. I'm busy.' And went back to pushing.

He stared at Connie in astonishment, shook his head with a smile and went. Swiftly. There was a junior mid-

wife standing at the lift, holding it for him, and he shot her a warm thank-you glance, then looked back over his shoulder at the senior midwife. She shooed him off, too. 'I'll page you when we get close.'

When the lift doors opened on the ground floor the first person he saw was Kelsie. His relief was enormous. He hadn't lost her yet. And she'd been with his gran in her time of need.

He allowed himself one brief, soul-enriching look and then scanned ahead. 'Where is she?'

'She's being assessed by the physician. She's okay, Connor. She was in a lot of pain but I think it's reflux, though they're ruling out cardiac or a clot. She demanded they bring her here.'

'She's a fighter,' he reassured himself more than Kelsie. Then glanced back at the lift. Kelsie had said hs grandmother was okay. Did he believe Kelsie? He should go back to the Wilsons. But he couldn't. 'I want to see her.'

'Of course you do. She wants to see you too.' Kelsie led the way. Knocked on a door and opened it on a room where a tall gangly man in a black suit stood beside the bed. Winsome looked pale, and very still, with her eyes closed.

'Ah. Connor.' The man put out his hand and Connor shook it briefly. 'I've given her something for the pain and she's a bit drowsy now. We're about to run an ECG to check her heart, and then we'll scan her, but I hear she's been on that train, living the high life again.'

'My fault. I went with her this time.' He stepped closer to the bed. Picked up his grandmother's hand

and squeezed it between both of his. Her eyelids fluttered and she smiled drowsily up at him.

He pretended to frown at her. 'You said you'd managed for eighty years without me.'

'I'll be fine. Soon.' Her eyes closed again.

She looked so pale, he thought. 'What about her bloods?'

'We're waiting for results. But she's tough. Given herself a scare, though.'

His heart squeezed with the dilemma of staying or leaving to go back upstairs. 'She's given me one as well.'

'She'll be fine with rest. I'll keep her in overnight.' The doctor's pager bleeped and he excused himself. Connor took a step to pick up the clinical notes when his own name was paged over the loudspeaker.

'Would Dr Black please go to Maternity immediately.'

He glanced up at the speaker. Torn. 'It's Connie's baby.'

Kelsie watched his indecision with a surge of empathy. Poor Connor. The struggle. He wanted to do everything. This was the Connor she knew. Bless him. All of it was good. 'You can't do everyone's jobs. Or save everyone. You go and do yours. I'll stay here until you get back.'

'She's the closest thing I've had to a mother for so many years. I love her. I don't want to let her down.'

Kelsie understood that. She understood a lot of things now. 'You couldn't let her down. Your grandmother is in good hands. The doctor is great. Go. I'll be here.'

He nodded. He trusted Kelsie to stay with her until he could return.

'You're right.' Unexpectedly, he paused and searched her face, said, 'I would have been there for you, you know,' before he dropped a swift kiss on her lips and spun away.

She heard his voice again as he disappeared. 'Hold that lift.'

Kelsie touched her lips with her fingers. He would have been where for her? She could still feel the imprint of Connor's mouth on hers.

She didn't understand his comment but wished she'd kissed him back, one last time, then hugged the feeling that he had trusted her with the most important person in his life. Anything else was too complicated to think about.

An hour later Connor was back. 'Baby Wilson has arrived!' There was immense satisfaction as well as quiet relief in his voice and Kelsie smiled.

'A bouncing baby girl who's taken to the outside world with a calm acceptance that's left her besotted parents very happy.'

She loved it that he glowed with relief. He was a very good man. 'I'm so glad you were there for them.'

He grinned at her. Almost buckled her knees with the power of it. 'Me too. Thank you for staying here so I didn't have to worry about Gran.'

'My pleasure.' She'd been glad she could help him but it was over now. Everything was over and she should go. They didn't need her any more. 'Dr Miles has been

back. Your grandmother's tests have all come back negative, as well as the positive result from the medication treating her reflux. So it all points to that being the cause.'

She pinned a bright smile on her face, even though she was suddenly feeling very flat for no reason at all. Which should have been bizarre with this handsome man smiling at her like she was the embodiment of Christmas. 'So everything has turned out well.'

Except now she needed to leave. 'And I have to get to my hotel. Now that you're back. Check my bag made it.'

His smile dimmed. 'I'll take you.'

She smiled, realising she couldn't help the swift lift in her spirits and that in itself frightened her. Very much. No. It was better to make the break now. Stop dragging out this painful feeling of loss. Leave Connor with his gran in private.

Though the reasoning was hard to pin down right at this second as she looked at Connor. She wanted to hug him and share his relief that his gran would be fine. All she knew was that this goodbye hurt. 'Don't worry about it. I can catch a cab.'

The humour had faded from his face. 'I said I'll take you.'

He couldn't leave the hospital and they both knew it. 'What about your grandmother?'

'Max will be here in a minute. We'll go as soon as he arrives. She'll sleep for a couple of hours yet and Max will stay with her.'

She shook her head. 'I'll catch a cab.'

'Not on Christmas Eve you can't.' Connor could feel

his frustration building. Why couldn't she at least let him do this for her?

Would this roller-coaster day never end? So much had happened and he didn't want her to leave until they'd had a chance to talk.

She was backing away towards the door and he followed her. Glanced once over his shoulder at his sleeping grandmother and decided this was better dealt with outside in the corridor than in a sick room.

'Goodbye, Connor. Give my love to your grandmother when she wakes up.'

What was she doing? Had he got it so badly wrong? Didn't the way they'd made love mean anything to her?

He suspected it had and they needed to talk about it. It shouldn't be rushed but she'd be out of here in seconds. Like she was afraid of him.

Connor fought to hang onto his feeling of impending doom. He wanted to ask her to stay. Give what they had a chance. But she was going. Leaning towards the exit as she waited for him to return her goodbye.

Tomorrow she'd be gone from the country. And he hadn't had enough time to know if they were right together or still so very, very wrong.

Though even in the brief time since they'd parted he had more faith in his own feelings for her than he had in Kelsie's for him—and damn right he was scared that she'd leave him at the last minute if he opened himself up to loving her again. What if he never recovered?

He ran his hands through his hair. She was the only woman, apart from his mother, whom he should have

told to come back, who'd torn his heart. Should he risk it all yet again, and ask her to stay?

He glanced up and down the deserted corridor but nobody was in sight.

For a moment he wished he'd never got on that damn train and met her again. 'Stop, Kelsie.'

She paused, turned back to him.

It was now or never and he couldn't bear the thought of never. 'I gave you my heart once before and you walked away from me. Unlike my mother, you didn't give me the chance to say come back, so I'm doing it now. I want you to stay.' But he was terrified he was going to lose at the last minute again.

It hadn't been the most romantic declaration. He couldn't believe what this woman did to him. How insane this entire crazy day had been. How desperate he suddenly felt. He couldn't believe he'd mentioned his mother. His loss. That he'd admitted he would be the one hurt if it didn't work out—so much for not putting himself out there again.

She shook her head. 'I can't. We're the same as we always were. On different sides of the world. But it was wonderful seeing you, Connor. Goodbye.'

So she'd missed the whole point. Though he had to admit it wasn't surprising seeing as his declaration had been so garbled. But he didn't believe distance would keep them apart.

Kelsie had no idea what she was saying. She was desperate to get away before she burst into tears. Her brain was all fogged again with the emotion this guy could stir up in her. Not all of it was good emotion be-

cause if she admitted she was wrong now then maybe she'd been wrong fifteen years ago and she'd been responsible for all that wasted time. It didn't bear thinking about. Not at this moment anyway.

She watched him run his hand through his hair. He did that a lot when he was stressed. And she had caused him this stress and she was sorry for that.

He was saying, 'Please. Let me take you to your hotel and we can talk. You said you're not leaving until tomorrow. And you don't even have to go then. Stay and have a drink with me.'

Almost with relief she seized on the argument her brain would listen to. Nothing had changed with him. This was why she'd run away from him before. He didn't listen when she said she needed her own space.

She took a couple of deep breaths. His face was serious. Determined, yet there was a vulnerability about him she hadn't seen before. It was that that made her pause. They began to walk towards the lifts together, even though she hadn't agreed.

Then he spoiled it. 'Do you really have to fly back to Australia tomorrow?'

Her voice quieted as a nurse approached. 'I have to. I have a ticket. And I start work in seven days. My patients need me.'

He frowned. Shook his head. 'Can't you delay your flights?' He pushed the lift call button with unnecessary force. 'Put them off!'

'Why?'

'I'm asking you to stay.'

'*I can't.*' Couldn't he understand she'd organised her life too?

'We need more time.'

And there it was again. *Give in, Kelsie. Do what I want.* She'd fought damn hard for her independence. Paid a huge price for it too, including the loss of the man in front of her. Had worked hard for respect in her profession. For the trust of the women she cared for. She'd like to see him fly away from his patients for her. He obviously didn't care about the women she'd looked after during their whole pregnancies. 'No, Connor. I won't do that.'

'I see.' No expression. How did he do that?

She wanted to stamp her feet and scream at him.

He stopped and in that same expressionless voice, 'Then I'm sorry I pushed you to stay.'

'Have a good Christmas, Connor. Give my love to your grandmother. I'll get my own cab.'

He sighed heavily and turned away and she couldn't help but wonder if her damned independence was worth the loss of this man—again.

Connor woke on Christmas morning and he'd never felt so alone. With sudden clarity he knew he didn't want to wake and feel like this ever again.

It wasn't too late. She hadn't flown home yet. He just needed a chance to tell her he would come to her in Australia as soon as he could.

He hadn't really expected her to cancel her flights. They'd discussed that, he thought with a wry smile. When he'd panicked and pressured her to suspend all

her flights and plans just because he'd said they should spend more time together. He couldn't say he blamed her for storming off.

But he wanted to explain more eloquently that he was now certain they were meant for each other. If he could just see her one more time he would let her know he'd wait for her.

That he'd fight for her.

To hell with it. He knew he was strong enough, determined enough to take that chance again or even as many times as it took. That risking everything for Kelsie's love would always be worth it—but he needed to stop rushing her. Let her come to that decision in her own way, in her own time.

Max had pulled some Orient Express Christmas Eve strings at his request and filled his special order so Kelsie would get his Christmas surprise before she left for the airport. There was a slim chance he'd have already missed her by the time he'd arranged his grandmother's discharge but he could deal with that.

Because once Gran was sorted he doubted he'd have much to do, and he could be on the next plane out to Australia, judging by the way Max had taken charge of Winsome since he'd arrived at the hospital last evening.

If he had missed her then, considering he and Kelsie had waited fifteen years to meet again, he could wait a few days more until he could arrange a flight. But he didn't want to wait.

Christmas Day and Kelsie woke to a blanket of snow outside the Ritz's windows. Her first white Christmas.

In a famous and luxurious hotel in a city she'd always wanted to visit. So why was her mood so black?

Ahh. She put her hand over her eyes. Not that word. Black.

Connor Black. It was too late now but she should have had that drink last night. Should have taken the chance that Connor was right. She missed him this morning.

Maybe there was still time to catch him before she flew out.

She scrabbled in her bag for the number of the hospital the nurse had given her and she dialled shakily.

The doctor had said Winsome would be able to go home early Christmas morning. But when she phoned the hospital they'd already left. Connor had picked her up already. The only good thing was that Winsome was now much more comfortable on the correct medication. Thank goodness it hadn't been her heart that was the trouble.

Kelsie wished she could say the same for her own heart. But she too would recover with the right treatment. Namely a flight as far away from London as possible and a whole lot of work, but first she had to get through the morning.

There was a knock at the door and she put the phone down as she glanced at the clock.

It was the arrival of breakfast, and when it was pushed in, it looked like a Christmas feast in miniature. A tiny, holly-decorated painted bowl of muesli, strawberries, honey yoghurt and steaming Earl Grey tea.

Under the silver dome was a tiny nativity scene, com-

plete with dozing animals, surrounded by curls of bacon and egg and French toast. It looked so cute she had to smile. Albeit a watery one. On the tray was a tiny, exquisitely wrapped box with a card and she smiled again as the waiter backed away.

He seemed to be waiting for her to open the card so she slid her finger under the seal and lifted the stiff folded paper out. She expected it to be from the hotel to go with the little unopened present.

Santa has been. There's something outside the door. Merry Christmas, Kelsie!

She looked up and as if he'd been waiting for her to read it the waiter stopped at the door.

'Someone has left you something outside your door, madam. Would you like me to bring it in?'

'Yes, please.'

It was a tiny carry-on suitcase, in gold, with a ribbon around it. She frowned as she circled it and then lifted it onto the bed to open. Inside lay a gorgeous little Christmas tree, sprinkled with gold and covered in tiny fibreoptic lights.

It looked suspiciously like the one from the Orient Express dining car. She guessed the suitcase was so she could fly it home. Why did that thought make her eyes sting and her throat close?

Was Connor here? Her heart leapt and she looked quickly up at the waiter. 'And the gentleman?'

The man shook his head mournfully. Obviously he was a romantic. 'There is no gentleman.'

She crossed to the dresser and plugged the little tree

in and watched it turn as the man left, quietly closing the door behind him. The tree spun and sparkled and shimmered like it had in the dining car where she and Connor had eaten together last night.

Tears stung her eyes but she blinked them away. Surely she'd done the right thing. And it was too late now anyway.

She turned back to the wrapped box on her breakfast tray and slowly unwrapped the stiff paper from the gift. Inside lay the silver charm bracelet from the Orient Express, complete with a tiny porter's hat like Wolfgang's, a miniature guard's whistle, a little train engine and a teddy bear.

There was a note.

I'm not asking you to stay. I'm asking if I can come and visit you in Australia as soon as I can arrange a flight.

'I think that would be wonderful,' she whispered to the empty room.

He was so much better at this than she was. She glanced at the phone again. One more try and she at least had the house number that Winsome had given her.

But that phone just rang unanswered too.

Time was running out and the airport waited. Maybe he would follow her to Australia, as he'd said. She could only hope so.

It took Kelsie two hours to get to the airport through the snow and as the cab driver dropped her off the radio

cheerfully informed them that flights had a two-hour delay due to the snow. Too long to wait. Too short to jump back into the cab and search for Connor.

'What you want to do, lady?'

She thought about the suitcase. 'Just drop me. I'll stay here until my flight opens.'

'You sure?'

'Yep.' She saw his shoulders lift and he pulled the car into the drop-off point. She paid him and the rat didn't get out of the car, just popped the boot so she'd have to lift her huge case out herself. Connor would never do that to her.

'Merry Christmas,' she said with her most winning smile, and he had the grace to look away. As she got out she heard his door open and he grumbled his way to the rear of the vehicle and heaved her bag onto the pavement for her.

'Good luck with getting that on the plane,' he said. Then he grinned, shook his head and wished her luck before he drove away.

Kelsie encouraged the wheels on her suitcase to ignore the snow, but they weren't listening so she tipped it on its side and dragged it, and her new little gold suitcase along with it, while the icy wind bit into her cheeks. It wasn't the only part of her that was cold.

Home would be humid. Christmas week would be sunshine and a hot wind. Sunburnt kids and ice-cream cake. Home would be great. But despite the promise of heat the words were only empty words as the wind continued to bite into her. Deeply. She'd blown it. Been a coward. But Connor had said he would come after her.

Inside the departure hall was chaotic. With the flight delays every available waiting space in the airport seemed to be filled with bodies and luggage.

And suddenly she knew. She didn't want to go. Didn't want to leave without seeing Connor one more time and telling him she loved him. He'd said he'd come to Australia but what if he never came? What if something happened to his grandmother and he couldn't come?

It was her own fault. She'd been a quitter. Waking up to Connor's gifts should have been the moment she grasped, not run away from. Should have jumped in a cab to him then and there.

And now it was too late. Her pride and her stupid independence had ruined it for her again. She turned around and dragged her suitcase towards the door but even that was difficult to traverse.

Then Kelsie saw Connor arrive and blinked. Or perhaps it was just someone she thought looked like him because she wanted him so badly.

No. It *was* him and she could feel a smile stretch right across her face. He must have been to her hotel. And the joy that had flooded her made no bones about the truth. She loved him. How could she have been so blind? It was as though for the very first time she could see who he really was. How wrong she'd been. Twice. She didn't deserve his love but she wanted it. All of it. She dragged her suitcases across the floor.

She should have known that loving Connor wouldn't take away her independence, it would bring out the best of herself. She'd so looked forward to travelling on the

Orient Express, but it seemed learning to love Connor
had been her true journey. If only he'd have her.

And here he was so it looked like he would have her.
The man was tenacious. Even now he was giving her
another chance when she'd been so determined to climb
on her high horse and fly off into the sunset. Fool. But
she was such a lucky fool.

She watched him cross the floor to her left. Striding
tall and straight and commanding. Connor, here, open-
ing himself up to the risk of being knocked down again.
She shook her head in wonder. He'd already been let
down by her so badly once before and she didn't think
she could ever be that brave.

Or maybe she could?

She saw him hesitate, glance around at the sea of
faces, and then he straightened and that determined
look she remembered from old crossed his face. His
eyes began to systematically scan the crowds. Look-
ing for her. She dropped the handles of her bags and
stepped forward towards him.

Connor felt a tap on his shoulder. 'Excuse me. Would
you like my seat, sir?'

He spun around and she was smiling at him. Sky-
blue eyes. Snub nose. That mouth. Here in the milling
crowds, looking up at him like she'd known he would
come.

Then she said something amazing. Something he'd
waited fifteen years to hear. 'It's not a seat I want to
give you.' She stepped into his arms. 'It's my heart. If
you'll have it.'

And there was love light shining from her beautiful

eyes. For him. He couldn't believe it. But he couldn't mistake it. She was lifting her face to his, waiting for his kiss. 'Merry Christmas, Connor.'

He gently touched his lips to hers. 'Merry Christmas, my love.' And he lifted her off the floor and spun her in his arms. 'I love you, you know. Always have. Always will.'

'I'm sorry, Connor. It was me who had the issues. I was scared of falling in love. Scared of losing my independence when I'd only just seen the possibilities. I put that on you. You never deserved it and I'm sorry.'

So many things made sense now. Even, perhaps, the man he was now. The way he'd organised everything when they had been younger. How he'd tried to think of everything. Kept her safe because he couldn't bear to lose her.

Connor looked down at her. Wonder and joy were bubbling inside him. 'We were both young. And I did organise you a lot. And when that blew up in my face I thought I could control my emotions and it wouldn't happen again. Until I saw you again and you had me back on the ropes.'

'You are the bravest man I know to take me on.'

He grinned. 'Not as brave as Max. For taking on Gran.'

She had to laugh at that. Then had a thought. 'You don't live with your gran, do you?'

'No. No way. I love her dearly but we'd kill each other.' He smiled. 'I have a flat near Tower Bridge. Scared, were you?'

'No. Just wondering if we had to live in England all

year round. The weather is very different from what I'm used to.'

'I'm sure I can think of ways to keep you warm. And Max and my grandmother will sort out their own lives.' He smiled at her. 'And *together*—' he stressed the word '—we'll decide the rest.'

She liked the sound of that. A lot. She remembered her presents and the little Christmas tree. Leaned up and kissed him. He tasted wonderful so she did it again.

He tilted his head. 'Hmm. What was that for? Not that I'm complaining.'

She lifted the sleeve of her coat and jiggled her wrist at him. The little Orient Express bracelet tinkled and caught the light. 'My gifts. They're beautiful. Thank you.' She looked at this tall and commanding man who had fought so hard for her. Had cared so much. 'I've only got me to offer you.'

'You are all I ever wanted for Christmas.' He leaned in and their lips met and Kelsie softened and sighed into this gorgeous man she was not going to waste another minute not loving.

'Merry Christmas, my love.'

He squeezed her in his arms and she felt surrounded by his love. It felt so right. He whispered in her hair, 'Welcome home.'

EPILOGUE

It was Christmas night one year later and Connor gently wiped the bead of sweat off Kelsie's brow as she breathed out slowly and surely.

No strenuous grunting or breath-holding, just slow breath after slow breath in the right direction, and already he could see that soon their longed-for child would arrive. He glanced at the clock. Five minutes to twelve. He smiled to himself. Kelsie had said she'd thought their baby would wait until it could have a birthday of its own and it looked like she had been right. It was obviously an independent little munchkin like its mother.

'I love you so much,' he whispered, and Kelsie's semi-focused gaze settled briefly and softly on his face before she closed her eyes again.

'Me, too,' she whispered back. There was no strain in her voice, just calm knowledge that all would happen as it should.

He'd watched her work with his nervous mothers over the last six months since they'd returned from Australia. They'd waited until all her women had birthed and then she'd been as eager as him to come back to live in England to spend time with Winsome and her new

husband, Max, and prepare their own home overlooking the Thames for their new baby's arrival.

He'd eased back from his research and spent more time working together with Kelsie in his fertility clinic, here at Saint Douglas's, meeting the gap for clients who had been successful in conception but were terrified about their pregnancies and labours, and his new mothers had blossomed.

The beautiful births he'd been privileged to watch over had taken on a serene quality he'd never seen before, and the other midwives were absorbing what Kelsie had to teach them. It was like the two of them had been destined to heal childless couples—just as they had been destined to heal each other—and the joy that brought made each day a blessing.

But this was his and Kelsie's birth, their own magic, and the wonder of the moment was upon them. He squeezed his wife's hand, glanced at the clock and smiled again as his daughter arrived gently into the world.

One minute after midnight, and baby Winsome Kelsie Black opened her eyes and blinked up at her father, her mother and the brand-new world. Accidentally her little arm lifted and she waved.

Kelsie laughed. Caught his eye and blew him a kiss. Whispered, 'I love you.'

And he whispered back, 'I love you, too.' He looked down at his family. His gorgeous wife, his gorgeous daughter, and the way his arm lay across them both.

He'd buy his daughter a present. And he knew the perfect thing. A train!

* * * * *

Merry Christmas
& A Happy New Year!

Thank you for a wonderful
2013...

A sneaky peek at next month...

Medical Romance™

CAPTIVATING MEDICAL DRAMA—WITH HEART

My wish list for next month's titles...

In stores from 3rd January 2014:

☐ Her Hard to Resist Husband — Tina Beckett

& The Rebel Doc Who Stole Her Heart — Susan Carlisle

☐ From Duty to Daddy — Sue MacKay

& Changed by His Son's Smile — Robin Gianna

☐ Mr Right All Along — Jennifer Taylor

& Her Miracle Twins — Margaret Barker

Available at WHSmith, Tesco, Asda, Eason, Amazon and Apple

Just can't wait?

1213/03

MILLS & BOON®
Book Club

Join the Mills & Boon Book Club

Want to read more **Medical** books?
We're offering you **2 more** absolutely **FREE!**

We'll also treat you to these fabulous extras:

- 🌹 Exclusive offers and much more!

- 🌹 FREE home delivery

- 🌹 FREE books and gifts with our special rewards scheme

Get your free books now!

visit www.millsandboon.co.uk/bookclub
or call Customer Relations on 020 8288 2888